UTTERLY

CW00520521

PAULINE MANDERS

This second edition (paperback) published in 2020 by
Ottobeast Publishing
ottobeastpublishing@gmail.com

First edition published in 2014
Cover design Rebecca Moss Guyver.

ISBN 978-1-912861-13-2

A CIP catalogue record for this title is available from the
British Library.

Also by Pauline Manders

The Utterly Crime Series

To Paul, Fiona, Alastair, Karen, Andrew, Katie and Mathew.

PAULINE MANDERS

Pauline Manders was born in London and trained as a doctor at University College Hospital, London. Having gained her surgical qualifications, she moved with her husband and young family to East Anglia, where she worked in the NHS as an ENT Consultant Surgeon for over 25 years. She used her maiden name throughout her medical career and retired from medicine in 2010.

Retirement has given her time to write crime fiction, become an active member of a local carpentry group, and share her husband's interest in classic cars. She lives deep in the Suffolk countryside.

ACKNOWLEDGMENTS

My thanks to: Beth Wood for her positive advice, support and encouragement; Pat McHugh, my mentor and hard-working editor with a keen sense of humour, mastery of atmosphere and grasp of characters; Rebecca Moss Guyver, for her boundless enthusiasm and brilliant cover artwork and design; David Withnall for his proof reading skills; Andy Deane for his editing help; the Write Now! Bury writers group for their support; Sue Southey for her cheerful reassurances and advice; and my husband and family, on both sides of the Atlantic, for their love and support.

CHAPTER 1

Decades of grime caked the surface of the block. Nick weighed it in his hand and traced the oak grain with his finger.

'We'll need–'

A piercing scream rent the air. It split the stillness, bounced across the chapel walls and reverberated high into the arched roof above.

Nick's mouth locked mid-sentence. His brain froze. He stared at Dave. And then another scream shattered the day.

'What the…?' Dave spun round and faced the doors, now widely open in the south porch. Shrieks and wails coursed around the portico.

'Come on! We'd better go and see.'

Nick didn't wait. Two long strides and he'd overtaken the middle-aged carpenter. He had no plan, just wanted to help. As he ran he imagined a catastrophe. At the very least a severed limb, a dog crushed beneath a bronze statue, an empty pushchair.

He took the porch steps in one bound. Sweat prickled in his short cropped hair. He paused, casting around the yard, catching his breath as he searched out the direction of the scream.

'Over there,' he shouted as Dave lumbered up behind.

Nick pointed past the mountain of wooden railway sleepers blackened with locomotive oil, the city of chimney pots, and the stacks of used bricks sorted into colour and size. He gazed into an open-fronted building with a corrugated roof. Broad, open stairs led up to wooden staging set at least ten feet high. Scaffolding poles served as rails. Under cover, but freestanding, a cast iron spiral staircase had been positioned for sale. A woman stood at its base, her head tilted upwards, both hands clasped to her mouth.

Now silence engulfed P Suffield's Chapel Reclamation Yard and for a second it was more chilling than a scream.

'There's, there's something up on those library stairs,' Dave whispered, tapping Nick's shoulder and breaking the spell.

Nick strained to make out the shape, as across the yard Patrick Suffield pushed past the woman.

'Come on, lad. Patrick may need a hand.'

Nick frowned. Had Dave seen something he'd missed? How did he know what to look for? All he could make out were ancient oak beams stacked on large racks at the back of the building. They threw the black painted spiral into patchy relief and played tricks with his eyes. Shapes merged and changed kaleidoscopically. He followed Dave.

An outline became more obvious. It sprawled on the metal staircase, one leg bent at the knee. He quickened his pace. 'Oh no!' Now he understood why his brain was having trouble making sense of it all. The form was a person and it followed the curve of the staircase. Only the lower half was visible from his angle.

Ahead, Patrick had hesitated, but now he stepped onto the staircase. Nick was already close enough to see more detail. He paused and waited with Dave and the woman, his brain numbed. Patrick eased his way past the scuffed shoe, the brightly chequered sock, and the exposed skin, mottled blue-black and showing below the trouser leg. The limb was rotated at an unnatural angle.

2

Nick let out a slow, silent breath and broke away from the small huddle. He circled around the base of the spiral staircase and stared upwards.

'Watch out, Nick! You're going to step in it,' Dave barked.

Nick stumbled and missed the pool of fluid, dark and ominous on the concrete. He gasped. Above, he caught sight of a man's jacket pressed against the grill of the steps. And then, his face.

'Oh Jee-e-eze,' Nick breathed.

It was bloated. Discoloured. The features hardly recognisable. The short blond hair looked unreal as it reflected the morning light.

'Is he…?' Dave asked.

'Dead?' Nick's voice almost failed.

'He's bloody hanging from a rope. We can't leave him like this.' Emotion sharpened Patrick's voice.

'Careful, Patrick. If he's really dead, it may be a police matter. Then–'

A wail seeped from the woman. It rose in pitch, gained strength and drowned Dave's words.

Nick lowered his gaze and stared at the man's neck. Now he could see a twist of coarse fibres pulling upwards. How hadn't he noticed before? 'No-o,' he moaned and turned away from the images behind the metal filigree and spindles.

'The rope's tied to the scaffold railing. Up there on the staging. See?' Patrick pointed. 'How the hell…?'

Nick didn't need to take a second look to work it out. The man had been suspended by his neck but hidden from view between the curving sides of the library staircase.

'But why didn't he stand up? Take the weight on his feet? Save himself?' Dave reasoned.

'I don't know. His hands aren't tied. Perhaps he was already out cold?' Patrick said.

Was it suicide, Nick wondered. He closed his eyes and shook his head, but in his imagination the bloated face kept staring.

'What's that at the top of the stairs, Patrick?' Dave's mellow tones dragged Nick back to the moment.

'Has he left a note?' Nick forced himself to glance back, urging his eyes higher than the blond hair. He caught his breath as metal reflected sunlight.

'What? Oh I see. Shike,' Patrick muttered.

'From down here it looks – are those cogs and wheels? It looks like the innards of a clock,' Dave murmured.

'It's nothing. Well, nothing to do with this.' Patrick looked down at them. 'Time to call the police, I think. Now clear off from here. If you go into the chapel you can sit down. We can make you a cup of tea, if you like.'

'But who is he?' the woman sobbed as Dave guided her towards the chapel.

Nick followed, struggling to make sense of it all and only half listening. He'd seen a dead body once before and it was one too many for his twenty-two years. His mind flew back to the incident six months earlier. He'd been the first to stumble across a drug overdose, a student looking so peaceful she could have been sleeping. At the time the encounter had taken his breath away, made his head spin and his stomach twist. But somehow this seemed different. It was so appalling he could hardly take it in.

He wondered if the screaming had primed him for something terrible, put him into a state of shock. Were his reactions on a slow fuse and any second now he'd feel the tightness in his lungs? He moaned as the bloated face zoomed before his eyes. He'd always thought a hanging dislocated the neck, but this looked like a slow strangulation. How else the puffy flesh, the purple-blue skin?

Nick dragged his feet as he traced his way past sections of iron railing and a cast iron deer. He paused before walking through the south porch. It was difficult to take on board that only a few minutes ago, the day had seemed so ordinary. One instant he was helping Dave choose parquet flooring blocks for an old dower house near Thorpe Morieux, and the next, someone screamed and he was staring at a man hanging from a rope. He shivered despite the watery sunshine.

Inside the chapel he found Dave and the woman already sitting on some wrought iron garden seats. The paintwork had flaked away and exposed the rust.

'Carol, this is Nick.' Dave spoke softly. 'He's our apprentice. He works with me at Willows & Son, the carpentry firm at Needham Market.'

The woman turned her mascara-blotched cheeks towards Nick, but made no attempt to smile. 'What are you going to do with that?' Her voice was rasping and hoarse.

For a moment Nick had no idea what she was talking about. He followed the direction of her gaze.

'Oh this,' he muttered. He still gripped a block of oak parquet flooring. 'I'd forgotten. We were choosing some when….' He raised it to look more closely.

She flinched.

'Sorry,' he whispered.

Please God, she wasn't going to start screaming again, he thought. Anxiety gripped his stomach as her mascara splodges morphed purple-blue and her eyelids puffed up into the man's face. He breathed faster, the chapel spun, and everything went speckled.

'Hey, lad, steady now.'

Nick heard Dave's words, distant and tinny. He felt a strong arm catch him around his waist as he stumbled to a bench seat. 'I'll be fine,' he muttered. 'Just need to sit down.'

'Put your head between your knees, Nick.'

Nick let himself flop forwards. He knew he was drifting. He let himself go.

***

When Nick opened his eyes he found himself stretched out on the bench. His head rested flat on the hard, unforgiving metal latticework. His calves tingled and throbbed. He cast around to get his bearings. Of course, he must have fainted and Dave had propped his legs up, no doubt trying to encourage blood back to his brain. But at six foot three, Nick was longer than the seat. His calves had taken the full weight of his legs as they lay across the iron armrest. His feet were leaden. He felt stupid.

'Ouch,' he groaned as he swung his legs off the armrest and tried to sit up.

'Hey, be careful.' Dave approached, smiling and carrying a mug of steaming tea. 'You fainted. Just sit quiet for a few minutes and you'll be fine.'

'Sorry. I'm sorry.' Nick rubbed his forehead. 'I don't know if I could face a cuppa. Not quite yet, Dave. You needn't have–'

'I didn't. It's mine.' He sipped the hot liquid and grinned. 'The police have arrived. They wanted our names

6

and details. I've dealt with all that, so I think we're free to leave.'

'Great. Can't think what came over me. How long have I been out?'

'Don't know. You looked as if you were catching up on your beauty sleep, so I left you for a while. Are you feeling OK now?'

'Yeah, think so.' Nick massaged the back of his legs, and tried to ignore the tightness developing in his chest as he remembered. 'I've never seen anything like that before,' he whispered.

'No. It's shocking. But....'

'But what?'

Dave sat down next to him. 'I remember when I was a kid going on a school trip to visit the World War One battlefields. You know the kind of thing. A coach trip and a couple of nights in something like a youth hostel but called a chateau.'

Nick nodded.

'I'll never forget seeing the Menin Gate Memorial. It marked the start of the main road out of Ypres to the front line. All those names of missing soldiers, presumed dead. But it was the museums and cemeteries that really brought it alive for me. I remember being shocked, angry, upset - but we had some great teachers with us. They said our reactions showed our humanity. We had to try to understand why we felt the way we did. And we shouldn't try to forget, but to put the memories where we could get to them, but in a more positive way.'

'So, how did that help when you saw that man... hanging?'

'I don't know exactly. I suppose I just tried to go through that process, as if I was back at the Menin Gate.' Dave gulped his tea. 'I didn't want to look at him. It was horrible. I wanted to blank him out. And then I realised it was because I imagined how any of my family might look if they'd been hanging there.'

Dave seemed suddenly restless and stood up. 'And then of course – I felt guilty for thinking those things. I told myself that behind the distorted body and face there'd been a real person. That's the image I needed to hold on to. The man when he was alive. Not what he'd become in death.'

Dave let his hand rest on Nick's shoulder for a moment. 'As I see it, the best thing I can do is to be practical and keep occupied. What I mainly feel now is sadness for that man.'

'So shock turns to realising how lucky you are? Then maybe guilt and… keep busy?'

'Kind of, but not quite. What did you feel, Nick?'

Nick didn't know what to say. He hadn't expected to be asked. This wasn't how his mates talked in the pub. He groped for the right words.

'I don't remember my thoughts, just looking and feeling numb. Then my chest went tight and I needed to breathe fast. I wanted it to all go away - but even when I closed my eyes, it was still there. And then I suppose I fainted.'

'Hmm, well at least you didn't feel the need to scream.'

Nick almost smiled. It was time to slip into pub talk. He knew he'd be safe with that. 'Yeah, Carol's got quite a pair of lungs on her.'

Dave nodded. 'We'll come back another day to pick up the parquet blocks. I'll go and have a quick word with Patrick.'

Perhaps Dave was right, Nick thought as he waited. Maybe he needed to confront his shock rather than smother it. Some months earlier he'd discovered he could control his fast, anxious breathing by singing. It was a useful trick. Now the singer in him tried to summon a song, any song and Bohemian Rhapsody surged into his mind. The words came fast, the beat was frenetic and the breath control all-important. He took a Freddie Mercury-sized breath, and filled his mind with the music and lyrics. He hummed and then sang softly. It seemed to help. By the time he walked with Dave to the Willows van ten minutes later, he felt calmer, the urge to hyperventilate at last curbed.

Nick fastened his seat belt. He knew the journey back from Horringer wouldn't take long, not with Dave at the wheel. He reckoned he was lucky to have him as his trainer. A year on the carpentry course at Utterly Academy and then his first year with Willows & Son had been both physically and mentally toughening in the best possible way. It was difficult to recognise himself as the same raw student who had once thought his future lay in an Environmental Science degree in Exeter. He was simply thankful he'd had the guts to change direction, return to Suffolk and pursue his interest in carpentry, before he'd wasted any more time. And as if to prove his toughness after seeing the body, he resolved to appear back to normal as soon as possible. After all, wasn't his head meant to be filled with carpentry, music, real ale and girls?

CHAPTER 2

Matt frowned. Nick's text message seemed unnecessary. Of course he'd be at the Nags Head tonight. Why ask? He'd always made it to the pub on Friday evenings. Matt shrugged and then had a thought. Maybe, just maybe there were going to be some new birds on the scene. He hoped that's why Nick was checking.

Sure mate, he texted back. He would have added one of those smiley faces with symbols, but somehow he found it difficult turning facial expressions on their sides. His basic android mobile didn't feature an emoji keyboard like the latest iOS; nor for that matter, was there a camera.

Matt dragged his mind back to his computer screen. Now that he'd switched courses and was no longer a trainee carpenter, it was time to change his image. He wanted to be a techie. A computing and IT techie, to be precise. He'd already grown the beard. It had been more of an accident than a plan, and when someone said it made his face look longer, he'd thrown his razor away. Now he wanted to use computing words to add to his street cred. *Shit* was yesterday, to be deleted. He needed new expletives, ones to reflect his course. He scrolled down the screen.

'Frag,' he hissed. He liked the sound, rolled it around his tongue and tried again. 'Frag!' It felt good with more volume. Sometimes his flattened Suffolk vowels distorted words – but not with this.

'What did you just say?'

Matt swivelled around in his seat. A furnace ignited in his face as he met the library assistant's gaze. 'I-I were lookin' up computer language, Rosie. How long you been standin' there?'

She held up a couple of books she'd been clasping.

'Just taking my daily workout. We still use books. They don't get back on the shelves by themselves, you know.' She glanced past his head to the screen. 'So, what's causing all the excitement?'

He couldn't help noticing how wisps of auburn hair had broken away from her loose ponytail.

'What does it say?' She frowned as she read. 'Oh I see. If you shoot someone in a computer game you fragment them. Charming.'

'Yeah, you frag 'em.'

'Sounds a bit... I don't know, a bit–'

'Rude?' Matt touched his sandy beard, just to be sure it still hid the fire beneath. 'What about this one?' he continued.

'G-I-G-O?' she spelt out. 'Guy-go? I think I've heard that one before. Garbage In Garbage Out. If you feed in rubbish data, you'll get rubbish results. Is this the kind of mind-stretching high tech stuff they're teaching you? Get a life, Matt, before you turn into a nerd like that Gavin guy. Sorry – I shouldn't have said that, but he stares at me and it gives me the creeps.'

Matt watched as Rosie moved away and headed for a bank of shelving along the far wall. He reckoned it didn't count as a stare if her back was turned. He shrugged and resumed his computer search.

Utterly library, despite its computer stations, photocopiers, printer scanners and rack of audio equipment, still exuded an air of the Edwardian. Perhaps it was the smell of the old wooden floorboards stretching the length of the room, or the ceiling with its gothic-styled beams. Matt didn't really care. He'd come to think of the library as a place of escape. Somewhere he could lose himself with a computer terminal. It seemed unbelievable to him that over a century before, Sir Raymond Utterly had built the place to impress - to tell the people of Stowmarket he was an entre-preneur, a business magnate, a success. And now his man-sion and grounds housed Utterly Academy. Rosie had once described it as a downturn in his fortunes, but Matt still didn't get what she meant. At the very least, he must have made a pile of money when he sold it.

The library door swung open and laughter breezed above the sound of raised voices in the corridor. Matt won-dered what all the commotion was about, and then Gavin darted in, wearing black skinny jeans and a tight purple sweatshirt.

Matt slouched further into his seat. He had no desire to talk to Gavin. He might be on the same course but that didn't mean he liked him. And what was the purple and black about, he wondered. Goth? Punk? If there was such a thing as vampire daywear, then Gavin was sporting the look; pasty-faced, thin and expressionless.

'Bot,' Matt muttered as he dropped his gaze and read the next word on the computer screen. 'Bot?' he repeated. It sounded good, but would anyone realise he was referring to a robot, an automated programme doing repetitive things like indexing webpages or sorting email? An outsider might think "arsehole", but would another techie or geek under-stand the real insult? If Gavin approached, he'd try it out on him.

Five minutes later, he had his chance. Out of the corner of his eye he spotted black drainpipes approaching. He held his breath.

'Hi Matt.' Gavin spoke in a soft monotone. 'You've got plenty of RAM. Want to try for a place in the quiz team?'

Matt pulled a face. He was about to say, *what, bot?* – but his tongue twisted around the words. The phrase disintegrated.

'It's your Random Access Memory we'd be after, not your mumbling.'

Matt opened his mouth to say *sure, bot* - but then closed it again. It sounded like *sure, boss* and that wasn't at all what he meant.

'Not very quick at answering questions, are we, Matt.' Gavin shook his head and moved on.

'Oh, go frag yourself,' Matt muttered and then inwardly grinned. He felt better. Frag could stay; bot might have to be dropped. He could try them out at the Nags Head that evening.

***

Matt pushed the heavy door. Voices, laughter, jukebox music and the smell of stale beer flooded over him. He stood for a few seconds and drank in the atmosphere. The Nags Head on a Friday night was already buzzing.

'What you waiting for? An invitation to come in?' The tones were hardly recognisable.

Matt looked in the direction of Nick's voice. 'Hi, mate.' He waved and let the door swing closed behind.

Nick lounged against the bar, one elbow resting on the counter top. 'Thought I'd get a couple in before everyone arrived.' He spoke slowly. His short brown hair was clumped together as if wet, his naturally open gaze, leaden.

Matt skirted past a group of drinkers. 'Everyone? You said everyone. So some girls are comin'. Right, Nick?' He searched Nick's face, hoping he'd see him grin, but all he caught were dark shadows beneath his eyes.

'Hence the tee,' Nick murmured, glancing at the design printed on the cotton straining across Matt's chest. He drained his pint. 'Afraid you may be out of luck, Matt. Even Kat can't make it this evening. So what you having? Your usual?'

'Yeah, lager. A pint if you're buying, mate.'

Matt pressed a hand to his chest and smoothed his tee-shirt, a recent find in a charity shop. He'd been attracted by its techie image and unremarkable colour, a kind of washboard grey. He wandered over to a bench seat in a quieter area of the bar and slumped down to consider his options. He reckoned he could either play along with Nick, pretending he believed the *out of luck with birds* line, or he could assume it was all a tease and act laidback because they'd be arriving any minute. The words *blue suede* drifted across from the jukebox, and for a moment drowned the raised voices and clinking glasses. He decided it was an omen and opted for cool.

Matt was still trying to figure out how to work frag into the conversation when Nick returned, slopping lager and beer.

'Here.' Nick handed him a dripping glass.

'Thanks. You OK, Nick?'

'Yeah, why?'

'Nothin'. It's what people say aint it? No need to jump down me throat.' He felt uncomfortable. Nick wasn't usually like this.

'OK, I've had a bad day, and I don't want to talk about it. How 'bout you?'

Matt pulled at his beard. Was he supposed to say something to cheer Nick up, or talk about the bad things and negatives in his own day? He didn't know, and he didn't want to get it wrong. He looked at Nick more closely and tried to read his face as the bass notes pounded from the jukebox.

'Hi!'

Nick spun around. 'Hey, I didn't see you come in, Chrissie.'

'I've just arrived. So, why the glum faces?'

Matt stared at Chrissie. He'd shared a workbench with her for the first year on the carpentry course at Utterly. He rarely thought of her now as twice his age and liked her direct, sometimes sharp approach, but she'd confused him. He'd tried to look sympathetic, not glum. He cast about for something to say, and opted for Nick's line.

'Bad day; we aint talkin' 'bout it. How 'bout you?' He grinned, pleased with his effort.

'Well, you sound OK, Matt. So what's up with you, Nick?'

'I went out to Suffield's with Dave today. Don't know if you've ever been there, it's that reclamation yard with the disused chapel.'

'Oh yes, just outside Bury. It's on the Ickworth Park road, isn't it? Before you get to the National Trust place.'

'That's the one. We were looking to pick up some parquet flooring blocks, and,' Nick gulped some beer, 'it seems it's also the place to hang yourself.'

The jukebox boomed out a final chord. Briefly there was quiet, and then the babble of voices rose in the bar, like tidal waters to fill the void.

'What you just say?' Matt coughed as a mouthful of lager caught at the back of his throat. He stared at Nick and then checked Chrissie's face.

'You are kidding, aren't you, Nick?'

'No, Chrissie. You asked about glum faces. I'm just saying it's been a bloody awful day.'

'Oh Nick, I didn't think. I mean... did someone–'

'Hang themselves. Yes. It was horrible.'

'Really? Strung 'emselves up?' Matt couldn't believe his ears. 'But d'you know who?' And then as an after-thought, 'Frag!'

'Afraid not.' Nick gulped more beer and then peered into his half-full glass. 'Anyone for another? Chrissie? You haven't got a drink yet. Ginger Beer?'

'Thanks, Nick.'

Matt held up his lager, still two thirds full. He reckoned if someone else was buying, he wasn't going to say no, but Nick was already out pacing him and that felt wrong. 'Just another half, mate.'

'Poor Nick,' Chrissie murmured as they watched him wander back to the bar. 'I don't think drinking's going to help.'

'No, but at least he aint hummin' yet, so maybe….'

'He's not upset? I think he is, Matt.'

'If you ask me, it's the livin' ones that come hauntin' us. Take Tom. I still wake up sweatin'.'

'I thought Tom was banged up and they'd thrown away the key, Matt.'

'I wish.' Matt tried to ignore the sudden lurch in his stomach. For an instant he saw his brother's sneering mouth and hard expression. Tom may have been only eight years his senior and a bully, but he'd recently upped the stakes from petty crime. He'd been involved in two people's deaths. Just thinking about it twisted Matt's guts. He'd always known his brother was a hard bastard. Now it was official and it terrified him.

'I think he's givin' evidence against the others. He could be out soon.'

'Then with any luck he'll be under a witness protection scheme. I bet he'll disappear with a different name to somewhere else. He won't come bothering you. He wouldn't dare show his face around here again.' Chrissie gazed at his chest and frowned. 'Were you going somewhere special tonight, Matt?'

'I thought Nick were invitin' some birds to meet us here.'

'Ah! Hence the new tee. Have you signed up for a sperm bank or–'

'What you talkin' about, Chrissie?'

'Or an infertility clinic,' Nick said as he set down their drinks. 'It's mad at the bar.'

Matt ran his hand over the image printed on his tee-shirt. 'What's wrong with a computer mouse?'

'Is that what it's supposed to be?' Nick's lips twitched. 'It's kind of stretched. Lost its shape, mate.'

'And the flex looks like a tail. It could be swimming.' Chrissie reached for her ginger beer.

'Scam. But I reckoned it were huggin' me. Kinda slimmin'.'

'No, it's sort of rounded the mouse, mate.'

'The colour doesn't help either; grubby underwear shade, and a giant sperm on your chest. It's not a good look, Matt. Believe me.'

Matt shifted his gaze from Chrissie to Nick. All he saw were smiles; ones that reached the eyes. He heard Nick laugh and in a flash he knew he'd got it right. The glum face had gone. 'You can borrow it if you like, Nick.'

Nick almost choked on a mouthful of beer. 'Thanks mate, but no.'

'Yes, Nick. Maybe you should wear it when you next sing with the band. It is tomorrow night isn't it? You are coming, aren't you, Matt?'

'I wish. No, I'm workin' the midnight shift at Tesco, up on the Bird Estate.' Matt pulled a face, but secretly he was quite looking forward to it. When he'd changed courses and gained a place on Computing & IT, the switch came at a price. He was no longer an apprentice carpenter and he'd forfeited earning the wages. Now he was a student, skint again, and in need of the cash.

Matt sipped his lager. 'But serious like, if you're ever in a tight spot and want to borrow it,' he let his hand drift across his chest, 'say the word. Just say the word, mate.'

He started to relax and enjoy the evening. Were people paid for donating sperm, he wondered. It was another thing to look up on the internet.

CHAPTER 3

'Lot number two hundred and sixty-four!' the auctioneer announced. 'A set of six, sabre-legged, Regency dining chairs.'

'We're on now, Mr Clegg,' Chrissie whispered. 'This is us.' She tried to keep her voice steady and suppressed the urge to grip her boss's arm.

'Now who will start me at six hundred pounds?'

Chrissie didn't dare crane her neck to scan the assorted people sitting behind. She didn't want to risk scaring away a potential bidder. Instead, she fixed her eyes on the chests and sideboards lined against the sale room wall, just to one side of the rostrum. She'd expected one of the senior auctioneers to be wielding the gavel. Saturdays were, after all, the big auction days. The younger members of the team generally only got their chance on the rarer Wednesday sales, but today Mr Prout junior stood supreme on the rostrum of Corps, Poynder & Prout.

She remembered all her hard work. This set of chairs had been her first solo project for the sale rooms. Ron Clegg had of course supervised, but she'd done the few repairs herself and then re-applied the French polish. Now she imagined the mahogany glowing under the auction room's harsh strip lighting. She felt particularly connected to Lot 264.

'Come on, come on. Somebody bid. Please somebody bid,' she murmured, willing a buyer to call out.

'Six hundred? Do I have six hundred anywhere?'

Chrissie held her breath.

'Six hundred? Thank you, sir.' The voice seemed unnaturally deep through the PA system. 'Do I have any advance on six hundred? Six-twenty? Six hundred and twenty pounds, anywhere?'

Chrissie let her breath escape and caught the auctioneer's fleeting gaze as he scanned the room. Was it just her or was everyone feeling the tension?

'Six-twenty…? Thank you. Six-twenty, I'm bid. I have six-twenty on my right.'

Chrissie felt the tension break as ripples of movement spread through the sale room. People shifted in their chairs, rustled their catalogues, and glanced at the new bidder sitting to one side of a display cabinet.

'Six-forty?' Prout junior directed his gaze back to the man standing near a bookcase.

Chrissie willed the bookcase man to nod. He must have, because the auctioneer started to chant out numbers, jumping through the twenties like a times-table, and at much the same speed.

'Six-forty, -sixty, -eighty, seven hundred, seven-twenty, -forty, -sixty.' She swayed to the rhythm, hardly daring to believe her ears as two bidders upped their stakes. Then like a symphony the bidding slowed, changed tempo, and under the baton of the conducting auctioneer, faltered at eight hundred. It ended with a lowered catalogue and a slow headshake.

'Any advance on eight-twenty? Do I have any more bids?' The auctioneer cast a slow glance around the sale room. 'Are we all done?'

Bang! The hammer went down. 'Sold for eight hundred and twenty pounds.'

Chrissie almost had to pinch herself. The Regency dining chairs had been sold. 'Yes,' she hissed, resisting the impulse to punch the air. 'We've done it, Mr Clegg.'

She sneaked another glance at the buyer near the bookcase and then grinned at Ron. It had been exciting. She felt so lucky - lucky to have sold the chairs for a good price, but also incredibly lucky to have an apprenticeship with a furniture restorer and cabinet maker. After her first year of carpentry at Utterly Academy, she could have been placed with a firm fitting roof joists, skirting boards and door frames, most likely on a building site and no doubt on a tight schedule. It would have been heavy, physical work. Her five-foot-two would have been a constant disadvantage, and her age and sex only grudgingly tolerated, probably just to demonstrate the firm's compliance with equal opportunities.

'You mean, you've done it, Mrs Jax. Never underestimate the effect of a good few coats of French polish.' A smile played around his eyes as he glanced down at the programme. 'Lot three hundred and ten; I'm curious. I'm going to stay a little longer, and see it go under the hammer.'

Chrissie was in no hurry to leave. This Saturday auction felt special. She nodded, and thumbed through the catalogue. So what was so interesting about this particular lot, she wondered. *Lot 310: Tortoiseshell veneered wooden box made for an automaton, possibly a singing bird. Mechanism missing. French circa 1890.* She frowned and read the description again.

'I didn't know you were interested in automata, Mr Clegg.'

'I'm not, but Marlin Poynder is, and he should have been the auctioneer today. I'm wondering if I should bid for it and sell it on to him. That's if he's not telephone bidding or something.'

'I don't think I noticed it,' she whispered, closing her eyes in an effort to try and picture the box.

'It was on the chest of drawers next to that hideous glass vase.'

Chrissie remembered the orange-flecked glass immediately. It was so repellent she hadn't given the box a second glance.

'It might be good for you to learn how to work with tortoiseshell. It needs some repair, Mrs Jax.'

She pulled a face. Tortoiseshell, ivory and animal skins weren't her bag. Working with them struck her as too close to taxidermy for her liking. It was hardly carpentry. She sighed, relaxed back into her chair and hoped against hope the automaton box went elsewhere. Beside her, Ron scribbled the closing bid against the next lot in the catalogue. His writing seemed so neat, despite the arthritis starting to make drumsticks out of his fingers and knuckles.

Time flew as the warm, slightly heady atmosphere in the sale room took over. The constant switch from boredom to excitement felt unreal as the lots came and went.

'Lot three hundred and nine,' the junior Prout's voice sputtered through the PA system.

She straightened in her chair and glanced at her catalogue. Yes, almost there. She hardly listened as the bidding closed rapidly.

'Now we move on to lot three hundred and eleven. Lot three hundred and ten has been withdrawn.'

Chrissie opened her mouth to speak, thought better of it and mouthed an exaggerated, 'Why?' at Ron. He frowned and then shrugged.

'Lot three hundred and eleven. A rosewood Georgian tea caddy inlaid with mother of pearl....'

'How strange,' Ron whispered next to her.

Chrissie sighed. She was secretly relieved not to be working with tortoiseshell, but her curiosity had been tweaked. 'Someone in the office will know why, Mr Clegg.'

'Come on then, Mrs Jax. I've been sitting for long enough. We can ask on the way out, and we'll be able to catch someone before the rush at the end of the auction.'

She watched as he stood up uncomfortably, and followed as he made his way slowly past a myriad of crockery, porcelain and glass items crowded onto oak and pine tables. All bore white labels with the lot numbers written in bold black. The auctioneer's voice, amplified through the PA system, seemed to follow them, but with each step his words lost their clarity. By the time they were out of the main sale room and standing at the reception desk, only the muted sound and rhythm of his words filtered through.

A young woman, probably in her thirties, looked up from the desk. The area behind was cramped. Stacks of catalogues jostled for space with phones, a card reader, computer and printer. A doorway led through to a large back room. Chrissie caught a glimpse of filing cabinets and more computer screens beyond.

'Can I help?' The woman smiled, looking both efficient and friendly at the same time.

'Thank you, yes. Lot three hundred and ten? The automaton box. May I ask when it was withdrawn from the sale, and why?' Ron spoke quietly. 'It's just that we were interested in it.'

A frown played across the woman's face. 'Just a minute, let me check.' She smiled at Ron again and then studied her computer screen. She clicked and scrolled, and with her eyes still on the screen murmured, 'The owner phoned this morning. It seems he's heard a major buyer has…,' she hesitated, as if searching for the right words, 'lost interest.'

'Ah, well that explains it. How very disappointing. And the owner is?'

'I'm afraid I can't give you his name, sir.'

'Of course. And I'd expected Marlin Poynder to be taking the auction here today as well. But it's nice to see the next generation working the rostrum so confidently. Mr Prout's son did well. A good sale.' Ron smiled at the woman. 'Our lot went for a good price. Please congratulate him for us.'

'I will. Aiden will be pleased. He stepped in at, shall we say... short notice. And you are?'

'Lot number two hundred and sixty-four.'

'The set of six Regency dining chairs,' Chrissie added for good measure.

They turned away from the desk. Outside, the late Saturday morning seemed to beckon through the large glass entrance doors. Chrissie paused in the doorway. Behind, she imagined the woman in reception searching through her computer files for the name. On the spur of the moment, the imp in her called over her shoulder, 'That would be the sabre leg set.'

The auction rooms were located in a Bury St Edmunds industrial estate to the east of the A14. Parked cars spread like an apron around the front and sides of the warehouse-sized building. Chrissie stood on the steps and let the October breeze massage her face and catch at her short blonde hair, as she scanned the area for Ron's van.

'Well, your car's easy to spot, Mrs Jax.'

Chrissie grinned. The TR7 might be more than thirty years old, but the vivid yellow paintwork wasn't the colour of a fading diva. 'Do you think so, Mr Clegg?'

For her part she loved the brightness. It never failed to lift her spirits. And besides, she had a history of mislaying parked cars, so the canary yellow was a blessing. She caught the slight movement as Ron glanced heavenwards.

'Goodbye then, Mrs Jax. Safe journey home.' He raised his hand, Chrissie suspected more to shield his eyes from the colour than a farewell salute.

She grinned again. The rest of Saturday stretched ahead and she felt on top of the world. She saw the world through rose tints. Even the huge circular towers and storage tanks of the nearby British Sugar factory looked more like contemporary sculptures than an industrial landscape processing sugar beet. The tall funnel-like chimneys seemed to billow white clouds as dense as candyfloss.

'Oh sugar!' she muttered, remembering her empty fridge. It was only a short drive to one of the nearest out-of-town supermarkets, but it still felt like an intrusion. She cursed under her breath and settled into the TR7 driving seat. She was looking forward to seeing Clive that evening and she'd promised to cook, so any thoughts of passing up on the Saturday supermarket crush were unrealistic. Experience had taught her that when he was the DI on duty and covering a weekend for Bury and Ipswich, arrangements could fly out of the window at the last minute. So if she wanted to avoid disappointment with her detective inspector, it was probably best not to hope for a meal out.

Chrissie listened to the throaty purr as the TR7's two litre engine responded to some throttle. She eased the wedge-shaped nose out of the parking space and headed for the nearest supermarket, her thoughts miles away. Ten minutes later she sighed as she pushed a shopping trolley past the open glass door and into the hustle and bustle inside. She glanced at the newspapers displayed on a stand in the entrance. Headlines leapt from front pages and like sound bites, she dismissed them as disconnected chatter - but they still fought for her attention. She read automatically, not registering the words. Two paces on and she stopped. What had the bold print shrieked?

She retraced her footsteps and picked up an Eastern Anglia Daily Tribune. *Man Found Hanging in Reclamation Horror*. Chrissie read the headline again and then hungrily skimmed through the text. Hadn't Nick said something about a hanging? 'Oh no,' she breathed as the name *Marlin Poynder* burned into her retina. 'But wasn't he the auctioneer…?'

The article was short on detail. She remembered Nick mentioning a reclamation yard on the road to Ickworth House, near Horringer. She guessed it was the *Patrick Suffield's Chapel Reclamation Yard*, as mentioned in the paper. Other than saying *a body had been found on Friday morning* and later identified, there was no information as to how or why Marlin Poynder had come to be hanging there in the first place – or if he'd died by his own hand. *It was too early to tell*, a police spokesman had said. Well, that had been twenty-four hours ago. She thrust the paper back onto the stand, frustrated by the lack of answers.

Chrissie pushed the trolley down the aisles, trying to ignore the prickling in the back of her neck. She had no idea what Marlin may have looked like, but the image of damaged tortoiseshell came to mind. 'Lot three hundred and ten,' she murmured.

Like a robot, she reached for items without thought. The self-checkout peeped as it read the bar codes, but she didn't take in the names on the screen. To be honest, she hardly noticed what she'd bought. It was only later, when she unloaded her purchases into her empty fridge that she wondered what had possessed her.

'How do I make a meal out of anchovies, plums, chicken breasts, Suffolk Gold cheese and ionised water for the steam iron?' she muttered. At least, she supposed, the chicken was free range. 'And anchovies? Are they fish farmed or wild?' Hopefully they'd enjoyed a good life before being netted. But ionised water? What had she been thinking? She shook her head.

CHAPTER 4

'We need to pick up those parquet flooring blocks this morning, Nick. First thing.' Dave tossed the words over his shoulder and slammed the van's rear door shut.

Nick lobbed his packed lunch onto the dash, and stepped up into the Willows van. He'd been dreading this. He knew they'd have to go back to the reclamation yard to collect the blocks. It was Monday and they needed to get on with laying the floor at the old Dower House, but somehow he'd hoped Patrick Suffield might have delivered the blocks. It could have been a kind of goodwill gesture to make up for the distress of finding a dead body draped over his stock.

'D'you reckon he'll give us a discount? You know, on account of us having to make two trips.' Nick couldn't quite bring himself to mention the hanging man yet.

'You must be joking. Patrick's a hard-nosed businessman. He's more likely to say prices have spiralled over the weekend and charge us more.'

'You're kidding me?'

'No, I've had dealings with him before.'

Nick waited until Dave had settled into the driver's seat before he mumbled, 'Heard it was one of the auctioneers from Corps, Poynder and Prout.'

He bit his tongue. He hadn't meant to say anything, but a vision of the dead man had surfaced through his thoughts again, just as it had all weekend. He'd been struggling to work on Dave's advice and replace his flash images of the dead man with an impression of the living one. It would have helped to know how Marlin Poynder had looked in life, but the bloated, discoloured face hadn't given much away. When Chrissie phoned to wish him luck before his Saturday gig, she'd described her morning at the auction. Something fell into place and Marlin Poynder became real. Nick was able to imagine him as a person with a life and occupation, standing on a rostrum, a gavel in his hand. He'd finally put some meat on the bones, as Chrissie might have said, and his breathing was easier as a result.

'I've never had any dealings with the auction house, myself. But it wouldn't surprise me if Patrick has.' Dave eased the van out of the secure parking area and drove at a sedate speed past the Willows & Son workshop and office.

'So you think they knew each other, Patrick and this Poynder bloke? But why didn't he let on? He must've recognised him when we found him hanging.'

'I don't know.' Dave half shrugged as he gripped the steering wheel. 'And anyway, seeing a dead body affects people differently.' He put his foot down hard and accelerated, jerking the van forwards into the main road. A sudden swerve to avoid an oncoming car, and then they were on their way.

Nick leaned back against the headrest as they whisked under the low, almost blind-angled bridge near Needham Lake and then up onto the A14. The ride was smoother once they were on the dual carriageway, and the panorama of ploughed, earthy clay fields soothed.

'So, did you have a good weekend, Nick?'

'Yeah. Seems a long time ago now,' he said as he watched a sugar beet harvester in the distance. It crawled along the skyline, a smaller truck at its side like some primeval beast with its young. For a moment he was transported back in time.

He remembered the gig. Jake and the rest of the band had been in high spirits but Kat had seemed distant and glum. By the end of the evening she'd told him about her air rifle target shooting session. She'd been training earlier that day. It hadn't gone well. Her coach had tried to be positive about the 50 metre distance but Kat didn't hold out much hope for the 2012 Olympic team, and selection was only a few months away. Nick recalled the smell of her perfume and the feel of her in his arms as he'd hugged her, but he hadn't known what to do when the tears streamed down her cheeks. He could have handled it better.

'How's that nice girlfriend of yours?'

'Kat? She'll be fine. So what dealings have you had with Patrick Suffield?' He closed his eyes as Dave surged up behind a Smart car and swung out to overtake.

Dave didn't answer straight away. He appeared to be choosing his words. 'Well, I remember one occasion when I phoned to see if he'd got something, a wrought iron pergola, and he said yes and gave me a price. Then, when I'd driven over he told me someone else had phoned asking for the same thing and if I still wanted it, I'd have to pay more. Once you're there and you weigh up the cost and time you'd spend looking elsewhere, it's easier just to settle for his price, but you hate yourself for paying it. No one likes being taken for a ride. I certainly didn't.'

'So you think he was just having you on? If anyone was going to be found dead, it sounds as if it should've been Patrick. What's a pergola?'

'It's like a tunnel or series of arches you grow roses or climbing plants over. We were building a wooden summer-house and decked staging for clients with a huge garden, and they asked for a pergola. Initially they wanted it in wood and then changed their minds, mainly because we'd botched up on the plans and quote. Wrought iron won the day, I'm afraid, and the boss told me to sort it out.'

The conversation drifted between the benefits of using wood for rose arches, preserved with a pressurised treatment, or using wrought iron. Nick relaxed as they headed to Bury St Edmunds and then out to Horringer. By the time they drove though the entrance gates of *P Suffield's Chapel Reclamation Yard* he'd almost forgotten his dread. Almost.

'Oh no.' Nick caught his breath.

It was immediately obvious they'd entered a crime scene. Yellow and black striped tape bowed in the breeze as it cordoned off a large section of the yard. A huge tarpaulin covered a frame enclosing the spot where the spiral staircase once displayed a suspended figure. Nick gulped as he noticed the policeman. He couldn't imagine a suicide calling for so much plastic tape and canvas. Murder seemed more likely. Why else would a policeman stand watch over the scene, like a sentry?

'Lucky for us, the parquet blocks were in the chapel,' Dave murmured. 'If they'd been closer to those library stairs they'd be evidence now and we'd never get to collect them.'

Dave parked the van next to a stack of reclaimed Suffolk bricks and moments later, they nodded to the policeman as they hurried past and into the chapel. They found Patrick in his office. Filing cabinets crowded the walls. Drawers were open; papers spilled onto the floor. He paced about, hissing into his mobile.

'So do you want it or not? You may have to wait for it but it's still a good deal - so don't insult me with offers like that. I can go elsewhere anytime, you know.'

Dave glanced at Nick and raised his eyebrows. A kind of *I told you what he was like, see what I mean* look.

Nick watched as Patrick turned mid-stride. The movement reminded him of a caged animal - frustrated, restless and wild. He felt his own unease surge.

'I can't talk now. Something's come up.' Patrick lowered his mobile, and fixed a pair of dark brown eyes on Dave. The tension was unmistakable. 'How long've you been standing there?'

'Just this second.'

Nick nodded, backing up Dave's words and hoping it would help defuse the air.

Light caught the side of Patrick's face, casting patchy shadows over sallow skin and making dirty smudges of the stubble near his mouth. He looked as if he'd aged ten years in just the course of a weekend.

'I see the police are here,' Nick mumbled.

'They haven't left.' Patrick almost spat the words. 'I think they've been searching for something.'

Nick frowned as he glanced past Patrick to the office filing cabinets and strewn paperwork. 'But what?'

'They said something about a weapon.'

'I thought he'd... hanged himself. I mean there was a rope around his neck, wasn't there?' Nick felt his cheeks flush. He hadn't meant to say so much or sound so interested.

'Yeah, but I'm starting to think it's just an excuse to go through my stock.'

'But why?' Nick caught his breath as he felt Dave's elbow connect with his ribs.

'We don't want to hold you up if you're busy, but we're here to collect those oak parquet flooring blocks, Patrick.'

'Yes, of course. A dower house out Thorpe Morieux way, you said.'

Nick nodded again but this time kept his lips buttoned.

'We'll load 'em into the van now, if that's OK, Patrick? I assume you're still trading and the police aren't interfering too much with business?'

'Not yet, but it's bloody difficult with half the yard cordoned off and the police creeping around.' Patrick shook his head. 'What I don't understand is why he came here to kill himself. We lock the main gates at night, and they hadn't been tampered with, so he must have... I don't know, had a key or got in some other way. I mean, why come here? It makes no sense.'

Nick was about to say there must be more to it, but bit his lip as he caught Dave's eye. He shrugged and shoved both hands into his pockets in what he hoped was a matey, I'm one-of-the-lads type of gesture.

'Come on then.' Patrick led the way.

'Find a loading trolley will you, Nick.' Dave turned on his heel and headed down an aisle. Nick imagined it once running between rows of chairs or pews. Now it weaved an erratic path alongside cast iron fireplaces. It seemed to him there was little trace of God left in the old chapel.

When Nick returned, pulling a platform trolley with mesh sides, he found Dave standing near the stack of parquet blocks, head bowed. Patrick was nowhere to be seen. 'Everything OK?'

'Yes. I was just thinking. We'll take the lot. Patrick didn't argue about the price, even said we could return what we didn't use. He seemed more interested in getting shot of me. That's not like him.'

'Only tough when he's got an audience?'

'He doesn't need an audience to play tough. You heard him on the phone, Nick. He didn't know we were there. No, he's probably got other things to worry about. Come on, let's get this lot loaded and out of here, before he changes his mind.'

It took six trips with the platform trolley to load all the blocks. The two builder's bags they'd kept in the van since Friday soon bulged horribly as they filled, despite the heavy fabric. Each was about one metre cubed in size and together they jammed into all the available space in the back of the van. Nick was sure they'd split. He imagined a torrent of sharp-cornered blocks pouring forwards and swamping him as he sat belted into the passenger seat; an avalanche of oak crushing him between windscreen and headrest, pushing on his ribs, stopping his breath and suffocating him. Not so unlike a hanging, he thought. The end result would be essentially the same. He took a sharp breath and hummed.

'Got everything in the van now?' Dave grinned and stepped up into the driver's seat. He'd already started the engine by the time Nick opened the passenger door.

'What's the hurry?' he muttered. 'We're not in some bloody race, you know. You'll make the police suspicious and it'll be me who ends up unloading the van for them.'

The policeman stepped away from the yellow and black tape, and beckoned. It was a command, not a greeting.

Nick swallowed hard. 'See, I told you so.'

Dave inched the van forwards, wound down his window and did all the talking. Nick was grateful for that. If he'd had to speak he was sure he'd have made their load of parquet in the back sound like blocks of compressed cannabis, the Dower House a commune, and Willows & Son organised crime. He concentrated on looking indifferent, but he suspected trying only made his eyes shifty.

'Right, on our way at last,' Dave said as he eased the van into gear and finally drove out of the reclamation yard.

'Substantial gates, wouldn't you say?' Nick stared at the iron bar gates, clad on the outside with corrugated sheeting. He hadn't taken much notice of them on the way in.

'Must be ten feet high.'

'Hmm.' Nick tried to remember Patrick's exact words. Hadn't he said something like, *must've had a key or got in some other way*? Well that stood to reason, if one looked at the gates.

They took a cross-country route towards Thorpe Morieux. With each twist and bend the van swayed and the builder's bags creaked. Nick loosened his seat belt and put a protective hand over his packed lunch. He was ready for the parquet avalanche, should it ever come.

'Why's it called the Dower House?'

'Beats me. It's not even close to Thorpe Hall, and that would be the obvious connection for a dowager.' Dave dropped a gear and accelerated.

'Maybe somebody wanted the mother-in-law well out of the way?'

'Could be a nickname that stuck, or even someone's idea of a joke. It's a Victorian pile with an Edwardian extension.'

'Sounds as confused as me.' Nick pictured the house, currently vacant and hidden away behind mature trees and a shrubby front drive. Only the tops of the chimneys were visible from the road. It would be easy to pass by without guessing it was there. He imagined it throwing off its shroud of damp moss and ivy, to reveal pale clay brickwork, as fresh and bright as the day it was built. Soon it would be liberated, watertight and someone's home.

The ride passed without incident and twenty minutes later, Dave braked hard on a corner and swung the van between two square stone posts. DOWER was carved into one and HOUSE, the other. There were no gates. Nick noticed holes in the sides of the stone. He guessed they'd once held iron hinges, taken when the gates were removed. He couldn't have said how long ago, he'd never taken much notice of gates before today.

'N-o-o; what now?' Dave slowed and banged the steering wheel with the flat of both hands.

Nick opened his mouth to speak, and then thought better of it. He scanned the scaffolding. It stretched from the ground to the roof and extended across the windows as if blinkering the very eyes of the house. Ladders and plastic shoots straddled the levels. A cement mixer and pile of sand were exactly where they'd been on Friday. The police car, however, was new.

'How did the police get here before us?'

'I don't know.' Dave's voice trailed into a groan.

Nick tried to think it through, as they parked next to the roofers' truck. Had Patrick set them up, he wondered. Had the policeman guarding the crime scene been suspicious and radioed ahead? Discovering Poynder's body had been grim, but today was turning into a nightmare as well. The apprentice release-day training was now fortnightly since starting his second year with Willows & Son. If it had still been every Monday, he'd have missed all this. Nick took a deep breath, waited for Dave to get out of the van, and then followed.

'What's going on?' he asked as they passed Jim, ruddy faced and carrying a load of slate tiles.

'All the drainpipes and guttering's been stolen. Sometime over the weekend, we reckon. The thieves must've bloody climbed the scaffolding to reach it. Bastards were after the cast iron and scrap metal.'

'I see they left your mixer and scaffolding. That was lucky.'

'Yeah, well.'

CHAPTER 5

'Bye, then. Will you be here next week?' Matt searched the girl's face.

'Yeah, need the money, don't I, but I'm dropping one of the night shifts. Two's killing me.' She yawned.

'Saturday? You'll be workin' Saturday?'

'Yeah, then I've got Sunday to recover.'

Matt watched as she pulled her coat tighter and crossed her arms as if to keep out the chill. It was the closest he'd got to asking a bird out on a date in months. He knew he couldn't consider working through the night, stacking shelves and taking deliveries at the back of the superstore, as a date. It was too much like hard graft. But it was good to pretend. 'See you then, Maisie,' he mumbled.

It wasn't cold. The autumn already promised to be the mildest on record since 1895. He'd read it somewhere on the internet. He was about to say something to that effect, but Maisie turned away and his moment had passed. Instead he watched as she walked through the empty car park, tight jeans tucked into Huggi boots, both arms wrapping her waist. He'd been right; working the night shift was a good way of meeting birds.

Matt checked the time on his mobile. 07:10. The shift had ended at seven and the Utterly canteen wouldn't open for another fifty minutes. If he went home now, he'd almost certainly throw himself onto his bed, burrow under the duvet with the faded Spiderman design, and die. The rest of Monday would be a write off. Except part of him didn't feel like sleep. His head was muzzy but his mind was still on the go. He was sapped of energy, his limbs felt heavy, and he couldn't tell if hunger or tiredness squeezed at his guts. An inner voice told him food wouldn't help, but he reckoned it was worth a try. Sausage, bacon and egg - that's what he fancied. It would set him up for his mid-morning lecture. *Then* he could go home and die.

He shivered. He knew it wasn't cold, but his body felt chilled, almost as if he needed to shut down. 'Diurnal clock,' he muttered. He'd read something about it some- where.

His brown Piaggio scooter waited like a faithful hound exactly where he'd parked it - and moments later, helmeted and with his denim jacket zipped to the neck, the two-stroke engine spluttered into life.

He idled past the trolley stations and sea of concrete, devoid of shoppers and beached cars. For a moment he im- agined himself the last man alive. Ultimate Man, a superhe- ro straight from his comic-strip books. He'd survived the plague, nuclear war and an asteroid strike. He was alone on the edge of an urban landscape and scanning for signs of life. He took his time. There was no hurry; the canteen didn't open till eight.

He skirted out of Stowmarket, looping east of the A14 and then back towards the town and the Academy. By the time he finally wheeled his scooter between the motorbike racks, it was still too early for the Utterly cooked breakfast. Someone caught his eye.

'Hi, Gavin,' he called as he balanced his helmet on the faux leather seat. 'You're early.'

'Could say the same about you.'

'Yeah, well I've just come off the night shift. No point goin' home first.'

'Yes, but do they pay you to wear their sweatshirt all day as well?'

'What?' Matt hadn't taken his jacket off. The logo was still hidden, stamped on the dark blue fabric beneath. Gavin couldn't possibly have seen it yet. He started to feel uncomfortable. What was it with Gavin, he wondered.

'What about you then, Gav? Why so early?'

Gavin fixed him with watery-grey eyes and then flicked his head back, a swift movement, twisting his neck as if cracking a whip. 'Not been sleeping well.'

Matt winced. The guy was weird. 'Bad luck, mate,' he murmured.

'So, now you're here, what are you going to do?'

'Eat, mate. Reckon the canteen should be openin' soon. Just need to stow this lot first.' He stripped off the jacket and packed it away with his helmet, then started to walk, a lumbering roll, shoulders hunched and head down. He knew Gavin was following. He couldn't hear the sand-creeper footsteps, but he sensed them.

When Matt reached the main entrance, he pushed the door hard, stepping through and letting it swing behind. He turned, half expecting Gavin to jump back and dodge the door, but there was no one. Nothing. Just empty space.

'Where's he…?' It didn't make sense. He couldn't have disappeared into the tarmac outside, could he?

The large entrance hall felt deserted and the pale marble flooring seemed to chill the air. Matt suppressed a shiver as he glanced up at a massive wall clock. He didn't bother to decipher the Roman numerals, the position of the hands were enough to tell him he still had six minutes to fill. He headed for the toilets.

By the time Matt walked up the main staircase leading from the entrance hall, he was better prepared for the day. He'd splashed cold water on his face, a kind of wake-up call, and now only a droplet or two still ran from his beard. With each heavy footfall, another spot seemed to leach into his sweatshirt, but at least he felt more alive, more *designer*. His nose caught the smell of bacon and sausages. He breathed in deeply, savouring the stomach-yearning cooking aromas as they drifted down from the canteen. He reckoned he'd been blessed with a slightly upturned nose for that very reason. To track food on a first floor level.

'Oh frag,' he muttered as he spotted Gavin mooching outside the canteen. 'I thought you'd pixelated off somewhere to get some kip.' He stared at Gavin for a moment, taking in his skinny jeans and soft-soled shoes.

'Already told you – sleeping's a problem. Weren't you listening, Matt, or are you just thick? Do you read the news?'

Matt blinked.

'You don't get it, do you Matt? You haven't worked out who I am, have you?'

'Look, mate – me insides are touchin'. Told you I needed to eat. I'll be listenin' and thinkin' a whole lot better with a plate in front of me.' He pushed past Gavin and into the canteen. There was no point in glancing back. This time he didn't care if Gavin followed. Instead he pictured a plum tomato, boiling hot and straight from a tin. He imagined the scalding splatter when he pierced it. Fork or knife, it would still be the same mini explosion of watery red liquid.

Memories of a different kind of explosion flashed back as tiredness pulled at his muscles. It might have been only sixteen months earlier, but the images were fresh enough. He didn't want to think about flying debris and the moment the Academy ovens went ballistic. Instead he focused on the woman behind the service counter as she lifted lids and then clanged them back onto stainless steel containers.

'No, no tomato, thanks. Extra beans instead.'

'Sorry, love. Baked beans haven't come through from the kitchen yet.'

'Awe ple-e-e-ease?' Matt tried his pleading puppy-dog face and tilted his head, dark sandy hair topping a ginger beard. She didn't seem to notice. Maybe she couldn't read sideways faces.

'So it'll be two bacon, two sausage and an egg.' She flicked a triangle of toast onto the plate and looked up, eyebrows raised. 'Anything else?'

'Can you throw in a cuppa for him, instead of the beans?' Gavin seemed to appear from nowhere, pressing up close to Matt, but directing his words at the canteen lady.

She stared at Gavin for a moment. 'Sure. You're the son of… that bloke, aren't you? Just been talkin' about it in the kitchen. Barbara said you're on a course here. Fancy seeing you.'

Gavin was far too close. Matt felt uncomfortable and slid his tray sideways. Why couldn't he just leave him alone? Matt rubbed his eyes and waited at the till, far enough away to watch but not catch his words. Gavin was shaking his head and staring at his foot; just the kind of thing Matt did when he didn't know something or there was a problem with his shoe.

'Shi-i-ite,' he breathed. Body language could speak volumes. And then in a flash he thought of *spam!* It suited

42

his new techie image better. After all, wasn't spam unsolicited and usually sent in bulk?

By the time he'd paid at the till, Matt felt more in control. 'Spam,' he muttered and slopped his tea. He carried his tray to a table near the plate-glass window, a modern addition giving a panoramic view across the Academy gardens. A quick glance behind to check Gavin was still talking at the service counter, and he reckoned he was safe to park his tray and tackle the bacon, sausages and egg.

'Hmm….' Egg yolk and bacon coated his tongue as he worked the first forkful around his mouth. The flavours exploded with each movement of his jaw. He closed his eyes and savoured the moment.

'There's egg on your chin.'

'Wha!' Matt half choked, swallowed and blinked away the blur. 'Where'd you–'

'Why didn't you wait for me?' Gavin banged a black coffee down, pulled a chair back from the table and sat, all the while fixing Matt with a steely gaze.

He felt skewered. A worm on a hook.

'And your sweatshirt's inside out.'

'Yeah, Gav. Did that when I freshened up. Reckoned on a designer look.'

'But the label's a give-away. It's rubbish. And the logo's still there. It may be on the inside – but it still shows through. We both know it's there.'

Matt forked a sausage. 'So what aint I heard, Gav?'

Voices carried, as a couple of early students pushed the canteen doors open. A burst of radio jingle drifted from the kitchen. Matt hoped his cheeks would stop burning.

'What's my name?'

'Gav. Why?'

'And my last name?' The grey eyes pierced, unblinking.

'Pointer.'

'Poynder. It's PoynDer with a D, Matt. Now do you get it?'

'Yeah, that's what I said. So?' He bit into the sausage.

'You must've heard about the man who hanged himself. The one they found at that reclamation yard, Friday. Now do you get it? Why I can't sleep?'

Something slotted into place. 'Are you sayin' he's–'

'My father, yes.' Gavin seemed to make the words formal, almost cold.

'You poor bastard.' Matt thought for a moment. 'So why d'you always say your name like it's got a T in it?'

Gavin leaned forwards. His tone changed. 'Because I like to draw a line, make a distinction. You see, he isn't my real father. So I'll have had a different birth name. I don't know what it was, but it won't have been Poynder.'

Matt couldn't think what to say. He was out of his depth. Drowning.

'Yeah,' Gavin continued, 'we're not so unalike, you and me. You turned your sweatshirt inside out to hide something. I drop the D and slip in a T when I say my name.'

'But why'd you want to hide your family? They're OK aint they? I mean, it's not like they're a supermarket chain. You're still upset, right? That's why you're not sleepin'.'

'I'm stressed out, Matt.'

Gavin stood up, scraping the chair legs on the floor. He seemed to sway, and strands of dark hair flopped across his pale forehead, a wild look crazing the grey eyes.

44

'But – you've got brothers? Sisters, right? You've still got your Mum.'

'How'd I know? I'm adopted.'

'No kiddin'! But your new family; you've still got 'em, even if they aint blood. Look, mate, is there anythin' I can do to help? I mean, after I've finished me bacon.'

Gavin didn't reply. Instead he shrugged and twisted away, pushing at the table and setting off shock waves. Coffee slopped from his cup as he snatched it up and ran to the door.

Matt blinked in surprise, forked more eggy bacon into his mouth, and munched. Words flew around his brain, like an electric storm. It was as if Gavin had thrown a grenade and Matt had taken a direct hit. If he closed his eyes now, he knew he'd be unconscious before his face hit the plate. Instead he concentrated on chewing and then mopping up the last of the yolk with the toast.

'Spam,' he muttered. 'Who'd 've guessed?' It was kind of sick. Sadness crept through his thoughts. The poor miserable bastard. And now Gavin, creepy Gav with the waspish tongue, was a celebrity - in a tragic way, and only by association, but still a celebrity. Matt shook his head.

A swig of tea failed to dislodge the bacon jammed between two molars. He sucked at his teeth. But why fix on me? What does Gavin want from me, he wondered. He thought of his own dad. He'd walked away when Matt was five. For all the contact he'd made since then, he might just as well have died all those years ago. At least that way there'd have been a reason for the silence and of course, some street cred. Had Gavin tried to trace his real dad? Matt guessed it was more than likely.

He massaged his eyes. It didn't help. The muzzy cloud was descending. What would Ultimate Man do? Power nap? An hour should be enough, he supposed. Mustering his focus, he set the alarm on his mobile, then let his head drift down, and down… and down.

***

'This isn't a bed and breakfast! Wake up.' The shrill voice cut into Matt's sleep.

'Uhh?'

'Didn't you hear me? Wake up. You're putting off the diners.'

'Uhh?'

'Look at you! Sprawled across the table. And your sleeve's got coffee on it. Are you on drugs or something?'

'What?' Matt sat up. His neck ached, his head spun.

'Are you OK?' The tones softened.

'I-I was eatin' me breakfast. Must've fallen–'

'Well the food's OK then.'

Memories returned as his brain rebooted. 'Beans would've been nice.'

'Come on, less lip. Now clear your tray and get out of here. I suppose you think they chose this colour to make it a rest room for you.' She started wiping the table with a damp cloth.

Matt picked up his tray. He quite liked the midnight blue paint. *Buzzzz. Buzzzz. Buzzzz.* The mobile vibrated and sounded its wake-up call.

He grabbed for his pocket and his plate slid across the tray.

'Watch out. Mind what you're doing!'

He killed the alarm. 'Sorry,' he mumbled. It was time to head for his lecture.

The rest of the day passed in a fog. He didn't notice Gavin at the lecture, didn't talk to anyone afterwards, just scootered home, crawled under his duvet and crashed out.

When he opened his eyes the following morning, everything seemed blurred. He stared at his arm and focused. Dried coffee marked his sleeve. His sweatshirt was inside out. Oh pixel, he thought. The canteen. Gavin.

A deluge of memories flooded his mind. He turned over, edgy and awake. He wrestled his duvet from under him, and with it, the last vestige of sleep. Why hadn't he asked more questions? What had he been thinking? Gavin would have told him anything. He sat up and the veil lifted. Now his brain was in gear. He flung back the duvet.

His laptop was by his bed, and within seconds he'd scooped it up, flipped it open and woken it from sleep mode. He keyed *Eastern Anglia Daily Tribune* in the search box and waited, chewing his lip. Seconds later he was onto the website. He was good at remembering number sequences, and he typed in the membership code for Utterly Academy. As long as Rosie never found out he knew it, he reckoned he'd be OK.

Tuesday's electronic edition popped up. He scrolled down the front page. He didn't know exactly what he was expecting to find; after all, a hanging on a Friday might be old news by Tuesday. *Thorpe Morieux* leapt off the screen as he scanned on. Hadn't Nick said he was working on a dower house out that way? He scrolled back.

Thieves used scaffolding to strip house, he read.

'Gutterin' an' drainpipes.' Matt sucked air through his teeth and browsed on. *A valuable bronze statue of Diana with Bow and Hound* had also been stolen from the garden. Who'd want Princess Diana *prancing across the lawn*, he wondered, but when he read further he realised she was some Roman Goddess with a penchant for hunting naked. That made more sense. 'Metal thieves who like nudes,' he muttered.

He didn't bother to look at more. Everyone knew copper, lead and just about all scrap metals were valuable. Thieves were even targeting the copper in earth conductors found in meter boxes outside peoples' homes. The yellow and green sheathing was the give-away. It was like an invitation to collect. There'd even been a spate of it on Matt's turf, the Flower Estate, though they'd never ventured down Tumble Weed Drive. Perhaps Tom had an influence, even from prison.

Skimming through the columns wasn't achieving anything. Instead he typed *Poynder* in the newspaper's search. 'Yeah,' he hissed.

It was only a short article. *Hanging Death Thought to Be Suspicious*, ran the headline. It seemed Police were *no longer treating the death of Marlin Poynder as a suicide*. Matt read the bit about the post mortem twice. It said *a head injury might have been instrumental in his death*, although Matt couldn't find any mention of how or when the head injury was supposed to have occurred.

'But there was a rope round his neck. The bloke was found hangin'.'

Matt didn't get it. Which bit of *a rope around his neck* didn't suggest some kind of strangulation?

He was intrigued, but he could see he wasn't going to get any further with the newspaper website. He pulled the screen forwards and closed the laptop. Matt reckoned if he wanted to find out more, then Gavin was his best bet. Trouble was, where to find him?

CHAPTER 6

Chrissie surveyed the worn leather. Cracks as deep as fissures traced the uneven wooden surfaces beneath. Time and sunlight had done their job so that now faded patches fatigued the green. The walnut edge along one side of the desktop had split away. It wasn't missing, just loose, and the central drawer wouldn't slide. She hoped the legs didn't need attention as well.

'Where to begin?' she murmured.

'Now come on, Mrs Jax. You've been doing this for over a year. You tell me how you'd go about repairing it.'

Chrissie took a deep breath. 'Well, it's a Queen Anne kneehole desk. I guess it's been put against a wall and there was a radiator close by. The carcass wood under the leather top, well it's probably pine or something. It'll have dried and shrunk. And then someone's tried to move the desk, lifting it by that edge. That's why it's split. The leather's had it.'

'Quite right. I knew you'd work that out, Mrs Jax. But tell me; what are we going to do about it?'

Watery October sunshine filtered through a window and caught the dust. For a moment the particles hung in the air, then swirled and danced, carried by unseen currents. Scents of pine, oak and mahogany mingled with linseed oil and beeswax. Chrissie took another breath, relishing the smells. Ron Clegg's workshop, an old barn with crowded bench tops and racks of tools, felt like a second home.

'I think the first thing to do is strip off the old leather. Then we can make good all the cracks underneath. Level it and repair the split edge. The drawer – well we'll have to take that apart. Do you know of a firm supplying new leather writing tops, Mr Clegg?'

'I do, as it happens. You're sounding like a professional. I think this calls for a mug of tea.'

Chrissie turned away, glowing with pleasure. Praise from Ron was praise, indeed. It only took her a couple of minutes to switch the kettle on, find the tea bags and make two mugs of steaming tea. She knew they'd sit on their bench stools and talk drawer runners and guides, leather tooling wheels and gold leaf, but she had other things on her mind. Now, before they started working on the desk, might be a good time to mention what she'd heard on the radio.

'I don't know if you listened to the news this morning, Mr Clegg, but it seems that auctioneer may not've killed himself.'

'Marlin Poynder? You mean it wasn't him they found?'

'No. I mean, yes it was him but they're saying he may have been murdered.'

'Really? But why? Why would anyone want to kill him? Ah you sure, Mrs Jax?'

'Well, it's what they said on the radio.' Chrissie thought for a moment. 'You knew him didn't you? His son's on the same computing course as Matt.' She tried to keep her tone light, didn't want to appear too interested.

Matt's text message had been short and to the point. She suspected he was excited by the association, and as always it was impossible to read anything into the words beyond their literal meaning. But that was Matt for you.

Ron sat quietly and sipped his tea. Chrissie waited.

'I knew him through the auction rooms.'

For a moment Chrissie couldn't tell if Ron was speaking to her or voicing his memories. He sounded wistful, his eyes focused somewhere else.

'He seemed a private sort of a man,' the soft tones were almost swallowed by the barn walls, 'and good at his job. He had a passion for automata. Obsessed with them. He was a family man, too. So his son hasn't followed him into the business, you say?'

'Well one of them hasn't. I don't know if he's got more than one. Maybe even a daughter?'

Ron must have caught her wry smile. 'Yes, a woman auctioneer. That'd be a first in the firm.'

'I'll drink to that, Mr Clegg.' She sipped her tea.

A distant rumble drew nearer. One two three, she counted in her head, and then the rotary beat boomed into her ears as the helicopter passed overhead.

'They're flying low today.'

Sometimes it felt as if Ron Clegg's workshop was actually in the centre of the Wattisham airfield itself, not on the perimeter lane. A year ago, she'd found the sound of the thundering engines unsettling. Now she hardly noticed, and when she did, the racket was reassuring, like an old friend. She pulled her mind back to Marlin Poynder.

'I've never really thought about automata before.' It was more of a statement than a question, but she hoped Ron would run with it. 'Are they sought after?'

'It's the French ones that collectors want. Mechanical singing birds in beautiful boxes.'

'So how's that different from a windup musical box, Mr Clegg?'

'Well, for a start, the birdsong comes from tiny bellows, not by a rotating metal drum pinging the teeth of a steel comb. And the mechanism is much more complicated than a musical box. Take the one Marlin showed me once. The bird bobbed up and down, moved its tail feathers, opened and closed its beak, and turned its head from side to side.'

'Good heavens.'

'Yes, and all the time the chirping and twittering was synchronised with the bobbing and beak movements.'

Chrissie tried to picture it. 'So it's a kind of adult's mechanical toy, Mr Clegg.'

'Exactly - beautiful, rare and valuable. The one I'm talking about was…,' he scratched his head, 'a Bontems one. Nineteen ten, maybe a little later.'

'So did Marlin Poynder act as an agent, you know, procure for other collectors? Or did he keep them for himself? It sounds rather an expensive hobby.'

As soon as the words were out, Chrissie realised what she'd said. Oh my God, she thought and bit her lip. 'I didn't mean….' Her face burned.

Ron didn't answer for a moment.

'It's difficult to believe he played in the major leagues, Mrs Jax. And anyway, the really valuable ones, the eighteenth century examples, are generally in museums now. This is Suffolk remember, and Marlin was based in an auction house in Bury St Edmunds. Hardly the world stage.'

Ron was right, of course, and she felt foolish. She'd allowed her imagination to fly. She was better sticking to evidence and hard facts. Wild conjecture was dangerous. She sipped her tea.

'Now, as we don't have cogs and wheels and leavers to strip that crumbling leather, you'd best pick a scraper and start removing it. If you're lucky, it should come off easily, Mrs Jax.'

In the event, the leather disintegrated as soon as she started working with the scraper. She found it difficult to lift an edge and any attempt to pull or tug merely made it fragment.

'Oh–'

She smothered the string of expletives exploding on her tongue. Pieces of ancient leather crumbled between her fingertips. She pushed her hair back, trying to cool her forehead.

'This might help, Mrs Jax.'

She spun around, frustration oozing from every pore. He stood, a paintbrush in one hand, a jar of clear liquid in the other.

'If you brush the water on where you're working, it'll make it easier, Mr Jax. It's probably a water-based glue sticking the leather, but if not, then–'

'Try a solvent – a lacquer thinner?'

She watched him nod. There was something about the way he stood. She knew he had arthritis, but he seemed to sag, as if he carried a sack of sand on his back, not a jar of water in his hand.

'Are you feeling OK, Mr Clegg?'

'Just a little shocked. And saddened, of course. That's all. Not every day you hear someone you know's been murdered.' He turned away and she sensed the matter was closed, the conversation over.

The rest of the afternoon passed quickly. There was no more talk. Chrissie scratched and scraped at the leather desktop while now and again, helicopters rumbled overhead. By four-thirty she'd removed all the remaining leather and glue.

'Time to call it a day, Mrs Jax.'

Chrissie didn't argue. Ron seemed quieter than usual, almost withdrawn. She guessed it was only to be expected if he'd known Marlin well, although he hadn't led her to believe that was the case. Was it all right to leave him like this, alone with his thoughts and memories? She didn't know, but one look at his face reminded her that grieving was sometimes best done in private.

'Would you like me to make you a mug of tea before I go, Mr Clegg?'

'That's kind, Mrs Jax, but really, I'm fine, thanks. You get off home. I'll see you tomorrow. Bye.'

Gathering up her hobo-styled bag, she lifted her hand in an informal gesture, something between a salute and a wave. Her slow-burning curiosity started to spark. Earlier, Marlin Poynder had been a talking point, but as of that moment he became a fascinating mystery. She made a decision as she pushed the heavy door open and headed into the courtyard. She needed to find some answers, if only for Ron's sake.

The late afternoon sun was sinking fast and cast long shafts of sunlight across the barn's weatherboard skin. Even the smaller brick building, Ron's second workshop, blazed. When she sat in her car, the light was so sharp she had to screw up her eyes against the dazzle as it fired from the skyline.

The track leading from the courtyard, with its ruts and potholes, rocked the TR7 as the tyres crunched over stones and sprayed gravel. She turned onto the Wattisham Airfield perimeter lane, pleased to escape the direct brilliance of the sun. She took the back route home to Woolpit, following the lanes as they wove between fields of ploughed-in stubble and recently harvested sugar beet. By the time she drew to a halt outside her end of terrace cottage, her mind was already flitting along a path and making plans.

She closed her front door, ignoring the junk mail on the hall mat. It could wait, she decided. Clive's waterproof jacket hung from a hook, along with her cagoule. She brushed past its horizon-red sleeve as she flung the car keys onto the narrow hall table. He'd left the jacket, she supposed, like an animal marking its territory. He'd passed it every time he walked down her hallway, but it still hung there. It would've been easy enough to flick from the hook and take it with him as he left. Was its continued presence a sign of his commitment to their relationship? Or was it a reflection of the remarkably dry weather they'd been having? She smiled. Either way, she felt lucky.

'Kettle,' she murmured and headed for the kitchen.

It was obvious she'd have to broach the subject of Marlin Poynder with Clive. After all, if it was murder, he was bound to be involved with the case. 'Hmm…,' but if she asked him straight out, he'd clam up. Professional confidentiality, and all that.

Brrring brrring! *Brrring brrring*!

She scrabbled for her mobile somewhere deep in her bag.

Brrring–

'Clive?'

'Hi Chrissie.' His voice sounded tinny. 'Things are rather busy this end.' The volume surged, then faded.

'It's not a good line. You'll have to speak up, Clive.'

'Sorry. I'm in the car, on speakerphone. Look, I need to talk to some relatives in Bradfield St George. Just wanted to let you know I'll be running late.'

'I didn't know you had relatives in Bradfield St–'

'I haven't, Chrissie. It's part of a murder investigation. I'll explain later but... why don't we meet up at the White Hart, about eight-thirty? If it's not too late to eat? They'll still be taking orders.'

'OK... if you're sure. I mean, if it's really busy we can meet up another evening.' Chrissie tried to keep her tone light.

'No, of course not. Eight-thirty, then.' The line went dead.

***

Chrissie stood on the old flagstones at the bar in Woolpit's White Hart pub. She thought it quite busy for a Tuesday evening.

'A glass of Pinot Grigio and a half of.... Is the Adnam's on tap?' she asked.

The barman nodded.

'A half of the Spindrift, then.'

She carried the drinks to a table in the corner, and was surprised to find the smell of beer and background voices strangely soothing. Clive hadn't arrived, but then he hadn't phoned, so she guessed he was still on his way. There were twenty minutes left before the kitchen stopped taking orders for food. She eyed up the specials scribbled on a board above the old fireplace. She reckoned they were more likely to be freshly prepared than the freezer-microwave combos on the regular menu.

Red Thai chicken with rice; Braised calf's liver with seasonal veg and sweet potato wedges; Fish cakes.... The writing was partly rubbed through. She pictured the dishes and her stomach rumbled. She sipped her wine.

No, she decided. She couldn't risk leaving the order any longer. It would have to be the red Thai chicken for her and the calf's liver for Clive. That way she could pinch a few of his wedges to eat with her spicy chicken. Two birds with one stone. She started to stand up.

'Clive!' She spotted him as he hurried in through the doorway.

He wore his work suit, but had shed the tie and loosened his collar. The short, auburn hair could have passed for an army cut. 'Sorry I'm late. Have you ordered?'

'I was just about to. Braised calf's liver OK? There's a half of Spindrift on the table for you. Why don't you sit down and I'll go and order.'

She watched him sink onto a chair and then headed for the bar. By the time she returned he appeared more settled.

'Did you find your relatives?' she asked.

He cast a heavenwards glance. 'The satnav tried to take me across a field. What a performance. How's your day been?'

'I finished earlier than usual. Ron called time at four-thirty so I was at home by five. He was rather upset when he heard the news about Marlin Poynder. I think he wanted to be left alone with his thoughts.' She paused, hoping he'd say something. Instead he drained his glass.

'Did you know he was a serious collector of automata? That's what Ron said.' Chrissie sipped her wine, conscious of Clive's searching look.

He let his breath escape slowly, a kind of resigned sound. 'I suppose it was a safe bet - you working out I'm on that case. Go on then. What's an autom–'

'An automaton? A mechanical wind-up toy with cogs and wheels, levers and springs, bellows and bells.' She flung her hand up expansively.

She watched his face, read the amusement in his eyes.

'According to Ron, he was... well he used the word, obsession,' she continued. 'I must admit I didn't know much about them, so I did an internet search after you phoned. I am now reliably informed, courtesy of Google. There's quite an international scene out there. Did you know there's even a new film out? Hugo. Do you want to see it? I think it's about an automaton that writes messages from the past.'

'Doesn't sound like my kind of film, Chrissie. So, are they valuable?'

'They can be. *Very* valuable. Do you think it could have a bearing on anything?'

He shrugged.

'Ron was..., well he found it difficult to believe he'd been murdered. Are you sure he was killed? Couldn't it have been suicide? Nick said he was hanging by a rope.'

'I know, but the pathologist found a head wound.'

'Couldn't that have come from the spiral staircase?'

'You'd think so, but no – he was struck on the head with something rounded. Those library stairs are nothing but sharp edges. It couldn't have come from them and forensics can back that up. And interestingly, whatever hit him was enough to knock him out but not kill him.'

They sipped their drinks for a while, each deep in their own thoughts. 'Ah, this looks like it's for us.' Clive smiled as a young man approached carrying plates of steaming food.

All contemplation of ropes and blunt instruments were swept aside as Chrissie caught the spicy aromas wafting from her plate. The next few minutes were taken up with cutlery, paper table napkins and finding space for side bowls of rice, vegetables and the sweet potato wedges.

'Why'd he have a rope round his neck? I still don't get it,' Chrissie said between mouthfuls.

Clive didn't answer. He loaded his fork with tender liver and gravy soaked vegetables.

Her thoughts raced on. 'So, are you saying he was on the stairs and someone knocked him out, then put the rope round his neck? And then what? Strung him up while he was still unconscious so he choked? To make it look like a hanging? A suicide?'

Chrissie shivered as she pictured the scene. She'd just described a well-planned, calculated murder.

'The thing is, Chrissie, what was he doing on the stairs in the first place? Although....' Clive's words were lost as he munched on sweet potato. 'Hmm, these are delicious. Do you want any more or can I finish them off?'

'No, no thanks. I'm on the rice now.'

They ate in silence, Chrissie savouring the chilli as the fiery flavours bit her tongue, while Clive seemed to eat mechanically. When he finally spoke, she had to lean forwards to catch the words. She couldn't be sure they were even meant for her.

'That's the puzzle - why would anyone climb those library steps? I mean they were right next to the stairs leading up to the first floor staging. If he wanted to get up there you'd think he'd just use the normal staircase. But he chose the spiral free-standing steps. They're not even connected to anything.'

'Are you sure he climbed them himself? Could he have been dragged up there after he'd been knocked out?'

'What?' Clive seemed to pull his mind back to her, as if he'd forgotten she was there. 'No, no signs of that.'

'Look, I'm going to get some sparkling water. My mouth's on fire. Do you want another beer?' She put her fork down, her hunger finally satisfied.

He didn't answer, just dabbed at the gravy with a wedge, seemingly miles away again. She left him to his deliberations and headed for the bar. A couple of late drinkers had just arrived and she waited while they ordered their beers, Suffolk accents so broad they could have been asking for rope, for all she could make of their words. By the time she returned with brimming glasses, Clive was sitting, back straight and eyes searching her out.

'Great! You got me another half. Thanks, Chrissie.'

'You looked as if you could do with one. For a moment back there, I thought you'd even lost the power of speech. Are you OK now?'

'Yes, of course. I think I've finally figured something out.' He leaned across and kissed her cheek.

'So are you going to share your eureka moment?' she asked, trying not to let him distract her with the kiss.

'Seeing as how you put me onto it in the first place, I suppose it would only be fair.'

'Come on then, share.'

'All this talk of automata - there was something like a piece of clockwork at the top of the library steps. Junk metal for scrap, Suffield said. But I think you may have helped answer a fundamental question. You said he was a collector, didn't you.'

'And you don't think it was junk metal?'

'Not any more, Chrissie.'

They passed the rest of the evening making plans for the weekend, Chrissie still glowing from her contribution to the case, and Clive resigned to his busy week ahead.

CHAPTER 7

Nick stopped the electric sander, pushed his ear defenders off and allowed air to waft over his sweaty head and short hair.

'Ahh,' he sighed, enjoying a moment's respite from the droning motor. It was turning out to be a sunny day and he was getting hot.

'Bloody bitumen,' he muttered. He'd grown to hate the stuff in the short time he'd been working on repairing and relaying the parquet flooring at the Dower House. He still didn't understand why, eighty years earlier, it had been so popular to use as the glue for the wooden blocks. He'd been chiselling and sanding off globs of the stuff, still hard and adherent to the underside of the oak.

He'd set the portable workbench on the old terrace and now he was enjoying the mild breeze and a view across the garden.

The French windows stood widely open behind him, and scaffolding spanned the back wall of the house. Tapping and knocking drifted from inside as Dave worked with a rubber mallet, easing the parquet blocks into position. It had been hard graft clearing all the old bitumen from the concrete floor and making sure the surface was dead level. At the start of the job Nick had felt more like a builder than a carpenter, but as Dave kept saying, preparation was everything.

They'd drawn lines from the walls to mark the centre of the room. Then, without using adhesive, Dave started from the centre and laid the parquet along the lines. He worked from a pile of prepared blocks, picking and choosing like a dry-stone waller while Nick kept him supplied with cleaned wood, having first checked the tongue and groove joints. Each parquet block was supposed to fit its neighbour.

'If we meet the walls and it's obvious we're going to have to cut off more than one half of the last row of blocks, then we'll need to shift the centre point. Adjust the lines,' Dave explained.

'A bit to the left, towards me,' Nick suggested about half an hour later.

Dave paced across the room and surveyed the lines. 'I reckon so.' He checked his watch. 'Time for lunch and this afternoon we'll take these up and begin applying the adhesive, starting from the–'

'Amended centre,' Nick finished. 'I'm going to eat outside. Might as well catch the last of this sun. D'you want me to fetch your lunch from the van as well?' He took the nod as a yes.

Nick slipped out through the French windows and around to the side of the house. At least the scaffolding hasn't spread round here, he thought as he scuffed through some fallen sycamore leaves, recent windfall but still too early for the glorious yellows and bronzes of late autumn. He glanced up at the old tree, branches almost touching the top floor windows, and for a moment felt its reassuring presence. And then its very size and closeness seemed to threaten.

'This house needs people living in it,' he murmured.

'Here, Darrel. Pass me the hammer, mate.'

Nick tensed. He'd thought he was alone. He'd forgotten about the roofers, overhead and out of sight. Jim's words had dropped downwards, as clear as if he'd been standing beside Nick, the tones as weathered as the owner's face.

'Police've been askin' questions,' a younger voice griped.

'Oh yeah? Just fishin' I expect.'

'You reckon? I'll bring some more tiles.'

'Nah, we'll be stoppin' for a break as soon as I got these last few hung.'

'You heard they came visitin' my place - sniffin' round me back yard?'

'No shit. I reckon someone's been braggin' down the pub.'

'Well, the bastards didn't find nothin' an' no one's made the connection with Vatry. I reckon I'm in the clear.'

'Hand me that tile, will you. Lucky you didn't fancy havin' a bronze in the yard. Might've been difficult explainin' that away.'

'Naked men? What'd I want with–'

'The one from here was OK though…. Nice tits.'

'Yeah….' The voices started to fade.

Nick relaxed his shoulders. He'd been right about the roofers. He hadn't liked them from day one. His insides gave a sudden growl as hunger surfaced.

'Lunch,' he muttered.

Dave had parked the van at the front of the house. Nick headed that way, determined not to get sidetracked by any further stolen words or bronzes. Luckily Darrel and Jim seemed to have disappeared, so he was able to concentrate on his mission. Five minutes later, he found Dave sitting on the terrace.

'You took your time, Nick.'

'Yeah, well it's a nice day. Here, I've brought everything that looked like your lunch.' He handed Dave a small cool-bag and thermos.

'Thanks. It's nice out here. The way they've laid out the garden... I could sit for hours just enjoying the view. You know there were statues dotted around? I heard they were stolen, along with the guttering and downpipes. Oh yes, and the front gates.'

Nick sat down slowly, conscious of the scaffolding behind. 'Can't say I noticed,' he lied.

'Some of the statues were cast in bronze, quite valuable I suppose.'

'Well they would be.' Nick slipped a couple of fingers inside the neck of his tee-shirt and eased it away from his skin. Where were Jim and Darrel, he wondered. He shifted his position slightly. 'How long 've we got once we lay the adhesive?'

The diversionary tactic worked. He knew Dave couldn't resist a technical question, and for the rest of the lunch break the conversation steered well clear of anything to do with metal theft.

The afternoon flew as they spread a small area of adhesive onto the concrete floor with a notched trowel, laid the central block and then worked outwards from it, laying more adhesive and blocks as they went. Dave tapped each tongue and groove joint into place with the rubber mallet while Nick darted between supply chain, chalk lines and adhesive. It was back-breaking work and hard on the knees.

'I thought I liked the herring bone pattern but to be honest, it's a bit of nightmare to lay.' Nick stood for a moment, stretching his back and gazing at the floor. 'I don't think I can look at it without remembering the pain.'

'What d'you mean? I thought you were meant to be fit. Tell you what, Nick - go and stretch those long legs of yours and get the chop saw from the van. Only one more block and I've reached this wall. And make sure you use the fence properly. It'll make it easier to cut the blocks straight.'

'Then we'll break for a mug of tea?'

'Dead right, we will.'

Nick hurried through the house. This time he thought he'd avoid the outside route. What he didn't overhear couldn't hurt him, he reckoned. As he searched through boxes in the back of the van, a large Mercedes saloon swept into the front drive. He recognised the driver as soon as he stepped out of the car. It was Mr Hale, the owner.

'Hello. It's Nick, isn't it?' The plump face broke into a smile. He stood for a moment, staring up at the front of the house while Nick closed the van doors, the chop saw finally recovered from a box.

'Hi, Mr Hale.' Nick thought him an old man, but Dave figured he probably wasn't even sixty.

'I'll be glad when we get shot of this scaffolding,' the man said, directing his words at the staging and metal poles. 'So how's the floor looking?'

'Pretty good. But come and see for yourself.'

Nick followed Mr Hale through the front door, their footsteps echoing on the bare floorboards in the empty hallway. They walked past the wide staircase leading up to the first floor and headed on towards the rear of the house.

They found Dave sorting through the pile of prepared parquet blocks, picking some up and then setting them down again.

'Everything OK?'

'Aah! Mr Hale, you startled me.' Dave's face blanched. 'Get a bit jumpy, what with that burglary.'

'Don't get me started. The bloody nerve of it. The garden statues came with the house, and the one of Diana hunting was actually quite valuable. Someone knew the house was empty, probably knew there was scaffolding. I bet the thieves were tipped off. You'd think it would be enough of a coincidence to give the police some leads. But no. Nothing. Bloody useless.'

'It's a dreadful welcome to your new home. So, how much longer before you move in?' The colour seemed to have returned to Dave's cheeks.

'The painters should be finished next week and then the carpets go down. We're due to move in Saturday week, not a day too soon. Now, how are you getting on with this floor?'

'It's going down well, Mr Hale. The old blocks will look really good when we've finished them.'

Nick nodded, his head buzzing with the roofers' words. He didn't trust himself to speak. The French windows were open and for all he knew, Jim and Darrel were outside and within earshot.

'So why don't you take the parquet right up to the wall?' Mr Hale continued, seemingly oblivious to Nick's inner turmoil. 'You've got enough, haven't you?'

'Plenty, but that's why Nick was fetching the chop saw. We need to cut some blocks, but we'll still have to leave a half-inch gap right at the very edge, to allow for any movement in the wood. Don't worry. It'll be covered by the skirting board.'

Nick didn't pay attention to the rest of the conversation; he was too busy with his own thoughts. In fact it was a surprise when he realised later over their tea break that he'd nodded when Mr Hale had suggested they work additional hours. 'Overtime? I agreed?'

Shike, he thought. I'm meant to be seeing Kat this evening. She'd been pretty gloomy about her Olympic hopes for the 50 metre target shooting. He didn't want to risk upsetting her, but to be honest, if it was a straight choice between cutting blocks with the chop saw or tiptoeing around a fragile girlfriend, the blocks had it hands down.

'OK,' he mumbled.

It was after six o'clock by the time Nick loaded up the van. They'd shut and bolted the French windows and then left through the front door, slamming it closed, latch down. He heaved himself up into the passenger seat and collapsed, exhausted as Dave revved the engine.

'We got a lot done in those couple of extra hours,' Dave said as he slipped the van into reverse and manoeuvred out of the driveway.

'Yeah. It looks good.' He hadn't thought about the roofers for a while, but one glimpse of the scaffolding brought it all back. 'Dave, have you heard of Vatry?'

'Who?'

Nick explained.

Dave didn't say anything. He seemed to be concentrating on the road.

'So, who or what do you think Vatry is?' Nick prompted.

'I guess he's a guy along the line.'

Nick wasn't following this. He waited while Dave braked hard at a T-junction and then accelerated away to the left. 'What line? Along what line?'

'The scrap metal thieves work in teams and networks. Put it this way, you can work as an opportunist or you can work on information. To be successful, first you need informers.'

'Scaffolders? Roofers?'

'Exactly, and maybe people like us, doing jobs in empty houses.'

'But you can't believe…. I mean nobody thinks we had anything to do with this?'

'Of course not, Nick. I'm talking generally. But the people who nick the stuff need to get rid of it. Vatry is probably the one with the contacts and a fat address book, the distributor with a list of dodgy scrap metal dealers. And I bet he knows a thing or two about bronzes, and probably any type of figurine, sculpture or statue as well. Some of it's going to be pretty hot. I reckon he'll have connections with other parts of the country or even abroad.'

Nick thought for a moment. 'Aren't they tightening the law, you know, about scrap metal? Don't the dealers have to keep records of where the metal comes from?'

'Don't make me laugh,' Dave snorted. 'Records can be forged. Addresses, names – all bogus. No, this is organised crime, but for metal instead of drugs.'

The engine grumbled as the van swung around a corner, forcing Nick sideways with G-forces he imagined worthy of a jet fighter. Jim, Darrel and Vatry, the names swirled in his mind as his stomach churned with the ride.

'Shouldn't we say something, I mean after what I overheard?' he asked.

'No point. The police need evidence. That's why they searched Darrel's yard. Just keep your head down and concentrate on the parquet flooring.'

They didn't say much for the rest of the journey, Dave focusing on the road and Nick deep in his own thoughts. By the time they reached Needham Market and turned into the Willows & Son entrance, it was twenty-to-seven and the daylight had faded. He guessed he'd better text Kat and let her know he was running late.

He pulled his mobile from his pocket and tapped out his message: *Been working late. Haven't got home yet. Need a shower and change. Do you want me to pick up Chinese takeaway? Could be round yours 8:30 earliest, may be 9:00?*

Before he'd had a chance to unlock his old Ford Fiesta, the reply pinged back: *9:00 too late to eat. Forget the Chinese. A drink at the Keys instead?*

Nick read the message. It was only a short drive from the Willows site to Barking Tye, where he still lived with his parents. He sighed. *OK*, he texted, not at all sure it was going to be an OK evening. He started the engine and slipped an Amy Winehouse CD into the player.

CHAPTER 8

Matt opened his eyes and stared at the ceiling. It was still only Friday morning, but already the prospect of another Saturday night shift filled him with dread. He needed the money and he wanted to see Maisie, but did he have to stack shelves and take deliveries? If only he could think of some other way to ease the cash flow.

He pulled his duvet snugly under his chin and half closed his eyes. Grubby white emulsion coated the expanse of plaster above. It had started to flake and peel in the corner nearest the window. The stains and blemishes blurred as he screwed his eyelids tighter. He knew if the merest chink of light filtered between his eyelashes, then the shapes would merge and reconfigure.

This time he hadn't been able make them into the image of a ghostly face, like the mask his brother had worn one Halloween. It had terrified an eight-year old Matt till pee ran down his legs and filled his shoes. Today the cracking paint had morphed into a frame and at its centre, a computer screen shimmered. Was it a message or a warning, he wondered.

He lay wrapped in his duvet and imagined himself a comic-strip hero. He'd be Geeko Dude, master of the QWERTY keyboard, the World Wide Web, and the universe. And like a Bond character, he'd have a pet chameleon to gaze at the screen and change colour with each key stroke, while he, Geeko Dude, would possess the power to switch between programmer, hacker or game designer. The dread churning in his stomach started to fade as he calculated he still had thirty-six hours left until the night shift.

Matt rolled over and buried his head under the pillow. It wasn't so crazy, he thought. One day, yes, one day he'd be like Geeko Dude. Not the bit about the weird lizard, but the clever bit; the programming and design part. People would pay him for his skills.

'Oh frag,' he muttered. 'Advanced text formatting. There's a teachin' session this mornin'.' He'd forgotten.

He groped for his mobile, his fingers finally unearthing it beneath the pillow. He checked the time. 10:00, he read. 'Pixels!'

He flung back the duvet and forced himself out of bed. He stumbled across his bedroom, catching a toe on his trainers. 'Ouch,' he yelped. There was barely time to sniff under the arms of a discarded tee, but he reckoned it was quicker than looking for a fresh one. Luckily it passed the test, so he didn't have to return it to the mound of yesterday's socks, jeans and sweatshirt. He threw on his clothes, grabbed a memory stick and headed for the door.

Moments later he sat on his most treasured possession, the Piaggio scooter, and accelerated over the concrete fissures in Tumble Weed Drive and away from the Flower Estate - and his mother's miserable bungalow. He'd yearned for a Piaggio Vespa but money was tight, so he'd settled for the second-hand Zip. Right make, wrong model. Tom had come up with the cash, and thank DOS he'd finally paid him off. The Halloween mask was small fry –Tom was capable of far worse.

It didn't take him long to ride to the Academy. Even as he stowed his helmet and locked the scooter, he was already thinking in HTML tags and angle brackets, the Hypertext Markup Language for browsers. He, Geeko Dude, was going to wrap up advanced text formatting at 10:30. 'I'll show 'em,' he told himself.

He skirted the side of the mansion building, sidestepping stragglers as they loitered in the unusually mild October weather, and then cut between an assortment of add-ons and prefabricated units. The computer lab, as the students called it, was tucked away near the language centre and a stone's throw from the car maintenance workshop. By the time he took his seat at a computer station, his tee clung to his back and beads of sweat stood on his forehead.

***

'OK, that's it for today.' The lecturer's voice cut above the fans whirring as they cooled the hard drives.

Nineteen students scraped chair legs on the floor as the session ended. Matt checked his screen. 12:30. Time had flown. So where was Gavin, he wondered. He didn't necessarily want to speak to him, just wanted to know where he was. That way he couldn't suddenly creep up and take him by surprise again. He was nowhere to be seen.

Following the principle of *last in first out*, Matt slipped away from the lab and headed for the canteen. He didn't hurry. It wasn't in his nature. Instead he took the shortest route, stepping through a side door and into a back corridor. Not many students ventured this way. The boiler room and service areas were off most people's radar, and the passageway felt dark and gloomy. He ambled on, thoughts centring on the hungry ache in his stomach and the possible food solutions. He imagined Geeko Dude writing a computational algorithm to solve the problem. His insides gurgled. 'On second thoughts…,' Matt muttered. Perhaps he'd forget the algorithm and just keep walking. The canteen and the choice at the service counter would hold the non-computing solution.

Someone flitted from a doorway a few yards ahead. Matt hesitated. The black skinny jeans looked familiar.

'Gavin? Hey, is that you, Gav?'

The figure turned, the pale skin seemingly even paler in the gloom.

'What you doin' along here, Gav?'

'I could ask you the same question, Matt.'

'Yeah, well I'm on me way from the lab to the canteen. Didn't see you at the HTML session. Why didn't you come?'

'I don't know. S'pose I didn't feel like it.'

'So why're you down here, then?'

'I don't know. Just wandering – exploring. Finding out what's behind all these doors. Don't you sometimes wonder, Matt? Aren't you ever curious?' The voice trailed away, wistful. Sad.

'Yeah, course. That's why I'm askin' what you been doin'?' Matt tried to read Gavin's face as he looked away.

'When I was little, you know, really young, I used to wander round our house and look under beds and in cupboards.'

'Why? Tom been hidin' your stuff too?'

'What? Tom? Who's Tom?'

'Sorry mate… I mean,' the skin burned under Matt's beard. He didn't want to bring his brother into this. 'Like an imaginary friend?'

'Tom? No I never had a Tom, if that's what you mean.'

'Then I reckon you were lucky, Gav.'

'Lucky? No way.' He started to walk and Matt fell into step alongside. 'Sometimes I found things. Things people had forgotten or hidden. It gave me a kind of power. It made me feel better.'

'Right, mate.' This was getting heavy. Matt felt uncomfortable and the sudden shared confidences were confusing. He wanted to say *you're weird, mate* but settled for, 'So, have you found somethin'? D'you feel better?'

'No.'

'Should've come to the HTML session, Gav.'

'Oh piss off, will you.'

'No, Gav, *you* frag off.'

They walked on, an uneasy truce developing as the narrow passageway widened into a main corridor, the artery running the length of the ground floor. Now the air buzzed with life. Students talked in groups, almost blocking the thoroughfare and making it nigh impossible to pass. They'd hit the lunch hour crush.

'Look, Gavin,' Matt muttered as he elbowed past an acne-pitted bloke with greasy skin. 'I'm sorry you're down. Me mates – we go drinkin' on a Friday. Join us, if you like. The Nags Head.'

Gavin didn't answer, just peeled off into the mass of students.

'Bot,' Matt hissed. How come he'd just asked Gavin out for drink, but Maisie... well, he hadn't even got her number?

And then a thought struck. Bot worked quite well. Perhaps he wouldn't trash the techie word quite yet.

***

'Still enjoying the course?' Chrissie shouted above the din.

Matt nodded.

The Nags Head was busy, even for a Friday. A handful of Stowmarket football supporters argued near the bar, and judging by the snatches of conversation riding on the beery air, feelings were running high.

'It sounds like there's a match tomorrow,' Chrissie mouthed.

'Yeah. D'you follow Stowmarket?'

'Does anyone?'

'The guys at the bar?'

Chrissie pulled a face. 'I wouldn't be so sure about that. It sounds like they may be changing allegiance. So what are you doing tomorrow, Matt?'

'Saturday? The night shift, I s'pose.' As he said the words he felt a crushing dread, so intense it overpowered the subtle clean taste of his lager. It became joyless in his mouth.

'It's a night shift, Matt. It doesn't take up the whole day as well.'

He glanced at her. She seemed to study his face.

'Well, what about doing something else instead? I mean, how about pizza delivery?'

'I aint thought... but, yeah; I've got a scooter, aint I?'

'You think?' Nick sat down, beer dripping from his glass. 'It's crazy at the bar. As long as it isn't Stowmarket colours, I reckon it'll still be there when you leave.'

'Oh my God, I came in the TR7. It's their home colours.'

'Yeah, it is kinda yellow, Chrissie. I don't s'pose it can get much yellower.'

'Oh shut up about the yellow, Matt.'

'I must say, I'd never put you down as a Stowmarket supporter. Will you be at the match tomorrow, Chrissie?' Nick gulped at his beer. 'Hmm, that's better.'

Chrissie narrowed her eyes. 'So how's the parquet going?'

'Ouch, that's mean. Did you hear metal thieves stripped the Dower House of its guttering and downpipes at the weekend? I reckon the roofers were behind it.'

'Yeah, I read somethin' about it. Also, a bronze Diana an' dog, 'cept they called it a hound. *Diana with Bow an' Hound.*'

'That's right. Dave said the garden statues had been taken as well; Diana hunting, or something. Have you heard of someone called Vatry?'

'A sculptor?' Chrissie asked.

A sudden shout and the sound of glass smashing onto the wooden boards drowned out Nick's reply. Matt twisted around to watch the ruckus.

'Right, that's enough, guys.' The barman stood tall. 'If you leave now, I won't call the police. Any more trouble and you're barred. Understand?'

Matt turned back, not wanting to catch anyone's eye. He kept his gaze low but a pair of legs in skinny jeans stood close by and seemed strangely familiar.

'Frag! How long you been standin' there, Gav?'

'A few minutes. Why?' Gavin seemed to sway, the tight-gripping clothes accentuating his stick legs and lean chest.

'You're doing that creepin' up thing again.' Matt's voice rose. Secretly he hoped his own clinging tee-shirt had a slimming effect and made him look svelte.

77

'I've heard the name Vatry before, if anyone's interested.'

'Gavin's on me computin' course,' Matt explained.

'Hi, I'm Nick. Yeah, what do you know about Vatry?'

'Oh, hi. I'm pretty sure I've heard Marlin–'

'That's his dad.'

'Not my real dad, you understand. I've heard him mention the name.'

'Marlin?' Chrissie cut in. 'That's an unusual name.'

'Yeah, Marlin Poynder.'

'Oh my G–'

Chrissie choked on her ginger beer.

'But you don't look at all like…,' Nick's voice trailed away.

Matt watched as his mates worked it out. Gavin might be weird and related to a possible murder victim, but he also knew stuff, and for the moment his willingness to tell put him centre stage. He shifted his chair to make space for him.

Music boomed from the jukebox.

'Great! The football fanatics 've gone and we're back to normal,' Chrissie muttered.

It didn't take Gavin long, once Nick bought him a lager, to enlarge on the double tragedy of his life – firstly, never feeling as if he belonged in his family, and now with this hanging, to lose his adoptive dad.

Matt's mind started to wander. He'd heard it before, and anyway, just about everything Gavin said was directed at Chrissie and Nick. Why was the star turn ignoring him now? I'm the one who invited him here this evening, he reasoned. Matt felt excluded, in fact pretty much the same way Tom used to make him feel. Uncomfortable. Undermined. Unimportant. He retreated into his thoughts and allowed himself to drift towards Saturday night and Maisie.

She was the reason he was working the shift in the first place. Well not Maisie herself. She just happened to be the first bird he'd talked to there. But that was the whole point. He'd reckoned on it being an opportunity to meet birds. He'd be nudging into them, easing past or helping them stack shelves, taking deliveries with them, and tea breaks. Yes, sharing tea breaks. The idea was to get up close; break the ice as it were, and have a reason to talk. He just needed some chat-up lines.

But there was a catch. Hard physical work didn't suit him. And then there was the problem of sleep deprivation, he hadn't expected to feel frazzled for days. So what was the smart thing to do? He resolved to get Maisie's number and ditch the shift. The trouble was he'd have to do the shift to get her number.

'Are you OK, Matt? You look kind of far away.' Chrissie's voice broke into his thoughts.

'What?'

'I said, you look kind of–'

'I must be going,' Gavin cut in. 'My mum, she's not my real… obviously, but she'll be worrying and I ought to be there for her.'

'Of course,' Chrissie murmured. 'And Gavin, well, we're really so sorry.'

Gavin stood up abruptly, knocking his chair back so that Matt found himself reaching out to catch it.

'Thanks for the drink, Nick.' He cast a half smile at the floor and hesitated.

Matt steadied the chair. 'Monday morning's lecture is somethin' 'bout *Digital Possibilities.* Maybe see you there, Gav?'

'Sure. Think you'll make it, Matt?'

'Yeah, Gav. Why shouldn't I?'

Gavin didn't answer, just shrugged and turned in one lithe movement. Matt watched as he dodged past the drinkers standing near the bar and slipped out into the night.

'You don't like him, do you Matt?'

'Why'd you say that, Chrissie?'

'Oh, I don't know. Just the way he–'

'He's upset. What d'you expect? He's just lost his father.' Nick drained his pint.

'Yes, you're right Nick. I wasn't thinking, just reacting. But we'll see you at the Academy on Monday if you're there, Matt. It's the fortnightly teaching day. Anyone want another?' Chrissie stood up, holding her empty glass.

'Yeah thanks, Chrissie. Another 'alf if you're buyin'. So, the teachin' aint every Monday any more then?'

'No. We're big, muscly, second year apprentices now. And just to prove it, I'm going to do the St Edmund Way walk with Clive. Right; drinks. Nick? Another half of Land Girl?'

Nick checked his watch. 'Yes please, I've just about got time. I'm meeting Kat shortly. What did you just say about your muscles?'

'Biceps and quads to die for. You're both invited to join us on the walk,' she said and headed for the scrum near the bar.

'Nick, was she bein' serious 'bout doin' the St Edmund thingy walk?'

Nick didn't answer.

'Nick?'

'Hum hmmm mm,' Nick hummed, drumming his fingers to the rhythm throbbing from the jukebox.

'You're hummin' again, Nick. Everything OK?' Matt asked.

CHAPTER 9

Chrissie felt unsettled. Meeting Gavin in the Nags Head the evening before had left her with a creeping unease. It seemed to her as if every day, layers of information were building up. The monochrome nothingness she'd imagined when she'd first heard Marlin Poynder's name now had colour, texture, a personality, and a son. She'd rather have kept Marlin at arm's length but fate seemed to be playing a different hand. It was making him real, bringing him closer, and she didn't want that. Yes, she'd always been curious, but this knowledge, this familiarity created a bond. It made her care, it gave her a sense of responsibility, and now it played on her mind. She ought to be able to do something. But what, she wondered.

Brrring brrring! *Brrring brrring*! Still preoccupied, she picked up her mobile.

'Hi.'

'Chrissie, I hope it's not too late.' Nick sounded weary. 'You haven't started your walk yet, have you?'

'No, I'm still at home. I was planning to leave for Lavenham shortly. Why?' She sat, clasping a mug of tea, her legs stretched out on the sofa and her feet thrust into a pair of slipper-socks. She'd considered the foot pampering an investment; after all, they'd be taking a pounding soon enough.

'It's just that, well Kat's having a bit of a crisis with her shooting. I think I'd said it's not been going well for her. Anyway, yesterday her coach told her to take a break from it for a week and I thought walking might….'

'Make her realise shooting's preferable to walking?'

'No, get her out and take her mind off it.'

'Sure, of course. Poor Kat. We were going to walk some of the St Edmund Way, have a pub lunch in Shimpling Street and then peel off and do a circular route back. How about we meet in the pub and then we can all do the circular bit together after lunch?'

'Great. What time do you think you'll hit the pub?'

Chrissie checked her watch. 'I don't know. Clive said he'd have dropped his kids off and be back in Lavenham by....' She did some calculations and then added an hour so there wouldn't be any pressure. 'We should be at the pub by about one o'clock, or maybe one-thirty.'

'Good. See you there then, Chrissie.' Nick rang off.

'Poor Kat,' Chrissie sighed. She knew she'd have taken it badly. The girl's father was a gunsmith. She was apprenticed to him, helping him run his gun shop somewhere out towards Somersham. Guns and target shooting were her life.

Chrissie turned her thoughts back to the day ahead. Walking boots and lightweight fleece; the list was short and the forecast good. Waterproofs? Clive's horizon-red jacket was still hanging in her hallway. Should she take it for him? No, she decided. A windproof was probably more than sufficient, and anyway, he was bound to have something high tech to fit the bill in his arsenal of walking gear. She swung her legs from the sofa and gulped the rest of her tea.

'Right, let's get this show on the road,' she murmured.

Ten minutes later and she was in the TR7, heading out of Woolpit. The soft-top was down and the mild October air breezed through her hair, pulling and tugging as she accelerated along the lanes and swooped around the corners. Vibrantly ripe rosehips peppered hedgerows, wild and overgrown. A pheasant ran from a grass verge, narrowly missing her beak-like bumper. She ignored the unease niggling at the back of her mind and concentrated on the road ahead.

Lavenham was a pretty village, Clive's home comfortable but tired. The house held too many echoes of Mary his ex-wife, for Chrissie's taste. They'd split before she'd met Clive, but judging by the décor, she could imagine what she'd been like. Fussy in a frilly kind of way, and dull.

She slowed to a halt and then reversed into a tight space outside. She knew he was back from his child ferrying duties because the black Mondeo was parked on the narrow concrete drive. Moments later, he was leaning over her driver's door and kissing her lightly on the cheek.

'I heard your engine from the end of the road. I think all four cylinders are firing.'

She laughed. 'I hope so. Did you get Ellenor and Josie to wherever they needed to get to?'

'Yes, no problem. My step-dad duties are completed for this weekend and now I'm free, with brownie points in the bag as well.'

She watched him smile. He made light of his divorce, seemed almost relieved Mary had left him, but he missed Mary's kids. She could tell. Now, she understood there was a second step-dad as well as the absent father in the mix. She'd decided to stay well out if it.

'Good,' she said. 'There've been a few developments. Nick and Kat have asked if they can join us on the walk, so we're meeting them in the pub for lunch.'

'Sounds good to me.'

She'd half expected him to throw up his hands in mock horror and say something on the lines of it not being a Saturday stroll, there'd be no time for lunch and an egg baguette on the move should suffice. 'You seem very re-laxed. Is your case going well?' she asked mildly.

'Have you got everything you need?'

She nodded.

'We might as well get to the start of the walk in your car then. If you just wait a moment, I'll put my stuff in your boot.' He turned on his heel and disappeared into the house.

So he didn't want to talk about work. Come Sunday evening, she knew his mind would be focused on the week ahead. That would be the time to casually drop the bit about meeting Gavin into the conversation. He might be more receptive then, she decided.

The next few hours were spent rambling the St Ed-mund Way. They skirted past the disused Lavenham Air-field, a relic from WWII, and followed the trail across the A134 onto the largely uninhabited patchwork of fields to the west of the main road. The sky was grey-blue and cloudless, the air warm but with a slight breeze. Chrissie started to feel the tensions of the past week drop away as she breathed in the scent of freshly ploughed soil and a faintly acrid tang of recent fertiliser.

***

Lunch had been eaten far too quickly. Chrissie could have lingered in the pub and happily rested her feet all afternoon, but Nick and Kat were itching to start walking, and Clive, well, he liked nothing better than to be striding out. She suspected his eagerness to get going was triggered by a de-sire to avoid talking about metal theft, a subject Nick had raised over a plate of sausage and mash.

As planned, they left Nick's Fiesta in the pub's car park and headed away from the St Edmund track to take a circular route over more isolated paths. Nick set a fast pace, with Clive and Kat hard on his heels. Chrissie found herself wondering if she should have worn thicker socks as one boot rubbed on her heel.

She slowed her steps and dropped behind a little to ease the soreness and enjoy the panorama. The ground sloped away into a shallow valley cut by small streams. Trees and woods capped the land, accentuating the hollows and raising the skyline. They made low hills out of the countryside. It was a gentle earthy landscape quilted with fields.

'Definitely rolling,' she murmured. 'Breathtaking. I should've brought my camera.'

A spark of irritation fired. She'd already walked several miles with Clive before the pub lunch. Why were the others speeding ahead, she wondered. Was this a workout? An endurance test? With head down, eyes on the path and feet mechanically pounding forwards, she might just as well have been on an exercise machine. No, she resolved to enjoy the scenery and the intoxication of the great outdoors.

The path skirted a wooded area. Chrissie gazed into the undergrowth as she walked. Red berry-like fruits blushed on waxy, needle-fronded leaves. Deadly, she thought. Yew trees grew naturally in the wild, but these looked as if they'd been planted. The mix of trees just didn't strike her as diverse enough to be natural, and some of the yews seemed very old.

The edge of a weathered flint building came into view, partially masked by tree trunks and dark green foliage. It was set well back from the track. Chrissie peered into the shadowy, dappled light. The end wall looked narrow and windowless.

'A mausoleum or tomb?' she murmured. She didn't recall seeing a church or graveyard marked on the map.

Voices carried on the breeze. They seemed to come from the far side of the building.

'It's OK, we're clear now. The walkers didn't see us.'

Chrissie froze. Were they talking about her friends who were probably already power-walking down to the brook ahead?

'Come on, get these railin's on the van,' the voice growled.

Van? How could anyone drive a van up here, she wondered, unless there was a track somewhere on the other side of the wooded area. And then Chrissie noticed the smashed concrete; it must have held the railings.

'Aww, stop complainin'. They're heavy 'cause there's lots of iron in 'em. Should get a good price.'

Leaves rustled and a branch cracked.

'This'd better be bloody well worth it.' The new voice sounded younger and nearer. Too near.

'Oh my God,' Chrissie breathed as a pulse hammered in her ears. It was time to leg it. She wasn't going to hang around and get caught up in this. With only one thought in mind, she turned to face the path.

A man in a grubby sweatshirt and jeans strode around the corner of the building.

'Oi! What the–'

She screamed. Fear and reflex took control. She bolted, springing forwards and gaining speed. One step, two steps, her foot snagged. It stopped dead on something rope-like and unforgiving. Her body flew on. The bramble trip-wire tugged back. Down she went. Desperation and panic shrieked as she hit the ground.

'Shit, let's get the hell out of here,' a harsh voice yelled. 'There's some mad woman back here.'

'N-o-o,' she moaned, wondering what had felled her. Frustration exploded, flipping her stomach and catching her breath. She scrabbled forwards, gasping as she pushed herself up onto her knees. She had to get away, had to distance herself. How had the others walked past and not realised what was going on? Bloody exercise machine syndrome, head down and blinkered view.

She staggered to her feet as a van door slammed and an engine revved. Were they going? It might only be a clever trick. Memories of a previous attack flashed through her mind. *Don't shut me in the mausoleum* she inwardly cried, as terror acted like touch paper. She launched into a run, as if her life depended on it. This time she watched out for each grassy tuft, rabbit hole and bramble as she covered the ground with desperate leaping strides.

The path sloped gently. 50 yards. 75yards. She started to slow.

'Hey, Chrissie.? Was that you screaming? Are you OK?' Clive's voice carried back up the track to her.

'Cli....' She hadn't enough air in her lungs.

'Chrissie?' Nick shouted from somewhere in the distance.

She slumped to the ground, ribs aching. Coarse long grass, nettles and stones greeted her as the soil struck cool through her walking trousers.

'Chrissie, what's happened? Have you hurt yourself?' Clive appeared around a bend in the track, trees to one side, open fields to the other.

'Didn't you see those men?' Her voice broke as she panted. 'Back there, Clive. If you're quick, you might just catch them.' She pointed back up the path.

'What's happened?' Nick's breath came in short bursts as he pounded up behind Clive.

'Back there, ransacking that mausoleum thing. Hurry, Clive.'

She watched as Clive hesitated, seemed to make a decision and then broke into run.

'Hey, Nick. Give me a hand up, will you.'

'What mausoleum, Chrissie?' He reached out and pulled her to her feet.

'Thanks. Didn't you notice as you walked past?'

'No, Chrissie. Hey Kat! Can you stay with Chrissie? I better go with Clive.'

Chrissie looked into Kat's flushed face, her hair a riot of toffee-coloured curls.

'I heard screaming. Are you hurt? Can you still walk?'

'Sure. I just…. Why did you all have to go so fast? It isn't a race.'

Chrissie tried to compose herself but as she stood, catching her breath and describing what she'd heard and seen, she felt mortified. Kat must think her panicky, hysterical and foolish. She'd been spooked like a rabbit. Now her cheeks burned, adding to the glow from her mad dash.

'Do you think the men have gone, Chrissie? Did they seem dangerous?'

'Oh no, Clive and Nick!' She didn't need to say more.

The same thought had obviously just struck Kat.

CHAPTER 10

Without much thought, Nick ran back along the path after Clive. The look on Chrissie's face haunted him. She wasn't by nature a screamer, but hearing her shriek had ignited a mix of alarm and urgency so compelling it still spurred him on. He must have covered at least twenty-five yards before he realised he hadn't any idea what he was going to do. Clive was ahead. That was the only certainty.

The words mausoleum and ransacking rang in his ears. It implied thugs and vandals only expecting a run-in with the dead. If that was the case, then he needed to sound enormous, angry and very much alive.

'Hey,' he bellowed, hoping the hooligans would take fright and bolt.

His heart hammered as he sucked in more air. With each bound forwards he yelled and shouted, closing the distance on Clive. He scanned the trees, his eyes searching the undergrowth to one side of the path, desperate to spot some hint of a tomb or memorial. He didn't know what to expect. He hadn't noticed anything when he'd passed, less than fifteen minutes earlier.

And then he saw the steely-grey flints, broken and split, set in mossy concrete and showing their glassy centres. The trunk of a large, squat yew blocked most of his view. He slowed his pace and bit back his rasping breath.

'Clive? Are you there?'

Panting, he picked his way from the path, over some brambles and then across sparse vegetation, starved of light under the yew's shady branches. 'Clive?'

'Nick? I'm round the front. Watch where you tread.' Clive's unemotional voice radiated authority.

'Thanks,' Nick breathed. At least Clive sounded unharmed. 'Have they gone?' he shouted, stepping over a broken concrete plinth and skirting the side of the building. He kept his head low, watching the ground.

'What the hell…?'

'Told you to watch your step.' Clive stood, mobile phone in hand and taking shots.

Nick focused on what he thought were sticks caught in clumps of material, the fine weave disintegrating and strewn on the ground. Twigs and canes spilled from a brown stained mass. He wiped his forehead and blinked to clear a trickle of sweat from his eye.

'They've broken in. Smashed down the door.' Clive turned his mobile to face the splintered wood and clicked.

'But what's all this on the ground? What were they after?'

'I guess they wanted the lead lining from the caskets or coffins.'

'But the contents….' In a flash, Nick realised what he'd been looking at. He felt his throat tighten. 'Oh that's sick.'

'Yes, bloody Neanderthals. No, don't go in. Some of the remains were liquid. And it smells bad. But it could have been worse.'

'Worse? How could it be worse, Clive?'

'Well, judging by the dog collar and some of the skulls, it was a mausoleum for family pets.'

'Animals? You're kidding me, right? I didn't know things like this existed.'

'Well, it's Victorian. Customs change, but I don't think we're looking at human remains, at least I hope not.'

A waft of pungent decay struck Nick. Strength drained from his legs. He sank down beside a section of concrete plinth and rested against the fractured stone. Holes punctuated its length.

'It's sick,' he repeated.

'Are you OK, Nick?' The tone was concerned, but the manner policeman-like. 'They took the iron railings as well.'

'How d'you know? Did you see the sick bastards?'

'No, but they dropped a section. It's lying up there, where they got access with a pick-up. We must've disturbed them. It looks as if they left in a hurry.'

Nick tried to marshal his thoughts. 'So what do we do now?' Action seemed preferable to thinking about skulls and rotting dog collars.

'I've already phoned the chaps at Bury. They'll send a patrol car over, and someone'll inform the landowner and come and board this up again.'

'And then I suppose it'll just end up on a list of break-ins and no one will ever be caught. Right?'

'Something like that.'

'Shike, it's the same where I'm working. All the guttering and some garden statues are nicked and even though it's obvious the scaffolders or roofers are behind it, no one can nail it on them. Traceability? Seems there's none for metal. I even heard them talking about a guy called Vatry, but Dave said there was no point in reporting it. Proof? It's impossible.'

'Vatry, you said?'

Nick nodded.

'That's an unusual name. I'll pass it on. Where are the girls?'

'I left Kat with Chrissie. I'll text her. Let her know we're safe, crisis over.'

Nick shot a text off and then scrabbled to his feet. While he waited for Kat's reply, he wandered over to where he imagined the pick-up must have parked. He needed to distance himself from the putrid tang cloying the air.

The railings had once been painted black and where the section had been dropped, a shower of flaking paint and rust speckled the ground. Nick bent to look more closely. The hinge gave it away. This wasn't a section, but one of a pair of gates. A metal shield was incorporated into the centre, like a coat of arms.

'A hound and a hunter,' he murmured.

He could just about make out the hunter was a woman, with a bow and only a wisp of cloth covering her modesty.

'A huntress?' Was there such a word, he wondered. He still held his mobile, and without any real thought, levelled it over the rusty gate and took a photo.

Ping!

He almost flipped the phone into the air with surprise. For a second he'd forgotten Kat, but the message alert pulled him back to the moment.

He read her text. *What's going on? Chrissie is fine. Do we walk back to u or wait here? K x.*

'What do you want to do, Clive? Carry on with the walk or hang around here till the police arrive?'

'Let's see what the girls want to do.'

Nick picked his textual words carefully. *Clive's phoned the police. Some dead animal bones and a bit smelly, otherwise OK here - apart from missing metal.*

Her reply flew back. *Be with you in less than 5. K x.*

Nick smiled. He might have guessed Kat would be itching to see what all the excitement was about, and true to her word, it wasn't long before footsteps rustled through the undergrowth.

'Are you both OK?' Chrissie's voice sounded overly loud.

Clive slipped his mobile back into his pocket. 'They'd scarpered by the time we arrived. That scream of yours must have done it, Chrissie.'

'Yeah, good on you,' Nick added. 'Must've galvanised them.' He felt a thwack as Chrissie swiped at his shoulder.

'Watch it. I'm still too fragile for metal jokes.'

'Well, you two were bloody lucky they'd run away. You weren't to know, and this could've ended very differently.' Kat seemed to direct her words at Chrissie.

'It's OK, Kat.' Nick picked up the wave of tension and gave her a hug. 'Look, shall we carry on with the circular walk?' He wasn't going to admit it, but he needed to get away from the mausoleum, and the stench of death wasn't getting any easier on his nose.

'Are the police coming?' Chrissie asked. When Clive nodded, she continued, 'Hey, I'll stay with Clive in case they come back before the police turn up. I've got at least one more scream in me.'

Nick saw the look she flashed at Kat. 'Why don't we all meet back at the pub?' he suggested.

'Yes, it could be a while before the police find this place. And if you head straight back, Chrissie, it'll be a shorter walk for you.' Kat squeezed his hand. 'Besides, we'll probably have done the whole circuit by then.' She dropped her voice, 'At the rate you walk.'

He bit back the *meow*. One person showing their claws was enough. He caught Clive's glance, followed his lead and kept the tone light as they agreed to all meet up in the pub.

'I'll give you and Clive a lift back to wherever you parked the TR7,' he promised. 'But I may need a pint first.'

***

The dent in the bodywork looked worse in Sunday's bright daylight than Nick had expected. He'd left Kat at about two in the morning, and driven back to his parent's home in Barking Tye. He needed a shower and to catch up on some sleep, but he'd allowed his mind to drift and the watery blackness of the early morning hours had cloaked the gate-post. It was a simple misjudgement, a lapse in concentration and the front wing of his old Fiesta had paid the price. He'd felt the car nudge the post, but at the time he hadn't stopped to look, just parked up silently and then crept in through the kitchen door. One day, he thought, he'd have his own place, but freedom and privacy came at a price.

Nick ran his hand over the grazed paintwork. At least no other car had been involved and Dave might know of some body repair place where he could get a discount. With any luck he'd keep his insurance company out of it.

CHAPTER 11

Matt finally plucked up courage to ask. It was now or never. 'Maisie, d'you want a lift on me scooter?'

He stood with his back to the door, blocking her path to the exit. It was a few minutes past seven in the morning and the Saturday night shift, spent taking deliveries and stacking shelves at the supermarket, had at last finished.

'Why?' she asked.

She'd stumped him. He been prepared for a no, but the why was a surprise.

'Because....'

'Because what?'

'Not many buses at this time on Sunday mornin' and... I aint here next week. This was me last shift. I'm deliverin' pizzas instead. Reckon it'll pay the same and I'll get more kip.'

'Oh yeah? So why'd I want to know what you're doing next week?'

'I thought....' Matt felt his cheeks burn despite the chill in the goods delivery area. He watched as she folded her arms, pulling her loose-knitted cardigan closer. He tried again.

'I might not see you next week an' I thought....'

'What?'

'So, do you want a lift or not?'

'It's a scooter, right?'

Matt opened his mouth, thought better of it, stared at the ground and nodded.

'OK, then.'

'You want a lift?'

'Yeah, I said OK, didn't I?'

'Right. Yeah, right.' Excitement fought with tiredness as he led the way through the exit and out onto the concrete forecourt.

'So where's the scooter?'

He pointed. The Piaggio was the only scooter parked between the motorbike stands.

She brushed past him and he followed, noticing the streaks in her bleached hair and how tightly her jeans hugged her thighs.

'It's a Piaggio Zip,' he called. 'Italian. Same people who make the Vespa–'

'Yeah, yeah, yeah. Do they only make it in brown?'

He pictured the spec sheet he'd read on the makers website. Did she mean for the year 2009, the year his Zip was made? He narrowed his eyes as he mentally read the print. 'White, black–'

'Stop. I don't want a list. I was making a comment.'

'Oh I see.' He didn't see at all. 'So where d'you live, Maisie?' he asked as he unlocked the stowage compartment under the seat.

'Stowupland. Have you got a helmet for me?'

'Oh spam.'

'That's a no, I take it.'

They stood either side of the scooter, her expression unreadable while he felt his face change through what he imagined was a shade card of crimsons.

'You've got to promise to drive slowly, Matt.'

'It's only 49cc and there'll be no one around at this hour if we take the back lanes.'

'OK.'

He couldn't believe his luck when she climbed onto the scooter seat behind and slipped her arms around him. It was as good as a date. No; better, he thought as he remembered the smattering of miserable encounters he'd had with other girls in the past.

He started the Piaggio and eased away, twisting the throttle. With his helmet on, he couldn't hear a word she said. So on Matt's suggestion, they'd agreed a system of right or left sided squeezes and taps as directions.

He wove slowly through the Bird estate and then, guided by Maisie, followed the road under the A14. He thought he was familiar with the back ways in the area, but she seemed to know a series of criss-crossing routes, some more like farm tracks than lanes. She signalled for him to stop when they reached houses behind some playing fields in Stowupland.

Disappointed, he pulled off his helmet and waited while she dismounted.

'Thanks, Matt. I can walk from here.'

'So which one d'you live in?' He looked around, hoping to see an obvious house she'd head for.

'Just around the corner. So whose pizzas are you delivering?'

'Ott's Pizza Place.'

'Well, I reckon if I order a takeaway, you'll find where I live.'

'I'll be deliverin' Saturdays and Sundays.'

She'd turned and hurried away so fast, he wasn't sure if she'd heard him.

'Saturdays and Sundays,' he called after her.

Matt pinched himself. Was this really happening? For once in his life he'd got lucky. It was only when he pulled his helmet back on that he realised he still hadn't got her number. 'Frag,' he muttered.

He took his time riding back from Stowupland, more or less re-tracing his outbound route. To be honest, he'd found Maisie's arms around him rather distracting, but now he was able to concentrate on both the road and scenery. He certainly hadn't noticed the vehicle dismantling outlet hidden behind high hedges and left to grow wild like scrubby woodland. He slowed and glanced in through the giant grilled gates. The name *TARV Auto Recycling* peeled on a large painted board. Cars were stacked two or three high. A huge grasping crane stood idle, its hydraulic piston rods glinting in the watery morning sun. Funny, he thought, how long he'd lived in the area and had no idea something like this existed.

He needed to get home and sleep. The hormone rush from giving Maisie a lift had run its course and the exhaustion of working the night shift was taking hold.

***

It was Monday morning and Matt felt very much awake. He'd slept on and off for the best part of twenty hours and now his mind was alive, primed for action and sharpened for the mid-morning lecture, *Introducing the concept of Algorithms, Data Structures & Computability*. He liked the idea of being a computational thinker. It was how he reckoned Geeko Dude processed the world.

He parked the Piaggio in the Academy motorcycle stands and let his hand linger on the faux leather cushioning as he locked his helmet in the under seat stowage compartment. Had it only been yesterday? He tried to picture Maisie as she might have looked comic-strip style - leaning into

99

his back, arms clasping his waist, and hair whisked into a twenty-eight mile-an-hour slipstream.

'Street cred high,' he murmured. But of course no one had seen. Why else had they taken the back routes? There would be no off-the-Richter-scale rating.

He glanced around, half expecting Gavin to appear from nowhere. There were virtually no students walking through the car park, but he checked again, just to be sure. Then he recognised the weathered blue paintwork of one of the parked cars. It was Nick's blue Ford Fiesta.

Matt headed for the canteen. He reckoned it would be the most likely place he'd find Nick before the apprentice release day session started at nine.

The canteen was busy and filled with the smell of bacon. Metal trays clattered across warming plates and spoons grated on steel containers, as servings of baked beans and scrambled egg were dolloped onto dishes. Sounds of Radio Suffolk filled the airwaves. Matt queued at the service counter and scanned the tables, searching for Nick's familiar profile.

'Hi,' he said when five minutes later he carried his platter of saturated fats and side order of baked beans to a window table, and sat down alongside Nick.

'Hey, Matt. How are you, mate?'

'I'm OK. You aint leavin' yet, are you?' He squinted at Nick's empty plate.

'No, I'm still drinking this.' He sipped a mug of tea.

Matt dug into a sausage as Nick told him about his weekend.

'No kidding? You mean it was some weird place for dead animals? That's… weird,' he muttered through mouthfuls of baked beans. The idea of little lead caskets for dead cats and dogs was just plain creepy. They talked on, unaware of the time.

'And then you clipped the gatepost? Frag.'

'Yeah, shike happens if you're me. And it was a bit more than a clip. So, what about Maisie? Did you get her number?'

He opened his mouth to answer, but his words were drowned as a student scraped back a chair and others gathered up backpacks.

'Hell, is that the time?' Nick muttered looking at his watch. 'Catch you later.'

'Yeah, see you at lunch, mate.'

Matt was left with his thoughts and a forkful of bacon. He figured he'd surprise Nick if he, Geeko Dude, sourced a replacement front wing panel for the Fiesta. Naturally the first stop would be a computer. There was at least an hour before his mid-morning lecture. Plenty of time.

The library was quiet, even for a Monday morning, and Matt felt self-conscious as he sauntered past the deserted library assistant's station. Where's Rosie, he wondered, as he peeped through the office doorway. Inside, Mrs Wesley the librarian seemed occupied with whatever filled her computer screen.

'Yes? Can I help?' Her tones didn't seem to invite a reply.

'Sorry, I was…. Is Rosie here today?'

Mrs Wesley glanced up from her screen. 'Oh, it's you. If you need some help, Martine is in.' As always, she spoke without looking at him directly.

'Thanks, Bill,' he said under his breath. There'd been a legendary striker who'd played for Stowmarket football team many years before, and the students' nickname for

Mrs Wesley had stuck. Matt had never quite understood the handle, but he liked its quirkiness.

'Thanks,' he mumbled again and headed for a computer out of the way near the corner. It didn't take him long to key *TARV Auto Recycling* into the search box. Moments later and he was on their website. It's a good deal, he thought, as *TARV* came up with a selection of panels for a Ford Fiesta MK3. So was it a right or left front wing? Had Nick said? He scribbled the phone number and opening times on a scrap of paper. Mission accomplished.

Fired by success, Matt typed *Vatry* into the search box, but – no leads, nothing. Perhaps he needed to take a fresh approach, start from the end product? He typed *bronze statue Diana with Bow and Hound* and waited.

'Bot,' he muttered as hundreds of thousands of results came up. There was every combination imaginable for sale on eBay. It seemed bronzes of Diana came in every size, with: bow or spear, deer, hounds, goat, stag, wings or even a moon-like headdress. And style? Classical, Art Nouveau or Deco.

'Frag.' He wasn't getting anywhere. It might help if he knew what it looked like, but there hadn't been a picture in the newspaper when it was reported stolen.

Without really thinking he keyed in *stolen metal* and then clicked on a stolen metal alert site. He scrolled through the pages.

'Yazoo,' he hissed. 'Result.'

'Wow!' Gavin leaned over his shoulder.

'Spam, where'd you come from?'

Gavin ignored the question and read, '*Solid bronze statue of Diana with Bow and Hound. Signed Edward McCartan. Thought to be worth–*'

'*In excess of two thousand pounds*. Yeah, I can read, Gavin.'

'And stolen from a garden only a week ago. *Thorpe Morieux*. Local. Now, I wonder why that interests you, Matt.'

'Pixel off!'

'So, are you selling or buying?' He stared at Matt for a moment and then smirked, 'You're not in the market, are you. It's more likely, you've seen or know something. Come on, tell.'

'I aint seen nothin' except your ugly mug.' He pressed print. 'Anyway, you're the one always snoopin' and creepin' around. What *you* seen, Gav?'

'Your computer screen, and that's fascinating.' He lunged forwards and cupped his hand over the mouse.

A bony shoulder pushed into Matt, edging him sideways as Gavin clicked on the top bar.

'What the–'

'Your search history, Matt. Vatry? Now why–'

'Hey, frag off, Gav.'

'Just stretching out the hand of friendship. Come on, time to split for the lecture,' and without waiting, he shut down the computer.

Matt searched Gavin's face. What was it with the guy? It didn't feel like friendship. He watched Gavin move soundlessly to the door, and then he was gone.

'Phisher.' He almost spat the word. 'Bloody spammer.' He stood slowly, his pulse thumping in his ears as he headed for the printer on a trestle table near Bill's office. He whisked the image of Diana with Bow and Hound from the paper tray and quickly folded it into his pocket. Had he allowed enough time to let Gavin get ahead? With luck he should be able to slip into the lecture without his new creepy friend.

He took a deep breath. Where was the Geeko Dude hiding within him? He imagined himself the comic-strip hero complete with a pet chameleon, now sporting a bronzed look and taking on the form of a Diana. What should he do?

'Frag,' he muttered as he let the library door swing behind him. 'Thought you'd gone Gav.'

'I remembered you'd something to tell me.'

'Oh, leave off will you? You're being a pain in the arse this mornin'. Why don't you tell 'bout your dad an' this Vatry bloke, for a start off?'

Gavin waved a finger. 'First rule, Matt. You have to trade. Give information to get some back.'

'You're just bloody phishing, mate. I aint got any.'

'Nor me.' Gavin twisted away, his skinny jeans clinging to his legs like a gymnast's tights, and his dark lanky hair tucked behind his ears, almost elf-like. He didn't look back, just hurried on down the main staircase and vanished amid the swarming students.

'Bloody spammer.' Matt let the insult roll over his tongue. He'd use that one again, he decided. The words worked, had a good ring and definitely fitted his techie image. Yes, Geeko Dude was alive and functioning. He headed for his lecture.

When Matt sat down for lunch with his friends an hour or so later, the world of computing seemed light years away from the hubbub of a canteen flowing with students.

'Hi, Chrissie,' he said as he pulled his tray closer.

She smiled weakly, and seemed to focus on a point in the centre of the Formica table.

Nick looked up from a plate of cottage pie. 'Hi, mate.' He suspended his fork mid-way to mouth. 'Should have had some of this, it's delicious, Matt.'

'Looks too much like mud, mate. You OK, Chrissie? Somethin' wrong with your sandwiches?'

'No, Matt. Just feeling….' She sighed.

'Hey, Nick. There's front wing panels goin' cheap at a car recycling place. I looked it up.' He pulled paper from his pocket and slapped it onto the table. 'It's not far from here. Might be worth givin' it a try. What d'you think?'

Nick unfolded the sheet, eyebrows questioning. He whistled softly.

Chrissie reached for the paper. 'What? Ahh… not the standard body shop, is it, Matt?'

'What d'you mean?'

Chrissie turned the paper for him to see. '*Diana with Bow and Hound*,' she read. 'I suppose you could try and mount it on a bonnet, but I don't think you'd be able to see through the windscreen.'

'Oh no.' Matt remembered scribbling TARV and the phone number. The scrap of paper had been on the desk next to the computer. 'Where the hell?' He checked his pockets and backpack. 'Frag. Gavin must've taken it. Snouty bastard.'

'It's…,' she paused as she read on. 'It's the bronze pinched from Thorpe Morieux. Looks very artistic. What's Gavin taken, Matt?'

'The details for the car recyclin' place. Why'd he do that?'

'I don't know. Probably wanting attention, you know, getting a rise out of you.' Chrissie lifted brown granary bread to her mouth and took a small bite. 'He was a bit like that when we met him at the Nags Head. Remember?'

'Here, pass the paper over an' I'll write down the name and number again.' He saw it in his mind's eye; in fact he could picture most of the TARV web page. It had taken him years to realise everyone's memory wasn't photographic, like his.

'Is it far away?'

'Ten minutes. Out towards Stowupland.'

They ate without speaking for a few moments as the clatter of plates and trays, conversations and laughter swirled around the canteen. Chrissie dropped a half-eaten cheese and onion sandwich back into its wrapper.

Matt sensed something was wrong. He'd already asked if the sandwich was bad.

'Heard 'bout your walk. Bloody metal thieves,' he said. He watched her as he blundered on, trying to be helpful. 'Looked up Vatry on the internet – nothin'.'

'Yes,' Nick chipped in between mouthfuls, 'and I mentioned the name to Clive on Saturday. He seemed cross enough to follow it up. Did he say anything more about it to you?'

'Only that he's working on a murder investigation, not theft. He'll hand it on to the organised crime team, but he didn't hold out much hope. Thought it would more likely sink into the basket of pilfering – unsolved. You were right about the grouchy bit.'

Nick put his fork down. 'I've an idea. How about you look on eBay for lead coffins for sale - animal size, Matt?'

'Yes, don't worry about the *one previous owner*, bit. In fact, that could be the clue, Matt.'

'Oh pixel off you two, you're havin' me on, right?'

Chrissie picked up a scrap of cheese, a fugitive on the Formica. Her tone seemed to change. She leaned forwards.

'Word of mouth might have more success. I'm up at the auction rooms again this week. I could put out a few feelers. Are you still working at Thorpe Morieux, Nick?'

'Just about finished there, maybe a couple of days more at the most. Depends how Dave got on without me today.'

'Hmm, it could be the last chance to sniff around the tilers.'

'Sorry, Chrissie but I'm not going anywhere near those guys.'

An idea sprang into Matt's mind. He spoke without really thinking. 'You could give 'em one of the pizza delivery flyers. Say you're advertisin' for Ott's Pizzas.'

'I don't know if they'd–'

'Hey, Matt. Have you got a job delivering pizzas?'

'Yeah, Chrissie. I start Saturday.' His face glowed beneath his beard.

'That's great.'

'Yeah, killer app.'

'Killer app? What are you on about, Matt?' she asked.

'Techie term. You know, a computer programme so fantastic you 'ave to rush out an' buy it. *Killer app*.'

'Like your pizzas?'

'Yeah, sort of. Well maybe not quite like the ones I'm deliverin'.'

'Hey, Nick!' All talk of pizza died as Seth and Andy, two first year carpentry apprentices shouted and came over to join them.

Matt moved his tray a little closer and concentrated on his chips.

CHAPTER 12

Chrissie ran her hand over the two pieces of old carcass wood, now glued together and forming one large section. She'd sanded it smooth. When placed back in the top of the Queen Anne writing desk, the two pieces would hold together as one. Movement would be allowed for at the edges. This time, with the new leather glued to it, there'd be no risk of splitting and fissuring across the centre.

'Central heating. The bane of our lives,' she muttered.

'That seems a bit extreme, Mrs Jax. How did the release day go yesterday?'

She stood with Ron in the barn workshop. She'd tried to immerse herself in her work, but she still felt agitated. Wood dust hung in the air and she rubbed her nose with the back of her hand as she gazed at the desk.

'Tea or coffee, Mr Clegg?'

'I don't think I've ever had a mug of coffee at this time of the day.'

'Of course, I wasn't thinking.' It was only his gentle way of a reminder, but now irritation with her own stupidity added to her agitation. 'You don't drink coffee do you, Mr Clegg.'

As she filled the kettle, her thoughts swirled around in her head. She'd felt like this since the fateful St Edmund Way walk. Her brain, usually sabre sharp, seemed to swim in tides of disconnected thought and emotion. Even analysing it logically hadn't helped.

'I don't think I've told you about my walk on Saturday, have I Mr Clegg,' she said as she waited for the water to boil.

Of course she knew she hadn't told him, and he must know it as well. Stupid, stupid, stupid, she thought as she set a mug of steaming tea on the bench near his work stool a few moments later. She needed to sharpen up, think before using these offhand phrases, think before screaming and think before sending her friends into danger.

'The weather would've been nice for walking on Saturday,' he murmured.

'Yes, it was. But it seems it was also ideal for raiding mausoleums.'

'Raiding mausoleums, Mrs Jax?'

She explained. She didn't spare her less than heroic part in the afternoon. It somehow helped, a bit like wearing a hair shirt in contrition.

'Ransacking animal graves for lead coffins and iron railings? What is the world coming to?'

'I know, it's horrible, Mr Clegg.'

'I suppose it's nothing new. There've always been grave robbers.'

'Anything for a fast buck.' She bit her lip. Another unthinking offhand phrase.

Ron stared into his tea. 'I don't suppose you've heard anything through Clive? Are the police any closer to finding out who... why Marlin was killed, Mrs Jax?'

Chrissie thought back over the weekend. To be honest, she hadn't asked Clive. The animal tomb raiders had already taken up the best part of his Saturday. While they'd both waited at the ransacked mausoleum for the police to arrive, he'd made some comment about Kat seeming a nice, sensible kind of girl. She'd interpreted that as implying she, by contrast, was some screaming airhead. So when she sensed he didn't want to be asked about the Marlin Poynder case, she hadn't pushed it. She'd felt too humiliated to risk irritating him further.

'No, he didn't talk about the case, Mr Clegg. I should've asked. He's been assigned to it, though.' An idea took shape. 'There is something I've just thought of. Is there a club or magazine for collectors of antique automata?'

'More than likely. Why, Mrs Jax?'

'I don't know, but wouldn't Mr Poynder have been a member? He may have written some articles, placed some advertisements or created some controversy. I don't know, just maybe an enthusiasts' club or society could point to someone or something.'

'I expect all that will be on his computer, don't you think. The police will have looked. Best leave it to them.'

Chrissie gulped down the last of her tea. 'Back to the writing desk then, Mr Clegg.'

Now she felt focused. The fog was lifting. If there'd been anything critical worth saying about how she'd behaved, Ron would have said it. Forget about Saturday's metal thieves, she decided. They were small fry; for the moment she'd concentrate on freshening up the tongue and grooves, and slotting the carcass-wood desk top into the surrounding edging. 'At least the supporting frame is sound,' she muttered.

As she worked with a chisel clearing the groove in a section of edging, she made up her mind to set Matt a small computer search task.

'Don't forget we're going up to the auction rooms tomorrow, Mrs Jax.'

'What? Oh yes,' she said straightening her back. She'd almost forgotten. There were a few feelers she planned to put out while she was there. She'd show Clive she wasn't an airhead. Now she had a goal, she felt better.

***

'So, tell me again, who are we collecting the pair of carver chairs for?' Chrissie asked as she slammed the passenger door.

'The Whittles. Nice family, this side of Hadleigh.' Ron started the van and drove slowly through the dry pot-holes and ruts peppering the track from his workshop. It was just after eight-thirty, and the morning air still held a chill. The passenger door rattled.

'Should've slammed it harder,' she mumbled under her breath.

'I gather Mrs Whittle is a bit of an online shopper,' he added, seemingly ignoring her mutterings. 'That's why she asked us to collect and repair before her husband saw them.'

'So she bid online at the Bury auction? Do we have any idea what state they're in, Mr Clegg?'

'She seemed a bit sheepish when I asked her, so I im-agine there'll be some work to do, Mrs Jax.'

Chrissie tried to picture the chairs. Ron had already described them as oak, gothic in style with caned seats and back panels. The arms had carved lion paws and the top of the backs, carved lion masks. She'd seen the kind of thing before, and the term *busy with barley twists* sprang to mind.

'Does she realise the repair could cost more than the chairs are worth, Mr Clegg?'

'I spent some time explaining that to her.'

Chrissie relaxed into the seat. The van swayed her gently as Ron turned onto the Wattisham Airfield perimeter lane. She glanced at the dense wild hedging, the security

111

chain links and barbed wire showing above the greens just starting to fade into autumn. She closed her eyes. Matt had sounded pleased to be given a search project. A quick phone call followed by a few texts the evening before and she'd got the feeling it wouldn't take much to turn him into an automaton enthusiast himself. All she needed now was to have some luck with her auction house feelers. She almost felt excited as she drifted into a dozing sleep.

'We're nearly there, Mrs Jax.'

Ron's voice cut into her dreamy state. 'What? Oh....'

Ahead, tall towers sprouting from the sugar factory reached into the sky like a gothic stronghold. Silver-stained lions roared fluffy steam and stretched their broken oak paws. She blinked and rubbed her eyes. She must've dropped off.

'Well, that didn't take us long to reach Bury.' She yawned and dragged herself back into the day as Ron turned off the A14 and headed northeast into an industrial estate. A slight anxiety now grumbled in her stomach.

A large notice printed with the words, *Corps, Poynder & Prout. Auctioneers and Valuers* stood at an entrance. Ron turned into the car park. A low warehouse-sized building sprawled in front of them, the glass doors of its front lobby glinting a mixed message of modern hard-nosed business amidst old fashioned values. They drove slowly, following the signs to the delivery and collection area at the side of the building. Ron pulled up behind a 4x4 and a dusty saloon car.

'Don't we have to go to the front office first for some kind of authorisation slip, Mr Clegg?'

'Mrs Whittle sent me the sale receipt and lot number details. We should be able to just collect from here.'

Chrissie rubbed her forehead. This wasn't at all how she'd envisaged things. How was she going to put out feelers from the collection bay? Past experience told her it would be manned by a porter who kept his hearing aids switched off. Not a good starting point for seemingly idle questions or whispered asides. And more to the point, she was unlikely to meet any of the other staff.

'I'll go in and see how the queue is doing, Mr Clegg.'

She didn't wait for Ron to say anything, but swung the van door open and hurried across the smooth tarmac. The side wall of the building was broken by two metal, window-less doors. The larger one was on sliders and opened into a vehicle loading bay, the smaller one was a standard six foot six and led into a cramped porter's office. She headed for the office.

'Hi, anyone here?' The door stood ajar, and she peeped in past the notice nailed to one side of the door frame. It read, *Ring Bell for attention*. She rang the bell.

The office looked more like a snug with its tatty Lloyd Loom chair, biscuit tin, kettle and old flyers for take-away pizza. She waited a few moments, guessed no one was coming and hurried further along the building to the open loading bay.

'Hey, hello,' she shouted, spotting a man dressed as a porter. He was bending over an open crate at the back of the bay and she recognised his smooth hairless scalp. He had doubled as a salesroom assistant at the auction, just over a week before. She supposed he was in his late twenties.

He straightened up. 'Can I help?'

'Hi, we've come to pick up some chairs,' she called.

He frowned and waited as she walked closer.

'We've come to pick up some chairs,' she repeated.

He held out his hand. 'Collection slip. Need a collection slip.' His voice had a nasal quality.

'Sorry, I haven't got–'

'Here, I thought you'd be needing these, Mrs Jax.'

'What?' Chrissie spun around. 'Mr Clegg! I didn't realise you were behind me.'

She watched as he handed the paperwork to the man. She waited, hoping to see a shrug, shake of the head or frown, anything to indicate she might be sent back to the main desk at the front entrance.

'I'll go an' find it,' the man said slowly. 'Two chairs. Will you need help to carry 'em?'

'I'll be able to say when I see them.'

The man stared at her face for a moment and then nodded.

So, there'd be no trip to the front office. 'Damn,' she whispered under her breath.

'I'll bring the van in here, ready to load them.' Ron must have read something in her face because he paused and then added, 'There's no hurry, Mrs Jax.'

While Ron headed out to the van, Chrissie followed the porter through double doors at the far side of the loading bay and into an area with a concrete floor. Metal-framed racks stretched along one wall and furniture stood in disorderly rows. He led the way, paper in hand, to a pair of large, dark-stained wooden chairs with uncomfortably straight backs. Paper tags with lot numbers hung from their arms. The broken carving was obvious, even at a distance.

'Victorian, and busy with barley twists,' she murmured.

She waited, her thoughts hustling in the silence while he checked the numbers and details against the papers. Now was the moment, if she was going to ask him anything.

Voices cut abruptly through the motionless air. She recognised the younger voice immediately. It was Aiden Prout. Last time, she'd heard him distorted through the PA system.

'Can you help this gentleman, Gray?' Aiden called.

The man checking the lot numbers next to her didn't react.

'Gray, we need your help.' Aiden picked his way through the line of furniture. The tone was sharp, each word perfectly enunciated.

'That seems correct. Numbers match.' The man's scalp reflected the overhead light as he turned to look at Chrissie.

'Ahem, Gray. I think Aiden wants you.'

'Mr Prout? Sorry, I didn't hear you.'

'That's OK, Gray. Would you go and help a customer, please? He needs your assistance moving a whole lot of small items out the front.' Aiden pointed across two chests piled next to a table. 'I'm sorry,' he added and smiled at Chrissie.

'That's all right. Actually I was hoping to ask you something, Aiden.' Chrissie couldn't believe her luck. She tried to sound relaxed, off-hand.

Aiden didn't say anything, just hesitated and then waited for her to speak.

'I was at the auction a couple of Saturdays ago. I don't know if you remember, but there was a tortoiseshell ve-neered wooden box made for an automaton. I think it was

French, around 1890. The mechanism was missing.' She paused, taking a moment to choose her next words.

'Yes, I remember. We don't have many lots withdrawn while the auction's running.'

'Well, I don't know if you noticed, but the tortoiseshell veneer needed repairing. We, I mean Ron Clegg's restoration arm of his business, wondered if the owner wanted it restored?'

'And you are?'

'Sorry, I should have said. I'm Chrissie Jax. I work with Ron.'

'Based out near the airbase? Wattisham, yes?'

She nodded and looked up through her eyelashes, hoping it would have a devastating effect.

'I can't give out owners' details. You understand that, don't you?'

'I know but I hoped perhaps you might–'

'Contact the owner for us,' Ron said softly. He seemed to have appeared from nowhere again.

Her cheeks torched like a flash fire. How much had Ron heard? She'd been too distracted to notice footsteps.

'I wondered what was keeping you, Mrs Jax.' His tone was mild. He extended a gnarled hand. 'Hello, Aiden. I'm Ron, Ron Clegg. We're here to collect those two carvers.' He turned to look at Chrissie as if waiting for her to continue, his eyebrows slightly raised.

'I w-was just saying how much we wanted to restore the tortoiseshell box.'

'Of course,' Ron murmured. 'And to collect those chairs.'

'Well, we've got a few minutes to fill before Gray comes back, so if you're interested, we could go to the front office and I can look up the details about the box.'

'Oh thank you,' Chrissie said in what she hoped was a disarming manner. She didn't dare catch Ron's eye, but fell in beside Aiden as they walked.

'You stood in at short notice to take the Saturday auction, I understand,' she said.

'Yes, usually I'd have familiarised myself with all the lots, but as it happened….'

'I know. Dreadful business. I thought you did very well. Poor Gavin seems to have taken it very badly.'

'Do you know him?'

Chrissie's seized her chance, hoping Ron wouldn't catch her words. 'Oh yes. Well, of course he puts on a front, but underneath…,' she lowered her voice. She talked casually about Gavin, all the time her intuitive antennae working overtime. She was ambiguous, skated over facts, and sparing with the truth. By the time they reached the front office, she'd convinced even herself that she'd known him for years and was almost part of the family. All the while Aiden seemed to relax and lower his guard.

'Marlin was so disappointed Gavin wasn't interested in the auction business, but to be honest, the rest of us were quite thankful.'

'I can well imagine,' she almost purred.

'Ah, we're here now,' he said as he led her past the main reception desk and into the office behind.

The receptionist flashed recognition and Chrissie smiled, pressing home her new status of VIP, virtually family.

'Good morning,' Ron said softly.

Aiden headed for an empty desk and logged onto a computer. His fingers flew across the keyboard and within seconds an image of a tortoiseshell box was up on the screen.

'That's the one.' Chrissie strained to see the writing. She leaned in, trying to find the sellers details amongst the description, lot number, estimated value and reserve price. Aiden reached for the phone on the desk and blocked her view.

'I'll ring Mr Ravyt now,' he said as he punched in a number.

'Mr Rav...it?' she said, sounding out the name as she'd heard it. 'Does he live locally?'

'Woodbridge.' Aiden paused as he listened to the ring tone. 'I'm surprised he didn't put it in the auction rooms there.'

'But Marlin is, I mean was the auctioneer here,' Ron murmured.

'Ah, Mr Ravyt, this is Aiden Prout from the Bury Auction Rooms.' He turned away so that his back was to Chrissie and Ron. Again, he blocked Chrissie's view of the screen. She gazed across the office to catch a pretty secretary watching them. She smiled a greeting and drifted to one side, trying to alter her angle to the screen.

Aiden swung round. 'Yes, he's interested. I think it's best if you speak to him.' He handed the phone to Ron who was now standing directly behind him.

She struggled to keep the frustration from her face. She'd missed the chance to speak to the Woodbridge collector, but one glance at Ron told her she needn't have worried. He'd decided to run with her scheming. For the first time since she'd been in the auction rooms that morning, the tension pulling at her guts started to ease. She was going to get away with this.

Fifteen minutes later the pair of Victorian carver chairs had been loaded into the van and Chrissie secured her seat belt as Ron drove slowly out of the collection bay.

'Well, I must say that was an eye-opener, Mrs Jax,' he said mildly.

Chrissie didn't comment, just clasped her hands and waited for him to say more.

'I'm curious. Were you driven by a desire to bring business into the workshop, or some kind of mad idea to play private detective?'

'Neither, Mr Clegg. I wanted to learn how to repair tortoiseshell.'

'Ah yes, for a moment back there I'd forgotten you were still an apprentice, Mrs Jax.'

She stole a quick sideways glance.

'Well, it seems this time you've achieved all three,' he said and smiled.

'So, do you think that's Ravit, spelled with an I, Mr Clegg?'

Now she had more to give Matt to help with his search, and there might be a trip in it to Woodridge for her.

CHAPTER 13

'So, have you done anything about that dent in your wing yet?' Dave asked.

Nick didn't want to think about the bent metal and scraped paint. It was on the Fiesta's near side, so he'd managed to ignore it each time he opened the driver's door over the last couple of days.

'I'm guessing it'll be a respray for the whole wing. And some filler, but don't forget you've got some rust to fix as well,' Dave said as he stood and gazed at the finished parquet floor. It had taken some hard graft sanding the wood to make sure it was dead flat once it was laid, and then two coats of sealant-finish to get it to its present state of glowing perfection.

'We ought to take a photo,' Nick said, standing next to him.

'I think a body shop would want to see the car, not a photo. Even if you're shopping round for an estimate.'

'I meant the floor, Dave.'

'Ah.'

Nick pulled his mobile out of his jeans and snapped.

'Need a proper camera to do it justice. What do you reckon to a panel from a car reclamation yard? Might be cheaper?'

'Car? Floor? You're all over the place today. It's not easy following what you're on about, Nick. Come on, time to pack up here and then we'll drop the leftover parquet blocks off at Suffield's. It makes sense while we're out this way.'

The words *drop off* triggered a memory. 'Shike, those pizza delivery flyers.'

'Now what?'

'Nothing, Dave.'

Nick wasn't exactly sure what had got into him. The unease creeping somewhere in the back of his mind was still there, but the floor was finished and in a few minutes Dave and he would drive away, leaving the Dower House for ever. The tilers had been like an occupying force, a constant presence always watching and listening. The phrase, *end-of-termitis* popped into his mind. Yes, that was it. Soon he'd be free to relax, be himself and forget about stolen metal.

It didn't take him long to load the last of the tools into the van. Glossy flyers touting pizza were stuffed into a pocket alongside the footwell. OTT'S, they shouted to his heightened senses and bubbled images of cheese with pepperoni topping. On impulse he grabbed a few and hurried to a battered vehicle parked on the far side of the drive. He lifted one of the windscreen wipers and slipped the paper under. For once he didn't bother to look up at the scaffolding to check for the tilers.

'Oi! What you doing?'

'Pizza. Mate of mine does deliveries,' Nick called as he glanced up towards Jim's floating voice and ruddy face.

'Mate's rates, yeah?'

'Yeah, just ask for Matt.'

Nick turned and strode away. He reckoned Jim was far too high on the roof to read the thoughts behind his eyes. There was nothing he'd said to make the tiler suspect a scam or duplicity, and he doubted he'd resist a discount.

Moments later, Nick looked into Dave's serious face as he climbed into the Willows van.

'Pizza flyers? Are you on commission, or something, Nick?' The tone had lost its good humour.

'Of course not, Dave. Matt's doing pizza deliveries at weekends now. He needs the cash. Anyway, he's got some crazy idea he'll find something out about... I don't know, that Vatry bloke.'

'What? Is he mad?' Dave started the van.

'Yes, more than likely.'

'So how in hell's name does he think delivering pizza to Jim will lead to Vatry? Or does he think they eat pizza together?' Concern seemed to replace the disbelief. 'And why? Why get involved?'

'I don't know. He just said to give them some flyers, that's all, Dave.'

'And if he finds Vatry, what'll he do then?'

'Look, I don't know. It wasn't my idea. He seems to have got a bit–'

'He'll end up with a broken nose.' Dave threw the van into gear and accelerated out of the drive, tyres spitting gravel and breeze gusting in through the open window.

'Jee-e-eze.' Nick hadn't thought it through. It was Clive who'd implied the police were as good as powerless in the face of organised metal thieving, and handing out flyers had seemed harmless enough when he'd been sitting in the canteen with a plate of cottage pie.

'It was Matt's idea to use a reclaimed wing panel for the Fiesta,' he added reasonably.

'Well, that's not such a bad suggestion, but I'd better come with you. For all I know, if you're with Matt you'll come back with a ton of metal and then concoct some idiotic way to pass it on to Jim, you know, just in case it leads somewhere.'

They drove in silence. Dave was right. He needed to distance himself. He already had enough on his plate without looking for trouble. There was his car to repair, Kat to keep happy, and band practice tonight.

Thinking of Kat reminded him. What had she said she did before taking a shot with her air rifle? Slow her breathing, yes, and then lock her rib muscles and very gently use her diaphragm. It sounded like a fancy way of saying *hold your breath*, but she'd laughed and added, 'The real trick is all in the mind. You have to empty it, focus on the target, and then, and only then… gently touch the trigger.'

'So how do you clear your mind, Kat?' he'd asked.

'Well, I imagine I'm floating in a pool and gazing up at a clear blue sky. I slow my breathing, relax my muscles, and in my mind visualise a kind of azure blue. Then I allow my eye to focus on the target. Nothing else exists.'

Remembering her words soothed him, but rather than pull a trigger he hummed.

'Is that Freddie Mercury you're humming again?' Dave asked.

'No, it's one of the numbers we're practising this evening. Jake's got this idea of adding a counterbalance harmony. It still needs some work.'

'Yeah, well it sounds like a chant, one of those Buddhist things.'

It didn't take long to drive from the Dower House to Patrick Suffield's reclamation yard. The parking area was almost deserted when they arrived, apart from a police car. Nick thought the yellow and black tape seemed stretched and tatty since their last visit. It fluttered and curved, nearly touching the ground. He imagined a good many policemen must have caught their feet and shins as they stepped over it. How else had it become so dog-eared?

'When will they take that tape and tarpaulin thing away?' he muttered to Dave.

'Soon, I guess. It was almost a fortnight ago.'

Nick tried to keep his thoughts fixed on the task in hand. 'I'll unload the parquet.'

Dave headed off to find Patrick while Nick fetched a platform trolley with mesh sides. It didn't take him long to transfer the wooden blocks from the builder's bag in the van and wheel them into the chapel.

'Hi,' he said as he spotted Dave talking to Patrick in the office doorway. 'I reckon there's at least a hundred in the trolley. D'you want to count them in?'

'Yeah, I'll show you where I want them.' Patrick walked into the main expanse of the chapel as he spoke, giving Nick a clear view into the office.

It was only a glimpse, but he was sure he'd recognised a head of dark lanky hair. In that flash of a moment he'd seen the slumping figure rise from a half sitting position and flit deeper into the office. The shape seemed familiar.

'Gavin?'

There was no answer.

What's Gavin doing here, he wondered. 'Is Gavin OK? I'm sure I just saw him.' But his words bounced off Patrick's broad back as they wove like a procession between wrought iron garden furniture and racks of stripped wood doors.

'You can stack them here,' Patrick said as he halted in front of a pallet.

'I'm sure I just saw Gavin Poynder. Is he OK?'

'Wasn't the bloke who died here called Poynder?' Dave murmured.

'Yeah, yeah. Gavin's often round here, well not so much this past year. Today's the first time since the incident. He's pretty cut up about it.'

'I'd have thought this was the last place he'd have wanted….'

'Yeah, Dave. But he used to have a Saturday job here when he was at school. He seemed to prefer it to the auction place.'

'Well, he's at Utterly Academy. Computing and IT now,' Nick said. After meeting him in the Nags Head the other evening, he could only suppose the chapel, with its old wrought iron and statues outside in the yard, must have appealed to the Goth in Gavin.

'So what'll he do? Follow into the family auction business?'

'I don't know. I hope so, Dave. His father's bloody gone now. Let's just say he was a useful contact and no one can afford to lose contacts these days. Gavin would be a handy connection for me if he joined 'em.'

Nick swallowed his shock in the face of such brazen materialism. 'Two, four, six,' he counted, as he placed the oak blocks on the pallet. It was the best comment he could make under the circumstances. Eighty-four blocks later, they were all stacked neatly and Nick had worked off the worst of his distaste.

'I thought you said one hundred,' Patrick said.

'As good as,' Nick murmured.

'Well, back to the office and I'll sort the paperwork out.' Patrick led the way.

The empty trolley rattled as Nick trundled it through the chapel's forest of old wood and iron. The rhythmic sound relaxed him. If Gavin was still in the office, he determined he'd say something sympathetic to him. He hoped it would make up for what he imagined was Patrick's bare-faced self-interest.

'Where's Gavin?' he asked when he reached the office. Apart from Dave and Patrick, the room was deserted. He scanned past the filing cabinets crowding along one wall, the paper-strewn desk top, computer, waste bin and shredder. The far wall had a recess, and tucked into the shadows, a door.

'I expect he'll have gone by now,' Patrick said, as he raked through some papers on the desk.

'I didn't notice anyone leave, but then we were counting blocks, Nick.'

'No, he probably went that way.' Patrick nodded towards the far wall.

'Gone where? He'll be distraught.' Nick made an effort to stop his voice rising.

'Through there. It's the old vestry, and there's a toilet and basin.'

'Are you sure he's OK? I mean he could've....'

'Nah, he's a drama queen. He'll 've gone that way to leave through the back exit.'

'But what if he hasn't?'

'You're bloody soft, mate.'

'Nick's right, Patrick. You wouldn't want another tragedy here. Police crawling over everything again?'

'Alright, alright. I've got your point. If you're so bloody worried, you go and have a look.' He stared at Nick. It felt like a dare.

'OK,' Nick said, hoping to defuse the tension.

He avoided any further eye contact and watched his feet as he picked his way through the office. The recess cast shadows across the door on the far wall. The handle was modern and he grasped it, turning and pushing, conscious of his heart thumping against his ribs. The vestry was deceptively large. It still had a full-length mirror, but now coats replaced any trace of priestly garments. He sensed no other presence.

'Hello,' he called softly. A narrow door to the toilet beyond was wide open. 'Gavin?'

'Is he there?' Dave shouted from the office.

Nick checked the toilet. 'No, I'll just have a look out the back door.'

It was wider and heavier than the inner doors. There were no bolts but the lock looked like a deadlock. You'd need a key to get in, he thought as he released the latch and pulled it open. Outside, a rough path disappeared into a wilderness of overgrown brambles. He couldn't tell if it led around the chapel to the main yard or to somewhere else.

'Gavin?' he yelled. There was no reply.

'If he's not out there, close that exit door and get the hell back in here.'

Patrick's voice jarred in his ears. It was time to focus. Gavin had vanished. 'OK, Patrick,' he breathed.

He closed the large heavy door, making sure the latch had engaged, and hurried back through the vestry. As he brushed against the coats and overalls, he caught the scent of cedar mixed with the sweet sharpness of limes. It hinted of a male fragrance. Aftershave? He couldn't imagine Patrick bothering with such niceties.

'Sorry,' Nick said as he joined them back in the office. 'But if we hadn't checked–'

'I knew he wouldn't be in there,' Patrick cut in. 'He was always one for hiding.'

'He's probably just shy.' Nick couldn't think why he was making excuses for him.

'Nah! He enjoys the attention. He's always liked to get a reaction. Enough of Gavin. Here's the invoice, less the returned blocks.'

'I'll hand it in when we get back to Willows.' Dave took the sheet of paper and folded it into his pocket.

A few minutes later, Nick checked his seat belt as Dave drove slowly past the police car and out of the reclamation yard. An overwhelming sadness rested like a cloud inside the van. It was almost impossible to shake off the sense of bleakness.

'Gavin's been really unlucky,' Nick said.

'I know, but the worst thing may have been him latching on to a hard bastard like Patrick.'

'Is it Patrick he's attached to, or is it something about the chapel and yard?' Nick let his voice drift away as he slipped into his own thoughts.

CHAPTER 14

It was Friday afternoon and Matt sat in the library. Most of the other students had bunked off for the weekend, but he still had some searches to complete. He'd received Chrissie's text message several days before, and now he checked it again. *Look up antique automata magazines, specialist meetings etc. Any Marlin Poynder references? Thanks C x.*

The second message was even pithier and had arrived more recently. *Anything on a Mr Ravit? Collects/sells automata. Lives Woodbridge. Thanks C x.*

Matt closed his eyes and visualised the screens of data he'd skimmed. There'd been an initial thrill when Marlin Poynder first came up on the Corps, Poynder & Prout website. It listed him as one of their auctioneers, with antique automata as his specialist area. The contact number was for the auction house, but there were no personal details and even the social networking sites had drawn a blank. Eventually he'd found a quarterly magazine devoted to antique automata, but he hadn't been able to access the articles, not without a membership name and password. He tried again now.

'Poynder,' he mouthed as he typed in the name. He thought for a moment and then deleted it and typed in Marlin Poynder. 'Password?' He'd already tried Gavin and the auction house phone number, but he'd done some web browsing since yesterday's attempt and he reckoned the big names in the field might be worth a try – in the same way people used favourite football teams or famous players as passwords. This time he typed in *Bontems*, the name of a well-known French automata maker. Not enough figures. He added the first name, *Blaise*.

'Wrong,' he muttered and tried *Malliardet*, a Swiss automata maker from the eighteen-hundreds. Nothing.

On a whim he kept the Swiss maker's name as password but changed the subscriber's name to *Ravyt*.

'Bot,' he muttered as he realised he'd mistyped the spelling. He was about to correct the *Y* when the screen page disappeared and flashed up the members' home page. He was into the site. 'Yes!' He punched the air.

'Now what?' The familiar voice broke through his concentration.

'Rosie!'

'What are you up to now? Starting a flame war?' She glanced over his shoulder at the screen. 'Antique automata? I'd put you down for something more electronic.' She swept a lock of auburn hair back from her face.

Matt stared at her. A flame war? Of course, he *could* start trading insults on the members' forum. That might throw up something interesting.

'Yeah,' he murmured. 'What you know 'bout automata then?' He'd done the reading; now might be the time to impress Rosie.

'Utterly Academy used to have one. It belonged to Sir Raymond Utterly.'

'Yeah? I aint heard of it.'

'It was stolen about three years ago. Apparently, it was unusual because it had two singing birds. It used to be kept in a glass case in the library here. I never saw it work. I think its innards were broken.'

'Well that'd be easy to trace if it came up for sale.' Matt tried to sound knowledgeable.

'Yes, particularly as it was a replica of the Utterly Mansion.'

'What? You're kiddin'. Who'd want a horrible thing like that?'

'Well, obviously not you. A collector, I suppose.'

Matt felt his face burn. He decided to ask if it was a Bontems, but her attention seemed to have drifted across the library.

'Oops. Bill seems to want me.'

'Bill? I don't see how you can tell.'

'She's looking at you, Matt. That's how,' and without a glance behind, she headed across to the librarian's office.

He caught Mrs Wesley's glare and smiled. She twisted slightly and nodded at Rosie, but he figured she'd been admiring his tee-shirt. It had a picture of a space invader from an early computer game on the front with the word PRIMITIVE in bold lettering above. Admittedly most of the picture had faded, but the letters stood out well enough. He reckoned it was a gem amongst charity shop finds.

He turned his attention back to the screen and pulled up the October edition. He skimmed through the articles.

'Nothing by Poynder, Ravit or Ravyt. Maybe there's a site noticeboard for small ads and notices?' he whispered.

It didn't take him a moment once he was into the small ads section. The type almost leapt off the screen. *Wanted: Automaton double bird mechanism, Charles Bontems circa 1920. To fit original inlaid casing 15 x 11 x 12 inches.* The contact was a landline with a Bury area code. Matt recognised the number immediately. It was the same as on the Corps, Poynder & Prout website. 'It'll be Marlin,' he breathed.

Matt turned his attention back to the members' home page and clicked on the *change subscriber details* tab. 'So, he's M C Ravyt and the address… Woodbridge.' He scribbled it down along with the phone number and email.

After an hour checking through the site and past editions of the magazine, Matt had collected the names and contact details of all the East Anglian members. They totalled six, and that included Poynder and Ravyt. It was time to query something with Chrissie.

He grabbed his mobile. *Chrissie, are you sure Ravit not Ravyt?* He pressed *send*, but while he waited for a reply, an idea stirred in the recesses of his mind. He needed to check some facts.

'Rosie said three years ago,' he murmured. That meant he'd have to go back to the 2008 editions. Matt typed *stolen automaton Utterly Academy 2008* into the Eastern Anglia Daily Tribune search box. The hairs on the back of his neck prickled when he read the report a few minutes later.

Rosie was standing near the printer, so Matt pressed *print* and sauntered over. 'Hi,' he said, trying to look cool.

She glanced at the paper churning onto the table. 'Hey, that's a picture of the Utterly automaton, isn't it?'

'Yeah. I looked it up.'

'It's quite distinctive, with those patterns across the front, don't you think?'

'*Satinwood and mahogany*,' he read. '*Inlaid to copy yellow brickwork criss-crossed with the lines and patterns of red bricks*.'

'Cream. I think you'll find they're… well they're the local ones from this area.'

'It's still gross.' He pulled a face.

'Clever the way the windows are done in that darker wood. And then the birds pop up out of the roof.'

'Yeah. It says rosewood.' He caught a glimpse of Mrs Wesley out of the corner of his eye. She was staring at his tee-shirt again.

'That woman,' Rosie muttered. 'What does she want now?' But before Matt could say anything, Rosie had turned on her heel. It seemed the conversation was over.

He scratched at his beard and gathered the sheets of paper. 'Frag,' he murmured. For once he hadn't said something stupid to Rosie, but she'd still flounced off. He let his breath escape slowly and flicked through the newspaper article as he ambled back to his computer station. He wondered if Chrissie might be interested. It seemed both the pop-up singing birds were damaged or missing, but he couldn't work out the exact details. He reckoned the journalist must have decided a photo was enough, because there was no mention of the measurements. So how to find out?

'I know,' he murmured as he remembered Rosie's words. 'Flame war.' He'd post a question on the magazine's noticeboard. Someone would be bound to know, and well, he could tag it with a pseudonym. He didn't have to sign the notice as Ravyt. Only the webpage manager would be able to trace which subscriber had posted it. Ravyt would have no idea. In fact, he might even answer his own question on the noticeboard discussion.

Matt thought for a moment. 'Yeah, I'll write as *Flaming Rose*.' Then he typed *Does anyone know the exact dimensions of the Utterly Mansion Automaton?* He checked the article again and added, *made by Charles Bontems*.

***

133

Saturday morning dawned cold and breezy. Matt gazed at his bedroom window and watched as raindrops hit the glass. They seemed to pause for a moment, as if daring each other to be the first to break rank, before drizzling down the pane.

'Typical,' Matt sighed. It would rain wouldn't it? His first day delivering pizza, and the heavens had chucked a bucket of water over Stowmarket. 'Flame,' he mumbled. It was like God's own inflammatory email. 'Yeah, flame.' He'd add that to his repertoire of frag, spam, bot and pixel.

He rubbed his beard and reached for yesterday's tee-shirt. The crumpled space invader might be captured on the tired cotton, but it looked ready to bite pizza. Matt eyed it up. What would a comic-strip hero do? He smiled, imagining himself as the ingenious and quick-witted Cap'n Starlight of the Space Hopper Corps. He sniffed the tee. Nothing a squirt of deodorant couldn't handle. If he hurried, he might reach Ott's Pizza Place in time to save the invader before it faded and flaked away from the cotton for ever. It was another race against time, another mission for the Cap'n.

He threw on his clothes and then held his breath while he squirted *Gym Fresh* under his arms. It made sense to apply it directly to the cotton. He pictured his hero, Cap'n Starlight shaking a rattle-can with protective shield written on the side. And all the while a huge sandglass in the sky counted down the minutes to ten o'clock. As each grain of sand fell, the universe waited and the space invader stretched across his chest grew fainter.

The Cap'n lolloped down the hallway, past the bathroom with its muted sounds of a power shower, and lunged for the outside world.

'Bye, Mum,' he shouted as he slammed the bungalow door. Three strides and he'd reached the Piaggio.

'Launching routine initiated,' he chanted, pulling the full space helmet over his flushed face. 'Ignition... take-off.' He was away.

Ott's Pizza Place looked pretty sleepy when Matt parked his scooter outside, ten minutes later.

'You're late.' A man with a scar running through one eyebrow looked across the counter.

Matt checked the clock high on the wall above the man's head. 'I was parking me scooter out the front.'

'Yeah well, we opened at ten. Have you got a rack for your pizza delivery box?'

He nodded. Nick had helped him fit it late Monday afternoon in the Academy car park.

'Then get the delivery box strapped on. You'll find one out the back. Might as well get it fixed on your bike now.'

'Scooter. It's a–'

'Primitive.'

'What?'

'Your tee – PRIMITIVE, that's what I'm reading. And the scooter, well that's a kind of primitive bike, isn't it?'

Matt looked down at his chest. 'It's a space invader. You know, like on those early computer games. It's kind of historic… primitive.'

'I thought you said your scooter was a Zip, not a Space Invader. That's what you said when you came round lookin' for a job last week. You've got insurance, yeah?' The man's eyebrow seemed to pucker around the scar.

'Yeah, course I 'ave.'

'For business use?'

135

He hadn't checked. 'S'pose so,' he mumbled.

'OK. It'll probably be quiet till lunchtime, but there's no knowing when some punter will order a fourteen-inch early-bird breakfast. So, get the box on that Space Zipper of yours.'

Space Zipper? Matt straightened up.

Out the back felt more like a storage area than a kitchen. There was a large stainless steel sink, food preparation area, dishwasher and an enormous fridge, but most of the space was filled with tins of olives, tomatoes and artichokes stacked alongside small wooden vegetable crates and tower blocks of take-away pizza packaging. Even without special eye filter protection, he spotted the heat & radiation-proof meteorite box. It was large and black, with straps and plastic snap-buckles. White lettering printed along its sides proclaimed *Ott's Pizza Place*.

He stood, as he imagined Cap'n Starlight would stand, legs astride and hands on hips. He surveyed the black box and made his plan. He'd move it carefully, get it outside into the open. That way no one would get hurt.

'Matt? What's taking you so long? Come on, get that delivery box and fix it on your bike.' Scarbrow's voice cut through the swing door.

Like an insect flying into electric filaments, the comic-strip illusion flashed, fizzed and died. He grabbed the box and hurried back.

Later, with it safely attached to the Zip's carrying rack, Matt lounged at a table and waited for his first call. Scarbrow had told him to memorize the Stowmarket street map, but that was the work of a moment, and now he was bored. He decided to wander behind the counter and take a look at the pizza oven.

The phone was attached to the wall near the gap in the counter. Something caught against his arm as he eased past.

'Frag,' he muttered as he knocked the receiver off and set a laminated notice swinging on its string. He turned and caught the awkward pendulum. As he replaced the receiver he looked more closely at the notice. Names and numbers were printed in columns on paper behind the plastic. The surface felt sticky, well thumbed.

'Didn't take you long to find the hot list.' Scarbrow tossed the words at him and then opened the pizza oven.

Matt felt the rush of heat. He ignored it, inhaled deeply, and savoured the aroma of pizza dough and mozzarella. 'Useful numbers?'

'You could say that. If anyone with their name, address or number on that list phones for a takeaway, we refuse. We know 'em from old. They're non-payers with a history. It's not your problem, but that list is – well they're cash only, and that's up front.'

'But don't most people 'ave to give a card number, if they're buyin' over the phone?'

'Yeah, but we've had stolen cards. Kids using parents' cards, people pre-ordering then coming in to collect and oops – lost their card on the way and no cash on 'em. People who order but never collect.'

'Like a hoax?'

'Yeah. We've even had the delivery lad roughed-up when the pizza's handed over. Lots of reasons to be on our hot list.'

'Frag, you're sayin' I could get attacked?'

'Doesn't happen often. I'm just saying why there's a hot list.'

No one had warned him there could be danger, and now the idea was planted, his anxiety grew. 'I'll check the list, OK?'

His stomach churned as he turned his back to the oven. Mouth-watering smells of pepperoni, basil and tomato wafted around as he studied the hot list. His photographic memory was automatic and immediate, but the associations always took longer and the food was proving a distraction, slowing him down.

'TARV? Aint that the auto parts recycling place?'

'Yeah, trouble there last year. Pissed out of their minds. Threw beer cans at the delivery bike. Threatened our rider.'

'Flame.' Matt was about to ask more, but the words died on his tongue. He'd seen the mobile number before. But where? The automata quarterly magazine? He closed his eyes and pictured the membership page. The connection snapped into place. 'Ravyt,' he murmured.

'Yeah, the police were called in the end.'

But Ravyt lives in Woodbridge. That's miles away. Why phone for a pizza from here, he wondered.

'I think they made some arrests, but I never heard any more so they probably let 'em off with a caution,' Scarbrow continued, seemingly unaware of Matt's distracted frown.

A customer hurried into Ott's. 'Hi, I ordered a Mar-gherita and an American Hot. Are they ready to collect?'

'Just coming out of the oven now.'

Matt stopped listening and withdrew into his thoughts. Maybe Ravyt's mobile had been nicked and it wasn't him ordering pizza? But then he'd have updated his membership details, wouldn't he? What if Maisie was on the hot list and he never got to ride out to her? Now that would be serious.

He checked the list again, but with only a first name to go on, he gave up.

It wasn't long before the first call for pizza delivery came through and Cap'n Starlight was finally scrambled for action. There was no room for further deliberation, it was time for the Space Zipper to take to the air. In the end Saturday turned out to be a busy day, and when he finally threw himself down on his rumpled duvet at a little after midnight, he didn't even have the energy to undress. So, he thought, Maisie hadn't called. He reckoned she was probably trying to play it cool, a hard catch. But he still had hopes for Sunday. He fell into a deep sleep.

CHAPTER 15

Chrissie read out the numbers on the pizza flyer as she tapped them into her mobile. 'I don't know what Ott's pizzas are like, but I know they deliver,' she called up the stairs. 'If they come out this far,' she added under her breath.

Upstairs, Clive padded from the bedroom. 'That'd be nice. For breakfast?'

'I was thinking more like brunch. Eat while we can.'

She knew he'd be heading for the shower. That's what he did when he got up. A kind of wake-up call. It had taken her a while to get used to the weekends when it was his turn to be the DI on call. They usually entailed restless nights and unsettled days. She felt unkind to think it, but she couldn't help wondering if he'd be better off getting called in to work. When he was busy, the time flew for him. The waiting was always the worst part.

'Hello, Ott's Pizza Place.'

'Hi,' she purred. It didn't take her long to persuade the man on the other end of the line that Woolpit was only a stone's throw from Stowmarket. She'd reckoned there wouldn't be many fourteen-inch prosciutto, mushroom and artichoke pizzas being ordered at that time on a Sunday.

'We'll deliver within the hour.'

She checked her watch. Brunch was about to be fast-forwarded to lunch. 'Thanks, and don't forget the extra tomato and mozzarella topping.'

The Victorian end of terrace cottage felt alive whenever Clive stayed. The floorboards above the kitchen creaked with his footfall, the immersion heater hummed and the pipes juddered as he ran the shower. She switched on the kettle and spooned freshly ground beans into the cafetière. By the time he came downstairs, the living room was filled with the warm aroma of a dark roasted Brazilian coffee. She watched him from the sofa as he poured himself a mug, and then sat beside her.

'Good morning, again,' he said, and kissed her lightly before sipping the rich brew. He left a faint scent of shaving foam and shower gel.

She cradled her mug in her hands. 'You seemed tired, so I left you to sleep on.'

'I had this weird dream and then I couldn't settle. My mind kept going over and over some numbers. I suppose by the time it was morning, I felt shattered.'

'Numbers? What was that about, do you think?'

'We never found Marlin Poynder's mobile. A bit of a mystery, I'm afraid. Anyway, we requested a log of all his calls and texts over the last couple of months. It came through on Friday. One of my DCs has been working on it, and… well I was looking at how far he'd got with it yesterday.'

'So those were the numbers? In your dream?'

'I guess so. Well, they weren't the actual numbers, but the numbers in my dream had voices. And some had names and faces. It was strange.' He set his coffee down and rested back into the sofa.

'Have you found any surprises? Anything unusual?' She tried to keep her tones even, her manner casual. 'From the phone records, I mean.'

'Too early to tell. Lots of what you'd expect. Family and the auction house. The last call was from his son Gavin, as it happens.'

'Poor Gavin,' Chrissie murmured, remembering his watery-grey eyes and pasty face.

'He didn't mention it when we interviewed him. We'll have to ask him about it. Could be important.'

Chrissie sipped her coffee. She'd learned early on that Clive tried not to think about work when off duty. However, when he was on call, his mind constantly wrestled with his cases. Even now, with his head back and eyes half closed, she guessed his brain was more than likely working on some link or clue.

'So why a pizza, I don't remember you ever ringing for a delivery before?' He turned and fixed her with a wide look, the hint of a smile playing around his mouth.

'Ah, well you'll understand when it arrives.' She kept her face passive, not wanting to give anything away. Secretly, she was disappointed he hadn't made any reference to metal thieves, bronze statues, or the mausoleum. Despite herself, the thought caused a pang as she remembered her airhead moment.

'Are you OK, Chrissie?'

'Yes, of course. Why shouldn't I be? I don't suppose anyone's come up with some leads yet on those grave-robbing clods? Or Vatry, by any chance?'

'Afraid not. I've passed on all the information and the team know I've got an interest. They've promised to keep me posted with any developments. I thought I'd already told you all this earlier in the week?'

'Yes, you did, but I just… well I hoped they'd have been caught by now.'

While the conversation wound around tracking active SIM cards, fashion trends in garden bronze statues, and traceability, she filled the coffee mugs again.

Rat-at-at-at-at-at! The metallic notes of the doorbell re-sounded down the narrow hallway. Chrissie checked her watch.

'I guess that'll be the pizza.'

'It's OK, I'll get it.'

A few moments later she heard the clunk and swish as Clive opened the front door.

'Matt? What are you…?'

'Come in,' Chrissie called from the living room. 'He's doing a weekend job to earn some cash.' She grinned, pleased with her little subterfuge as the heavy footsteps pounded down the hall.

'Have you got time for a coffee, or do you have to ride straight back?'

'Jeez, that sounds good.' The words came like a muf-fled groan from behind the visor.

'Then hand over the pizza. And take your helmet off, Matt,' she said, as her home filled with hints of prosciutto and the smell of warm cardboard.

Without a word he passed the pizza box to Clive and then yanked at his helmet.

'I 'ave to wear it. See, I could be a target while I'm waiting at the door.'

'Don't be daft, Matt. This is my front door and you're in Woolpit.'

'You haven't been attacked, have you?' Clive's voice sharpened.

'Nah, but I've been warned 'bout some places. TARV's for a start.'

'TARV? In Stowupland?'

'Why, you heard of it, Clive?'

143

'No. I mean yes. But it was nothing to do with assaulting delivery riders, Matt.'

'Come on, Clive, the pizza. It may need a few minutes in the oven, or is it still hot enough? Matt, have you got time for a slice?'

'I reckon an extra few minutes before I get back won't hurt.'

She caught Clive's eye. A mixture of an unspoken, *you sly minx*, and amusement passed between them as he opened the box.

***

Chrissie smiled as she remembered the pizza. It had been fun calling Matt out.

'You seem happier today,' Ron said, glancing at her and then dropping down a gear. The engine complained as the van ground up Quay Street to Market Hill.

'I like Woodbridge. It's… well it's as if we've stepped back in time.' She could have added that her lighter mood might also have had something to do with Clive.

Monday had dawned cool, but already a slight breeze had driven away the clouds and the day was brightening. When she'd arrived at the Clegg Workshop, Ron suggested she might like to come with him to collect the tortoiseshell box. She'd leapt at the idea.

'Now remember, Mrs Jax, leave me to do the talking.'

She bit her lip.

Ron drove into the market square. The red brickwork of the Shire Hall overshadowed the van on one side, while ancient timber framed houses crowded the narrow pavement on the other. The square seemed quiet. Chrissie suspected few drivers ventured this far. Tight, steep roads and one-way systems kept most of the shoppers down on the flatter ground and closer to the River Deben and the car parks.

They left the square through the southwest corner and followed the road.

'Not far now, Mrs Jax.'

'Did you know Utterly Academy used to have an automaton? Sir Raymond Utterly apparently commissioned it.' She'd slipped Matt's copy of the newspaper article into her shoulder bag. He'd been right, she had been interested. And now she wondered if Ron would be interested too.

'Yes, I think I remember hearing something about that. Marlin again.'

'Marlin Poynder, Mr Clegg?'

'Yes. He said it was an important example. I'm trying to think why.'

Chrissie was about to explain about the mechanism working two singing birds, but Ron had already slowed and was indicating to turn. Ahead, a narrow driveway led between what she guessed must have once been a small coach house and stabling for a couple of horses. It was on a modest scale, but still smacked of the wealth and prosperity of an earlier age.

'Something between a town house and a country pile,' she murmured, as she gazed up at pale bricks and a three-storey façade with sash windows. 'I think Mr Ravyt should be able to afford a fair price for the tortoiseshell repair. Front door or tradesman's entrance, do you think, Mr Clegg?'

'Now come on, Mrs Jax. We haven't met him yet. He was perfectly charming on the phone.'

Before they could make a decision, the front door opened and a man wearing tinted glasses strode out.

'Mr Clegg?'

He was younger than Chrissie had expected. She'd imagined a middle-aged man with the features of a turtle.

'Mr Ravyt?' She felt her face colouring.

'Hello. Mr Clegg?' He stepped forwards and shook Ron's hand. 'And?' He held out his hand to Chrissie.

'Mrs Jax. I'm Mr Clegg's apprentice,' she said, catching her breath as his signet ring dug into her hand. The chemistry was wrong. She knew there shouldn't have been any, and yet she was reading all kinds of subliminal signals.

'This way, if you'd like to follow me, please.'

She watched him as he spoke to Ron. She guessed he was in his mid-thirties. He was built like a greyhound, with dark hair and Celtic complexion. His voice almost purred. And his accent? Had she caught a soft burr? Hints of Scots or Irish perhaps?

They walked around the side of the house and into a surprisingly large walled garden. Despite her distaste, he must have heard her sharp intake of breath.

'Yes, it's beautiful, isn't it, Mrs Jax.'

'Who would have guessed such a large garden, virtually in the middle of Woodbridge?' she murmured.

'Deception,' he purred. 'Things are rarely what they seem. Take the so-called tortoiseshell. In reality it comes from a turtle. All is deception, Mrs Jax. Even the tortoiseshell covering my simple box hides another surprise.'

She thought for a moment. 'You mean, when it opens it gives life and song to a bird, hatches a different species of egg to its own, so to speak?'

He laughed, a softly musical sound. 'You're sharp, Mrs Jax. I like that.'

She looked at Ron, bit her tongue and turned her attention to a late flowering rose.

'I keep this locked,' he said as he pulled a bunch of keys from his pocket. 'Can't be too careful.'

Mr Ravyt led the way into a brick outhouse. It was arranged like a small workshop, with a rack of tools and workbench. Chrissie recognised the box immediately. It sat in solitary splendour on a soft linen sheet. She sensed a change in his demeanour. Perhaps it was just the tint in his glasses adjusting now he was out of the sunlight, but his face seemed to harden and his voice sharpen.

'So what do you think, Mr Clegg? Can you fix it?'

They waited while Ron examined the box. She watched as he ran an arthritic finger over the gilded silver disc in the lid before setting it down carefully. Chrissie knew from her internet reading that the disc flipped open and the mechanical singing bird popped up, or at least it would if it was complete.

'Well, as you know, sea turtles are an endangered species. It's illegal to use new shell, so I'll have to re-use salvaged pieces. The match won't be perfect, and of course there may be colour and thickness variations. But I've got a selection of tortoiseshell saved from the backs of old hairbrushes, hand mirrors, damaged boxes, et cetera. I think I can get a nice finish using them. And of course the bottom of the box needs replacing, but thankfully that was never tortoiseshell.'

Mr Ravyt didn't say anything, just thrust his hands into his pockets and waited.

'The mechanism is missing. If you're planning to put it back, then it would be easier before replacing the bottom. Do you have its mechanism, Mr Ravyt?'

'I'd hoped putting the damaged box in the auction would arouse interest, set a few tongues wagging. And it did. In fact I almost acquired a suitable mechanism. Someone led me to believe,' he paused and then continued more slowly, 'but I'm afraid that's a long story and proved a dead end. When Aiden Prout phoned and gave me your name, of course I assumed you knew of one. Am I right, Mr Clegg?'

Chrissie felt the bite in his question. She watched Ron, hoping he'd keep the man hooked. Instead he changed tack.

'My main contact was Marlin Poynder. I've done a fair amount of work for him over the years, and I'm used to keeping an ear to the ground for anything of interest to him. But to be honest, Mr Ravyt, everything's gone silent since his... death.'

'So you know, sorry, knew Marlin. Collecting antique automata... it's a small, competitive world, Mr Clegg. We tend to keep our contacts to ourselves, at least the important ones. I guess that's why he never mentioned you. But I'm still a little surprised I've never heard of you before.'

'I'm a cabinet maker, not a horologist. I expect there's more of a call for mechanical repairs. Most of my work for Marlin was furniture repair and restoration. If he'd bid for the box, he'd almost certainly have asked me to repair the tortoiseshell veneer for him. But as for the mechanism, I can't say who he'd have used.' His voice trailed away.

Chrissie stared at the ground. Ron was sounding like an old pro and she didn't want to do anything to break the spell.

She guessed Mr Ravyt must have thought the same, judging by his body language. He moved away from the door, freeing up their exit and then stood looking out through the window. It was shaped like a half circle and

148

some of the panes had been replaced with amber coloured glass. It disguised the chill already gathered in the air.

He finally broke the silence. 'I'd like you to do the repair for me, Mr Clegg. Marlin Poynder had a good eye and he was a good judge. I don't have a cabinet maker among my contacts, so if I'm happy with your work, I may use you again. And, if I'm out your way, I may even drop in at your workshop. Get a measure of your setup.'

'Good. Then I'll wrap the box up,' Ron said, as if there'd never been any doubt. He lifted one edge of the soft linen.

'Here, let me help you, Mr Clegg,' Chrissie said.

Without another word, Mr Ravyt started to lead the way back to the van. This time Chrissie caught a different view of the garden.

'Wow,' she said as she spotted a graceful figure emerging from between young closely planted silver birch.

'Subtle but striking, don't you think?' Mr Ravyt said, following the direction of her gaze.

'It's beautiful,' she murmured.

'Yes, Diana, the huntress. I love the way the bronze has weathered over the years. It's a question of finding the right place for things, don't you think?'

They walked on, around the side of the house. Moments later, she sat in the van with the tortoiseshell box carefully cocooned in the linen and safe on her knee.

'Goodbye, Mr Ravyt,' she said as he shut the van door for her with a flourish.

'Well, that was interesting, Mrs Jax.' Ron eased the van forward, slowly negotiating the narrow driveway.

Chrissie didn't answer. She needed to get beyond her dislike of Mr Ravyt and make her brain work rationally.

They drove through Woodbridge and joined the by-pass. 'We can't like all our customers, Mrs Jax. We just have to be able to work with them.'

'I know, Mr Clegg, but something you said back there set me thinking. This may sound a bit convoluted, but let me try and explain.'

'I'm listening, Mrs Jax.'

She tried to organise her thoughts before continuing.

'When they found Marlin's body, there was something like the innards of a clock near him. When you mentioned the word horologist, well it struck me a clock-maker would be able to tell if it was the right mechanism for Mr Ravyt's box.'

'Or if it was made for a completely different automaton.'

'Exactly my point. And if it's incomplete or damaged, only someone with clock-making skills would be able to say for sure. Don't you see how it could link Mr Ravyt?'

'Or, depending on the type of mechanism, implicate him less, Mrs Jax.'

'I know.' She tried not to sound disappointed. 'But what I'm trying to get around to is, do you know of a horologist who'd have that type of expertise? Someone not in Mr Ravyt's pocket?'

'Yes, as it happens, I do know a good horologist. Known him the best part of my life.'

'I thought you would, Mr Clegg. Now we need to know if the clockwork found near Marlin was meant for Mr Ravyt's tortoiseshell box.'

'We, Mrs Jax? I think you should slip the name of the expert horologist to that nice DI of yours, and let the police investigate.'

'Yes, that's what I meant.'

'And remember, Mrs Jax, we've got the box.'

'Of course, that's a point. The police can seize it as evidence and then the expert's got both the mechanism and the box, and I won't have to handle the tortoiseshell.'

'Oh, I think after all this we should repair the box, Mrs Jax. It'll look very suspicious to Mr Ravyt if we don't start work on it.'

'Do you think so, Mr Clegg? I hadn't thought of that.'

CHAPTER 16

Ping! Nick pulled his mobile from his jeans and read the sender ID. Why was Chrissie texting, he wondered. *Need a beer – c u & Matt Nags Hd 6pm?*

He'd always enjoyed meeting up with Chrissie and Matt at the Academy on the release day Mondays, but now he was in his second year the teaching was only once a fortnight and it was still a week away. He checked the time. Dave had said he'd go with him to TARV's after they'd finished in the workshop for the day. They hoped to find a front wing panel for his Fiesta. He reckoned he'd need a beer after that.

Ok, c u there, he texted back.

Monday was flying. Nick had spent the day helping Kenneth, one of the other carpenters at Willows. Together they were bending wood laminates in the workshop while Dave drove out to Lavenham to talk through some plans for a bespoke fitted wardrobe with a customer. He was just clamping the last forming mould into position when he heard Dave's familiar voice.

'Kenneth, Nick, how's it going?'

'Hi. Perfect timing. We're just about done here for to-day.'

Nick looked up from his work. 'How was Lavenham?'

'Good. It'll be a nice job. I'll draw up the plans tomorrow and get an estimate out ASAP. There'll be a nice set of open sliding drawers for you to work on, Nick.'

'Oh yeah?' Nick pulled a face but secretly he was pleased.

Dave checked his watch. 'If you get a move on, we should just about make it before they close. No time for a cuppa.'

They decided they'd both take their cars to TARV's. From there, Nick would drive on to the Nags Head and Dave could continue home. Nick led the way. He'd found it earlier on a Google Earth aerial view, but as he followed the road to Stowupland, it felt very different from the ground. High, overgrown hedges blocked any view of the auto recycling yard he knew was hiding somewhere. He almost sailed past the huge gates, their metal grilles shrieking a silent warning to keep out, but then at the last moment he caught a glimpse of the weathered notice, *TARV Auto Recycling*.

He hoped the neglected, down-at-heel appearance translated into a cheap, good value front wing. A mixture of excitement and curiosity drove him into the yard.

'Here goes,' Nick muttered as he parked in front of a prefabricated structure on low brick stacks. It would have passed for a shabby mobile home, if there hadn't been a notice nailed to one side. He got out of the Fiesta as Dave drew up.

'Well, what d'you think, Dave?'

'It's pretty much what these sorts of places are like.' Dave surveyed the scene. 'There's plenty here. We should be able to find something.' He pointed to a low-rise city of car shells stacked three or more high. 'I'm guessing they're already stripped and ready for the crusher.'

'Hey, can I help?' A man appeared in the doorway of the office. Nick reckoned he was in his early thirties.

'Hi, I'm looking for a replacement wing.'

The man, thickset and with powerful looking shoulders, pulled the office door closed before stepping down onto the hard-packed rutted ground. He moved slowly, hints of a menacing swagger vanishing as he looked from Nick to the Fiesta. It felt as if minutes passed as he stared at the dented scratched wing, bear-sized hands on hips.

'You're welcome to look around.' He gestured to unbroken lines of cars parked on the other side of the yard and stretching as far as an old chain-link fence. 'But I've some Fiesta body panels already removed. Obviously there's an extra charge for those.'

Nick glanced at Dave, hesitated, and then said, 'We'll have a look at what you've already got dismantled, if that's OK.'

'Yeah, sure. This way.' He led them to an area beyond the office. Racks and stands constructed from scaffolding were laid out with space between, like supermarket aisles but with weeds and brambles sprouting.

'Wow!' Nick could hardly take it in. Ahead, exhaust pipes, hubcaps, wheels, old chrome bumpers and wing mirrors were stacked in haphazard order. Cars and engines had been dismantled and then brought together in an open-air warehouse that extended into an old Nissen hut.

The man turned to face Nick, obviously pleased with his reaction.

'How long have you been running a car recycling yard here? It must've taken years to collect all this.'

'Yeah, we've been here a while. I heard it were small, more of a wrecking yard before TARV took it on. I'm the manager, Dodge Carner. People call me Dodge, after them American cars. Right then; Fiestas - this way.'

He led them between racks of body panels. Just the mention of America, and Dodge had developed a roll to his walk, like a broncobuster with a six-pack. They stopped in front of some Fiesta parts, near the entrance to the Nissen hut.

'Here, take your pick.' Dodge stood to one side as Dave slid a front wing down.

'That's lucky, it's a near side and in good shape. No rust,' Dave said as he turned it over. 'And it's in a damn sight better state than the one on your car at the moment.'

'So who's doing the work for you, or are you doing it yourself?' Dodge dropped his gaze, as if he didn't care.

'An accident repair place out Great Blakenham way. Trying to keep the costs down.' Nick hoped he sounded suitably strapped for cash.

'I know of someone nearer. Whatever your bloke's charging, bet you mine's less. What d'you say? Are you interested?'

'Well, if you give me his number….'

'I can do better than that. I'll give you his card.'

'Either way, we'll need this wing,' Dave muttered.

Back at the office, five minutes later, Nick read the card Dodge handed him. 'Mustang Carner?'

'Yeah, me bro likes American cars as well.'

'Your brother?' Dave parroted.

'Yeah, well I wouldn't be recommending anyone else, now would I?'

'He's on this site?'

'Yeah, he's beyond the Nissen hut.'

'Then I reckon I should get something off this wing if I use him.'

'First see Mustang, then we'll talk money. Just drive straight on, and follow the main track.'

Dave got into the Fiesta and Nick drove. 'What d'you reckon?' he murmured as they wove past a mountain of old tyres.

'With a name like Mustang, I'd say he was born to it. For what you're wanting I guess he'll be OK, but we'll check him out.'

Mustang, when they found him, was a younger, smaller version of Dodge. He had the same jet-black hair and heavy brow, the same swagger, and Nick even detected the same timbre to his voice. There was no doubting they were brothers, but Mustang's eyes seemed closer set and sharper, his manner faster. Dodge might be older, but Nick reckoned Mustang was the brains in the outfit.

They'd disturbed him as he worked on a Volvo. He seemed irritated; almost inpatient as he wiped his oily hands on a rag before crouching to look at the Fiesta's wheel arch and wing.

'Lift the bonnet, mate.'

Nick released the bonnet catch and waited. He smothered the urge to hum.

'Caught it on a gatepost, you say? No other cars involved?'

'Yeah, that's right, and I'm not claiming on insurance. So I need to keep the cost down.'

Something flickered behind Mustang's eyes. 'And you said Dodge was providing a wing? Yeah, I can cut you a deal.' He stared at the ground. Nick guessed it was an act. He'd already have a price in mind, one for the insurance company, but something completely different if insurance wasn't involved. He was more than likely weighing up how much he could get away with.

'Could you give us the names of other customers you've done work for?' Dave asked.

'Yeah, sure.'

By the time Nick and Dave left, they had a quote and some names and phone numbers on a sheet of paper.

***

'So you left the wing at TARV's?' Chrissie sipped her ginger beer. 'Oh no, they've got a darts match in here tonight.'

The Nags Head was busy for half past six on a Monday evening. Nick sat, legs stretched out under a small table and with half a pint still in his glass. It had seemed so simple and logical when he'd described the visit to his friends.

'I mean, if you decide to go to the place in Great Blakenham, will Dodge want more for the wing? Sting you?'

'Or he could say it's gone, just to get back at you,' Matt added.

'I hadn't thought, I mean he seemed OK. Both of them seemed pretty straightforward,' Nick said, remembering Dodge's broad open face and heavy brow. 'To be honest, I don't think Dodge has the brains to do that.'

'I wouldn't bet on it.'

'Yeah, Chrissie's right. And somethin' else. Ott's Pizza Place don't deliver to TARV.'

'Why? Too far out?' Nick sipped his beer.

'Nah, roughed up the delivery bloke. Might've made the headlines. Yeah, I'll try an' find out more, if you like.'

'Oh shike, p'rhaps I shouldn't have gone there,' Nick mumbled into his glass. But Dave had seemed OK with the place. 'They gave me some names of satisfied customers,' he added, as if that made it all right.

'Well, contact them. I assume they're genuine.'

Nick pulled the quote and names from his pocket. 'No surnames,' he said, reading the neat handwriting.

Across the bar a couple of darts players chalked up their names on the scoreboard. They used first names only. Admittedly it looked like a pre-match warm up, but maybe it wasn't so suspicious to leave out surnames, Nick figured.

Matt leaned across and looked at the paper. 'Darrel. Could be a last name round these parts.'

'Or the name of a pizza. A *Darrel* - Dolcelatte, with drizzles of olive oil over fennel, sorrel and chanterelle,' Chrissie added.

'Not at Ott's, it aint. Hey, you're kiddin', right?'

Nick watched Chrissie laugh. She'd seemed quite tense earlier when she'd told them about her visit to Wood-bridge, and then almost annoyed when he'd said it was only a tortoiseshell box. Now she sipped her ginger beer and seemed back to her normal self, diverted by his description of the Carner brothers.

'Do you still have that picture of the stolen bronze from Thorpe Morieux, Matt?' she asked, breaking his train of thought.

'Diana with Bow an' Hound? Yeah, it'll be in me backpack, I expect. Why?'

'Yes why? Whatever made you suddenly ask that, Chrissie?'

'Because I'm damn sure I saw it, or one very similar to it, in Mr Ravyt's garden in Woodbridge this afternoon. I've been racking my brains trying to think why it looked familiar and it's just struck me now. Talking of fennel and sorrel and chanterelles reminded me of his garden.'

'Was it signed Edward McCartan? The statue?'

'I never got that close to it, Matt. It just… well it's beautiful. I can see why someone would want it.'

'Sounds like something you should tell Clive about, Chrissie.'

'Yeah, an' that reminds me. That Ravyt bloke. I found him on the antique automata collectors' site. But it's weird, the mobile number on Ott's hot list with the *don't deliver to TARV* note was the same as his.'

'What are you trying to say, Matt?'

'I don't know. Seems odd, that's all.'

Further talk died as around them, calls for double-sixteens drifted from the darts players. A misthrow and then raucous whooping filled the bar as a dart landed with a heavy clonk and slid along the wooden floor.

'Sounds as if the warm up's going well. Anyone want another, before the bar gets busier?' Chrissie asked.

'I'll pass, thanks Chrissie. I want to phone those numbers and, well I'd better get home. I'm bushed and I haven't eaten yet.'

Out of nowhere, a wave of exhaustion swept over Nick. At eight-thirty in the morning and full of energy, he'd wondered why they were using strips of constructional grade veneer as laminate. 'Couldn't we just cut our own from solid wood?' he'd asked. Now, ten and a half hours later he was thankful Kenneth had spared him that effort when he'd said, 'Time's money and anyway, cutting the laminate strips also wastes a lot of wood.'

He drained his glass. 'Look, Chrissie, if all this with Mr Ravyt is worrying you, then tell Clive.' He stood up. 'I don't know what else to suggest. See you guys on Friday.'

As he left the bar, he wondered if he'd been a bit hard on Chrissie, but for his own sanity, he knew he had to keep focused and throw his energy into the carpentry. He barely had enough spare to cope with Kat, let alone anything else. And the thought reminded him of another call he wanted to make.

Out in the car park, he pulled his mobile from his pocket and pressed *contacts*.

'Kat?' he said, as the familiar warm *Hi* travelled back across the airwaves. 'How are you? Feeling more positive?'

But the warmth left her voice as she answered, 'Not a good day, Nick. In fact, not a good moment. Do you mind if I call you back later?'

'Sure. I just hoped you were feeling more upbeat, that's all. Look I can't stop to chat either, I'm just on my way home. Speak soon....' But he didn't get a chance to say *bye* before the line went dead.

A sinking feeling caught at his stomach. Perhaps he shouldn't have phoned her, but it was difficult to get it right, gauge the moment. He decided to steel himself and phone the references instead. Maybe those calls might go better. He tapped out the number written on the paper alongside Jim's name and listened as the ring tone repeated. A crackly voice cut in, 'If you want to leave a message, speak after the tone.'

He killed the call and slipped his mobile back into his pocket. It was time to drive home.

CHAPTER 17

Matt double clicked on the maths module file and waited while it opened. Tuesday morning was quiet in the Academy library and he was tucked away near the window at a computer station. He didn't expect to take long completing the maths coursework, and then he could indulge himself in what interested him more - a search for reported incidents at TARV, and a check on the antique automata collectors' website. He also needed to decide what, if anything, he could do to entice Maisie out on a date. She still hadn't ordered a pizza.

He sighed. Nick and Chrissie had seemed more amused than concerned the evening before at the Nags Head. He corrected that thought; they'd taken Mr Ravyt's mobile number seriously enough, but not Maisie and her lack of contact. Nick suggested offering her another lift back home after her night session at the supermarket, but Matt didn't fancy getting up that early. Chrissie's alternative option of hanging around in the supermarket car park at the beginning of her shift didn't cut ice either.

'Uncool, uncool, uncool,' he muttered. But Cap'n Starlight of the Space Hopper Corps could never look uncool. If he waited, setting sun crimson-red behind his white helmet, the Piaggio propped at a jaunty angle….

The maths module file opened and pulled his attention back to the screen. He'd never had a problem with maths and the module was basic; a kind of catch-all syllabus to ensure everyone on the course was up to speed with fractions, decimals and percentages, along with graphs and geometry. It was supposed to help him use maths to solve problems and make decisions in his everyday life.

'So,' he murmured, 'how's that work with Maisie?'

There'd be no geometry involved, for a start. He guesstimated the chances of meeting her before work and of her saying *yes* to a lift. However, what were the chances of getting her number, or her saying *yes* to a date? That was likely zero. If he multiplied to get the overall odds, it was a suicide mission but, if he added, it still didn't look good.

A shadow fell across his computer. He sensed someone behind him as the patch of gloom hovered and then moved on. He swung around. 'Frag, Gavin. What you doin' creepin' up on me like that?'

'You'd be surprised what I see when people think no one's looking. A flashcard of your soul.'

'What you on about, Gav?'

'I'd hoped for a screen of porn. Something hot. Last time, it was TARV Auto Recycling and a stolen bronze Diana. This time, maths. Are you depressed?'

'No, I'm doin' me coursework, that's all. Anyway, that Diana bird wasn't wearing much. What 'bout you? Are you still feelin' down?'

Gavin's whole manner seemed to change. The straight confident back wilted and his eyelids drooped, cloaking his watery-grey eyes. 'Yeah, well it's not good at home at the moment. Just trying to distract myself.'

Matt watched, uneasy as Gavin pulled a chair back from the desk and sat down at the computer station next to his. He tried to say something sympathetic, but the words died in his mouth. No one usually sat there. A draught from the window in winter and blazing sun in summer usually ensured that. Why else would Matt choose the place next to it?

'What you doin', Gav?'

He didn't answer for a moment, but flicked the dark lank hair back from his forehead. 'Thought I'd do my maths coursework, Matt. Any objection?'

'No. No, mate.'

Matt cursed under his breath as he checked the time at the bottom of his screen. The morning wasn't going according to plan. Gavin's constant needling was starting to get under his skin.

The library doors swung open and girls' voices breezed in. A couple of students, now with muted voices and smothered giggles, headed for the librarian's office. One had a backpack swaying from a single strap slung over her shoulder. It struck Matt as sexy. The leggings clinging to her thighs beneath a six-inch skirt also helped. He hadn't noticed her around before and the sight of her set him thinking about Maisie. What did Maisie do during the day? Could she be a student here at the Academy? He hadn't liked to ask, but if he'd not seen this one before, it was possible Maisie could be a student here without him knowing.

He leaned across to Gavin and without considering the consequences, whispered, 'Have you come across a student called Maisie? Bird with streaky bleached hair and fantastic legs?'

'Why?'

'Met her at the supermarket a couple of weeks ago. Just wondered, that's all.' Matt turned his attention back to his computer screen. He could almost feel Gavin's eyes searching his face.

'I've got half a password to access the Academy computers, if that'll help.'

'What d'you mean, Gav?'

'I was hanging round in the admin office last week. Compassionate leave, and all that. Anyway, I watched Glynnis putting in her password. You know Glynnis, the one with bright red lipstick and glasses? I got the first few characters but....' He reached for a scrap of paper from his skinny jeans. 'Here, she keyed in nine characters but I wasn't fast enough to get them all.'

'Thanks mate.' Matt looked at Gavin's spidery writing. 'It's her email address and then this password, right?'

'Yeah, well you'll have to work out the last bit. Look, I need some air. I'll be back in half an hour. Be here, right?' He stood up and a thin smile flickered on his pale lips. 'Oh yeah, and when you've cracked it, I want to know the password too.'

Matt watched as Gavin walked across the library. He couldn't put his finger on why, but he reckoned Gavin had engineered the whole thing: the library visit, the matiness, and then that smile. 'Lazy bugger, an' then he'll use her password for bot knows what. If there's any trouble, he'll say it was me. Bet he will.'

He turned his attention back to the screen, his pulse thumping in his head. What could he do? What would Geeko Dude, the comic-strip hero and master of the keyboard, World Wide Web and universe do? Fail to break the password? Comic-strip heroes couldn't fail, but he figured they could subvert. He had thirty minutes. The pressure was on. It was time for Geeko Dude to step up to the mark. His fingers flew across the keys and seconds later he was on the Eastern Anglia Daily Tribune site with *TARV Auto Recy-*

cling in the search box. He found the article he was looking for, dated 20th November 2010.

Police were called to a disturbance, he read. After skimming through the report, he reckoned brawl would have described it better.

It was an argument over a pizza. Possible charges were referred to as: *common assault*, *disturbing the peace* and *drunk and disorderly*. It appeared that *Jim Birstell* and *Darrel Birstell*, both *local tilers*, had been visiting the auto recycling site. They'd been drinking at the time and things had *got out of hand when tempers flared*. The delivery bloke didn't get much of a mention.

'An' all because someone didn't get extra pineapple toppin'?'

But Geeko Dude was still on a mission and milliseconds later he'd logged in to the members' page of the quarterly magazine devoted to antique automata. He was curious. Were there any replies to the notice he'd posted as *Flaming Rose*?

He almost punched the air as he read: *The Utterly Mansion Automaton was announced in the Suffolk Echo of 1920. It was described as being 15 x 11 x 12 inches in size and being of a particularly unusual construction because of its double bird mechanism. I trust this answers your question. I am intrigued. Does Flaming Rose ever masquerade as a Tortoiseshell Butterfly? M C Ravyt.*

'A Tortoiseshell Butterfly?' Matt murmured. The seconds were counting down. He knew there wasn't time to post a suitable reply. That would need further thought.

With lightning speed and still in Geeko Dude mode, he clicked *print*, logged out and shut down the computer. A moment later and he was rebooting. This time he'd make sure Gavin couldn't track his internet activity. As long as he also retrieved Ravyt's message from the printer, he'd be safe.

Matt pushed back his chair, and primed himself to launch across the library. The printer was on a trestle table near the librarian's office and the sheet of printing, already ejecting into a tray. It was time to move. One stride, two strides – and then he spotted the two students. The sexy one had slipped her backpack to the floor and partially blocked the doorway into the office. Now she bent to pick it up. The other girl appeared from deeper in the office. Legs, bottoms, ankles – he was mesmerised. Stride three turned into a saunter. But the momentum of his upper body still propelled him.

'Flame,' he squealed, as he swung a leg forwards and kicked his ankle.

The next steps came at higher-speed. He saw the trestle table. Stretched out his arms. Caught at the edge. Gulped air. Heat spread up from his back and chest, prickled across his neck and burned his cheeks. He tried to slow his breathing as he stood, supporting his weight on the table.

'So what's the hurry?'

'Oh, hi.' Matt swallowed hard and stared into a pair of widely open eyes. Smudges of colour on the lower lids seemed to broaden her face.

'Did you want this?'

He watched, fascinated as she shrugged the single strap from her shoulder and let the backpack slide to the floor. It was a simple, careless movement. Then she reached for the sheet of paper in the print tray.

'Here,' she said, and handed it to him.

'Thanks.'

'Come on, Arolla. We'll be late.' The other girl seemed to scrutinise Matt as she spoke, then turned towards the door.

'Yeah, thanks again, Arolla. What course you on?' He stuffed the paper into his back pocket.

'Not yours. You must be… Sport Sciences or something?'

Matt heard the giggle; saw the other girl's shoulders hunch, and his cheeks flamed again.

'No, I could see him as a long-jumper, April. Really I could.'

'Oh yeah?' He glanced down, hoping to hide his glowing face. Flab hugged his midriff. It blocked a view of his feet, so he straightened a leg and waggled his foot for inspection.

'Oh yes, definitely,' Arolla murmured.

'Now that's enough out here.' Mrs Wesley appeared from her office. 'Haven't you all got some work to be getting on with, or somewhere else to go?'

'Yes, of course. And thank you for ordering those books.' Arolla smiled at Mrs Wesley and Matt was transfixed.

Off to one side, the library door swished open. Matt heard it but he wasn't going to look.

'Yes, inter-library loans are usually pretty fast,' the librarian continued. 'And as you say, you can't beat a good colour plate. You don't always get the same feel for a painting when you see it on a screen, but I don't need to tell you art students that.'

Arolla nodded, while April put a hand to her mouth and smothered a yawn.

'Hi. Is this a printer demonstration?'

The familiar voice didn't surprise Matt. He'd been expecting Gavin.

'No, it is not. Now I really must get back to my office.' Mrs Wesley almost spat the words. 'If you need any instruction with the printer, one of the library assistants will help you.' She turned on her heel.

'Bye, Arolla, April,' Matt mumbled, then flashed a smile. He'd have tried the sexy one, just with a corner of his mouth, if he'd thought of it in time.

'You were meant to be breaking a password, not chatting up....'

Matt looked past Gavin and watched the girls as they left the library. 'Yeah, well Maisie could be history. I rather fancy me chances with that Arolla bird.'

'Have you even started on it, yet?'

'Nah, been distracted, Gav.'

'I told you I wanted it.' Gavin drew himself up, puffing out his ribby chest and narrowing his eyes, but as he stared into Matt's face, the tension seemed to drain. A sly, more calculating expression smoothed the lines on his face. 'I think you've been in here too long. How about a coffee?'

'Only if you're buyin', Gav.'

Five minutes later, Matt sat at a table in the canteen and pulled the tab off a can of cola. His mind tingled with the nervous excitement of the starting gate. He reckoned a sweet fizzy drink was the fastest way to get the sugar high he craved. He needed his brain sabre-sharp if he was going to play Geeko Dude's subterfuge game. Gavin sat opposite and sipped a coffee, eyelids hooded, dark hair flopping forwards.

'Are the police any closer to catchin' your dad's killer?' Matt asked, as an opening ploy.

Gavin rested his cup on the Formica surface and leaned back, tilting his chair. 'I thought I'd told you before. He's not my real dad.'

'Yeah, whatever. But are they? Any closer?'

'They don't tell me much. After all, I'm only the adopted son. Not important enough.' He stared at the ceiling for a moment. 'It's been the same all my life. Like finishing second in a race.'

Matt gulped his cola and then tried to hold back the fizzy burp.

'That's why I refused to go into the auction business. A real son would have joined the firm, been pleased to, no doubt. But I'm not. Why should I make the world believe he's my dad? He never acted like one. Not to me, anyway.'

'So how do real dads act, then, Gav? I mean, mine buggered off when I was five.'

'Did he? Well you had five years more than me. You were lucky.' He let his chair tip back onto its front legs and leaned towards Matt.

'Don't know 'bout that, Gav. Don't remember much before I was three. Never got to know him; see, I was too young.'

'But that's my point. He never wanted to know me or what my interests were. It was always me having to learn his trade. Always about his interests in automata, Titanic memorabilia, and anything with a Liberty's mark stamped on it.'

'The Titanic?' Matt was almost sidetracked.

'Yeah, he even dragged us to Northern Ireland one summer, just so we could see where it was built. What a bloody wet holiday that was.'

He sipped some coffee. 'Actually, there may be some news. The police, or rather DI Merry, want to speak to me.' The same thin smile flickered on his lips. Matt recognised it from the library.

'But you know why he was killed, yeah?'

'The police were asking about his automata collection. But like I said, no one tells me anything.'

'But you must know loads about automata, Gav.'

'Yeah, and the Titanic.'

Crashing metal rang out across the canteen as trays clattered onto the service counter. Matt caught his breath. His stomach pitched.

'Careful, Doris,' someone yelled from the kitchen.

'What's up, Matt? You've gone a weird kind of colour.'

'I'm fine, Gav. You're makin' me jumpy, that's all. Just… give me a moment.' A pounding rhythm pummelled in his head.

'I want the password, Matt.'

'What for?'

'None of your business.'

'Yeah but, Gav, I don't need it for me. See I've met Arolla now. Give me a reason, mate.'

Gavin's watery-grey eyes turned on Matt like steel rapiers.

'Flame, Gav. No need to take it like that.' The sugar-high kicked up a gear. 'Here,' and he delved into his jeans' pocket and pulled out the scrap of tatty paper, 'here, if you want it, you work it out.'

He threw the paper onto the Formica, but Gavin didn't make a move.

'I've told you before, I collect information. I'm an opportunist and that password could be useful.'

'Then do it yourself, Gav. Or don't you know how?' Matt stared at him and waited. He hoped he looked tough.

'I'm the one doing the favour round here. Helping you find that Maisie student. I thought you were a friend. So, are you?'

'Breakin' a password don't prove nothin', Gav. Hangin' out together, that's what mates do.'

'Oh, yeah?'

'Yeah. So if you're a mate, I'll see you down the Nags Head, Friday.' Matt stood up, still fired by glucose. 'Thanks for the cola.' He turned his back on Gavin and headed for the canteen door. 'Frag,' he muttered to himself, hardly able to believe what he'd just said.

There was only one place to go, the library, and he walked, the hint of a swagger in his step. His mind buzzed. Already he was on to the next thing.

How would Geeko Dude handle the Maisie Arolla choice? As a maths problem? He set it out in his mind as he went.

Firstly, if he considered Maisie, he knew where to find her and she'd spent eight minutes on his scooter with her arms around his midriff. And what about Arolla? She'd called him an athlete and he guessed he'd find her hanging around the arts department. He'd already worked out the chances of success with Maisie, and they weren't good. Chances with Arolla? Probably not great either. But combine both and the chances with one girl improved, in a random winning-the-lottery kind of way. He had the answer to the Mais-olla question. He fancied both and it made mathematical sense to keep trying with both.

CHAPTER 18

Chrissie read Matt's text message again. *Hi. I've found a notice on the automata site - posted by M C Ravyt. Tortoiseshell Butterfly mentioned. Is it your box? Will bring printout on Friday, Nags Hd. Matt.*

It didn't make sense. What made Matt think a tortoiseshell butterfly had anything to do with the box she was repairing for Ravyt? Or rather, she would be repairing, just as soon as she'd finished the Queen Anne writing desk.

'You're frowning, Mrs Jax. Is everything all right?'

'I think so, Mr Clegg. Just puzzled by Matt's text. Something about tortoiseshell butterflies.' She slipped her mobile back into her bag and smiled at Ron. He stood, arms crossed and with his weight on his best leg, the arthritic knee slightly bent. She turned her attention back to the desk. It was the star piece in the barn workshop.

'It looks good, doesn't it, Mr Clegg?'

'It does now, Mrs Jax.'

Chrissie ran her hand over the new leather top. The olive-green colour with the gold scrolling-pattern tooled around the edge seemed to bring the wood alive.

She remembered the moment when she'd unrolled the new leather and discovered it was slightly larger than the rebate in the top. Ron had explained she'd need to trim the leather with a scalpel, but not until glued in position. She'd waited impatiently until the specially thickened wallpaper paste had soaked a little into the leather and it was ready to stick onto the carcass wood. If Ron hadn't helped her align the tooling so that it ran parallel to the edges of the rebate, it could all have gone horribly wrong.

'A rolling pin?' she'd queried.

'Yes, Mrs Jax. You start from the centre and work any excess paste and air pockets to the edge. And don't press too hard. Don't overwork the leather.'

'Good job I've let my nails grow,' she'd murmured as she ran a fingernail along the edge of the leather, feeling through it to the wooden boarder.

'And angle the blade away from the rebate when you trim the leather, Mrs Jax,' he'd warned. 'That way you'll undercut it and the brighter shade on the underside of the leather won't show at the very edge.'

Had it only been yesterday she'd done all that? And now it was Wednesday and the day was flying fast.

'Tea, Mr Clegg?'

He didn't answer but pulled the top right-hand drawer out, slid it back, and then repeated the action. 'It slides properly, now. Well done, Mrs Jax.'

'So that's a yes for tea?' She turned away, hiding her glow of pleasure. A *well done* from Ron was a furniture restorer's Olympic gold.

By the time the kettle boiled and she'd handed Ron a mug of tea, she was thinking about the next task.

'Once I've given the desk a good polish and buffed it up nicely, do you want me to make a start on Mr Ravyt's box? Or I could give you a hand with those oak chairs if you'd prefer?'

She indicated the Victorian gothic dining chairs. Ron had dismantled one of them. Arms, uprights, legs, crossbars and a carved panel lay alongside the seat. It looked as if it had transformed into a flock of broken creatures born of darkly stained oak.

He didn't answer for a moment, but sipped his tea. She waited.

'Have you spoken to Clive yet, Mrs Jax? You know, about what we'd discussed on Monday.'

'No, not yet. He was on call at the weekend and he's been pretty busy since, but I'm seeing him tonight. Do you think we should wait and see what he says before starting the box?'

Chrissie heard the deep sigh as Ron put his tea down on the workbench.

'I could take some photos of the box, if you like. I'm pretty sure my camera's still in the car. What do you think, Mr Clegg?'

'Photographs? Now that's a very good idea.'

'Insurance. It would be like a kind of an insurance, Mr Clegg.'

'Covering our backs is how I'd think of it, Mrs Jax.'

'Right, I'll do it now.'

Chrissie left her tea and hurried out to her car. It was only as she returned, camera in hand, that she realised he still hadn't said when she could start work on the box, nor if it was to be a solo project.

The tortoiseshell box, still swathed in the soft linen cloth, had been placed out of harm's way at the far end of the barn workshop. She approached it now, her mind more on Ravyt and composing the shots than on how to repair it.

'You might as well bring it down this end,' Ron called.

She set it carefully on a workbench near him and pulled back the layers of material. The gilded silver disc on the top was the size of a saucer, its underside polished like a mirror to reflect the singing bird when it popped up. The tortoiseshell stood out well against the pale cloth, so she left the box on the linen and angled her camera to get good close-up shots of each side in turn, top, bottom and the inside.

'I can just about make out a name,' she murmured, as she zoomed in on some faint lettering.

'Does it say Bontems?'

'I can make out the B of Bontems easily enough, but the letter before could be a C or an L. I can't make it into a B for Blaise, I'm afraid.'

'So, it wasn't made by the great man. Makes it a later piece by his son or grandson.'

'Seems so, Mr Clegg,' she said as she scrolled through the images on her digital camera. 'I'll load them onto my computer this evening.'

'You can start by marking where there's damaged or missing shell and where it's come away from the wood underneath. Look through my collection of old tortoiseshell scraps and see if you can find pieces to match the patterns. We don't want the repaired patches to stand out.'

Chrissie smiled. It was his way of saying yes you can start working on the box. Typical Ron, she thought.

By the time her workday ended, she'd spent some hours searching through Ron's old salvaged fragments. She was also familiar with every millimetre of the box. Although she still didn't like or approve of using tortoiseshell, she'd developed a grudging respect for the material and its owner, the unfortunate sea turtle. She'd learnt the shell was keratin and when heated could be bent or married with other pieces of the shell. And if she was lucky the fish glue, originally used to glue it to the carcass wood of the box, would also soften with heat and re-stick the tortoiseshell.

But her knowledge was still theoretical. Tomorrow she'd start work in earnest. 'It's all in the preparation,' Ron had said.

As she drove home, she turned her mind to the evening ahead. How was she going to tell Clive about Ravyt without irritating him? She imagined him saying, 'Don't interfere, Chrissie.' And then she'd get annoyed, the evening would be ruined and he wouldn't take her suspicions seriously. She knew it.

She changed down a gear and accelerated out of the bend. What had Ron said? It's all in the preparation? The yellow paintwork of her TR7 caught the early evening sun as high hedges gave way to views across flat earthy fields. In that moment she had an idea.

***

Rat–at–at-at-at-at! The doorbell's metallic notes sounded down the narrow hallway. Chrissie sat at her small kitchen table and listened. If it was Clive, now he'd use his key; if it *rat-atted* again, then it wasn't. Soft clinks and rustles gave her the answer. She guessed his habit of always pressing the bell once before entering was his way of acknowledging something. This was her home, and while he still had a house in Lavenham, this one was hers.

'I'm in the kitchen,' she called. The aroma of fresh coffee floated on the air.

She'd already set up everything. Her camera was connected to her laptop and she'd transferred the images of the tortoiseshell box into a file she'd previously named and dated. She wanted to appear as if this was still a task in progress.

'Sorry, I'd meant to get this done before you arrived. Have you had a good day?'

She half turned her head as he bent to kiss her cheek lightly.

'Hi,' he said and glanced at the screen as she clicked to open the file. 'What are you doing?'

'Oh, just something from work today. There's some fresh coffee. It's in the cafetière if you'd like some, or there's beer in the fridge.'

She waited, pretending to be busy with the computer while he looked in the fridge. When she heard the top come off a bottle, she opened the first image, filling her screen with a shot of the tortoiseshell box. She sensed his eyes on her again.

'I give up, what is it?' He took a gulp straight from the bottle and stared at the screen.

'I took the photos because we've got a bad feeling about this customer. Ron thought we'd better have some record of what the piece was like before starting work on it, in case we have trouble with him.'

'Yes, but what is it?'

She had his complete attention now. 'See this gilded saucer-like thing?' She outlined it on the screen with her finger. 'That's supposed to flip up and then a mechanical bird pops up and sings.'

'It's an automaton?'

'That's right. How did you know?'

'Well, to be honest, I hadn't heard of them before you told me Marlin Poynder was a collector. Remember?'

She nodded and turned to watch him as he drank some more beer.

'After that meal in the White Hart, you set me thinking.'

She waited, not sure where this was leading.

'You see, I hadn't realised the significance of the clockwork thing we found close to Poynder's body. But after what you'd said, I got it checked out by an expert. Turns out it's an automaton.'

'Really?' She tried to kill the, *I knew it would be* in her voice.

'Yes, and a very unusual one. The mechanism works two singing birds, except the birds are missing.'

'Two singing birds? Not one?' Shock, surprise, disbelief; she tried to process the information and her guard went down. 'But... but I thought the mechanism might fit this one.'

'What are you talking about?'

'Well, I....'

She had to think fast. The implications flashed like lightning.

'Oh God, Chrissie. Have you been meddling again?'

'No, not exactly.' Her face scorched.

'So, what's this box got to do with anything?'

She didn't answer.

'Come on. You can't half tell me and then leave me hanging in the air.' He softened his tone. 'Your face says this could be complicated. Come on, bring your coffee and let's go and sit down. I promise I won't say anything till I've heard you out. Remember, this is a murder investigation, my investigation. You have to tell me.'

Chrissie felt her hopes for the evening spinning away. Clive was listening, but she hadn't planned it like this. Did she really want to tell him the full extent of her scheming, snoopy ways? Her stomach lurched.

'Promise you won't call me stupid or get cross or irritated, and… you may need another beer. It's a long story, Clive.'

Without saying a word, and still holding his half-finished beer, he opened the fridge door and reached for a second bottle. He led the way into the living room, lined up the two bottles on the coffee table and settled into the sofa.

His air of controlled calmness daunted Chrissie but she followed, carrying the cafetière and her mug of coffee. She hoped the aroma would make it feel less like an interrogation or a confession. More like a friendly chat over drinks, she thought. She sat next to him, took a deep breath and tried to quell her quietly churning stomach.

'Right,' she began, 'I suppose I have to start at the auction in Bury on the Saturday, the day after Marlin Poynder was found dead at Suffield's.' She spoke slowly, explaining how Ravyt had withdrawn the tortoiseshell box from the sale.

Once she'd started telling, it became easier. She skipped the details of how Matt hacked into the antique automata collectors' site, merely disclosing his discovery of a posting by Poynder.

She sensed Clive's interest and launched into an account of her next visit to the auction house, shamelessly airbrushing her behaviour.

'You mean you just walked in to collect Mrs Whittle's chairs and Aiden Prout asked if you were interested in mending Mr Ravyt's box?'

'Yes, something like that, Clive. I'm afraid I can't remember the exact words now.'

She ignored his raised eyebrows and continued with a description of the Woodbridge visit and Ravyt's garden.

179

She explained her suspicions unemotionally. It was the only way Clive was going to take her seriously. In the end she ran out of words and her tongue felt dry against the roof of her mouth. She sipped her cold coffee and wondered if she'd managed to come out of her account smelling of roses.

'You haven't touched your beer,' she said sweetly.

'I was concentrating on what you were saying.'

Silence hung in the air while she watched his face, not sure how he was going to react.

'Have you still got the printout of Diana with Bow and Hound?'

'Yes, I think it's still in my bag. I'll get it in a moment, but....' She smiled. It was going to be all right. He wasn't irritated and he wasn't acting as if he considered her an airhead. Without thinking she started to voice her next concern.

'I've got a few things playing on my mind, Clive.' She watched a muscle flicker in his cheek.

'Let me guess,' he said. 'Any news on the metal thieving front? Not as far as I know, I'm afraid. But I might tipoff the organised crime boys about the sighting of Diana in Mr Ravyt's garden.'

'Hmm, and the expert you used. Was it a local horologist? Anyone from around here who could be in Mr Ravyt's pocket?'

'Wooah, you have got it in for the guy, haven't you Chrissie? But no, it's some expert on our books from London.' He leaned forwards, reached for the already opened bottle, and swigged back the rest of the beer. 'Anything else troubling you?'

She thought for a moment. 'Well, yes. Have you any idea what's happened to the casing for the double bird mechanism? I mean is there a maker's name or serial number on it that might tell you more about it? What to look for?'

'Come on, Chrissie. If I told you, you'd probably try and track it down, and repair that as well. Just to tempt some crook out into the open. You're not safe.'

'Now, that's not fair, Clive. I'd keep you in the loop if I found it. But, while we're still talking about the murder, well kind of, what about Gavin? Did you ever find out what the last call was about?'

Clive didn't answer for a moment, but stared at the coffee table, as if remembering an interview. 'He's a troubled young man. I'm not sure I've got to the bottom of that yet.' He looked up. 'Are we done with questions now?'

'Almost. What about eating? Do you want to walk up to the White Hart yet?'

He slipped his arm around her and gently pulled her closer. She didn't remember hearing his answer.

CHAPTER 19

Nick slammed the Fiesta door and locked the car. He wasn't sure why he was bothering. Who'd want to steal it with a ravaged front wing? He'd drawn up next to the secure parking reserved for the Willows & Son vans and out of habit glanced through the chain-linked fence at the loading area to the workshop.

He pulled his mobile out of his pocket and checked the time. No wonder it seemed deserted. It wasn't even eight o'clock yet. The other carpenters would be arriving over the next ten minutes. But with his mobile already in hand and nothing else to distract him, why not try Jim's number again? He'd given up trying to raise Darrel. The number from Mustang had drawn a blank, but Jim's had at least been answered before cutting out. The early hour might trigger his curiosity. He pressed ring and waited.

'Yeah? Who's that?'

Nick couldn't tell if it was a poor signal or Jim's voice, but the words could have travelled through a gale.

'Hi, I've been given your number by Mustang,' Nick said, as a hundred yards behind the Willows site a commuter train on the Norwich to London line hurtled past.

'Who? Who's this?'

'Mustang gave me your number,' Nick shouted.

Nick waited, but there was no sound from Jim. 'Hi. Can you hear me? Is that Jim? Mustang gave me your number. He said he's done some work for you.'

'Yeah?'

'I was thinking of getting him to repair a wing on my Fiesta and he said I should ring you. See what you thought

182

of his work.' The words tumbled out as he rushed to finish before Jim cut the call.

'Oh right, yeah. Who'd you say you were?' The voice was gruff, no longer hostile.

'Nick. I'm Nick. So what work's Mustang done for you, Jim?'

'A respray. Yeah, he did a good job. He's got all the kit. You know, a sprayin' booth and all that.'

'So you'd use him again? You'd recommend him?'

'Yeah, and he's done work for my nephew. Did a good job for him, too. Nick, you say?'

'Yes, why?'

'A Fiesta with a damaged front wing? You aint by any chance been working over Thorpe Morieux recently? Layin' a floor?'

'Y-es.'

'Hey, over here!' Wind almost howled through the phone as Jim's voice faded for a second. 'Sorry, I'm up on a roof at the moment, Nick. But yeah, you gave us those pizza flyers. We were laying the roof tiles. So you know Dodge as well?'

'Well–'

'Yeah, make sure Mustang gives you mate's rates. Say it from me.' The phone went dead.

'Shike!' Nick's head buzzed. Now he understood. He'd just spoken to Jim, the weathered tiler with a voice to match. 'Shike, shike, shike!'

He thrust his phone into his pocket, and leaned back against the Fiesta. The bodywork felt cold but solid. He closed his eyes, took a deep breath and let the cool morning air breeze over him.

Moments later he heard tyres crunching over rough concrete as the first of the carpenters arrived. A car door closed, footsteps approached.

'Are you OK, lad?'

Nick opened his eyes. The sudden rush of anxiety had passed.

'Morning, Mr Walsh. Yeah, just a heavy night, that's all.' If only, he thought. Chance would be a fine thing. He suspected Kat's coach had recently counselled less on the boyfriend front and none on the sex front. At least he hoped that was the reason. He felt mildly edgy as he watched the elderly foreman scrutinise his face.

'Just as long as it doesn't affect your work, Nick.'

Mr Walsh pulled a bunch of keys from his jacket and unlocked the gates to the secure area. He didn't open them, but walked on past, slowly making his way along the side of the workshop. When he reached the side entrance door, Nick knew he'd unlock that as well and the working day would be set to begin.

No point in hanging around out here, Nick thought, but before he'd taken a step, Dave drove in. He waited as tyres screeched and Dave skidded to a last-minute halt parallel to the Fiesta.

'Morning, Dave. Thought for a moment you were going to take out my other wing.'

'Bloody cheek. Why? Are TARV's doing two-for-one deals?'

As they walked together through the side entrance, Dave paused and asked, 'Did you ring those numbers Mustang gave you?'

184

'Yes. Just now. And you'll never believe this, but the guy was up on a roof. Turns out he's Jim - the tiler working at the Dower House the same time as us.'

'You're kidding.'

'No. Mustang resprayed something for him. He seemed happy with it. And while we're talking deals, Jim seemed to think if I mentioned him, I'd get a better rate.'

Nick waited, expecting Dave to explode, wag his finger and say something about shady deals, stolen goods, and nothing but trouble would come from mixing with the likes of Jim. But Dave didn't say anything, just headed into the office-like sitting area, seemingly untroubled by Nick's revelations. Nick shrugged and followed.

Inside, the room smelt stale. Its assortment of plastic stacker chairs and comfy favourites in grubby fabric exuded the feel of a well-used room. Filing cabinets stood along one wall and Mr Walsh stooped over a table and studied a large sheet of paper with a plan of the work schedules. He looked up to speak to Dave, but his words were lost as Kenneth clomped in heavily, followed closely by Tim, a thin wiry carpenter.

Another train thundered along the line. Nick checked the time. It was eight o'clock, the commuters were on track and Needham Market would be waking. There was just one thing he needed to settle before concentrating on his work.

'What d'you think, Dave? About the connection with Jim?' he asked a few minutes later when he'd got Dave's attention again.

'Relax, Nick. Even if some of Mustang's other business isn't strictly legit, does it matter as long as what he does for you is OK? It's pretty common to mess with insurance companies in accident repair claims. He's not welding the front half of your chassis to the back half of another chassis. It's only a replacement wing and paint job, you know.'

'Yes, you're right.' He took a long slow breath. 'I'll phone at lunch and fix a date.'

The morning passed quickly enough. Dave asked him to work out how much wood they needed to order for the wardrobe in Lavenham. Dave's plans were easy to follow. The skill was in knowing the dimensions of the timber supplied from the timber merchant and how that translated into what they needed to cut from it - a three-dimensional puzzle with American cherry doors.

While Dave checked his calculations, Kenneth asked to borrow Nick. It required two pairs of hands to assemble the laminated wooden pieces into a sinuous bespoke-designed chair.

'Wow, it looks ace. Unbelievable how the wood keeps those shapes,' Nick said, remembering clamping the veneer strips, one glued to the next in the forming moulds, at the beginning of the week.

They stood in the workshop admiring the chair, Nick a million miles away from any thoughts of Jim, Dodge or Mustang, and Kenneth quietly modest.

'What did you think of TARV's? I never heard. Did you find what you wanted on Monday, with Dave?' Kenneth asked.

'What? Yeah, I think so.' Nick dragged his mind back from thoughts about laminating wood. 'There's an accident repair place, kind of attached. Mustang Carner. I thought I might get him to do the work.'

'Hmm, yes. I've heard he's good.'

'Really?' Nick felt relieved, pleased and stupid, all in one rush. Why hadn't Kenneth said that on Monday when he was helping him with the forming moulds for the wooden strips? But Kenneth wasn't much of a talker. Nick swallowed his irritation. Dave was right. He should relax; keep a sense of proportion and his humour.

'Well, thanks for that, Kenneth.'

Even Kat seemed to think he needed to lighten up, as she called it. Humming and breath control weren't enough.

'You need to clear your mind. Meditate,' she'd said.

'As well?' He'd tried to keep the sneer out of his voice, but looking back on it now, perhaps he'd used too harsh a tone. She'd taken his reaction personally when really, he'd only been thinking of himself and his image.

'Meditation doesn't mean you have to be a Buddhist, Nick,' she'd countered. 'No orange robes. It might help to clear your mind, give you a calmer, more peaceful outlook, that's all.' She hadn't mentioned it again but at the time her face spoke volumes - her hurt and his insult.

He found he was staring at the chair while his thoughts raced. He reined them in and focused on the sinuous shapes of the laminated wood, but it only made Kat more real. There was nothing else for it but to text her and ask about meditation. He figured she'd rise to the bait. His taking an interest in meditation techniques was a small price to pay for a decent date. He hadn't thought to ask if she meditated herself, but if she did, then perhaps she could teach him; if not, they could learn together. As Matt would say, a win-win situation.

While Kenneth walked around the chair, stooping, tilting and examining it from every angle, Nick let his mind leaf ahead through his diary. Saturday afternoon would be a good time for meditation instruction, he reckoned - after band practice in the morning and before the John Peel Centre gig in the evening. If he played his cards right, she might come to watch him sing at the gig. And if not, well maybe it was a sign. There were always plenty more fish in the sea.

'Nick. Hey, Nick!'

He turned to see Dave had walked into the workshop from the office-like sitting area, some plan drawings in his hand.

'Oh sorry Dave, I hadn't realised you were standing there. Do you want me for something?'

'Yes, we've been asked to drive over to Mendlesham. A friend of the boss needs bailing out. The joker tried to hang some old stripped-pine doors and well, he's made a pig's ear of it. Apparently he's got a houseful of guests due at the weekend, so we'd better get going now.'

'Right, I'll put some lengths of pine in the van.'

'Good. We've got what's left of today and we'll probably have to spend tomorrow on it as well. So look lively and don't forget anything.'

'Yeah, yeah, yeah - clamps, wood glue, nails, hinges – I'll load the van.'

'And make sure the circular saw's in, Nick.'

It was like flicking a switch. All thoughts of Kat flew out the window as the challenge of fixing a botched job filled his mind. He'd been an apprentice long enough to know they'd more than likely have to work on the door frames as well as the doors. Today was only a Thursday but already it felt like a Friday night, with everything to look forward to.

***

Nick breathed out, almost a sigh. He'd arrived early. Only a couple of Friday drinkers sat on stools at the bar in the Nags Head. The jukebox was silent, and the flat screen blank. He stretched his legs out and rested back against the wall, almost tipping his chair. The pint glass felt cool in his hand as he tried to blank out the memory of the journey from Mendlesham. What had possessed Dave? Which part of his brain made him step on the gas when he got on the A140? Was it simply the sight of a straight road and long inclines?

Nick had sat in the passenger seat, his stomach lurching as they skimmed over brows of hills only to plunge into hollows, his jaws clamped on the rising bile. Some alien force had once again turned Dave into a rally driver from hell.

He raised his glass and sipped. If it hadn't been for the speed cameras, he was sure Dave would have broken the land speed record for a white van. Nick reckoned he'd have died of motion sickness long before all four wheels finally left the ground. He stared at the old wooden floorboards. They weren't sticky but they smelt of beer. They were reassuring and grounding. He sighed.

'Hi, it's Nick isn't it?'

'Hey, I didn't notice you come in. Hi, Gavin.' Nick covered the surprise in his voice and smiled at the goth-like creature. He could have sworn he was thinner, more stick-like than ever.

'Will Matt be in?'

He checked his watch. 'Yeah, next fifteen minutes, I guess. If you're getting a drink, come and join me while you're waiting.' He'd spoken without really thinking. He'd rather have kept his own company, but Gavin's pasty sadness made him feel sorry for the guy.

Gavin returned surprisingly quickly with a long straight glass filled with blue liquid. His eyes seemed to come alive as he watched Nick looking at it. 'It's lemonade with blue curacao. Cool, don't you think?'

'I don't know about that. It looks like antifreeze.' Nick waited as Gavin pulled up a chair. 'Weren't you over at Suffield's reclamation place last week? You disappeared before I had a chance to say hi.'

'Maybe.'

'Yeah, we were returning some parquet blocks. So what took you over there?' The words had slipped out too fast for Nick to stop. 'Ah - sorry, Gavin. I didn't think.'

'It's OK.' A half smile moved the thin lips. 'When I got there, I found I couldn't be in the yard. I couldn't face where it had happened.'

'I'm not surprised. So you slipped away through the vestry?'

Gavin didn't say anything, just stared at the blue liquid.

'So where does it go, out the back of the vestry?'

'What's it to you?'

'I don't know. Nothing I suppose, but when you disappeared I checked out the back, in case you were ill or something. There's a path. I reckoned it had to lead somewhere. Just curious, that's all.'

Raised voices filled the bar as a couple of men, still in their work gear, surged into the pub on plaster-spattered trainers. Nick looked up, hoping Chrissie and Matt had arrived. He only just caught Gavin's hushed tones as he scanned the bar.

190

'If you follow the path, it takes you to Suffield's house.'

'What?'

'Yeah, the old preacher's house.'

'Is that where it goes? Of course, for the chapel. I guess you know it pretty well. Suffield said something about you working there on Saturdays when you were a kid.' Nick bit his tongue before anything else slipped out. Suffield had come across as a selfish moneygrubbing bastard and there was no point in upsetting Gavin.

'Yeah, Suffield taught me loads. But I've helped him too. Turns out I've a good eye for things. I try to pay him back.'

'You owe him money?'

'No, Nick. He's been good to me. I tell him when I think something's valuable. Repay like with like, that's what I say.'

Nick sipped his beer. There was something unnerving about Gavin's watery-grey eyes. They seemed hard, cold as steel and at the same time sad. He looked away, just catching a change in Gavin's expression. What was it he'd seen? A smirk? He glanced back, but the face was a mask.

It was Gavin who spotted Chrissie and Matt first. He stood up as soon as they entered the pub and sidled over to them. Nick stayed where he was, a sudden waft of cedar and lime cutting through the scent of beer. It transported him back to the vestry with the coats and overalls hanging on the hooks. It was the same aftershave. 'Gavin,' he breathed.

Matt hurried over, Gavin on his tail. 'Hi, mate. Have you booked your car in yet?'

'This coming Monday. Should be able to pick it up by the end of the week.' Nick caught Gavin's look, now a slightly hangdog droop. 'Are you going to try one of Gav's lemonade with blue curacao drinks?'

'You're bloody jokin', right? Chrissie's gettin' me a lager, mate.'

It felt awkward with Gavin being there. His initial celebrity status was wearing thin. He was too weird, too uncomfortable to be around. Nick decided to ignore him. After all, he reasoned, he'd spent the last fifteen minutes talking to him. Instead he sat back and watched, trying to read the faces: Chrissie, animated as she talked and laughed; Matt, shifting on his chair; and Gavin.

'I printed this lot out for you. Thought you'd be interested,' Matt said as he handed several sheets of folded paper to Chrissie.

They were both too preoccupied with the paper to notice Gavin. But Nick picked up the change in him. He'd seen it earlier. The eyes came alive, the mouth line changed. It became thinner, almost cruel, and for a moment, Nick felt uneasy. And then it was gone and only the sad expression remained. It happened so fast he wondered if he'd really seen it.

'Look, I'd better get going,' Nick said and drained his glass. 'I'm seeing Kat. I'll be in trouble if I'm late. Haven't been home yet. I need to have a shower and change.' He had to get away.

'See you at the day release on Monday,' Chrissie called as he left.

CHAPTER 20

Matt shivered as he rode the Piaggio out of the Nags Head car park. The temperature was plunging, there was no moonlight, and only minimal street lighting. It was starting to feel like winter. He followed Chrissie's tail lights for a short distance before peeling off and heading towards Tumble Weed Drive. He wondered if she was driving home or over to Lavenham and Clive, but he hadn't thought to ask. He was just pleased to be shot of Gavin.

'I get the feeling you don't like him,' she'd said thirty minutes earlier as they watched Gavin slink out of the bar.

'Dead right. He's mega weird,' he'd muttered, and now he muttered it again, almost fogging his visor.

'He kept mentioning Maisie.'

'Yeah, that's why I told him I was seein' her, just to shut him up.'

'And are you?' she'd asked.

'Not yet, but I reckon I'll try an' meet her tomorrow – well I got to now.' He'd felt his guts twist. Was it the Tom effect, or Maisie? As he'd downed the last of his lager, he'd realised something. Not every flutter and stomach lurch was Tom related or bad. This was excitement. His brother had never triggered that emotion.

By the time he'd reached Tumble Weed Drive, parked his scooter and stowed his helmet, creepy Gav had long been forgotten and scary Tom consigned back into custody. Now his mind filled with Maisie and comfortable fluttery excitement. He ambled through the gloom to his mum's front door. Her bungalow was modest, even by Stowmarket's standards, but he'd always considered being a semi-detached anchored it to something. It made it belong, even if only to next door, and by association suggested a kind of permanence. He fumbled with the key and pushed the door.

The hallway was dark. He listened, but there was only silence. A stale smell of frying hung in the air and he followed his nose to the kitchen. Dirty plates in the sink told him his mum had already eaten and he supposed she was probably out playing bingo. Overwhelmed with a sudden pang of hunger, he grabbed slices of bread and mopped leftover fragments of burnt bacon from the pan, now cold with congealed fat on the cooker.

'Hmm…,' he murmured, and bit into the budget bacon butty.

Stomach assuaged, he headed for his bedroom and settled onto his bed. He needed to decide how to impress Maisie tomorrow. He opened his laptop. It was time to look up some ace chat-up lines.

**

Saturday morning dawned later for Matt than he'd intended, and the unscheduled oversleep drove plans for a carefully coiffed appearance out the window. He dressed in a hurry, throwing on clothes, raking fingers through his short hair and rubbing sleep from his eyes. He scratched at his beard and then patted it back against his face. There was no time to check in the mirror, but he left his denim jacket open so as to give a casual jaunty air and expose his latest charity shop find.

By the time he reached Ott's Pizza Place, the mild churning inside had settled into hunger rumbles.

'Morning, Matt,' Scarbrow called from behind the counter. 'Like the tee. Yeah, *BYTES FOR ALL* – very clever.'

Matt glowed. 'Neat, aint it? An' the *delivering's* covered, as well.' He looked down and touched the words stretching across his chest.

CLOSER LINKS
FASTER CONNECTIONS
BYTES FOR ALL

Some of the lettering had started to flake off, but the meaning was clear enough from Matt's angle.

'Ah, that's what it says. You had me for a moment on that first word. There's a C before *LOSER*. So it's *CLOS-ER*, not–'

'Yeah, an' faster. Any pizza goin' wantin'?' Matt surprised himself with his boldness, but he reckoned he counted as staff. He hoped it gave him privileges.

'Before you start asking for freebies, get the delivery box attached to that Space Zipper of yours. Then if you're lucky, there may be a slice of Gipping Special.'

As Matt lugged the black box with white lettering out to his scooter and set about fixing the straps, he conjured up flavours of tomato, mozzarella and tinned tuna.

'Flamin' poser,' he muttered. 'Gipping Special, my arse. More like tomozza an' tuna.'

But he knew it was a lucky day; Scarbrow liked his tee and there was pizza waiting on the counter, or maybe out the back. It was a sign. Things were going to go well with Maisie.

When he sauntered back into Ott's, he hoped the Cap'n Starlight swagger showed in his step. Scarbrow was busy on the phone taking the first order of the day, and Matt waited, catching one half of the conversation.

'So that's an American Special... extra pepperoni, and a... yes the Mexican Hot... both fourteen-inch? To be delivered... who do you know? What... and promised mate's rates?' One eyebrow puckered around the scar line as Scarbrow looked across at Matt. 'Says you're a–'

'It'll be Maisie. Say yeah, an' get the address. It'll be Stowupland.' His stomach flipped. He could hardly believe it, but then he figured, when you're a Cap'n in the Space Hopper Corps you make your own comic-strip luck. She'd phoned for a delivery and that meant she fancied him. That's all that mattered.

'You'll have to make up the difference. It'll come out of your wages, OK?'

'What? Yeah, s'pose so.' If the Mexican Hot was meant for him while Maisie ate the American Special, then he was hot all right, and the deal sounded OK. His skin burned beneath his beard. Of course, in his comic-strip books, Maisie would be the hot Mexican. He wondered if he should try an American accent. Is that what she wanted?

Scarbrow spoke into the phone again. 'Stowupland? Yeah, OK then.' He scribbled an address. 'Thirty minutes.'

It felt like forever before the pizzas were cooked and ready in their boxes. Matt, now on special secondment to the American section of the Space Hopper Corps, scooped them up and power-walked to his scooter. Moments later he was riding away, the two-stroke engine whining as he accelerated towards the Stowupland Road, the precious warm cargo safely in the transporter box behind his seat. He took the most direct route, only one thought in mind. Earthy fields sewn with winter wheat sped past in a blur of twenty-eight miles per hour. Soon Stowupland was almost history and he was on the Gipping Road. A sharp left and he was there.

He parked outside a terrace of late Victorian cottages. He pulled off his helmet and checked the address. A blue front door beckoned while his heart pounded a rap rhythm. Cap'n Starlight seemed to fade, leaching downwards into his space trainers as he lifted the warm cardboard containers out of the delivery box.

'Frag,' he muttered, trying his best Suffolk-American accent, but his ears heard only Suffolk. He loosened his denim jacket.

The front door opened as he walked the front path.

'Flame,' he hissed as he caught his shin on a child's trike abandoned on the gravel.

'Hey, good timing, mate.' The voice was rough, but the face young, wind-burnt more than tanned. Matt reckoned he was in his late-twenties. The man stood in the open doorway.

'Maisie?'

'There aint no Maisie here, mate. I'm Darrel. Ott's pizzas, right? You look well dosselled.'

Matt handed over the warm boxes.

'So where's Maisie? I thought she made the order. Sure she's not inside?' He looked down and checked the name at the bottom of the paper. Birstell. His guts twisted. Now he made the connection with the newspaper report on TARV's.

'Don't get clever with me, mate. I've already said once, *she aint here*. Now piss off. Me pizzas are gettin' cold.'

'But....' He backed away. His calf collided with the trike. 'Ouch.' He flung out his arms, ready to hug air. Denim parted. His tee was exposed.

'Hoy, watch out, loser,' Darrel sneered. 'Bloody fool. You've even got it written on your chest. It's official. *LOSER.*' He held up one hand, making the L sign with his thumb and first finger.

A quick sidestep and Matt was in balance but still moving. He spun, hopes shattering as he turned his back on Darrel and bolted. Harsh laughter followed as he rammed on his helmet. He jumped onto the Piaggio and turned the ignition key. He gunned away, twisting the throttle as if his life depended on it. The pounding in his ears finally slowed as he approached Ott's Pizza Place.

'Are you OK?' Scarbrow asked the sweating Space Rider minutes later.

'I could've died. Phishin' hell, it was the TARV bunch again.'

Scarbrow pushed a segment of Gipping Special across the counter. 'What're you sayin'? I thought it was a mate.'

The recovering Space Rider explained and then bit into tomato, mozzarella and tuna while Scarbrow added a name, address and number to the hot list on the wall. The warm cheese seemed to wrap itself around the hurt burning through him. Tomato dropped onto his tee. Tuna wedged between a canine and premolar, but a glimmer of hope doggedly struggled on.

***

Matt drew up and killed the two-stroke engine. The supermarket car park was virtually empty, just a few cars – mainly staff arriving and leaving at the beginning of the Saturday night shift. He sat on the Piaggio, all thoughts of comic-strip heroes blown away. A cold, leaden feeling weighed heavy in his stomach. It matched his mood better than the earlier fluttering excitement. The shadowy gloom made it difficult to see if any of the figures in the distance could be Maisie. He pulled off his helmet and a breeze chilled his face as his eyes searched the darkness beyond the lit area.

'A bit like waitin' for Tom,' he murmured.

He knew from his past about waiting and disappointment, the moment when hopes were dashed. It had happened often enough with Tom. As a ten-year old he'd waited in vain, willing the next footsteps to herald his big brother. But there was always some reason why Tom didn't arrive or couldn't take him on the promised treat. He never did get to see Tom having that tattoo. What if he never got to see Maisie either? He swallowed back remembered defeat.

A figure crossed a pool of light cast by the car park lighting. Matt recognised her immediately and his thoughts boomeranged back from the past. His limbs froze, as his guts wrenched. He watched, drinking in the long legs and streaks in her bleached hair.

'Hi, it's Matt, isn't it?' she said as she walked towards him.

He couldn't tell from her face if she was pleased to see him.

'Are you back here doin' the night shift, then? Pizza delverin' not workin' out for you?'

'I…,' his tongue wouldn't move. The ace chat-up lines dried in his mouth.

'Well, I see you've got a delivery box on your scooter. Tryin' to hold down two jobs then?'

'No, see… why didn't you order a pizza? I went to Stowupland deliverin' this mornin' an' thought it'd be you. Don't you like 'em?'

She didn't answer, just fixed him with a wide-eyed stare. 'Have you brought one for me? Is that why you're here?'

'Yeah, no…I mean yeah, I would bring you one but you aint ordered. I just done a delivery out this way an' I hoped I'd see you as I was passin'.'

'Oh.'

'I could bring you a Mexican Hot?'

'Persistent, aint you? Don't know if I could eat a whole one.'

'I could help you…,' and his face flamed beneath his beard.

'Are you chattin' me up?'

'No… yeah.' Had he seen that line on the site? 'I like pizza an' well, we could go for a drink sometime?' The words came in a rush.

'Are you askin' me out for a drink?'

'Yeah, an' a pizza, if you like.'

'I've a better idea. What about pig racing?'

'What?'

'Next weekend. Give me your number an' I'll text you.'

He scribbled it under the last delivery address and handed the dog-eared scrap to her.

'It aint where I live. I've just delivered a couple of six-teen-inchers there. Reckon they were sharin' too.' He watched as she read the number.

'OK, but no promises. So don't come lookin' for me if I don't text. I'm going to be late. Bye.' She tossed the words over her shoulder as she started to walk.

'Yeah, an' I gotta get back to Ott's. If they sack you for bein' late – text me an' I'll give you a ride back to Stowupland,' he called after her.

A musical chuckle breezed back. She raised a hand in the air, not quite a wave but definitely not a two-fingered salute or L sign.

CHAPTER 21

Chrissie leaned forwards as she repeated her question. 'But what's pig racing, Matt? Out-running the police?'

'Nah, I looked online. It's like ferret racin'.' Matt shifted his tray to make room for Nick. It was the Monday apprentice release day and she was in the Academy canteen with her friends. They'd just sat down to eat lunch.

'So? Tell me more.' She held up her hands. Something between *I give up* and an appeal for information.

'I've heard of it. Never been, but I've seen it on a notice once in Coombs.' Nick closed his eyes as if picturing the words. 'Pig Racing, Hog Roast & Barn Dance.'

'What? So you eat the losing pig?'

'Nah, Chrissie. You get a load of pigs runnin' along a short track an' bet on the winner. That's what I read.'

'Who cares where you take her? You asked her out and she said yes. That's the point, right?' Nick mock-punched Matt's shoulder.

'Well, I'd care.'

'You're not like most people, Chrissie.'

'What's that supposed to mean?' But secretly she was pleased. Who wanted to be like most people?

She bit into her egg and cress sandwich, savouring the malty wholemeal as she studied Matt's face. He wasn't giving much away, but she guessed this could be a ground-breaking date for him.

'Why you lookin' at me like that?'

'Just thinking, that's all.'

'About those things I printed out for you?'

'Yes, those as well.' She sipped her water and made a decision. She'd share her suspicions. She didn't think Clive would mind, and anyway, she suspected Matt had already guessed.

'The Utterly Mansion automaton – its innards could be what they found at the top of those library steps.'

'How the hell did it get there? Didn't you say it'd been stolen from here a few years ago?' Nick stared at his plate for a moment before adding, 'Look I don't want to think about it. OK?'

'Yes, sorry, Nick.'

'It'd explain why notices were posted about it on that website,' Matt murmured.

'But they were your postings, remember?'

'Yeah, some of 'em, Chrissie. D'you want Tortoise-shell Butterfly to reply?'

'Maybe.'

'Can't you two just give it a rest?'

'You're starting to sound like Clive, Nick.'

'I know who'd know. Seems to 'ave his snout in most things.'

'Just leave it.' Nick shovelled some lasagne into his mouth.

'Not Gavin. You don't mean Gavin, do you, Matt?' She had a bad feeling about this. 'Anyway, why would he know anything, unless his father.... You don't think Marlin Poynder had anything to do with it? Stay out of it, Matt. And keep Gavin out of it as well. Sorry, what were you going to say, Nick?'

The conversation moved on, winding between Nick's John Peel Centre gig on Saturday night and dropping his car off for bodywork repairs that morning. The level of laughter and clatter rose as more students crowded into the canteen. Chrissie found she was listening with only half an ear. Her thoughts kept drifting back to Ravyt. He had to be involved in some way; she felt it in her bones. She just needed to work out how.

***

Chrissie woke early. The apprentice release day hadn't taxed her physically, and apart from a lecture on how to set up your own business, there hadn't been much to stretch her brain. She'd exhausted the topic of Ravyt, and now her restless thoughts turned to Sir Raymond's automaton. Gavin was too young to have been at the Academy three years ago when it was stolen, but she reckoned Marlin Poynder, as a local auctioneer with an interest, would have known of its theft at the time. It had been all over the local newspapers. Matt had a printout. Did Marlin know what he'd find at the top of those library steps, she wondered. Did he deal in stolen goods? Was he a fence?

She sighed. Of course Clive, if he was there with her now, would say it was all speculation. The expert hadn't confirmed it was the Mansion automaton yet. He seemed to be taking forever, but she'd already decided it was going to be Sir Raymond's. It was too much of a coincidence not to be.

She rubbed her eyes. It was no good; she wasn't going to be able to doze off again.

'Tea,' she murmured, and pushed the warm duvet to one side and swung her legs out of bed.

Forty minutes later she'd downed a mug of tea, showered, dressed and was in her car thinking of the day ahead. She assumed she'd be working with Ron on the Victorian gothic-styled dining chairs. The repair of the tortoiseshell

204

box was complete and apart from a final polish, it was ready for Ravyt to collect. Pity, she thought. It would have been interesting to visit his Woodbridge place again and get a chance to look more closely at Diana, maybe see inside the big house and more of the automata collection.

'No,' she murmured as she accelerated out of a corner and changed up through the gears. 'No, no, no. Don't meddle. Leave it to Clive and the police.' But visiting and observing, that wasn't meddling, she reasoned. It was just part of her day-to-day work.

She drove through low lying mist as first light pushed back the night. By the time she turned off the Wattisham Airfield perimeter lane and rocked over ruts and potholes, daylight had added a colourwash of late October hues. She parked the TR7 in the courtyard next to Ron's van.

'Morning, Mrs Jax,' he said as she stepped into the barn workshop. 'You're early. How'd the release day go yesterday? Learn anything interesting?'

'We had an outside speaker. He gave us a talk on setting up a business. You know, tips on how to avoid the pitfalls. It was good. You should have come along, Mr Clegg. You'd have enjoyed it.' She turned away to hide her smile.

'I'm not going to put up my charges, Mrs Jax.'

'I know. You're an artist and a craftsman. I'm going to put the kettle on. Do you want another mug of tea?'

'Websites, advertising, was it about that kind of thing, Mrs Jax?' He held out his mug, warm dregs in the bottom.

'Yes, but the most important thing, the lecturer said, was to have a good product.'

'And ours come damaged. So, that lets me off the hook.'

'Not quite, Mr Clegg. Still need a business plan.'

She made fresh tea, her thoughts following the same thread. Perhaps that's why she felt at sea about this Ravyt business? It was she who needed the plan.

'You're looking very serious, Mrs Jax.'

She settled onto a work stool and sipped her tea before answering. 'Have I got time to give the tortoiseshell another polish before Mr Ravyt comes to collect it?'

'He phoned yesterday. Said he'd be here this morning at about ten o'clock.'

She gulped in surprise, almost scalding her throat.

'How much more polishing did you have in mind? I thought you'd already done a pretty good job with the jewellers rouge, Mrs Jax.'

She coughed. 'Thanks, Mr Clegg. Adding almond oil to make a paste of it was a good tip.'

'Hmm.'

Chrissie wasn't sure why she'd felt such a bolt of surprise, and a rush of heat seared through her cheeks. She rummaged through her bag until the worst of it had passed.

'Have you lost something, Mrs Jax?'

'No. Just checking I hadn't left my mobile at home. So, can we take the clamps off the carver yet?'

She glanced across the workshop at the dark-stained oak dining chair. A length of webbing ran around the seat and several more stretched across the back. The ratchets on the webbing looked like giant beetles crawling over the chair. Not so much gothic as just plain creepy.

'So why not use bar clamps?'

'Difficult to get an even pressure with all that barley twist turning on the arms, legs and back uprights. Better to use a web cramp. A useful tip, Mrs Jax.'

The second chair was still in pieces. Its back was more damaged than the first and the repair was taking longer. She walked over to Ron's workbench, mug in hand, and examined the piece he'd been carving. A scrolling leaf and edge of lion mask were already morphing out of the wood. She pictured it fitting where a section had split away and been lost.

'Wow, it's going to look fantastic.'

'When it's stained to match, you'll hardly notice.'

She finished her tea and then settled to cleaning away old glue still caked to the mortise and tenon joints of the dis-articulated chair. Time flew as she concentrated on her task. Helicopters rumbled overhead while Ron tap-tapped a mallet against a spoon-bent gouge. The sounds had a rhythmic soothing quality, like a percussion-based masterpiece. She hardly registered the distant sound of tyres spitting grit on the entrance track.

'I expect that'll be Mr Ravyt arriving early,' Ron murmured. 'If you want to do some last-minute buffing, you'd better be quick, Mrs Jax.

'What? Oh….'

She grabbed a soft duster and as good as sprinted to the tortoiseshell box. It was wrapped in the linen sheet, but with a few deft movements she had it free. By the time the door opened, she stood near the box, looking as if she'd been polishing for hours.

'Good morning Mr Ravyt,' she said, taking care not to catch Ron's eye.

Ron laid his mallet and carving gouge to one side and eased himself off his stool with slow stiff movements.

'I found your workshop more easily than I'd expected, Mr Clegg.' The voice lilted softly, but Chrissie detected an underlying tension. She caught the blueness of his eyes as the tint in his light-sensitive glasses faded.

'There she is,' he said, looking past Ron. 'She looks magnificent.'

'What?' For a second Chrissie wasn't sure if he meant her. And then she realised he was gazing at the box. His tone made her skin crawl.

'Yes, I hope you're pleased with our work. All it needs now is its mechanism and it'll be complete.' Ron emphasised each *it*, as if making a point of removing the gender.

'Yes, yes… but let me have a look. The tortoiseshell glows… and with the gold. Such warm colours, even from here.'

He moved quickly, covering the distance in a few strides. He picked up the box, turning it in his hands and examining it from every angle.

Chrissie watched, mesmerised as he set it back down on the linen. His fingertips lingered, as if reluctant to let go. A gold signet ring with initials glinted on one finger and she leaned closer, concentrating on the letters. He laughed and lifted his hand away, leaving sweaty marks in its place. The innuendo was gone in a flash, but the impression lasted longer.

'Irresistible,' he murmured.

'Yes, it's cleaned up well,' she said, and wiped away his smudgy prints with the duster. She hoped her disapproval shrieked in his face.

'I'm impressed,' he said, turning his back on Chrissie and facing Ron. 'Now I'd love to have a look around your workshop, if that's all right with you, Mr Clegg?'

'Of course. We've several projects on the go, at the moment.'

While Ron and Ravyt slowly toured the workshop, Chrissie wrapped up the box again. As she folded the linen, his fingers played across her memory. She banished them with a shiver, but then remembered the ring. With a surge of determination, she focused on the image. There should have been a scrolling R, but all she'd seen was a capital M and A.

'And a small C. Yes, a small C between the M and A,' she whispered to herself. 'Mc A or M c A?'

The crowded shelves, stacks of wood and the machine tools baffled their voices, but now she caught snippets of conversation as they passed within spitting distance, only a workbench separating her.

'So you'd be interested in restoring more of my automata?'

'Yes, it's nice to tackle something a little out of the ordinary. We don't get to….'

They moved on and the words were lost.

'R? Definitely no R for Ravyt,' she murmured.

Unable to explain it, her mind drifted to the snippet she'd overheard. It would be interesting to work on more of the automata casings, she thought. And there'd be more opportunity to snoop on Ravyt. 'I bet Ron won't mention charges or present a bill.'

She'd realised when she'd worked as an accountant that clients rated her services as highly as she rated herself or, put bluntly, by how much she charged. But that seemed a long time ago. 'I bet he'll be under-selling his skills again,' she said softly.

'Are you going to the auction rooms in Woodbridge this coming Saturday?' The lilting tones floated across.

She looked up. Was Ravyt asking her? 'What? I–'

'I'm afraid I won't be able to make it. Is there something of particular interest in the sale, Mr Ravyt?' Ron replied.

'Yes, there is. Will you be going, Mrs Jax? I expect with your interest in automata you wouldn't want to miss it.'

'I-I… of course. It's in my diary.' She smiled, hoping the pause hadn't given her away.

'I look forward to seeing you there. What is it they say? A tortoiseshell butterfly flaps its wings, and across the other side of the world…?'

Oh my God, the website postings. Her stomach lurched. 'Not a tortoiseshell butterfly, Mr Ravyt. Really I don't think–'

'Ah, but I do,' and the blue eyes narrowed as his expression hardened. 'Perhaps you prefer - a flaming rose drops a petal, and across the other side of the world…?'

Ron broke the moment. 'Well, if that's everything, Mr Ravyt, how would you like to settle your account?'

Ravyt pulled a wodge of notes from his pocket and licked his thumb, ready to count them off. 'I assume a ten per cent discount for cash, Mr Clegg?'

Chrissie turned away, her head reeling. He thinks I'm Flaming Rose, her inner voice screamed. And not only that, he thinks I'm an expert. Saturday? Woodbridge? Did I say I was going? Had she lost her mind, she wondered. But despite the alarm bells, part of her was excited. This could be a lead that finally led somewhere.

Ten minutes later, with Ravyt and his tortoiseshell box gone, equilibrium was restored.

'What's being auctioned on Saturday, Mrs Jax?' Ron asked.

'I haven't a clue, but I had to pretend I knew. I'll check their website this evening. I can look through the catalogue online. It has to be automaton related. Stands to reason.'

'Well if it's anything to do with a casing for a double bird mechanism, or a single mechanism that'll fit his tortoiseshell box – let the police deal with it, Mrs Jax.'

'Don't worry, I'm not stupid. Of course I'll tell Clive. If he'll listen,' she added under her breath.

'Hmm… what was all that about a tortoiseshell butterfly and then a flaming rose? What was he trying to say, Mrs Jax?'

'I think it was a reference to the Chaos Theory. You know, one small thing can alter the course of something, and set off a chain of reactions with spectacularly unforeseen consequences elsewhere.'

'Hmm… I think he was referring to you.'

'If it was me, then I'd be a tortoiseshell cat. Curiosity, and all that.'

'And we know what happened to the cat. Be careful, Mrs Jax. It's one thing to look through the catalogue of sale items, but you don't need to go to the auction as well.'

'I know. But we may be onto something, Mr Clegg. Did you notice his signet ring doesn't match his name?'

CHAPTER 22

'Watch out,' Nick yelled, as a car accelerated towards them.

Dave cut tighter into the bend and took the corner at speed. Brakes squealed as the oncoming car veered toward the hedge. And then they were past.

'That was bloody close,' Nick muttered, as he looked back to check the car was OK.

He rested back in the passenger seat, closed his eyes and breathed out slowly. It was always like this when Dave drove, even his own car. They'd left the Willows van at work and Dave was dropping him off home as he passed Barking Tye.

'When will your car be ready? They've had it the best part of this week.'

'Mustang said he'd ring and let me know. Probably Friday, so hopefully I'll collect it tomorrow. Can you give me a lift, again?' He kept his eyes closed. Witnessing one near miss was enough.

'Yeah. I should think so.'

Nick sensed the car was slowing. He waited for the hollow clicks of the indicator, and the jolt as Dave braked hard. He reckoned it was safe to look.

'Are you OK, lad? You've gone a bit green around the gills.'

'Yeah. I'm fine, thanks.' He wasn't, but there was no point in mentioning the rising bile and motion sickness. He knew Dave didn't rate it. Instead he loosened his seat belt and opened the door. Cool air bathed his face. The sweat evaporated but his guts still complained.

'You've been quiet all week. Are you going down with something?' Dave let the engine idle as he turned a questioning face and waited.

'Everything's fine.' Nick attempted a smile. He'd wanted to keep it to himself, but he should have guessed nothing got past Dave. Trust him to notice, he thought. Easier just to tell.

'The thing is, I'm between girlfriends – but that's OK. I feel good. Really, I do.' He got out of the car. There wasn't more to say, and anyway, Dave clearly wanted to get on home.

'I'm sorry. Kat seemed such a nice girl.'

'Don't be,' Nick said and slammed the car door.

Nick stood outside his parents' house. Shrubs and clusters of long ornamental grass softened the unforgiving lines of the modern brick as the light faded around him. He raised his hand in a parting salute as Dave threw the car into gear and launched back into the road. He watched, distracted for a moment before his mind replayed the closing scenes. No explosion, not even a slow fizzle, just a thoroughly modern text.

It's not working for me. I'm sorry but I've been thinking about this for a long time. It's over and we need to move on. Please don't try to contact me. Kat.

She'd sent it three days ago, late on Monday and like a nasty stinging insect, he'd felt the sharpness of the stab, but the full reaction had taken longer. Now a dull burning replaced the numbness. In fairness to her, it wasn't a surprise. Meditation on Saturday afternoon hadn't been the fun-packed hour he'd anticipated. Sitting in silence, while shutting out the world had only served to distance her. And what's more, there'd been no sex afterwards.

'Big mistake.' He sighed and kicked the gravel. Grit showered the gatepost, the same gatepost he'd driven into almost three weeks earlier, after the fateful St Edmund Way walk with Kat.

'Big mistake,' he repeated.

A memory from the Saturday gig flashed back. Perhaps he shouldn't have signed his name on that girl's shoulder, but she was a fan and insistent. She'd wanted the entire band to write a message. Jake had written in felt tip scrawl, just above her left breast.

'Over my heart,' the fan had said.

Kat hadn't been amused.

He pulled his mobile from his pocket and deleted her text. It had festered long enough amongst his messages. It was time to stop thinking about her and make a clean break. He headed for the kitchen, emptiness dragging at his core. For a moment, hunger replaced his humiliation and licked his wounds.

'I'm home, Mum,' he called and headed for the fridge. Its cold polished steel exterior matched his mood.

Brr brr, brr brr! His mobile almost leapt out of his hand.

'Hi. Kat?' Hope answered without checking the caller ID.

'Nick?' The harsh voice hit like a punch in the stomach.

'Is that…?'

'Yeah. It's Jim. If it aint safe to speak, don't worry – just say yeah an' no. I'll get it.'

'What?'

'We got an understandin', right? Worked the same site, remember? Over at Thorpe Morieux. We talked about

214

your car. Mustang's a kinda mutual acquaintance, yeah? It's turned out I've had a chance to… let's say, put in a good word with him regardin' that. He knows we're kinda connected.'

'What?'

'And you gave us a flyer. Promised mate's rates.'

'Oh yeah, I remember. Pizza. You want pizza?'

'Nah, not today, mate.'

'What then? It's about my car?'

'Catch on quick, don't yer? But it aint your car. Not today.'

'So…?'

'One of your work vans. Seen it parked in Lavenham. Church Street. Need some details. How long's the owner away?'

'Pardon?'

'You heard. How long's the owner away?'

'Look, I don't know. I've not even been there. What's this about?'

'We need details. Find out, and fast. I'll ring tomorrow and you'd better have what I want, if you know what's good for you.' The call cut out.

'Shike!'

A thousand volts shot through his mind. What the hell was he going to do? He flung the phone down as his knees buckled. He sank. A breakfast-bar stool with a buttock-shaped seat broke his plunge.

'Oh no-o-o,' he moaned and gripped the counter. He needed to empty his mind and think. He needed to… meditate.

He went through the rudimentary steps: closed his eyes, distanced himself, relaxed, and breathed. As the whirlpool in his brain slowed, he finally floated in an azure pool.

'Hello, dear. Everything all right?' His mother's voice cut into his consciousness.

'What?' He dragged himself back. 'Oh hi, Mum.'

Calm washed over him as his mother busied around in the kitchen, opening cupboards and putting pans on the hob. With the anxiety in retreat, he knew what he had to do.

He figured Dave must have visited Lavenham at least a couple of times to talk to the customer about the fitted wardrobe. That must have been when the Willows van was spotted. But they hadn't started work there yet, and as far as he knew, nobody was away. The more he relaxed, the clearer it became. He realised he couldn't give Jim any information, even if he'd wanted to. But he could pretend to.

'I've got a few calls to make, Mum. Give me a shout when tea's ready.'

He didn't wait for her to reply, but picked up his phone and strode to the back door, new purpose to his step.

'Where are you going, Nick?'

'Outside. I can think better out there.'

The gathering darkness of early evening veiled him as he shut the door. He stood near the back step and tapped in an automatic dial name.

'Chrissie? Hi. Look, something's come up and I need to speak to Clive.' He didn't wait to listen to her questions, he knew they'd sap his resolve and slow him down.

'I'll tell you after I've spoken to Clive. Promise I will.'

Moments later he had Clive's number. His heart pounded into his throat as he listened to the ring tone.

'Answer, answer,' he hissed under his breath. He knew he might not try again if Clive didn't.

'Hello, DI Merry speaking.'

'Clive, it's Nick. I'm sorry to bother you but something's happened and I need your–'

'Oh hiya, Nick.' The tones were relaxed and friendly.

He took a deep breath. 'Remember a few weeks ago when we were walking and those bastards ransacked that mausoleum thing?'

'Yes.'

'And I told you there'd been metal stolen from where I was working as well? Guttering and a Diana bronze. A place in Thorpe Morieux?'

'Yes, go on.'

'And I said I thought it was the tilers. I'd overheard them talking. A bloke called Vatry was mentioned. Anyway, Jim, one of the tilers phoned me just now. He wanted to know about a house in Lavenham. He'd seen the Willows van parked outside and… well, judging by the way he spoke, I guess they're planning a break-in.'

Nick waited, listening to the silence. 'Hello? Are you still there?'

'Yes, I was thinking. How'd he get your number?'

'Ah, that's a bit complicated.'

'I'm listening.'

He tried to explain.

'So you rang him for a reference for the accident repair place attached to TARV? Go on, surprise me. He gave a glowing recommendation, yes?'

'Yeah. Why?'

'Hmm... this can't be the first time someone's fished for information about where you're working. What do you normally do?'

'Shrug and walk away. Never tell them anything.'

'So why not do the same now?

Nick swallowed and pictured the azure blue. 'I did, but he got ugly. Said he'd ring again tomorrow. I don't think he's going to be shrugged off so easily.' Nick paused. He knew he had to get the next bit right. 'I thought maybe you'd consider setting up a sting. Catch them red-handed. You said it was difficult to trace the metal back to where it's stolen. This could be an opportunity.'

'Hmm... look, keep fobbing Jim off. I'll have a word with a colleague in organised crime. Someone will call you if they're interested, OK?'

'OK, and thanks, Clive.' He killed the call.

His tension seeped away slowly, like melting ice. He'd done it. He'd made the call. He was using his brain and fighting back. So, had he toughen up? Was he handling it? Mouth still dry, he rang Chrissie back.

***

'Have you heard from Mustang, yet?' Dave asked as they broke for lunch the next day.

The American cherry had arrived from the timber yard that morning, and they'd been sorting through it in the Willows delivery bay, ready to start work on the built-in wardrobe. The faint scent of the wood carried through the workshop air.

'No, I haven't heard anything yet. Do you think I should call him? He's probably masked up and busy in his spraying booth. I thought I'd wait for him to call me.'

'He's more than likely stopped for lunch. You want to know if it's ready, don't you?'

'Yeah, of course,' Nick said and followed Dave to the office-like sitting area. 'Tea?'

He pulled his mobile from his jeans and parked himself on a plastic stacker chair. While the kettle hissed beside him, he listened to Mustang's ring tone. He was about to give up when a rough voice answered.

'Carner's Accident Repair.'

'Hi. Nick Cowley here. Is my Fiesta ready to collect yet?'

'Nah sorry. I should've let you know. The new wing's rubbed down, an' lookin' good. It's ready to spray, but I'm havin' trouble matching the colour with the rest of the paintwork.'

'How d'you mean?'

'See, I ordered the exact blue an' it should've been spot-on. It's the right colour code for that Ford model an' year. Unfortunately the rest of your paintwork's degraded. I reckon it's been kept outside.'

'Yeah, but the rest of the car looked OK to me. Same blue it's always been. Is the new paint that obvious? I mean, it can't be that bad a match if it's the right colour code.'

'Well if you really want me to go ahead. But I was goin' to try a different....'

'OK, OK. So it's not going to be finished today. Will it be ready by Monday?'

'Yeah, I hope so. Want to get it right, mate. Don't like turning out a substandard finish.'

'OK, but let me know what–'

The call cut out. Disappointment smarted.

'Trouble?' Dave asked.

'I don't know. Says he's having problems matching the paint.'

'It happens.' Dave bit into a doorstep-sized sandwich.

'Yeah, but it's nothing special. It's not one of those metallic finishes. Just plain blue for a Ford Fiesta. I bet he hasn't even started yet and he's just playing me along to give himself more time.'

'Why d'you say that?'

Nick shrugged. He wasn't sure. He'd expected Mustang to sound frustrated but there'd been no emotion at all.

'Look, get used to the idea you haven't got a car for the weekend. Now make the tea will you, before we all die of thirst. The kettle boiled ages ago.'

'Yeah. And you can make me a cuppa too, while you're about it,' Kenneth said as he stepped through from the workshop.

Kenneth's arrival foiled any opportunities to tell Dave about Jim's call the evening before. Instead, Nick squeezed the teabags against the sides of the mugs and handed round the tea. He'd wait for another moment, he told himself.

He settled back on the plastic stacker chair and tucked into his cheese roll. Losing Kat had hurt, at least it had four days ago, but as he munched on the cheddar and pickle, he reckoned there could be advantages to freedom. It was a licence to play the field. And if he had to choose, would he pick Kat or the car? He knew it wasn't a fair question but he surprised himself with the speed of his answer.

'Fiesta, it has to be the car.'

He looked up from his roll to catch Dave watching him.

CHAPTER 23

Matt scrolled through his messages. He supposed it didn't really count as subject reading for his digital life module, but he still hadn't heard from Maisie and he couldn't resist checking.

Ping! The mobile jumped in his hand. A flutter of excitement exploded. Then died.

'Nick,' he muttered and opened the text.

Car not ready to collect. CU Nags Hd. May need lift home after.

He checked the time. It was still early Friday afternoon. Students were beginning to slough off and the mansion building had a muted, forsaken air. He headed to the library and slipped past the vacant librarian's station. He reckoned there was time to check through the Woodbridge Auction Rooms' catalogue again. One last look, in case he saw Chrissie in the pub that evening.

'Nothin' here.' He sighed.

The sale goods were listed under their lot numbers. They started from one and rose through the hundreds, with items grouped broadly into categories: glass & ceramics, silver, jewellery, pictures & art, furniture, rugs, and small & sundry items. There wasn't a section for automata or clocks. Not this Saturday. He supposed that would've made it too easy, and then Chrissie wouldn't have needed his help.

'Bot,' he muttered as he tried the web page search box again. It took him to the category headings, but it wouldn't drill down further.

'Don't even say who's sellin' the stuff.'

He would have looked for names he'd seen on the collectors' website, but the lots were like orphans and their source anonymous. Owners were shrouded in mystery, at least as far as the catalogue was concerned.

He gave up and checked his mobile for any new messages.

'Oh pixel,' he moaned, 'still nothin' from Maisie. Don't she realise it's Friday?'

CHAPTER 24

'I'm sorry, Chrissie. It's the way cases go. Sometimes sifting through all the information doesn't throw up any leads. More questions than answers.' Clive made it sound so reasonable.

'I know. I was sure there'd be something in the sale catalogue.' Her mobile felt hot against her ear. She'd only been talking for a few minutes, and was reluctant to let him go. 'And it's not just me. Matt couldn't see anything either.'

'Don't involve Matt.'

She bit back the sharp retort. It was late evening and she sat alone in her living room. She guessed it was going to be another long Friday for Clive. Not a good start to his weekend on call as duty DI.

'I couldn't get to the viewing. It's so frustrating. I just know there's something important being sold. I'd recognise it if I saw it,' she said quietly.

'Have you wondered why Mr Ravyt told you about the auction?'

'I thought…,' her words dwindled as she remembered his visit to the Clegg workshop.

'I mean, why would an avid collector tell another collector about something coming up for auction?' Clive's voice soothed. It was more of a spoken train of thought than a question.

'I doubt he thinks I'm a collector. An expert maybe?'

'My point is - you might want it as well.' A hint of exasperation mingled with the background voices from his end of the call.

'Oh. Yes I see what you're getting at. Two bidders would push up the price.'

'So, either he's selling and thinks you may be interested in buying, or he thinks you're selling something and therefore you won't be bidding.'

'What?' She needed time to take in the implications.

'Are you still with me, Chrissie?'

'Yes. I was just thinking. They don't put the seller's name in the catalogue.'

'And people don't always use their real names.'

Oh my God, she thought. Clive can't know about Flaming Rose, can he? She hadn't told him, but his team might have looked on the website.

She forced her voice to sound steady. 'Now I'll definitely have to go to the auction tomorrow. And before you say anything, I know you're busy. I'll get Nick to come with me. He's just broken up with Kat and his car's still with the accident repair place. Seemed a bit down, at the Nags Head earlier.'

'Hmm… what time's the sale?'

'Ten o'clock. Why?'

'I might make it, or even send one of my DCs, but no promises. And don't let on you know me. Tell Nick as well.'

'So you think it could be important?'

'I'm not sure. Now I must be getting on. It's busy this end.'

Chrissie sighed. She supposed she was holding him from his work. 'Thanks, Clive.'

'Sleep tight, Chrissie.' The call cut out.

***

'Come on, hurry up.' Chrissie watched Nick slump into the passenger seat. He looked rough. She suspected he'd been awake half the night. Probably tossed and turned and finally fallen asleep in the early hours. It had been like that for her three years ago when her husband Bill died.

'Come on. We're going to be late.' Anxiety sharpened her tone.

'I thought you said it started at ten.'

'It does, but we need to look round the lots first.'

She threw the TR7 into gear and accelerated out of Barking Tye.

'I want you alert, Nick. On the top of your game, not semiconscious.'

'I've got half an hour.' He closed his eyes. 'A14 and then A12?' he asked, resting his head back.

'Yes.'

'Thought so.'

She sought speed. She craved straight sections of dual carriageway sweeping over the Orwell Bridge and circling Ipswich. She wanted to drive, not concentrate on twists and bends while the greater part of her brain wrestled with the auction.

The engine hummed and purred through the gears as it ate up the miles. Soon Chrissie slowed.

'Wake up, Nick. We're almost there.'

She took a turning from the roundabout and headed east, directly into Woodbridge. Not so pretty as driving up from Quay Side, she thought, but the shortest route to the auction rooms. The road sloped in front of her towards Market Hill. School playing fields gave way to ancient beamed houses.

'I see it. It's on the left. Just before the pub. Stop,' he yelped. 'You'll miss the car park.'

Chrissie braked and swung in.

'Over there.' Nick pointed to a narrow space near a wall. 'We can just about squeeze in. Go for it.'

'Well you seem to have woken up,' Chrissie muttered as she tugged down hard on the steering wheel.

They had a plan. Nick suggested they split up and work separately. That way, with limited time, they'd cover more of the lots.

'I'm guessing we're most likely to find whatever it is, in the Small & Sundry Items,' Chrissie added. 'And once the sale's begun, note down the buyer's card number if you think the lot might be important.'

'Are you going to register to bid? You know, get your own number?'

'Hell, I'd forgotten that. Yes. I suppose I ought to.' She tried to keep the rising panic out of her voice. She hadn't expected to waste time queuing when she could be searching.

Nick strode ahead. Chrissie followed past heavy double doors already thrown open for the auction. A dusty mildew scent of unwanted furniture hung in the air. Under foot, age-worn red bricks had been laid in a higgledy-piggledy manner. They led her onwards, giving the impression of a passageway created from an outside walkway. Along both sides, chairs, wardrobes, corner cupboards and all manner of sale items flanked the way. She glanced at the lots as she hurried past. It was like entering a time tunnel back into history.

A handful of people meandered along the passageway in front of her, and she nipped between them. The uneven bricks descended, following the steep slope of the ground. At last the roomy passage ended with a wide doorway to her left.

'Nothing automaton related yet,' she muttered and stepped into a large wooden-floored hall. 'Oh no,' she groaned. It was crammed with sale items, and hummed with the commotion of bargain hunters talking and moving between the lots.

The enormity of her task struck home.

While she queued to register, she cast an eye around. She spotted Nick's short cropped hair as he disappeared through a door leading off one side of the hall. She guessed he was heading to another room of sale items. No sign of Clive or Ravyt yet, she thought.

Finally armed with her buyer's ID number printed across a laminated card, and a catalogue thrust into her bag, she did a circuit of the hall. Nothing. She checked her watch. Only fifteen more minutes. If she was fast, she could run a cursory eye over the lots in the side rooms, but she also needed time to find the right spot to sit when the auction began. She hesitated, wavering between search or sit.

'Hello, Mrs Jax. You look quite excited.'

'What?' She turned and stared straight into a pair of tinted glasses.

'Gets the pulse racing without having to do the workout, don't you think?' The lilting tones made his words sound harmless, almost conversational.

'Just about time for one last look,' she said and started to move away, conscious of the minutes counting down.

'Oh, I think the time for that has passed, Mrs Jax.' Ravyt touched her arm.

She flinched, then forced herself to relax. She had a part to play, she told herself. Sit, don't search - she could do that.

'Then let's find the best spot to sit, shall we?' she said, inclining her head and smiling sweetly. She hoped she sounded confident.

He led the way to some chairs on the far side of the hall. Ravyt must have wanted to watch everything, because it was a vantage point commanding a good view of the rostrum, other bidders, the entrances to the side rooms and the doorway out of the hall. If he had a gun, she thought, he'd control the room, the auction and the building. Oh no, and me as well.

'I see you're expecting to bid,' he said, as she pulled her catalogue out of her bag and held it ready with the laminated card.

'Hmm.' She'd noticed a battered cabinet, probably circa 1900, with glass-fronted drawers for displaying spools of coloured thread. She supposed if she had to bid, she could bid for that, but she didn't know the lot number. She buried her head in the catalogue and searched. Ron was going to kill her.

Ravyt opened his catalogue and turned to the Small & Sundry Items. She watched out of the corner of her eye, hoping for a clue.

She was about ask him about his collection and what his first pieces had been, but the room hushed and her opportunity passed. Excitement rippled through the hall as latecomers hurried to their seats and catalogues rustled. The auctioneer mounted the rostrum. And then it began.

'Lot number one. A Victorian mahogany butler's tray on a stand....'

228

Chrissie listened with half an ear and gazed around her. Behind the dreamy façade her brain worked double-time as her eyes combed the hall. Where was Nick? And Clive, was he skulking somewhere amongst the bargain hunters? As long as Ravyt didn't suspect anything, she'd be all right. A knot of unease tightened in her stomach.

Something caught her attention. She looked again. Across the hall someone stared, then glanced away. It was over in a flash, but there was no mistaking those watery-grey eyes. Gavin? It can't be, she thought.

'Lot number twelve… hanging hat rack with mirror, slight damage to the mahogany….'

She peered again. He slipped further back, stepping behind a man in a granite-coloured sweater. It was definitely Gavin; pale skin, dark hair and a tight skimpy jacket zipped to the neck. And the way he moved was instantly recognisable. Half hidden, and now blending with the man's sweater, he must have thought he was invisible as he watched. But the intent expression wasn't directed at her.

It took a moment to work out. It was fixed on the man sitting next to her. Ravyt. Her mind spun.

'Lot number eighteen….'

'It's a bit slow this morning. Not many wanting to bid, Mrs Jax.' Ravyt spoke under his breath as he leaned to-wards her, the smirk barely disguised.

'Perhaps they're waiting for the big one.' It was a bit clichéd, but too many thoughts ricocheted in her head to allow something better.

The smirk paled.

'A small Brainerd & Armstrong Co. spool cabinet….'

Oh no, she thought. Already?

'Twelve glass-fronted drawers….'

This was the battered cabinet she'd thought she might bid for. She gripped the laminated card, now sweaty in her hand, and slid her bag to the floor. A movement on the far side of the hall distracted her. She saw it was Nick. Had he found something? She guessed he'd just come through from the side room, and hoped he'd make a sign.

He shook his head. Not subtle - the meaning was clear to her. Nothing found yet.

'He doesn't seem to want you to bid for the spool cabinet,' Ravyt murmured.

'What?' and then she realised he'd seen Nick's signal as well. 'He doesn't sew, he wouldn't understand,' she countered, nerves sharpening her words.

Now she was going to have to bid if she was to save her cover.

'Twenty pounds. We'll start the bidding at twenty pounds....'

She waited, heart pounding.

'Twenty anyone? No...? Ten then. Ten pounds... anyone bid me ten pounds?'

Chrissie raised her laminated card.

The bidding followed fast and with the sudden ferocity of a shark attack, and then abruptly it was over.

'Well done, Mrs Jax. Only thirty pounds.'

Was Ravyt being genuine or laughing? She couldn't tell. The tinted glasses under the bright strip lighting obscured his eyes.

As the adrenaline rush subsided, a thought struck Chrissie. Why hadn't Ravyt asked who Nick was? Wasn't he curious? Wild theories took root. Still aware of Nick as he coasted around the hall, she determined not to make any eye contact, and focused on the catalogue. One mistake was enough. Don't do anything so obvious again, she pleaded in her head and hoped telepathy would carry her message to Nick.

The auctioneer rattled through the lots while Chrissie followed the items. She ticked them off as they sold, each fall of the hammer racking up the tension.

'Lot three hundred and eight. A wooden rocking horse….'

'It's taking forever,' she sighed as exhaustion swept over her.

'We're almost there. Not much longer now.'

If it hadn't been for the cynic in her, she might have mistaken the lilt in his voice for compassion. She shifted on her seat and checked the catalogue. Only forty more lot numbers. What was she missing? And then with lightning clarity, the words leapt from the page.

Doll's House.

Of course! She looked again.

Lot 313. Doll's House, wooden, circa 1920. Front opening. Some minor damage to roof towers.

She closed her eyes and imagined something box-like and in the image of Sir Raymond Utterly's mansion. With the mechanism removed, it would have been simple to cut the whole front panel free and hinge it to open. Ingenious. A doll's house.

The auctioneer banged the hammer. 'Sold for eighty pounds to the man with card two hundred. Next – lot three hundred and thirteen. A doll's house….'

She gulped. This was it.

'I'll open the bidding at fifty pounds.' The auctioneer scanned the hall. 'Fifty pounds anyone? No…? Twenty pounds then, twenty pounds anyone? Come on, someone must want it at twenty pounds…? Fifteen then?'

'Oh no,' she gasped. 'It's worth more than that. Loads more.'

Ravyt leaned towards her. 'You should've put a fixed reserve on it, Mrs Jax.'

'Thank you, madam,' the auctioneer boomed. 'I have fifteen. Eighteen… eighteen pounds, anyone?'

Across the hall, a young woman with a child smiled and lowered her card.

'Eighteen pounds, anyone?'

Chrissie groaned. If she was right about the doll's house, Ravyt should be bidding.

And then he made his move. He straightened in his seat. Up went his hand.

Yes, I've got him, she thought.

'Thank you, sir. I have a bid of eighteen pounds. Twenty?'

The bids rose in fives and petered out at forty pounds. Finally Ravyt smiled; a self-satisfied curve of the lips, so slight even the movement seemed tinged with meanness.

'It's mine,' he whispered. 'And for only forty pounds.'

While the auctioneer moved on to the next lot, Ravyt turned to Chrissie, eyebrows raised. 'Why put it in a sale? Why not sell privately?'

'Less suspicious. And this was a particularly sensitive item, wouldn't you say? Perhaps the seller isn't greedy.' Chrissie spoke in rehearsed phrases while inside she shrieked, *I've got to tell Clive. He's got to stop Ravyt collecting it. What do I do now*?

'Let's not play this game any longer, Mrs Jax.' His tone was matter-of-fact as he dropped the pretence. 'We both know who the seller is. There'll be something you're after. What is it?'

'Apart from the spool cabinet? How about… lunch?' She kept her tone smooth, despite the knot in her stomach.

'What about your friend? That young guy. The one who doesn't sew.'

'Ah.' The knot tightened. 'What about him?'

'Don't worry. I saw him leave… with a guy more his own age, only minutes ago.'

'What?'

A slow smile spread across Ravyt's face. 'Can we assume he doesn't eat lunch?'

'I-I think I'll give him a call. I'll meet you in the main entrance. Ten minutes?' Chrissie grabbed her bag and struggled to her feet. She didn't wait for him to answer, but hurried between the chairs, stooping so as not to distract the auctioneer.

Once outside, pulse still racing, she crossed the road. An archway led through a timber framed house. She stood, catching her breath under its ancient beams. It was safe there and easy to keep a watch on the doorway to the auction rooms. She pulled her mobile from her bag.

'Blast.' Her phone had been switched to silent and she'd missed Nick's text. She opened it now, hands shaking.

It's lot 313, she read. So he'd worked it out as well, and judging by the time of the text, thirty minutes sooner than she had.

She pressed Clive's automatic dial number.

'Answer, damn it. Answer,' she hissed.

'Hi. Chrissie?'

233

'Oh, thank God. Clive, you've got to stop him. It's a doll's house–'

'Wow, slow down.'

'Sorry. Look, the casing to the automaton - it's been made into a doll's house. It's the spitting image of Utterly Mansion. Lot three hundred and thirteen. Ravyt won the bidding. You've got to stop the auction people releasing it to him. It's stolen goods. It must count as evidence in some way. You've–'

'Slower, Chrissie. OK, I've got the lot number.'

'You've got to hurry. There's no time. The auction's about to finish.'

'OK. I'm on it. A doll's house?'

'Yes, lot three hundred and thirt–'

The call cut out.

'Damn.' She hadn't had time to ask Clive where he was. And Nick? Ravyt might have been lying, but if he wasn't lying, why would Nick leave with someone? 'Damn,' she repeated.

Across the road, people were starting to emerge from the auction rooms. No one carried any sale items yet. Queuing to pay and collect always took time.

'It must have just finished,' she muttered. 'I've got to find Nick.'

She took a deep breath and crossed the road back to the auction rooms, dodging cars as they turned out of the car park.

Mobile still in hand, she pressed Nick's automatic dial number. She focused on the wide passageway leading up from the hall as she held the phone to her ear and waited.

'Oh no.' She spotted Ravyt's wiry figure.

He seemed to fix his tinted glasses on her. Those around him kept looking down and checking the uneven bricks underfoot, but he walked straight, no deflection of his head. Spooky, weird, threatening – whatever his intent, she felt immune. And then she smiled. He'd helped her make a decision. She'd never be hungry enough to eat lunch with him.

Nick's ring tone continued unanswered and then cut out.

'Hello, Mrs Jax. Shall we go and collect our sale items?' Ravyt stood a little too close.

'I'm going to collect mine next week. But don't let me stop you.' She stepped back.

'Hmm… lunch then?'

'Another time. I'm sorry.' She pulled a wry face, looked at her mobile pointedly and then slipped it into her bag.

'Ah. Your friend.'

She shrugged. He was bound to draw whatever conclusions fitted his nasty little world.

'You play complicated games. Well, another time, perhaps.' He smiled, at least his mouth did. The tinted glasses held no expression as he began to move away.

'Goodbye, Mr Ravyt.' Chrissie retrieved her mobile from her bag, pressed redial and waited for Nick to answer.

CHAPTER 25

Why, Nick wondered, should whispering, 'Hi,' make Gavin bolt?

He wasn't going to let him get away this time. No slipping through vestries and down bramble paths. The auction rooms might be packed with sale items, but as far as Nick was concerned, he had him in his sights and he was as good as bagged.

He concentrated on the dark, lank hair as it bobbed and swerved ahead. He dodged past a chest of drawers and raced up the wide passageway. Gavin nipped between the double doors. Hard on his heels, Nick hurtled sharp left into Market Hill.

It was more difficult in the open. Saturday shoppers strolled as if time had no meaning, their eyes only on window displays. Nick as good as hop-scotched past them, crossing the market square and leaving the Shire Hall behind. Gavin darted along a narrow pavement where timber framed houses huddled shoulder to shoulder. Nick lengthened his stride.

'Gavin. Stop,' he called and sidestepped another shopper. His phone hummed and vibrated. Silent mode felt frantic inside his pocket. He ignored it.

He looked again, but Gavin had vanished. Frustration tightened Nick's chest. And then he spotted a walkway squeezed between the buildings. Gavin's rat run. It had to be.

'Gav-in,' he panted as he launched himself along it. The worn paving bricks sloped gently. Five leaping strides and he was out the other end. Bright autumn light dazzled as he soared over unexpected steps and straight down into a graveyard.

'Where the…?' He skidded to a halt.

Before him the ground dipped away steeply. Headstones jostled with stone sarcophagi and angels, haphazard in their alignment, and all resisting the slide down the hillside. Below, a magnificent church stood grey in flint and stone.

Nick paused, drinking in the peace and scanning the scene. No movement, no sounds, no people. No Gavin.

'Shike. I've lost him.' There were just too many directions Gavin could've taken if he didn't want to be found.

Nick stepped off the path into the rough-cut grass between the graves. Easy to hide behind a tombstone, he thought. That's if Gavin hadn't already nipped into the church or out of the graveyard again. The area felt as secure as a wide-meshed string bag. There was nothing for it but to do a slow circuit and catch his breath.

He kept to the upper contours of the slope. Houses high on the hill backed directly onto the graves, no gardens and no fencing between. It felt otherworldly, a step back in time.

His mobile burst into vibrations. 'Bloody phone.' This time he didn't ignore it.

'Nick? Where are you?' Chrissie's irritation transmitted across the airwaves.

'Church.'

'Why? Are you OK? You sound… out of breath.'

'Yeah, I've been running.'

'What? You disappeared.' Her voice sharpened.

'It was lot three-one-three, wasn't it? Did you see who bid for it?'

'Yes. But… where did you say you are?'

'I can't explain now. If you walk across Market Hill, there's a church on the other side, just down the hill. I'll see you in the graveyard.'

Nick cut the call. There was still a chance Gavin could be hiding close by. The trail was getting cold but he hadn't completely given up the chase yet. More to the point, he knew Chrissie's irritation would soon be forgotten. She'd be hurrying across, curiosity firing her stride. He reckoned two people were more likely to flush Gavin out than one.

He crept between the graves, pleased to be free of the hectic atmosphere in the auction hall. When he glanced to check the roadway entrance again, he spotted Chrissie as she rushed in from the bottom end of Market Hill. He straightened and waved.

'Hi,' she said, breathless as she joined him, 'What's going on?'

'Let's just sit where we've got a good view of everything while we talk, OK?'

They settled on a grassy ledge. 'I nearly missed the doll's house,' he began. 'It was pushed under a table. Was the bloke with tinted glasses Mr Ravyt?'

'Yes, and he won the bidding for it.'

'Wow, really? You had your head buried in the catalogue most of the time. That's why I sent you the text.'

'Yes, thanks for that. Well spotted. Clive's going to block its release.'

'Right, but why was Gavin there? I thought auctions weren't his thing. He spent most of the time watching you and Mr Ravyt. I didn't see him bid for anything.'

'Yes, I noticed that too,' Chrissie murmured as she gazed across the graveyard.

'Well, I can't be very good at this undercover stuff, because Mr Ravyt was watching me… watching Gavin.'

Chrissie frowned.

'I decided I'd work my way through the bidders and get close enough to say hi to Gavin,' Nick continued.

'So, what did he say?'

'Well that's the weird thing. He bolted before I'd had a chance.'

'How very strange. So you followed him?'

'Yeah, and I lost him somewhere here.' Nick stared at the church tower.

'Well I got the feeling, I'm probably wrong, but I think Ravyt would get more pleasure from Donatello's bronze of a naked David than a semi-nude Diana hunting with a bow and hound.'

'What are you on about, Chrissie?'

'I don't know how to put it; just something about Ravyt today. He thought you were my toy-boy. And he'll have known Gavin was looking at him. So when you left with Gavin, he saw it as… well, put it this way, he was pleased to point out you'd left, not only with someone more your own age, but also male. Why would Ravyt even think to insinuate stuff like that unless it reflected his own tastes?'

'Probably just trying to get a reaction from you. So he thought I was your toy-boy? Hey, but you don't look that old!' Nick laughed when she pulled a face. 'And he implied Gavin…? And me…? But so what? Gavin has that intense way he looks at everyone.'

'Your right, and if Gavin doesn't want to be found, I suppose we should leave him.'

'That's assuming we'd be able to find him.' Nick frowned. Chrissie really didn't seem quite herself.

CHAPTER 26

Matt swaggered into Ott's Pizza Place on Sunday morning. He'd practised the walk. Admittedly the bathroom mirror at home only allowed him to view the upper half of his body, but he reckoned if he got the shoulder move right then the rest would follow.

'Are you OK, Matt?' Scarbrow asked, looking up from behind the counter. 'You weren't like that yesterday.'

Matt smiled. Then he remembered. The website said *smile*, so he pulled his mouth into a sexy half-smile and murmured, 'Men with swagger don't ask. They just do.'

'What did you say? Men with swagger? You're…. You can still deliver pizza? Right?'

'What?' Matt dropped the smile and resumed the slouch. 'You think I'm kiddin'? I researched it on the net. Honest. Swagger's the new cool.'

Scarbrow fixed him with unbelieving eyes as one eyebrow puckered around the scar.

'I can show you.' Matt shifted his weight, scuffing his trainer on the fake-wood flooring.

'The swagger?'

'Nah the site. You've got a computer out the back.'

Scarbrow hesitated. 'All right, I suppose we're quiet. But don't get any ideas. You're here to deliver pizzas. Remember?'

'Yeah. Course I remember.'

He resumed his swagger and moseyed past Scarbrow and the pizza oven. The kitchen and storage area out the back had a counter with a computer. It stood next to boxes and crates, and where cherry tomatoes jostled with fresh basil. When Scarbrow sat at the small screen and ordered supplies, the area doubled as a makeshift office. Until now, Matt hadn't been allowed anywhere near the keyboard with its scent of Italy, but Sunday was turning out to be special. And lucky. As of nine o'clock that morning, when Maisie sent her text, Matt had a girlfriend.

He slumped onto a stool near the screen and pulled his mobile from a pocket. He needed to read it again, just to be sure he hadn't been dreaming.

Hi. Got it wrong - pig racing not this week. Meet 4 coffee instead? Wednesday? Maisie. She'd added a smiley face tag at the end. He hoped it wasn't code for *this is a joke, you gullible prat, and I'm laughing at you.*

When he'd first opened the text, a thousand butterflies took flight in his stomach. Even now, hundreds of gossamer wings fluttered and skimmed as he thought about coffee and Wednesday.

'Don't touch the computer,' Scarbrow called, his voice preceding an eruption as the door burst open.

'I was waitin' for you,' Matt murmured, his mind still drifting.

'OK, OK. Give me some space then.' He elbowed Matt off the stool, sat down and switched on the computer.

Matt tried not to be too obvious, but his eyes were drawn to Scarbrow's hands. They might be good at working pizza dough but they were slow and hesitant as he keyed in the password. Predictable, Matt thought. Ott's Pizza Place; all one word, lower case and some of the letters replaced with lookalike numbers – 0tt'sp122ap1ace. Yes, he had the entry code.

'Right,' his boss said and stood up. 'Show me. And fast, coz no one's out the front.'

A moment later and Matt was on Google, searching *how to swagger*, and then playing a YouTube clip.

'Amazing,' Scarbrow murmured. A phone rang, shrill and demanding on the other side of the door. 'Right, close it down. That'll be the first order ringing in.'

'Yeah, OK.' Matt closed Google, logged off and followed him out.

'Stowupland? And the house number?' Scarbrow spoke into the phone as he glanced at the hot list. 'Did you say a Mr Darrel Birstell?'

'No. Not Darrel,' Matt yelped. The butterflies were forgotten as his guts seized.

'Sorry, but we're no longer doing mate's rates. Why? Too many mates.' Scarbrow turned to face Matt, and still holding the receiver, continued; 'Yeah I know you got mate's rates last week but... I don't care who this Nick is. Think of it as an introductory offer. Yeah. And there's still a charge for delivery.'

'Birstell's the... he attacked the last delivery guy at TARV's. Remember?' Matt wailed.

Scarbrow turned his back and took visa card details.

'OK then. About thirty minutes.'

'What you tryin' to do? Get me killed?'

'His visa payment went through OK. Anyway he didn't attack you last week. Just walk normally and you'll be fine.'

'What?'

'No swaggering, or whatever you call it. Toughen up. I'm running a business here. Now get yourself organised while I get these two sixteen-inchers in the oven. Be pleased no money's coming out of your wages this time.'

'Oh yeah, thanks a bunch.'

What did he just say? Thanks? Matt couldn't believe his own meekness.

'Frag,' he muttered. His boss was a bastard. This time he'd keep his helmet on when he got to the address. And he'd put the pizzas on the doorstep before ringing the bell, so he had time to scarper before Darrel even knew he'd been there. He straightened his back. Cap'n Starlight had a girlfriend, and a plan.

Ten minutes later the pizzas were loaded in the transporter box. Cap'n Starlight pulled his face into the sexy half-smile and fired up the Space Zipper. He twisted the handgrip accelerator and launched onto the road. The two-stroke engine whined. The Stowupland Road beckoned. The Piaggio strove for comic-strip speed as the Cap'n held one thought on his space helmet Heads Up Display. The mission plan.

He recognised the Victorian terrace and singled out the blue front door. This time he slowed to a halt and left the engine idling. He scanned the front path for hazards, then unloaded the pizza boxes. The door was closed. No one in sight. The delivery drop was the work of a moment.

As he leapt back onto the Space Zipper, the front door opened.

'Hey!' Darrel yelled.

Cap'n Starlight lifted one hand in the air, thumb and forefinger outstretched in the shape of an L. 'Loser,' he mouthed as he accelerated away. 'Operation Extra Pepperoni successfully completed.'

The returning hero rode past earthy fields. They were sewn with winter wheat, but all he saw were furrows of promise. Matt glowed. Sunday was working out better than just plain lucky. It was comic-book inspired. He pulled up, wanting to prolong the moment before riding the last mile back to Ott's.

Beep-itty-beep! *Beep-itty-beep beep*! His mobile burst into life. 'Oh bot,' he muttered as he grappled with gloves and helmet, and dreading it was Scarbrow, or somehow Darrel.

'Hiya.' It was Chrissie's voice.

'Mornin'. Thank bot it's only you. I'm on me Piaggio, out deliverin'.'

'Sorry. Just a quick question. The police want to speak to Gavin and, to cut it short, he was at the Woodbridge auction yesterday and did a runner. Any idea where he'd go? Apparently he's not been home and he's not answering his phone.'

Matt scratched his beard. 'Don't know.'

'Well phone if you think of anywhere. Oh, and we discovered the casing. It'd been made into a doll's house. Bye.'

'I've a date with Maisie,' he said, but Chrissie had gone.

Cap'n Starlight crashed back to reality.

Chrissie was always so clear. No double meanings or innuendo, but he felt battered by her sound bites. The torrent of information was unexpected, and his re-entry into the here and now too sudden. 'Frag,' he muttered as his thoughts foamed like white-water.

'Break it down into key words,' he told himself.

'Casing – doll's house. Auction – Gavin. Police – Gavin.' He put on his helmet. 'Bloody Gavin.'

The rest of the ride back to Ott's only took a few minutes. The warm inner glow of success remained, but his mind worked overtime. He found Scarbrow busy loading pizzas into the oven. They were for some customers to collect.

'I'll wait out the back for the next delivery call.'

'OK, Matt. I'll shout when I need you.'

Once the door had swung shut, he headed straight to the computer. It was the work of seconds to switch it on and key in 0tt'sp122ap1ace. He reckoned Suffield's Chapel Reclamation Yard was somewhere Gavin might head for. He remembered Nick mentioning Gavin and the yard in the same breath a few times. But where was it exactly? Matt wasn't sure. He keyed it in the Google search box and waited.

'Yeah, I see. Out on the Bury – Ickworth Park road,' he whispered as the map came up with a red balloon marker. He clicked on the balloon. As he scrolled through the pages advertising P Suffield's business and the catalogue of reclaimed items for sale, a key word jumped from the screen. *Lead*. There were *lead pipes*, *lead guttering*, and *lead liners for wine coolers* listed.

'Wine coolers?' Weren't they plastic with reflective tin foil? Something you stuffed in the freezer first, or packed with crushed ice?

He typed *wine cooler* into Google, and then as an afterthought added *lead liner*. The search results came up with a surprise. *Georgian wine cooler,* he read.

'Mahogany? In the shape of a sarcophagus?' He couldn't believe his eyes. Did they use wine coolers in those days?

A key word stood out. *Sarcophagus*. He looked again. *Sarcophagus-shaped wine cooler with lion-mask handles*.

'Sarcophagus.' He rolled his tongue around the word. It made him think of death. Wasn't it a kind of oblong-shaped box? He clicked on the site and images of antique wine coolers popped up. 'Flamin'….'

He couldn't believe it. They were made of wood, most seemed to have a lid and all would easily have taken at least a dozen bottles. 'Of course. The lead liner's waterproof for the ice. Makes sense. No plastic back then.'

Hadn't Chrissie said she'd stumbled on an animal mausoleum as it was being ransacked, close to the St Edmund Way walk? Animals in lead coffins, but she'd used words like casket and sarcophagus. Square, oblong shapes.

He looked at the pictures on the site again. Something pinged in his brain. The size was quite large. A dog's casket would fit a wine cooler.

'An automaton casin' becomes a doll's house. So why can't a lead animal coffin become a lead liner for an antique wine cooler? Yeah, up-cycling. Reckon they'd get more for it than meltin' the lead down. Flamin' genius.'

Matt scratched his beard. It didn't automatically follow that P Suffield's lead liners had once housed the mortal remains of well-loved dogs, but Labrador Fido might have been tipped out to make space for vino blanco. It was a long shot, but maybe not completely crazy.

A phone shrilled on the other side of the door. Oh bot, Matt thought. Can't get caught using the computer. 'He'll kill me.'

With half an ear on Scarbrow's voice and the other half listening for the door to swing open, he shot off an email to Chrissie. He added links to the P Suffield's site and the antique wine coolers. Then he logged out and closed.

'Is it a delivery?' he shouted and moved towards the door. He reckoned a swagger might be in order, after all it was turning into one flaming brilliant Sunday.

What had the website said? 'Men with swagger don't ask. They just do,' he murmured.

CHAPTER 27

Chrissie stood at her kitchen window and gazed at her apology for a garden. More of a Post-it Note than handkerchief in size, and choked with herbs and wild flowers. Rose hips beaconed red on a dog rose and pink-purple flower spikes of rosebay willowherb were already dying back to seed. Sunday was proving a slow day. Clive was busy with what he called *developments in the case*, and she'd been left alone with her thoughts. Even Sarah, a friend in the village, was away for the weekend. There was nothing else for it but to do battle with the weeds and tame the herbs in her garden.

Ping!

She'd left her mobile on the small kitchen table-cum-desk. Great, she thought as she opened the text. Matt's got back to me. But it felt more like unwrapping a parcel than a message. She'd stripped off the outer brown paper only to reveal an inner layer of pretty novelty paper. He wanted her to open an email he'd sent with links.

Intrigued, she sat at the table and opened her laptop. A few minutes later she'd clicked on the links. All thoughts of weeds and flowers gone-to-seed flew out the window, as she concentrated on the Georgian wine cooler. It took a few moments to get her head around what Matt was suggesting but the more she thought about it, the more she was convinced he could be right. Clive had never held out any hope of catching the thieves or of finding the stolen mausoleum goods, but this had to be a line worth pursuing.

She made a decision and forwarded Matt's email to Clive with a brief covering message. No point in burdening him with details, she thought, as she pressed *send* without adding her intention to go and check it out for herself.

Between gulps of tea and bites of croissant, Chrissie gathered up her bag, camera and car keys. A quick look at a map, and then she was slamming her front door and starting the TR7. She opted for some fast straight road.

'A14 up to Bury and then out on the road towards Ickworth House,' she murmured as she accelerated onto the slip road. 'Get this over and done with.'

By the time Chrissie turned off the dual carriageway, she'd started to feel excited. A harmless adventure, she told herself as her pulse raced in time with the engine. The road out of Bury twisted and turned as it swept through farm and parkland. Large houses, built in prosperous times a few centuries earlier dotted the route. Beautiful Tudor brick chimneys coiled and corkscrewed above peg tiles and thatch. The landscape appeared richer and better manicured than around Woolpit and Stowmarket. She slowed when she saw the sign *P Suffield's Chapel Reclamation Yard* and buoyed up by the journey, she turned through the large metal-clad gates.

It seemed at least a dozen people with a house to reno-vate or a garden to dress were visiting the reclamation yard that Sunday. While cars manoeuvred around stacks of pav-ing stones and bricks, Chrissie waited impatiently to park. She quickly lost herself in the mix of serious customers and curious browsers, and headed into the old chapel. She fig-ured the lead liners would be indoors or under cover, oth-erwise they'd fill with rainwater and never sell.

A cursory glance at the arched roof above brought her back to reality. It reminded her of her own mortality and Marlin Poynder's death somewhere out in the yard. It even instilled an ethereal feel to the wrought iron garden furniture displayed where pews and chapel chairs once stood. The air held a chill. She needed to be careful.

Moving quietly and keeping close to the wall, she started a slow circuit. She tried to blend in with the stacks of parquet blocks, wooden bannisters and racks of stripped wood doors. Progressing from wood to metal, she stepped amongst the collection of fire grates and surrounds. And then she spotted the lead liners.

'Oh my God,' she whispered, but caution kept her moving. She decided to linger near the assortment of taps and check no one was watching before making her way back to the liners. A gentle rummage in her bag, and she'd retrieved her camera and was ready for action.

'Oh look. They've got some old white enamelled ones,' a man said as he strode towards her.

The surprise must have shown on her face.

'Sorry... I was talking to my wife about the taps,' the man said, and quickly turned to mutter, 'Try to keep up,' to a woman behind. By the time he'd directed his attention back to the taps, Chrissie had slipped away.

Camera in hand, Chrissie sidestepped a couple of metal grates and then squatted behind a fire surround. There was no mistaking the marks and residue on the bottom of the liners. She saw the outline of where a dog had lain and rotted; on another, the marks from the metal on a collar. It was like looking at ink splodges and trying to read something into them, except they weren't so banal. She knew what had rested there.

She flicked onto automatic focus and zoomed in for close-ups: front, back, and sides of all three liners, then shots down inside them. The automatic flash went off several times. She held her breath. No one seemed to notice the brief flicker. The fire surrounds must have screened her.

She stepped away, and without appearing to look, took some wide-angle views. There was too much ambient light this time to set off the automatic flash. These shots would show the liners positioned amongst the stock in the chapel. First identification, now evidence she thought, and dropped her camera back into her bag. It was time to leave.

***

Chrissie threw her keys onto the narrow hall table and hurried into her kitchen.

'Success!' she hissed and punched the air. Had she got time for a mug of tea? No, she decided. Get the photos to Clive, first.

Excitement and euphoria sped her hand as she imported the photos to her laptop and then attached them to an email for Clive. He might be sitting at a desk or driving somewhere in his car; either way, she was desperate to pass on her discovery. It was like tossing a hot potato.

'It's brilliant,' she murmured, and like Matt, she fired off a quick text telling Clive she'd sent an email.

While the kettle boiled, she paced her tiny kitchen, still too high on success to settle.

Brrring brrring! She snatched up her phone.

'Clive? Did you get my photos?'

'Yes Chrissie. What the hell did you think you were doing?'

'I drove out to Suffield's Chapel Reclamation Yard. People do, you know. In fact, quite a few were looking around for stuff. A Sunday pastime. I just happened to have my camera with me, that's all. Why?'

'You bloody fool. You walk into a crime scene, poke around, and then warn them by taking photos? They could've taken your camera. You could've been injured. Why couldn't you just leave it to us? Now I've got to send someone up there before the liners vanish into thin air.'

Chrissie bit her lip. Her bubble had burst and she'd landed with a bump.

'Well? Did you stop to think, just for a moment, before you went tearing up there?'

'Yes. No – I mean I don't think anyone noticed me. They were too busy. And… maybe you should send someone anyway. Isn't it somewhere Gavin hangs out?'

She listened to the silence on the phone.

'Clive?'

'OK, maybe you have a point. Just don't,' he seemed to catch his breath, 'don't meddle, Chrissie. Have you got that?' He ended the call.

She wasn't going to say yes. She was too angry and deflated. And anyway he hadn't given her a chance to answer.

CHAPTER 28

Nick studied the drawings. 'So it's a modular unit construction?' It was Monday morning and he was pleased to be back in the Willows workshop with Dave.

'That's right. We'll make and assemble the frames here in the workshop,' Dave said as he sipped a mug of tea.

'And the dividing panels are in solid cherry?'

'It's a bespoke fitted wardrobe, Nick.'

'Just seems a bit of a waste, that's all.'

'You haven't been over to Mr Sops' place in Lavenham yet. Nice place. Huge garden. No expense spared, though I can't help thinking oak might've been more in keeping.' He paused and stared into his mug. 'The staircase is a bit of a challenge. We'll screw the frames to the dividers once we've got them upstairs. You'll need to watch out you don't lose the top of your head as well.'

'Low beams? Small doorways?'

'Afraid so. They didn't cater for six-foot-pluses in those days, Nick.'

'So how long do you reckon before we're working over there?'

'Should be before the end of the week. So no more wasting time. Less talking and more working.'

Nick wrestled with his conscience. For the hundredth time he wondered if he should tell Dave about Jim's phone call, the one nosing around for information several days ago, after Dave had given him a lift home. Nick had been dreading the follow up demand, but there'd been nothing from Jim since, not even over the weekend. Nor had anyone got back to him from the police. Perhaps none of it had happened and it was all in his imagination, except Mustang was still holding onto his car. Coincidence or Jim's doing? He pushed the thought away.

While Dave nursed a mug of tea, Nick picked out a long, wide section of the American cherry. 'I could saw this down, split it and join it side-on. But it seems a bit too nice to use for dividing panels. Nicer as a door panel, don't you think?'

'Hmm. Lift all the pieces like that out and we'll use the ones with the nicest markings for the door panels. We'll cut those ones thinner.'

'Or we could take off more with the thickness planer,' Nick suggested.

The morning flew as Nick used the band saw to divide the wood into thinner sections, while Dave worked on making the frames. The drone and squeal of the saw made conversation impossible and provided a soundtrack that grounded Nick firmly in the workshop. No place for flights of fancy. No time to worry about Mustang. No thoughts of Jim. No clashes of conscience. Instead, he focused on passing the sections he'd cut through the thickness planer before working on their side edges, ready to glue.

He felt a tap on the shoulder. 'We're stopping for lunch, Nick.'

'OK. I'll be with you in five.'

He didn't put his tools down straight away. Instead, Nick lingered at his workbench. He needed some fresh air and he knew if he told Dave, then the *if you're not happy with the dust extractor, wear a breathing mask as well* line would soon be burning his ears.

He slipped out through the loading bay and took a deep breath. Cold air stung his nose and caught at the back of his throat. Funny, he thought, how summer had lasted so long this year only to vanish overnight. Did the weather systems know it was the first day of November tomorrow? Even the leaves were finally yielding. Greens were now yellows and browns, waiting for the wind to take them. He pulled his phone from his pocket.

'Bugger, a missed call.'

At least it wasn't Mustang or Jim. He'd put their numbers in his directory so he wouldn't get caught off guard again. This caller was unknown. He pressed *ring back* and waited.

'Hello. DS Crip speaking.'

'Hi, I missed your call. I rang back to… who did you say you were?' Nick was still processing the female voice.

'Detective Sergeant Crip.'

He swallowed hard. 'The police?'

'Yes. And you are?' The tone sharpened.

'Nick. I'm Nick Cowley. What's…why did you phone me?' His heart hammered against his ribs.

'Well, I thought you phoned us. Last week. You reported someone taking undue interest in a property you're working on.' She let her voice hang in the air, half question, half a statement of fact.

'Ye-yes….'

'I'd like to know more details. Talk to you about it.' The voice almost purred.

'Now?' He steadied his tone.

'If you like.'

A gust of wind caught an old sheet of packing cardboard, lifting and dropping it as it cavorted across the concrete.

'Look, I don't think I can speak here. Don't get me wrong, I want to talk to you.' He stopped, almost biting his tongue as he realised how he must sound.

'No problem. Do you want to drop in at the station?'

'I'm at work. My car's being repaired so I'd need a lift. People would ask questions.' The beat in his chest felt like a reggae shuffle as he waited for her to speak.

'I suppose… yes I could talk to you at your home. Where do you live?' she asked.

Nick gave his address. 'Well, it's my parent's house,' he said, and then felt a little foolish.

'That's OK. I'll call in around five o'clock.' More business-like and with no trace of a purr, she added, 'Remember - I'll need as many details as possible.' She rang off.

'Wow.' He breathed out, long and slow.

He tried to clear his thoughts and picture the azure blue, but his mind preferred to wrestle with something else. What did she look like? 'Bet she does firearms training,' he muttered. And then he thought of Kat and a sudden pang caught him by surprise. One girlfriend with a penchant for shooting had been one too many. A second would be madness. He wasn't going to repeat that mistake.

'Lunch,' he murmured and headed back into the workshop, the unsettled feeling close to excitement.

Body odour, wood dust and stale tea permeated the air in the office-like sitting area.

'Any news about your car?' Dave said looking pointedly at the phone in Nick's hand.

'What? Oh I see.' He realised he was still holding his mobile. 'No. I was just about to ring,' he lied, and without really thinking pressed Mustang's automatic dial number.

The smells around him evoked the atmosphere of a men's locker room, heavy on masculinity and buoyed up with *can do*. It was infectious.

'Mustang? Nick Cowley here.'

'Hi.'

'My Fiesta. When will it be ready to collect?'

'The paint I ordered should arrive on this afternoon's delivery, so….'

'You promised on Friday it'd be ready today. This is starting to piss me off.'

'Yeah, a cock-up at the delivery end, I'm afraid. Useless bastards. They do this every now and again. I've got other work booked in. Messes everyone up.' His tone seemed to say, poor me.

There was a pause. Nick imagined him drawing on a cigarette. Poor Mustang? To hell with that.

'When will my Fiesta be ready to collect, Mustang?' He let an edge creep into his voice.

'That depends.'

'On what? The delivery truck? A hold up on the A14? If there's an R in the month? This is getting ridiculous. It's only Ford standard blue.'

'Yeah. But as I said, it depends. See, we've got a mutual friend an' he's been waitin' on you. So it depends on you.'

'What?' Nick thought he'd explode. 'What are you talking about?'

'I think we both know Jim.'

Nick bit on the expletives ready to fire from his mouth. White-hot anger seared his lips. He wanted more than ever to set up a sting, but he needed to use his brain. He was supposed to be Jim's mate.

'Jim, the roofer?' It was more of a choking sound than spoken voice.

'Yeah.'

Nick kept his tones low. 'You should've said sooner. I'll give him a call. He never got back to me, so I assumed he wasn't interested any more. Consider it sorted.' And then as an afterthought, 'Of course I'll expect a double discount for the repairs and paint job.'

'Oh yeah?'

'Too right. Recompense for all the aggro, plus standard mate's rates.' Nick killed the call.

'Is it ready to collect yet?' Dave asked brightly.

***

Dave slowed to a halt and kept the engine running while Nick got out of the car.

'Thanks for the lift home. See you, usual time tomorrow.' Nick slammed the car door. He was about to raise his hand in farewell but before he had a chance, the engine revved, the wheels spun and Dave accelerated away, launching a storm of loose chippings.

'Bye,' Nick said to the trail of exhaust fumes.

He hurried past the shrubs and ornamental grasses and in through the kitchen. He reckoned he had time to either explain to his mother that a detective sergeant was about to arrive and interview him, or take a quick shower. He wondered if the freshen up and change of clothes routine might be seen as trying too hard, so he braced himself for the mother-alert option. Besides, she'd need to know why DS Crip was coming, otherwise she'd hover in the background, her curiosity toe-curlingly obvious. The modern downstairs open-plan living hadn't been designed with police questioning in mind.

A nondescript graphite-coloured car drew up quietly outside the house. Nick checked the time. Five o'clock on the dot.

'That'll be DS Crip. Now give us some space, OK Mum?' he said as he went to open the smoked glass front door, excitement quickening his stride.

'Hello. Nick Cowley?' She held up her police ID card.

He looked past the card and into a pair of remarkably blue eyes, a peachy-coloured complexion, short brown hair and a chiselled nose. Each feature wasn't exactly pretty, but put together the effect was striking.

'Nick Cowley?' she repeated and slipped the ID card into the pocket of her light coat, the colour of butternut.

'Yes. And you must be DS Crip. Come on in.'

She'd sounded larger on the phone, he thought as he led her through to the sitting area.

'Please, take a seat,' he said, indicating a grey leather sofa with steel frame. He flashed his killer smile and sat down opposite. 'So, you work with Clive Merry?'

'Indirectly. I'm with organised crime. He was the detective you first spoke to, wasn't he?' She smiled. It was the *I'm the one asking the questions* kind of a smile. A warning.

'So, why don't you start by telling me about the call you got last week?'

He wouldn't have known where to begin, but DS Crip seemed to have a sense of order. She jotted things down in a small notebook, and when she spoke, she had a way of tilting her head to one side.

'So you first came across Jim with Darrel when you were working at the Dower House in Thorpe Morieux?'

'Yes, that's where the guttering, downpipes and gates were stolen. Also, a bronze from the garden, I believe.'

'Diana with Bow and Hound. DI Merry filled me in with some of the background. But I don't understand why Jim thinks you're a mate. Are you sure you haven't met him before? Maybe you know Darrel, the nephew? More your age group?' The edge was back in her voice.

'No way,' he protested, and then realised she was playing him. He explained about the pizza flyers, but his words sounded ridiculous, even to his own ears.

'So how do you explain Jim had your mobile number?'

'My Fiesta.'

'Your car?' She tilted her head. 'How does that come into it?'

'TARV. The auto recycling yard near Stowupland.'

He told her about Dodge and Mustang, and as he talked he, got the feeling she already knew most of what he was telling her. No doubt it was part of the *give him plenty of rope* ploy. He reckoned she was waiting to trip him up and catch him out. Enough rope to hang himself, as the saying went. Except there was nothing to catch out.

'Surely you recognised the names when Mustang Carner gave them to you?'

'No. Why should I?' Nick kept his tones even. 'By the time I went to TARV we'd finished the job at the Dower House. I'd forgotten all about the tilers working on the roof.' He waited, his mouth dry.

She let the silence hang in the air, then scribbled something in her notebook and leaned back. He got the feeling she didn't believe him.

'Look – up until then I'd hardly said a word to Jim. And I never clapped eyes on Darrel, at least not his face. They were up on the roof, working. We were inside laying a parquet floor. Anyway, there are hundreds of Jims, or rather Jameses. It's a common name round these parts. And as for Darrel? It could've been a surname.'

'Hmm….' She didn't sound convinced.

'Look. You're in organised crime. You're trained to see links because it's your job to see links. I'm a carpenter. Give me a mortise and tenon and I'll tell you if the two pieces fit. That's my limit on links and connections.'

He watched as she wrote something down. Probably mortise and tenon.

'And this is the connection I hadn't seen coming,' he continued. 'Mustang had to spell it out for me today.' He paused, marshalling his thoughts before launching into Mustang's call about the fictional non-delivery of the blue Ford paint and the real reason for the delay. 'So I told him I'd speak to Jim this evening,' he finished.

'Is there anything else you want to tell me?' she asked.

'Apart from the fact that I've got to ring Jim and I've no idea what to say to him? I've never been to this house on Church Street, and I've never met Mr Sops. I think I start work there on Thursday. Oh, and I want my car back.'

'Everything's obviously coming to a head. You're going to have to tell Jim what he wants to know and fast, otherwise we won't hook him.'

'So what do I say?' He glanced into her amazingly blue eyes, and then embarrassed, looked away.

'Tell him you'll have the information for him tomorrow.'

'But what about my car?'

'Your car will have to wait, I'm afraid. We need time to speak to the house owner and set everything up. I'll get back to you tomorrow. I promise. Now ring Jim, while I'm here.'

'What?'

'If you put your mobile on speaker, then I'll hear what he says.'

'Talk to him now?' A flash tide caught him by surprise. 'But–'

'Is that a problem?' Her tones bit.

'No. I just….' He breathed out slowly. 'I'm just a bit nervous, that's all.'

He knew she was watching him. Testing him. Triggering the moment when she called his bluff. But knowing it didn't help. He closed his eyes and tried to picture the azure blue. His pulse slowed. 'OK. I'm ready now,' he murmured.

It took him a moment, fumbling with his phone, to find the speaker option. Then he pressed Jim's automatic dial number and waited.

'Hi Jim,' he cut in when he heard the harsh tones. 'It's Nick. No, you said you were going to call me.' He held his mobile in front of him to make sure the detective sergeant would hear the speaker clearly.

'What the bloody hell you playin' at?' the voice shouted across the sounds of a cement mixer being cleaned in the background. 'I got people waitin' on this. If you don't tell me what I want to know, then we'll work without you. And don't' expect to see your car again.'

'Calm down Jim. I'll be over at Mr Sops' on Thursday. That's when we start putting the wardrobe in. Till then I'll know nothing.'

Nick held the phone further away as the speaker volume crackled and distorted with Jim's anger. Across from him on the grey leather sofa, the DS mouthed something.

'Wednesday?' he mouthed back.

She nodded.

'OK, OK, Jim. Chill. Only winding you up. Mr Sops is away on Wednesday.'

'Back on Thursday,' the DS mouthed.

'He's back for Thursday so he'll be there when we start work on the wardrobe. Now I want my car, Jim.'

'No, you joking bastard. Not till after the hit.' The call cut out.

Silence filled the room. It felt like the end of a round in a heavyweight boxing contest. He was battered and bruised, and ready to have water poured on his head by his coach.

'Well done,' she murmured. 'Now I've a lot to set up.' She got to her feet and glanced towards the top of the open-tread stairs. 'You can make that cup of tea now, Mrs Cowley.'

'Oh no-o,' Nick groaned. 'She promised....'

A knockout would've been preferable to the embarrassment.

CHAPTER 29

Matt cut along a narrow passage surrounded by a tangle of rooms. He dodged between old filing cabinets and haphazard stacks of chairs abandoned in doorways, his thoughts running ahead unchecked. He was following his preferred route back from the computer lab. He'd already nipped through a side door into the Academy's old stores, service and boiler room areas, and now he headed for the corridor linking the goods delivery bay with the main corridor.

As he walked, his mind wrestled with the *Introduction to Digital Possibilities* module. The nine o'clock practical and teaching should have been a two-hour session, but he'd left early. It hadn't taken him long to learn how to use a small stand-alone computer board to connect to his computer, along with a *drag-and-drop* programme. With portals in the stand-alone board to plug in temperature, motion and light sensors, he'd partway designed a rudimentary burglar alarm. He was fired with excitement.

But something else triggered his pulse and launched a million butterflies into gastric flight. Maisie. He had precisely thirty-five minutes to make it to the centre of Stowmarket for the coffee date. He would have preferred McDonald's or the burger van to coffee, but Stowmarket didn't boast a McDonald's and the van only came on Thursdays and Saturdays. Today was Wednesday.

'Hi.' The voice came from nowhere.

'Aah,' Matt screamed. He leapt sideways, his heart vaulting. It choked his mouth.

'What the hell?' he gasped, and raked the shadows with frenzied eyes.

A figure hunched in the darkness of a doorway.

'Gavin? Is that you?'

'Yeah. What of it?' a voice grated.

'Nearly gave me a flamin' heart attack, that's what. Anyhow, what you playin' at?' Relief triggered anger.

'You're a jumpy bastard, aren't you? So what's your hurry, Matt? The lab's in the other direction. The practical session doesn't finish yet.' Gavin stepped from the doorway into the virtual light of a low energy bulb hanging ten yards away. 'Where are you going?'

'Frag, Gav!' Matt stared at a wraith-like creature. 'Are you OK? You look kinda ill.'

'Never felt better. Marlin's dead. Home's a nightmare. The pigs have raided Suffield's, and Patrick's been carted off somewhere for questioning. I can't sleep and I haven't eaten. Yeah – never been better.' A thin smile shadowed across the pale face.

'You're….' Matt frowned. 'You're kinda joking. Yeah?' Sarcasm had never been easy, particularly in the dark. And now Gav was talking about pig racing? He pulled his mind back from Maisie and drag-and-drop programmes.

'You're gaping like a fish, Matt.' The sneer was pointed, sharp enough to hook and cut.

'Yeah, but… I don't get it, Gav. Why're you down here? I aint seen you around all week. Are you hidin' or what?'

Gavin clapped his hands, more of a slow dripping sound than hollow smacks. Was it the sarcasm thing again, Matt wondered.

'Fast to catch on, aren't you?'

'What?'

'The thing is, I need time before I face home again. I can think here, at least I could before you came along and started staring at me. I need…. How much cash have you got?'

'What?'

'Cash. Are you deaf or just plain stupid?' Gavin moved closer. 'Come on. Hand over what you've got.'

'But–'

'You'll get it back.' His tone softened. 'We're mates. Right? So help a mate out.'

'Yeah, but I reckon you'd be better seein' a doctor. They could give you some pills. You know, help you sleep or–'

'I don't need to see a doctor.' His voice rose in a spiralling squeal. 'I don't like them. What I need is money. Now what've you got?' Gavin lunged at Matt.

'Ouch. Let go.'

Gavin's fingers squeezed as he gripped Matt's forearm.

'Y-o-u-c-h. Get off. I aint got time for this.' He pulled back hard.

Searing heat dragged on Matt's skin. He could have been back in the playground with the school bully giving him a Chinese burn, except now he weighed in at thirteen stone against Gavin's eight-and-a-half. Matt twisted away. Gavin lost his footing and slewed across old tiles.

'Let go, you bastard!' Matt screamed, shaking him off. The sweatshirt tore, rending somewhere near the top of his sleeve as the stitching gave way. 'Now look what you've done.'

Gavin's grasp had broken. It was over.

'Oh bot, I'll be late,' Matt yelled. He reached into his pocket, grabbed a fistful of small change and flung it onto the tiles. He didn't wait, just hoofed it to the tune of coins spinning and rolling behind him.

'Don't look back,' he muttered as he puffed his way to the main corridor. 'Oh graphene,' he croaked when he looked at the clock in the main entrance hall. 'Twenty-five minutes.'

Four minutes later he was helmeted and hunched over the Piaggio. His ribs burned, his thighs ached. 'Bloody Gav,' he gasped, as he turned the ignition key and twisted the accelerator.

The wind caught the cotton of his sweatshirt, worrying his sleeve and whooshing up to vent one armpit, the one with broken stitching. His mind raced as the wheels turned. Gavin? The bloke must've gone crazy. Maisie? Twenty minutes and he'd be meeting her. But what would he say? What would they talk about? Would she like him? More butterflies took flight.

It didn't take him long to ride into the centre of Stow-market. He parked behind one of the charity shops where chairs, crockery, black sacks of clothes and an ornamental birdcage had been left. Oddments and unwanted items queued at the rear entrance. He stowed his helmet and straightened his tee-shirt. Chrissie had told him to wear something clean. She'd also once remarked that blue suited him, so he'd put on the only clean blue item in his wardrobe that morning - a long-sleeved blue sweatshirt. The tee was a last-minute addition. He'd slipped it on over the long blue. At least it disguised the flapping armpit.

He hurried past the market place and headed for Costa. His dark, sandy hair felt wet as he combed it quickly with

267

his fingers. A bead of sweat trickled from his hairline. He wiped it away and pushed the coffee shop door. Oh frag, he thought. The swagger. Was it too late to get the shoulder move right?

A wall of sound filled his ears: coffee shop babble, espresso machine chortle, cups chinking, and cutlery grazing. The mouth-watering scents of chocolate, coffee and caramelised milk filled the air. The website had said *smile*, so he pulled his mouth into the sexy half-smile and scanned the place for her. She sat at a table near the large plate-glass window. Relief and excitement overwhelmed him.

'Hi Maisie,' he mouthed.

She waved.

He kept his eyes fixed on the streaks in her blonde hair as he cut between tables.

'You look as if you've been running,' she said.

'Well I 'ave.' He took in the half-read newspaper, the coffee cup two thirds full. 'Am I late?'

'My bus arrived early.'

He drew a chair back from the table and started to sit down.

'Don't you want any coffee?'

'I… yeah, sorry. I didn't think. Just came straight to you. I better go an' queue up. Do you want anythin' while I'm there?'

It felt like forever to Matt as he waited in line for his double latte to be prepared. He wished he'd asked for a can of cola, and then he'd already be back sitting with Maisie. Instead steam jetted while milk frothed. When he finally set the tall glass mug of pale milky coffee on the table, the butterflies had settled and his hair had dried. He pulled the cuff of his torn sleeve back from the coffee.

'Do you study music, then?' Her question caught him by surprise. She lowered her gaze and eyed his tee-shirt.

'Those penguins. They're…,' she read out the print on his tee. '*CONDUCTOR*. Right? Like for an orchestra. The conductor at the top is a penguin using one stick. The… *SUPERCONDUCTOR*'s got two sticks, one in each wing. It's a music thing, right?'

'Yeah, and the *SEMICONDUCTOR*'s got a broken wing in a sling.'

'And a stick. He's holding a stick in his broken wing. He's only half conducting, right?' She raised her eyes and held his gaze.

For a moment, nothing else existed.

'It aint about music, Maisie. It's about electronics. It's a kind of play on words thing. Conductor, semiconductor and superconductor – they're materials for conducting electrons. See I'm studyin' computin' and IT and, well I reckoned the tee was cool.'

She didn't say anything, just sipped her coffee, so he continued, 'They use semiconductors to make transistors. In computers.'

'Well I don't get the electronics, but I like penguins. It makes sense for penguins to conduct orchestras.' She laughed. 'You'd be the penguin with his wing in a sling. Why's your sleeve dangling like that? Better squeeze the coffee out of it.'

Matt found himself telling her about his trip back from the computer lab.

'So this weirdo's hanging around in the store rooms and jumps you? Doesn't sound like someone who's depressed.'

269

'He don't look well and he's got reason to be depressed.'

'Yeah, but when my dad was depressed, he sat around doing nothing. Wouldn't have had the get-up-and-go to jump someone. Maybe it's a bit like your penguins.'

'What you mean, Maisie? A play on words? Electronics? Music? How's it like my penguins?'

'What I'm trying to say is - you can see things in different ways if you know more stuff. I don't know about electronics, so I see penguins conducting music. But I got experience with depression, and it's - too weird for depression. It's not depression like my dad's.'

Matt had never found girls easy to talk to before. Chrissie didn't count, of course. But Maisie was somehow different. He didn't quite get all she was saying but that didn't seem to matter. He felt at ease with her. Words didn't swell in his mouth, explode and then choke him mid-sentence as they did with the others. She made him feel he could swagger.

'I've got to go, Matt. I start my shift at twelve.'

'What?'

'Sorry, but I'll be late if I don't go now. I'll call you. Really I will. Bye.'

Before he'd struggled to his feet, she was already halfway to the plate-glass door, and then she'd gone. Matt stared into the cold dregs of his double latte. So what had he learnt? Her pink highlights caught the strip lighting and almost fluoresced. She worked part time in a clothes shop in Stowmarket. She liked penguins.

CHAPTER 30

'So, do you know if they've arrested Mr Ravyt?' Ron asked as he took his mid-afternoon tea break with Chrissie. The light was fading outside as a November wind rattled the barn workshop boarding.

'No, Mr Clegg. They can't arrest him for bidding for something he says he didn't know was stolen. They can't prove he knew the doll's house was made from the automaton casing. I know he knew, but I've no evidence. Nothing cast iron. It's hopeless.'

A helicopter rumbled overhead.

'I'm still convinced he had something to do with Marlin's death,' she continued. 'He must have known before anyone else that Marlin was dead, otherwise why withdraw that tortoiseshell box from the auction? And….'

Matt's printout of the emails flashed through her mind. 'He definitely knew about the Utterly Mansion automaton.'

She sighed, almost defeated. 'He bought the casing on Saturday, Mr Clegg, or at least tried to. And to my mind that makes him guilty. The workings were at the top of the spiral stairs where Marlin was found. Too much of a coincidence, don't you think?'

Ron didn't answer for a moment, just stared into his tea. 'If he had killed Marlin and he'd wanted the Utterly Mansion automaton, don't you think he'd have taken the workings with him? Why leave them with the body? It doesn't make sense.'

'Well, why do you think he did it?'

'I don't know what to think, Mrs Jax. We don't have enough facts. There has to be a motive and I can't see one.'

'Doesn't mean there isn't one. What do they say? Money, jealousy and sex – that's what drives people to kill. I bet you it'll be one of those.'

'What does Clive say?'

'He won't discuss it. Says I'm just speculating.'

They didn't speak for a few seconds as the helicopter's engines thudded into the distance. Even the sounds of the rotary blades and autumn gusts couldn't drown out the memory of Ravyt's voice. Chrissie pictured his face, heard his tones, relived the moment when he'd told her Nick had left the auction rooms with a young man. No, she thought, Ravyt had emotions all right. It was the nature of his appetites she questioned. She doubted if they were strictly mainstream. Who knew what currents flowed deep beneath that cool exterior?

'If I didn't know better, Mrs Jax, I'd think you'd lost your mind when you bid for that spool cabinet.' Ron's quiet tones broke into her thoughts.

'What? What are you saying, Mr Clegg?'

'I'm trying to illustrate a point. On the face of it, there was no earthly reason for you to bid for that spool cabinet. But see you in the context of an undercover automaton expert and it all makes perfect sense.'

She watched the hint of a smile creep across his face as he swirled the dregs of tea in his mug.

'Just wait till you see it, Mr Clegg. You'll eat those words. Is it still all right if I borrow the van to collect it from Woodbridge tomorrow?'

She'd arranged to pick up the spool cabinet on Thursday lunchtime. Ron had said it was a trip she could make by herself.

'Of course. Now let's get back to work.'

When Chrissie drove home after work that evening, she felt quietly excited. There was plenty to look forward to. She'd be going out for a meal with Clive in a couple of hours' time, and then there was the trip to Woodbridge and the spool cabinet tomorrow.

Just one thing gnawed at the back of her mind. Matt's text message.

Maisie & me - coffee ok. Need to look up depression. See u Friday, Nags Hd.

CHAPTER 31

Nick lifted the last dividing panel into the Willows van. The frames and doors were already stacked neatly inside and secured against the sides with straps. He'd wrapped dust-sheets around some of the pieces so that the richly grained American cherry heartwood would be safe on the journey.

'I think that's the lot,' Nick called. He reckoned if Dave was driving the cross-country route to Lavenham, then the panels and doors would need the equivalent of a rally car harness seat belt if they were to arrive in one piece.

'Have you got the spare battery packs for the cordless drills charged and in, Nick?'

'Yup.' Nick slammed the van's rear doors.

Thursday had dawned bright but chilly. The early autumn sunshine seemed to give little heat, but at least it promised warmth later in the day. Nick hugged his sweat-shirt closer as he waited for Dave. It was a good feeling, just knowing Jim and Darrel would've been nicked yesterday. Man, it was good.

'You've not met Mr Sops before, have you, Nick? He's an interesting bloke. You'll like his house,' Dave said as he headed towards the driver's side of the van.

'Yeah, but I'll need a helmet for the beams, right?' Nick hoped Mr Sops didn't know he'd helped set up the sting. It might prove awkward to explain.

'Come on then, lad. What you waiting for?'

Nick stepped up into the passenger seat. It was as if a weight had been lifted from his shoulders and a light switched on. He felt seven feet tall, and the world without Jim and Darrel seemed full of extra colour.

Dave eased the van out of the Willows secure parking area and across the rough concrete alongside the workshop. The American cherry swayed with the van, but nothing rattled or shifted.

'Everything secure, do you think?' Dave asked.

He was still turning to look when Dave hit the accelerator. Nick lurched towards a heartwood panel, then jerked backwards to the windscreen.

'Let's rock an' roll,' Dave shouted.

'Wooah,' Nick groaned.

The journey wove through Bildeston and Monks Eleigh, then on to Lavenham. They swooped over flat hilltops and rolled around sharp corners, following the route cut by mighty streams. Nick's stomach bucked and reared with the ride, but he gripped his seat belt and imagined Jim's face when someone stepped from the shadows and said, 'You're nicked.' He reckoned it had to have been a few shades greener than his own.

'Nearly there,' Dave murmured as he slowed into Water Street. Ancient beamed houses pushed sloping first-floors over narrow pavements. They turned into Church Street and drove at jogging speed up the gentle hill.

'It's up here on the left,' Dave grunted.

The final sharp left nearly did for Nick. His stomach heaved. He clamped his jaws and focussed on the police car parked on the side of the road.

'Looks as if something's going on here,' Dave muttered and drew in behind the patrol car.

'Is this Mr Sops' place?' Nick asked and looked at a long-fronted beamed house a few yards back from the road. 'Is there a side entrance or a way round to the back? Or do we unload from here?'

He felt confused. The police were meant to catch Jim and Darrel red-handed yesterday. So what were they doing here now?

'We can drive round the side but it looks busy. Best leave the van here till we know what's going on. Come on, Nick. We've a lot to do today.'

Dave got out of the van and led the way to an oak front door, stained dark but weathered and with iron hinges, knocker and handle. A small porch protected it from the worst of the elements. He lifted the knocker and let it fall against its strike plate – a cast iron mermaid striking her tail against a small iron rock. Nick thought it incongruously maritime for a town built centuries earlier on the success of its wool and cloth industry.

Moments later the door was opened by a middle-aged man. 'Ah good, you've arrived. Come in, come in.' He gestured with theatrical exaggeration.

'Good morning, Mr Sops. I've got Nick with me today,' Dave said.

'Yes, yes, of course. From Willows. Hello.' He nodded briefly at Nick and then continued, 'I seem to be overrun this morning so you'll have to excuse me if I leave you in a minute. I have to get back to the police. Now don't stand in the doorway. Come on in.'

'Yes, we noticed they were here when we parked. Is everything all right, Mr Sops?'

'No it is not, Dave. I've been burgled.'

'What?' Nick couldn't help himself. The words just erupted with his shock. 'You've had stuff taken?'

'Yes. It's horrible. It's as if the place has been... violated.'

Nick winced.

'That's terrible, Mr Sops,' Dave said quietly. 'Was much taken? Anything damaged? Are you OK?'

'I was out all day yesterday.' He spoke as he led the way through a room which served as the hallway. 'I didn't get back till late last night. Everything seemed the same as usual in the house, well as much as you notice when you come in tired.'

He turned as he reached the stairs. They were built into the far wall and curved upwards beside a Tudor brick fireplace and chimney stack. 'It wasn't till this morning and it was daylight that I realised I'd been burgled. I looked out of the window at my garden and my statues had gone.'

'What? Statues? Were they bronzes?' Dave said and glanced at Nick with a kind of *we've seen this before* look.

'Yes.' Mr Sops climbed the stairs with heavy feet.

'So have the police caught anyone yet?' Nick asked as he stooped to avoid a low beam.

'You're joking. They're still here taking photos and casts of tyre treads.'

'Did you have many bronzes?'

'Four. The thieves must have got into the garden by coming round the side of the house. And the police think they did it on Wednesday in broad daylight. I bet no one even noticed when they loaded up a van. The bloody nerve of it.' He led them into an L-shaped bedroom running the width of the house. 'Now, you'll be working in here. Anything you need?'

A window looked out across the garden and Nick walked over to peer through the small panes of glass. A lawn, formal flowerbeds and shrubs stretched for almost a hundred yards. Tyre tracks scarred the grass. Plants with their roots exposed lay amongst scattered soil near a garden

277

trellis. Part of the access around the side of house was cordoned off with yellow and black striped tape. It told the tale more eloquently than words, and Nick's heart sank. He realised Mr Sops was watching him.

'Yes, I should have said. They took my old iron garden chairs and table. And I'd been stupid enough to leave the wheelbarrow and watering cans out. Metal again, so you can guess they grabbed the lot. It's the bronzes that break my heart though.'

'Bastards,' Nick muttered.

'If you've no last-minute changes to what we agreed, Mr Sops, then I think we can unload the van and get started. At least my pencil marks are still here,' Dave said, running his hand over the plaster on one of the walls.

It was hard physical work carrying all the frames, panels and doors from the van to the bedroom. Between trips up and down the narrow staircase built into the old walls, Dave talked about Mr Sops. 'He's got a studio at the back of the house, you know. He makes statues and models out of clay and composites. Very artistic. I think he said he used to design theatre stage sets sometime in the past.'

Nick wasn't really listening. His mind was too taken up with trying to work out what had gone wrong. Jim and Darrel were supposed to be caught red handed, not get away with four bronze statues and a pile of old garden stuff. If they were still at liberty, it could only mean trouble. He reckoned it wouldn't be long before he got the next call. They'd want more and more information about Willows' customers.

In the end he couldn't contain his agitation any longer.

'I need a pee-break,' he told Dave.

Alone at last, he pulled his mobile from a pocket and pressed an automatic dial number. He waited, listening to the ring tone, confused butterflies tingling his anxieties.

'Hello. DS Crip, speaking.' She sounded distant, her voice small.

He pictured her amazingly blue eyes and almost faltered. 'Hi, it's Nick, Nick Cowley speaking.'

'Yes? Everything OK?'

'Yeah. Well no. I'm at Mr Sops' place – about to put in a wardrobe, and just about everything metal in the garden's been stolen. The bronzes. The lot. I thought you said you were setting up a sting. You were supposed to catch the thieves in the act. But the police are crawling all over the place and they're too late. It's already been pinched.'

'Thanks for calling, Nick. You've done your bit, and we're grateful, but stay out of it now. OK? And at least this way you might get your car back.' She ended the call.

'But–'

It was no use. He was talking to air. She'd gone. He stared at the ground and tried to collect his thoughts. Poor girl must've messed it up, he decided. It was the obvious explanation.

'I bet she's in trouble with her DI,' he murmured, and then imagined the blue eyes, serious and sad. The thought helped. Not the sad eyes, but knowing it was she who'd messed up and it wasn't his fault. The police had blown it. He reckoned it absolved him of responsibility.

By the time he rejoined Dave in the bedroom, his stomach had settled and his mind was back on the wardrobe. As they started bolting the frames between the upright dividing panels, a thought struck him. If Jim contacted him again, then it would be an excuse to phone DS Crip, and who knew where that might lead.

'Must find out what her first name is.'

'What did you say, Nick? Must fasten what?'

'I said I must ring Mustang. Find out when my Fiesta will be ready, Dave.'

CHAPTER 32

Matt slumped onto a chair, hunched down and logged on. The computer screen shielded him as he cast around the library. He'd already checked as he came in, but fear made him look once more. Was Gavin lurking somewhere in the shadows? Was he hiding on the other side of that bookcase? Matt shuddered. After meeting him on the shortcut yesterday, he felt as if Gavin might pop up from anywhere.

Coffee with Maisie had driven everything out of his mind. He'd wanted to live in the moment for as long as he could. Maisie smiling, Maisie liking his penguins and talking about music; it was a first date and she hadn't told him to get lost. That had to be a success. He reckoned it was down to his lucky tee, so he hadn't changed it or the coffee stained sweatshirt either. He was still in the moment. But when he'd walked into the Academy that morning, the memory of Gavin came rushing back with the ferocity of a kick in the guts.

Maisie had reckoned it wasn't depression, but Matt didn't see how she could say that. It stood to reason the guy was depressed. Sure, he was weird as well, but put the two together and you were bound to get something odd - someone like Gavin. Everyone gets depressed, he thought, so everyone's an expert, right? He typed *depression* in the Google search box.

'Graphene,' he muttered as hundreds of sites came up. It was easy reading and he mentally ticked off the symptom boxes as he skimmed the screen. *Can't sleep*, well that sounded like Gavin. And then he read, *can't get up in the morning, can sleep till midday*. So which was it, he wondered. 'Can't be both, stands to reason.'

Feelings of hopelessness and worthlessness typify depression, he read. 'Don't sound like Gavin,' he muttered and cast a glance towards the door. 'Anger an' self-pity, more like.'

The further he read, the worse his confusion became. The obvious stuff made sense, but *bipolar* had him stumped. *Hallucinations*? *Delusions*? *Psychosis*? How could he tell, Matt wondered. And when did *mood change* become *suicidal thoughts*? As for *changes in eating habits and weight loss or gain*, it seemed both were typical of depression. Matt finally toyed with the idea he was depressed himself. He smoothed his tee-shirt over his ample belly. Depression or big bones?

'Nah, I got big bones,' he muttered.

As he sat, reliving his encounter with the Goth apparition lurking in the stores area, a sudden thought struck. What if Gavin was suicidal? What if he planned to kill himself?

'Oh bot,' Matt hissed. A mate would go and search for him. Make sure he was OK. But Gavin wasn't a mate. Gav thought he was, but he wasn't. He was just a scarily weird guy.

The library door swung open. Matt held his breath.

'Arolla,' he whispered.

His relief must have shown, or his whisper ricocheted, because she caught his eye and smiled. He watched as she circuited the library, stopping off at the printer station and the librarian's office before heading towards him.

'Hi,' she said as she breezed past. 'What kind of music do penguins conduct then?' She didn't wait for an answer, but moved on down the library.

'What?' Matt looked down at his chest and bulging midriff. The *SEMI* and *SUPERCONDUCTORS* were partially hidden by the desk. 'That's the second bird to….' Something clicked in his brain. What if Gavin wasn't depressed, but everyone just assumed he was?

***

Chrissie pulled into the side of the road and took the call.

'Hi Clive. Everything OK?' She couldn't help but sound surprised. She'd only kissed him goodbye a couple of hours earlier.

'I've just remembered. Did you say you were driving to Woodbridge today, Chrissie? To pick up that - what was it? Yes, a spool cabinet - from the auction rooms?'

'Yes, in Ron's van. I'm driving there now. I've only just this minute turned out of his track and onto the airfield perimeter lane. You must be telepathic. Why?'

'Good. I've caught you in time. I've just had a message from someone in the organised crime team. I don't think it's a good idea for you to go anywhere near Woodbridge today. OK, Chrissie?'

'What? No it's not OK. You can't expect me to alter all my arrangements without giving me a proper reason. You getting a call from organised crime doesn't tell me a thing. What am I supposed to say to Ron? And the auction rooms, for that matter?'

She guessed he was irritated, but there was no way she was going to cancel her trip without more of an explanation from him.

'OK, OK, but don't tell anyone. And that includes Nick and Matt. Right?'

'Right,' she said, intrigued and riled in equal measure.

'OK, all you need to know is that the organised crime boys have set up a sting. Seems the thieves have taken the bait. A whole load of iron garden furniture and bronze statues, marked with trackers. Now if my suspicions are correct, I reckon some of the bronzes might be heading to our friend, Mr Ravyt. If he even gets wind of you in the vicinity... well I think it's best if you stay away. Now do you understand, Chrissie? Not Woodbridge and not today. OK?'

'Great. Someone's finally doing something about that slippery bastard. At least you phoned before I'd gone far. Have you....'

'Have I what?'

'With your telepathic skills, have you ever thought of pursuing a career in the police? You know, like a consulting medium? A psychic or something?'

'Yes, and I love you too, Chrissie. Bye'

She stared at the mobile, now lifeless in her hand. He'd sounded quite animated, excited even. He was probably right to warn her off. She would never have told him, but secretly she'd planned to drive past Ravyt's house. So, did it give her a nice warm feeling to know Clive was thinking about her, or did it irritate her? She was still trying to work it out when her mobile leapt into life.

Brrring brrr–

'Yes?'

'Chrissie. Hi. Look, I think I know where Gavin's hangin' out. Can I 'ave Clive's number?' The voice sounded breathy. Something like a small jet engine whirred in the background.

'Where are you, Matt? Are you OK?'

'The toilets. The number, I need it now.'

'I'll text it to you. So where is he, then?'

'I think 'es livin' rough in the Utterly stores area. Could be wrong, but I saw 'im there yesterday.'

'What? At the Academy? Matt, why didn't you tell someone yesterday?'

'I had other things on me mind, Wednesday. Thanks Chrissie. Bye.'

***

Matt stood near the hand basins and read Chrissie's text. He knew he couldn't make a call in the library, but he'd figured the toilets on the first floor would be private enough. He imagined Gavin as a goth-bat with comic-strip styled ears listening through walls and doors. When he'd first walked into the gents he'd spotted the hot-air hand drier. It had proved to be his saviour, doubling as a voice scrambler when he'd spoken to Chrissie - a masterstroke worthy of any comic-strip hero. He checked the cubical doors again and tapped in Clive's number.

'Hi. Clive?' he whispered as soon as he heard the ring tone cut. He thrust one hand under the drier. The motor whirred into action.

'Hello? Hi? DI Merry speaking.'

'Clive. It's Matt. I've got some information for you.'

'What? Who's speaking? I can't hear. There's a lot of noise on the line.'

'It's Matt. Ouch! Flamin' drier.' Pain seared through his skin. He snatched back his hand and flapped at the air. The motor cut out.

'That's better. Less interference. Who's calling?'

'It's Matt. I heard you were lookin' for Gavin Poynder.'

'Gavin? Go on.'

'Well, he was in the Academy stores area yesterday.'

'Is he there now?'

'Don't know. I don't want to go back an' check, not on me own. He was really weird. Creepy. Do you think he could try and top 'imself?' Matt listened to the silence. 'Clive? Are you still there?'

'Yes. Why do you say that about Gavin killing himself? Did he seem suicidal?'

'How'd I know? I'm just sayin' he looked ill. And scary. I've web browsed depression and it says about toppin' yourself.'

'Hmm, I thought he'd go to Patrick Suffield's place.'

'Yeah, but he told me Suffield's been picked up by you lot.'

'Did he now? Well we released him yesterday evening. Look, Matt. Don't do anything. I'll send over one of my sergeants. If you'd show him where the stores area is, that would be helpful. OK?'

'How… I mean where'll I meet…?'

'DS Stickley will ring your mobile as soon as he arrives. Will you still be on this number?'

The main door to the toilets opened and a student hurried in. Matt gasped. All he saw was a pair of skinny legs in charcoal denim jeans dashing to the urinal. Was it Gavin? His stomach lurched. He looked again. The guy was too tall to be Gavin. He waved his hand under the drier and the motor burst into life.

'Yeah, I'll be on this number,' he hissed into his mobile and cut the call.

Matt had spent too long standing next to the porcelain and tiles with the smell of stale pee overwhelming his senses. His nerves felt like shredded Beef Jerky. He bolted back to the library and slumped down at his computer station.

When the call came, he felt calmer. More focused. He was deep in advanced HTML and working on some exercises set for the following morning's teaching session.

'Oh bot,' he muttered as he pressed speak and stumbled from his chair. 'I'm in the library,' he wheezed, as he headed for the door.

'DS Stickley, here. Is that Matt Finch?' The voice had a sharp grating quality.

'Yeah, Matt here. No need to shout.'

'I'm at the reception desk. Main entrance.' He'd quietened his tone, but it still rasped.

It took Matt a few minutes to hustle himself along the first floor corridor, past the canteen and down the main staircase. He spotted the sergeant immediately. DS Stickley's taupe-coloured windproof blended perfectly with the pale marble tiles in the entrance hall, but his leather shoes shrieked policeman.

'Hi. I'm Matt.'

The sergeant nodded briefly and showed his ID card.

'OK. I'll take you where I last saw him,' Matt said and led the way. He snaked along the marble flooring, sidestepping and pushing past students more intent on talking than walking. He kept his eyes on the ground, hoping no one would guess the policeman behind was with him. The marble flooring changed to wooden boards as they followed the corridor. The walls seemed to press in as grey heavy-duty carpet replaced the wood. The students thinned out and disappeared. Even the temperature chilled as they wove further and further.

'Where does this lead?' Stickley asked, his footsteps catching at Matt's heels.

'If you keep straight on, you'll reach the delivery area. If you cut through here,' Matt turned sharply left into a small passageway, 'we're into the stores.'

'What were you doing hanging around here?' The voice held shards of suspicion.

'It's a shortcut. There's a side entrance through this way. It gets you outside, not far from the computer lab. I do computin' an' IT.' Matt slowed to a halt and turned to face Stickley. They stood directly under the low energy light bulb, casting shadows which merged with gloomy door-ways.

Stickley held a finger to his mouth.

Matt listened to the silence. All he heard was his heart beating.

'OK, I thought I heard something. Where exactly did you see him?'

'Along here. He was standin' in one of these door-ways.' Matt moved slowly, almost too afraid to look in case Gavin was there, strung up by the neck. 'Yeah. This'll be the one.'

Stickley pulled his smartphone from a pocket and using its torch, shone a beam into the doorway. Something glinted.

'Frag. That'll be one of me coins.'

'Leave it.' Stickley commanded and kicked the door. It flew open. He raked the blackness with the tiny shaft of light.

'Is he there?' Matt whispered.

'Gavin? We're coming in. We want to help you.' Stickley's voice soothed like a pan scourer. In one rapid move he stepped into the room and flicked the light switch. A single unshaded bulb burst into yellowy light.

'Gavin?' Matt echoed.

A stack of wooden chairs towered amongst tables. Filing cabinets clashed with writing desks for space.

'There. Over there.' Matt pointed to a corner.

'What the…?' Stickley picked his way around more chairs and poked at a stack of carpet tiles with the toe of his shoe. Sweet wrappers and a couple of old newspapers nestled amongst what must have once been a canvas blackout blind. It lay on some of the tiles, arranged like a mattress. An empty cola bottle rolled onto the floor.

'Looks like someone's been sleeping here.'

'Poor bugger,' Matt muttered.

'Well, what have we here?' Stickley squatted and looked closer. 'Seems our friend has left his mobile.' He thrust his hand into his windproof and pulled out a plastic evidence bag. Matt watched, fascinated as the DS slipped it deftly in.

'Right, now let's see if it'll turn on.' Stickley played across the keypad and fingered the sides of the phone through the plastic. 'No. It's dead. Best leave it to our tech boys. They'll get it to work, no trouble.' He dropped it into his pocket.

'So if Gavin aint here, where do you reckon he is?' Matt glanced back into the passageway. The chill from the floor was starting to strike through his canvas trainers.

'I guess we'd better check the rest of this corridor and the other rooms down here.'

Twenty minutes later they'd searched the area, but there was no sign of Gavin.

'I'll phone the DI.' Stickley turned his back. 'Hi, Sir,' his voice cut like a cheese grater. 'It seems the Poynder kid's been living rough here, but he's gone now. Left a mobile behind.'

Matt only half listened as the DS asked questions and took instructions. 'OK, Sir. I'll leave everything as it was… yeah, in case he comes back.'

As long as Gavin wasn't hanging from the back of a door by his laces, then Matt didn't care too much where the spooky weirdo was. Odd he'd left his mobile, though. So was the guy depressed? He still hadn't worked it out.

A gurgle rumbled under the *SEMICONDUCTOR* penguin with the broken baton and its wing in a sling. Matt smacked a hand over his stomach. He needed food.

CHAPTER 33

Chrissie sipped her ginger beer and watched Matt's face as he read his text message.

'I hope it's better news than my last text from Clive,' she said, raising her voice to compete with the jukebox.

Matt ignored her. He seemed riveted to his mobile.

'Let me guess. Is he working late again?' Nick asked as Adele's powerful voice soared above the strong beat. He tapped his foot to the rhythm.

'Got it in one. This Marlin Poynder case seems to have suddenly taken off. That's great of course, but it would have been nice if he'd been able to come with me to Sarah's fish pie and strudel fest this evening. It'll be fine going by myself, she's my friend, after all. But....'

For a moment the jukebox paused between tracks. The Nags Head bar erupted with laughter as someone slammed a pint glass onto a table. Chrissie sat back and let the sounds of Friday night drinkers wash over her. It somehow soothed and comforted.

'Well I've got some good news. I can collect my car tomorrow.'

'Fantastic! That's great, Nick. Do you want a lift?'

'Yes please. If you're sure, Chrissie.'

'No trouble. Well I think this calls for a celebration. Is anyone ready for another drink? Nick? Matt?'

'What?' Matt looked up. He seemed rather distracted.

'Another drink, Matt?' Chrissie repeated. 'What's got you so riveted then?'

'Maisie.' His face flushed crimson from his beard to the roots of his hair. 'She wants me to give her a lift tomorrow. Back from some communal apple pressin'. S'pose it counts as a date.'

'Maisie? Is she a cider drinker, then?' Nick asked.

'They've got cider at the bar, if you're going to become an expert. It'd make a change from lager, Matt. I'm sure I saw a barrel of Slack Alice. The barman said it was mellow with a slightly tart finish.'

'Or,' Nick added, 'you could try a Bramley Wiggins – a race winner.'

'Oh pixel off you two. So they're letting you collect your car, right?'

'Yeah, Matt. That's why I'm celebrating.'

'Yeah, but what'll they hold over you next time?'

'Next time?' Nick drained the rest of his Land Girl in one gulp.

'Well, they've done over the place where you're workin' and they aint got caught. That's why the Fiesta's ready to collect, right? They'll reckon they're onto a good thing with you. They'll want more. What'll they use to twist your arm next time, mate?'

'Matt's right, Nick. Except they probably think you're one of them by now.'

'It's not my bloody fault the police messed up.'

Chrissie hid her smile behind her glass. If Clive hadn't said something about trackers, she wouldn't have known the sting, as Nick called it, was still going according to plan. But she'd been sworn to silence.

'What's so amusing, Chrissie?' Nick's face was stony with indignation. 'What's there to smile about?'

'I was just wondering what the bronzes were like – you know, if any of them might appeal to our friend Ravyt?

Maybe a statue of an older, muscular Poseidon or a young sinuous Eros?'

'Who knows. They'd been stolen before I'd ever set eyes on the place.'

'What you talkin' about?' Matt butted in.

'Statues of male Greek Gods. Poseidon – he's a god of the sea, and Eros – he's a god of sexual desire and attraction. I was just wondering about Mr Sops' taste in garden statues.'

'Well, he's got a mermaid door knocker,' Nick murmured.

By the time Chrissie had struggled back from the bar with a small glass of ginger beer wedged between a pint of Land Girl and a pint of lager, the jukebox was belting out Madonna and her pumps were splattered in beer.

They all drank a toast to the Fiesta's new wing.

'Hey, Jake,' Nick shouted above Madonna. 'Over here, mate.' He turned to Chrissie and added, 'He's giving me a lift to band practice.'

Nick waved and his guitarist friend edged towards them from the bar, sipping his overfilled glass as he walked. By the time Chrissie left about twenty minutes later, she felt happy and relaxed.

The drive back to Woolpit didn't take long. A shower and a change from her working jeans into a smarter pair, a shimmering loose turquoise vest under a grey suede leather biker jacket, and she was ready to face fish pie and strudel.

When Clive phoned later that night, he sounded tired.

'How's it going?' she asked 'You missed a good fish pie.'

'What? Oh yes, sorry about that. It's been mad here. I told you we found Gavin at Patrick Suffield's place on Thursday afternoon, didn't I?'

'No.'

'It seems a long time ago now.' The sound of his yawn got in the way, like a speech impediment. 'I'm sure I said something.'

'You said you'd made a breakthrough and you needed to do everything by the book, otherwise it wouldn't stand up in court.'

'Ah yes, that's right. We needed a medical opinion to see if we could interview Gavin. But as it turns out, by the time he'd been assessed and passed fit enough late this afternoon, the prints were back and we'd discovered a lot more about that phone.'

'What phone?'

'The one we found in the Academy stores. You know, where Gavin was sleeping rough.'

'Oh yes, Matt said something about that. So was the poor guy suicidal?'

'No.'

'Well that's good. And the phone... why'd he leave his phone, unless it just slipped out of his pocket?'

'It wasn't his phone.'

'So why...? Whose...? Oh my God. It wasn't Marlin Poynder's missing phone, was it?'

Clive didn't answer. She guessed that meant she was right.

'So how did Gavin come to have it?' she said softly voicing her thoughts. 'No wonder you're doing everything by the book. Have you finished for tonight?'

'Not quite yet. We've got Suffield back in again, and this time he isn't covering for Gavin.' He half laughed, more of a weary sound than amused. 'It seems we'd got him so rattled by those stolen lead animal caskets, he's more interested in looking after his own skin than Gavin's.'

'Well, I guess this is going to run into tomorrow morning then. You must be exhausted.'

'Yes, but at least we're getting somewhere at last. I'm sorry Chrissie, but you know how it goes.'

'OK then. I'd better let you get on. Good luck with it all, and give me a call in the morning.'

'Sleep tight.'

'Bye,' she ended, reluctant to let him go.

Her mind buzzed with sound bites. She'd wanted to ask more, but she knew he wasn't going to tell. She'd just have to make sense of the crumbs he'd already thrown. But the picture she was building wasn't the one she'd expected.

CHAPTER 34

Saturday morning dawned overcast and threatening to drizzle. By ten o'clock, fine rain blew in gusts on an easterly wind. Nick hugged his anorak tighter. He'd wanted to collect his Fiesta for so long and now the day had arrived. He pushed aside the misgivings spiking his excitement and watched the wipers as they swept across Chrissie's windscreen. The rhythmic strokes beat out of time with the pickaxe hammering inside his skull.

'Shouldn't have had those vodka chasers,' he muttered.

'What? Excited?' Chrissie asked, seemingly oblivious to his pain.

'Yeah, and a bit hung over. The blue had better be a good match after all the buggering about.'

'So it was a good band practice then.' She changed up through the gears and accelerated out of Barking Tye.

'Do you know where you're going, Chrissie?'

'Kind of.'

'Well, it's probably easier to take the Newton Road and then come at Stowupland from the west. I'll direct you when we get closer.'

Nick closed his eyes. He knew Chrissie was hopeless with directions but for the moment his main priority was to give the fat, protein and rehydrating hangover cure a chance to work. He reckoned bacon and eggs washed down with a mug of tea was as good as anything he'd read about. And breakfast ten minutes earlier had been on those lines.

Nick sensed a change in the sound of the engine. He opened his eyes as Chrissie dropped her speed. 'Take the turning off to the right here,' he said.

They drove along a lane with a high overgrown hedge on one side and sloping earthy fields on the other. 'It's somewhere behind all that. It's a huge area, but you'd never guess from the road. Just keep going for the moment. Yes… just here and there's a fork in the road. Keep right. There, on the left.' He pointed to huge gates with metal grilles and a weathered notice, *TARV Auto Recycling*.

She indicated and slowed.

'No we don't turn in here. If we keep following the road it skirts the site and there's a separate entrance for the accident and body repair workshop.'

'Are you feeling any better?' she asked as they kept on past the gates.

'Yeah, I'm good. Hey, why would you park there?'

A car had drawn off to the side of the road. It was at an angle, and for a moment Nick wondered if it had run into a ditch, except it was facing outwards. The driver and a passenger sat in the front seats watching them as they passed, the car blending with the autumn shades of a nearby oak and the long grass.

'I don't know. They look as if they don't want to be seen.'

***

Matt flipped his visor down and set off in the direction of Haughley, a mile or so northwest of Stowmarket. Excitement churned his stomach. Scarbrow had said he could start Saturday morning at the Pizza Place half an hour late, but he reckoned he'd get away with slipping his ten o'clock start time well beyond that.

Riding the Piaggio with the wind and spitting rain gusting against his denim jacket, Matt felt every bit Cap'n Starlight of the Space Hopper Corps. If he had a tee with an apple on the front, he'd have worn that as well. It could have passed for a planet. Instead he'd settled for one sporting a picture of a bottle top with crimped edges.

Judging by Maisie's text, communal apple pressing, along with the bottling, was an annual event and took place all day. Her mum, along with some friends, hoped to bag an early slot on one of the presses, and Maisie was expected to take an interest and help. She reckoned it'd be OK for her to steal away after an hour or so. Matt saw himself as her saviour. A comic-strip hero.

He gritted his teeth and twisted the accelerator while the engine whined. Soon he was riding past the local recycling and waste disposal collection site, and out on the old road parallel with the A14. Large woods vied with ploughed fields as he zipped on. It wasn't far before he spotted the first notice and an arrow pinned between fence posts.

'Thought they were makin' cider,' he muttered, but the notice definitely said apple juice.

He followed a car as it turned off the road and along a track to a car park, roughly gravelled and near corrugated metal barns and outhouses. Matt parked his scooter and stowed his helmet while people unloaded baskets and boxes brimming with apples from their off-roaders and hatchbacks. A festive excitement hung in the air as fruit escaped and bumped along the ground, only to be chased and recaptured.

He slipped through the gate and trailed behind the general drift to the main barn, feeling as out of place as raw beefsteak in a vegetarian soup kitchen.

'Hi, Matt.'

He turned to see Maisie in pink wellingtons, skin tight jeans and a transparent pack-a-mac, several sizes too large and with bright flowers printed all over. She looked damp.

'It aint mine,' she said by way of explanation.

'I like it Mais, it looks kinda retro.' Matt hoped the Mais abbreviation made him sound cool. 'So how does it work, this pressin' business?'

'It's a community sponsored thing. They've hired three presses this year so the pressin' bit's free. You bring your own apples but pay a small amount for the bottlin' bit. I guess it's a chance to do somethin' with your extra apples and windfalls before the winter sets in.'

'So why don't it become cider?'

'They heat the bottled apple juice in a water bath. Kills the yeasts and stuff. Makes the juice last without goin' bad. Stops it fer…ferm….'

'Fermentin'?'

'Yeah. Do you like cider, then?'

Matt opened his mouth to answer and then thought better of it. This was a trick question. If he got it wrong he could blow the whole Maisie thing. Instead he said, 'I think we better get goin'. I'm meant to start work in half an hour, Mais.'

'Yeah, OK then. I've got a helmet with me this time. It's a spare I borrowed from a neighbour.'

Wow, Matt thought. If that aint commitment, then what is?

While Matt waited as she collected her helmet and said goodbye to her mother's group of friends, the smell of crushed apples filled his nose. It was a heady mix of fruity sweetness and damp grass. He breathed it in, happy and relaxed in the moment. He imagined the taste of cider.

A few minutes later Maisie sat behind him on the Piaggio, arms around his waist.

'We can take the back roads from here to Stowupland. It'll be quicker,' she shouted.

***

Nick watched the wild, shrubby hedge through the rain spattered window as Chrissie drove slowly and followed the road.

'You can get from the auto recycling yard into Mustang's repair place from inside as well.'

'Why didn't you say, Nick? I could've driven in through those gates back there.'

'It's not really an official route, and anyway…,' he let his voice drift as he pictured the yard, 'I'd have to speak to Dodge. He'd want to know why we were cutting through his place.'

The road ahead, already narrow, dwindled to single track. Chrissie kept glancing at the hedge.

'You're sure it's this way?'

'Yes. Look, you can see the gates just up there, same as the auto recycling ones'

They turned into the entrance, and drew up outside Mustang's workshop.

'Hey, that's my Fiesta. There.' Nick pointed to a dark blue car parked next to a transit van and a BMW saloon. He didn't wait for Chrissie to switch off her engine, but sprang out of the TR7. His muzzy head, intra-cranial pickaxe and slight nausea were forgotten as he hurried to look at his car.

'Yes,' he murmured as he ran his hand over the re-paired wing. Rain covered the surface so that his palm left a trail, but beneath his fingertips he felt the hard, glossy paintwork. It was luxuriously smooth. He stroked it again.

'Fantastic.'

Chrissie got out of her car. 'Happy?'

He knew she didn't need an answer, he guessed his face probably showed it all: the relief, the excitement, the pleasure. Memories of Jim, Mustang's threats and the rob-bery - they all faded away as he drank in the vision of his repaired Fiesta.

'Hi there.' Mustang walked from his workshop. 'I thought I heard a car and voices.' He nodded briefly at Nick. 'It's all ready for you.'

'Thanks, that's great, Mustang.'

'I'll wait out here while you settle up, Nick.'

'Is the TR7 yours as well,' Mustang tossed over his shoulder as Nick followed him into the workshop.

'You must be kidding. I can hardly afford one car.' Nick sensed the undertones.

Mustang sat down at a small table. It served as the desk in an office-like alcove off to one side of the spraying booth. With its air seals and extractor ducts, the booth could have been a theatre suite in the way it was separated from the main body of the workshop. The transaction was swift, clinical and in cash. One hundred and twenty pounds seemed ridiculously good value considering it included Dodge's wing, and Nick wasn't going to argue. He under-stood the terms of the deal. It just knotted his guts, that's all.

'Thanks,' he muttered as Mustang threw the keys on the table.

He snatched them up, thankful to get his hands on them at last. There was no point in hanging around to ask more questions about the paint, Mustang would only turn ugly. It was time to leave.

Nick tried to look cool as he walked out of the workshop door. It was a huge effort to suppress his eagerness. The keys were burning into his hand and he was desperate to break into a run. He took a deep breath and slowed his stride. He knew it was a weakness to care and he guessed Mustang would be watching. All he wanted was to get behind the wheel of his car and drive it away as fast as he could. If the tyres spun, and spat mud and gravel as well, then it would be all the better.

'Everything all right, Nick? Are we good to go?' Chrissie called from her car as a black Jaguar turned in through the iron gates.

He held up the keys and waved.

***

Chrissie watched as Nick strolled towards his Fiesta. The body language was wrong. He'd waved his keys as if everything was OK, but the walk was too stiff in its slowness. Not at all like his usual ambling gait when he was happy. Unease seeped into her mind and joined the moisture inside her car from her wet anorak and hair. She shouldn't have stayed out in the rain so long, nosing around Mustang's yard.

Mustang appeared at the workshop door and waved at someone. Not at her. Not at Nick. She tensed.

The swoosh of tyres cutting through water prickled her senses. She flicked a glance into her rear-view mirror. An inky black Jaguar sleeked across the yard and drew to a halt alongside Mustang.

'Morning Mr Vatry.' Mustang's words carried in the damp air, drifting in through her open car window.

'There's a car parked on the side of the road a stone's throw from Dodge's entrance. I didn't know what it was doing there, so I came in this way. Can't be too careful. Everything OK here?'

Hearing the voice was like a kick in the solar plexus. She didn't need to look. She knew instantly. She'd spent a couple of hours sitting next to him at the auction. It was Ravyt. His accent, with that hint of a soft burr was as distinctive as a fingerprint. Oh my God, she thought and slid lower into her seat.

'Yeah, it all seems fine here, Mr Vatry. I'm not expecting any more collections or deliveries today after this customer's gone,' Mustang answered.

Chrissie heard a car door slam. Was it Nick's Ford or the Jaguar? She decided the Ford.

'What? The customer with that blue Ford Fiesta?'

'Yeah. Why, Mr Vatry?'

'The driver… that bloke I've seen him before.'

'Well you might've. He's Nick. One of Jim's contacts.'

'And the TR7. Where's the driver?'

'I don't know, Mr Vatry. It was a bird with short blonde hair. She brought Nick here. I heard her talking only a moment ago.'

'Oh no,' Chrissie breathed, as her heart hammered. Should she wind up her window, lock her doors and phone for help, or start her car, jam it into reverse and back out of the yard at high speed?

'I'm pretty sure I've seen the TR7 before as well. Outside a furniture restorer's. Bird with blonde hair, you say?'

'Yeah, Mr Vatry.'

'Hmm, well I don't want them snooping around here. Get rid of them.'

The Jaguar engine purred. Gravel crackled under tyres. A ringtone cut through the air.

Was Ravyt leaving? Chrissie tracked the noises, her senses sharpened by fear. But the sounds seemed to disappear off to her left, not back through the entrance gates. Before she'd had a chance to work out where the Jaguar had gone, Mustang's voice boomed across the yard.

'What? You're saying Jim and Darrel....'

Of course, he was answering his call. Speaking into his mobile. Chrissie trained her ears back onto Mustang.

'The police have picked them up? This Nick guy? What the hell...?'

Chrissie didn't wait to hear the rest. She sat up, rammed the gear leaver into reverse, started the engine and let out the clutch with a bang. Back she shot. She pulled hard left. The tail end of the car swerved. She hit the brakes and spun the wheel. Wafts of burning rubber filled the air. She slipped into first gear and aimed for the gates.

***

Nick headed for his Fiesta. He paid no attention to the black Jaguar as it swung through the entrance, but walked around his car one last time, his mind buzzing as he took in the new paintwork. Mustang seemed to be talking to the Jaguar customer, so he was safe, but the drizzling rain was starting to seep into his sweatshirt where he'd left his anorak open at the neck.

He unlocked the Fiesta, got in and slammed the door. He slipped the keys into the ignition and glanced across at the TR7.

'Where's Chrissie?' he muttered. Tiny beads of rain covered her windscreen where the wipers had kept it clear on the journey. He strained to see through the glass, but it was hopeless. Droplets ran down his own windscreen, merging to form little rivulets obscuring his view. He could just about make out the back of her seats, but no head, no driver, no Chrissie.

He thought he'd get out and check, but the Jaguar started to move. He waited as it drove past him and through Mustang's yard. But it wasn't heading for the iron gates.

'Aha, I bet it's missed the auto recycling entrance and Mustang's directed it the back way through to Dodge.' But where was Chrissie?

'Oh shike,' Nick hissed as Chrissie's car leapt into life. The engine roared, the brakes squealed. A yellow streak ricocheted across the gravel and concrete.

'You bastard,' Mustang yelled, and sprang towards the Fiesta.

'What the hell?' Nick shouted and turned the ignition key. All he registered was Mustang's rage as he bounded towards him shaking his fist.

Nick threw the car into gear and slammed the accelerator. The car surged forwards. He flicked on the wipers. Ahead, it was forty yards to the iron gates. Behind, Mustang shouted. He gripped the wheel.

'No-o,' he shrieked as Chrissie's car slewed across the gates and stalled. He swerved and doubled back. Mustang still came at him. He veered to the left. Mustang lunged at the car. He missed. The car shot on.

He snatched a glance in his rear-view mirror. Mustang was climbing into the transit van.

'Shike!'

The Fiesta bucked and lurched over gritty ruts. He checked his mirror. The bastard was following in the van. What the hell was going on? He focused on the track ahead.

***

'Come on, come on, come on,' Chrissie shrieked at the engine. 'Start, damn you, start.'

She'd skidded on the gravelly, wet concrete. She'd done all the right things and steered into the skid. But then she'd braked. She'd had to; otherwise she'd have wrapped the TR7's wedge-shaped nose around the grills of the gate.

Then she'd stalled.

Now as she rattled the ignition and pumped the accelerator, the engine wouldn't catch.

'Bloody car,' she howled. She'd flooded the engine and if she carried on, she'd flatten the battery as well.

Her hand shook as she brushed away a hot tear searing down her cheek. Across the yard Mustang shouted while Nick burned rubber like a boy racer. She watched, almost unbelieving, as Mustang jumped into the transit van. The sound of engines revving and brakes squealing rose to a crescendo, then died. They weren't driving at her; they'd disappeared towards Dodge's auto recycling yard.

Chrissie reached for her phone. Ravyt? Vatry? One voice, two names? Had she lost her mind?

CHAPTER 35

Matt accelerated away from the communal apple pressing. The Piaggio was sluggish with Maisie on the back, but the loss of speed was more than offset by the feel of a bird hanging onto him.

'This back route better be quick, otherwise Scarbrow'll flamin' kill me,' he muttered.

Maisie squeezed her arms tighter as he hit twenty-five miles per hour, top speed for the scooter's load. The wind caught at her plastic mac and cracked and slapped it against the carrying rack behind. Rain gusted against his chest and ran down his visor.

'You should've worn the mac,' she shrieked, but it was difficult to hear her as the airstream took her words.

'What?'

'Take the left fork,' she yelled and tapped his left thigh.

He nearly wobbled off, but signalled and changed course. With half a mind on Maisie, he hardly noticed the road as the engine buzzed and whined. Soon he recognised the tall, overgrown hedge and he was zipping past the *TARV Auto Recycling* notice. He felt Maisie wave at a car parked to one side of the road.

'Do you know 'em?' he shouted.

'No.'

They travelled on, the road narrowing and the surface roughening. He hardly glanced in at the next set of gates, but something familiar and yellow caught his eye.

'What you slowin' for?' Maisie yelled.

'I know that car. What's Chrissie doin' blockin' the entrance?'

He turned back and idled between her front bumper and the gatepost, stopping next to her open driver's window. He pushed up his visor.

'Hey Chrissie? Why're you parked like this? Are you OK?'

She sniffed and rubbed her hand across her face.

Maisie pulled off her helmet. 'Is something wrong?'

'Yeah, Chrissie. Say somethin'.'

Matt strained to follow Chrissie's feverish words. He couldn't tell if she was excited or crying. Could she be both? 'So you're worried about Nick?'

'We could ride after him, if that'd help. What do you say, Matt?' Maisie pressed his arm.

'Well, 'ave you called the police, Chrissie?'

'Yes. Yes of course. I've phoned just now. They're on their way.' She tried the ignition, the motor whinged but nothing fired into life.

'Come on, Matt. It'd be fun.'

'But what we goin' to do, Mais?'

'I don't know. Come on, it's exciting.'

He watched as she shoved her helmet back on, stretched both arms up in the air and shrieked, 'Onward!'

He gulped. It was a now or never moment. Another make-or-break decision with Maisie. He sensed it wasn't the moment to say *but I've got to start work in half an hour, Mais*.

'Chrissie, could you phone the Pizza Place? Say I'll be late.' Pulse racing, he flipped down his visor.

***

Nick powered on. He'd driven the route with Dave the first time they'd visited, but it had been in the opposite direction. He caught a flash view of the city of car shells stacked three or more high in the distance. He remembered the large Nissen hut and the scaffolding racks piled with everything from exhausts to hubcaps and wheels. He hoped the track would lead him in that direction. Then he'd be able to find his way out.

Adrenaline surged through his veins as he followed the rutted gravel trail. He guessed Mustang was close behind in the transit van. Could he outrun him to the main exit? Had Dodge closed the gates?

'Shike!' he yelled as the van streaked into view in his wing mirror.

The van was gaining on him. Nick turned sharp left off the track. He lurched across a muddy rut and onto a pathway. Behind, the van tried to follow, swayed and caught a pole carrying an overhead electric cable. Nick heard the crunch and swung sharp right back onto the track. Ahead he saw the Nissen hut. He was going to be OK.

The Nissen was much larger than he remembered. He gritted his teeth and careered alongside. He swung round the end of it. The black Jaguar was parked outside. Nick swerved.

Dead in front, Dodge sat in the cab of a tractor with caterpillar treads and a hydraulic articulated arm. A grabber on the end had its jaws open, metal fangs ready to pick up the shell of a car for stacking. It faced away from Nick, as if guarding the hut.

Nick slammed on the brakes and stole into an aisle between scaffolding racks loaded with chrome bumpers. Like a Stealth Bomber, he crept on, easing his way past Dodge as the grabber speared through the empty windows of the car shell, off to one side.

'Ye-e-e-e-s,' he breathed. It was going to be OK. He could outrun the monster on caterpillar treads.

Gears grated, and pistons hissed. Metal scraped on metal. The monster jarred and shuddered as the driver's cab turned.

'What the–'

It was too late. Dodge had seen the Fiesta. The grabber, still holding the car shell, swung towards Nick. It powered across, smashing into a post carrying the overhead cable. Down it came. Metal crashed across scaffolding racks. The cable wrenched itself free from its fixings. Sparks flew. Exposed electric wire fizzled.

In front, Nick's path was blocked by the shattered post, the car shell and live cable. Behind, he was hemmed in by an avalanche of chrome bumpers. He was trapped.

***

Matt twisted the accelerator grip and launched across the gravel-strewn concrete. He had no idea where to head, so he wove past shallow puddles as Maisie squealed and yelped at his back.

'Over there. That way, Matt,' she yelled, waving her arm and flapping a hand in front of his helmet.

He aimed for a gap in some old chain-link fencing and hit a rutted gravel track. The front wheel bounced, almost taking flight across a pothole. He was fired with adrenaline and testosterone. He was Cap'n Starlight of the Space Hopper Corps and the bird on his back was a missile-throwing Galactic Rider. They were racing to save the universe.

The Piaggio engine whined and droned. The front tyre ate stones, the rear spat grit. Scaffolding racks of car parts stretched like supermarket aisles from the sides of the track. Ahead, a transit van angled across the gravel as if discarded.

'Watch out.'

Matt slowed.

'Must've just happened,' Maisie shouted.

The bonnet had crumpled. Metal gleamed beneath grazed paint. The radiator grill hugged a pole while fluid dripped and oozed, forming rivulets of rusty water. The driver's door gaped open. Inside, the dark interior looked empty.

'Anyone in there, do you think?'

Matt felt Maisie twist to look closer as they edged past. He didn't want to see. Instead he gazed upwards at the pole. It was alarmingly angled, as if a javelin had been thrown from the sky. Off to one side an overhead cable sagged.

'No. Nothing. Don't stop, Matt. Keep goin'.' She patted his shoulder.

The track curved. He rode onwards, soon following ruts alongside a large Nissen hut. A sense of foreboding started to erode the testosterone-induced Space Hopper shields. He clamped his jaw and twisted the accelerator. He kept an eye on the cable. He reckoned it was bound to lead somewhere.

They burned around the end of the Nissen, swerved to avoid a solitary black jaguar, and skidded to a halt.

'Frag!' He stared at a mechanical monster on caterpillar treads.

'No. Over there,' Maisie screeched. She waved her arm and pointed to something off to the left.

A figure ran, bobbing between the scaffolding racks and headed towards a heap of chrome bumpers.

A thickset man with powerful shoulders shouted from the monster's driving cab, 'Go on, Mustang. Get the bastard. I've trapped him in his car.'

'No,' Maisie screamed.

The running figure reached the bumpers. Something flashed. The figure jerked. Then fell.

'What the flamin' hell?' Matt knew it wasn't Nick. The hair was black, the figure too short. Was Nick's Fiesta amongst that heap of chrome and scaffolding?

Then he saw the fractured pole, pointing to heaven like a broken fingernail.

'The cable,' he yelled. He pushed up his visor, and with the power of the desperate, yelled, 'The electric cable's down. He's been electrocuted.'

A howl from the monster's cab rent the air. 'No! Not my brother. Not Mustang.'

No one moved. Maisie slipped her arms around Matt's midriff, squeezing the rain-soaked denim of his bomber jacket tighter.

A sudden clunk cut through the silence.

'That's a car door. Someone's openin' a car door.' Matt strained to make out the direction of the sound. 'Hey, it's comin' from over there.'

He pointed to a blue Fiesta hidden between the scaffolding racks and amongst the heap of metal and chrome.

'Nick! It's Nick. He's OK.' He raised his voice and shouted, hard enough to bust his guts, 'Don't open the door. Stay in the car, mate. You're safe if you stay in the car. It's like a Faraday cage. Stay where you are till the electricity's turned off.'

Relief turned to anger. 'Hey, Dodge. You're Dodge, aint you? Go an' turn the fraggin' electricity off. Then someone can help your brother.'

A man stepped out of the Nissen hut, as if to walk to the black Jaguar.

Maisie pushed up her visor. 'I wouldn't come out here. An electric cable's down. The place is live. A bloke's just been electrocuted. I'd stay where you were - unless you want an electric shock.' She put her head closer to Matt so that her helmet bumped against his.

'You aint half clever. What's a Faraday cage, Matt?'

Police sirens sounded in the distance.

CHAPTER 36

Nick followed the others into the interview room. He glanced at Chrissie but her face was stony and gave nothing away. Maisie's eyes seemed to dart from person to person. She looked how he felt. Nervous. And Matt? He held his helmet as if it was a lifebelt, hugged to his midriff.

The room was larger than he'd expected and he supposed Clive had chosen it for that reason. Windowless and silent, the focal point was a table fixed to the floor. It dominated the room. Apart from some wooden chairs, there was no other furniture. It felt oppressive. He cast around, looking for the CCTV cameras. No one sat down.

Clive's voice cut across the stillness. 'It was lucky for you TARV's was being watched and the police got there before anyone else was injured. I think you've probably heard by now; Mustang Carner didn't survive the electric shock.' He spoke quietly. His manner seemed weary.

'I thought you'd be more comfortable waiting in here than in the main reception. I'm afraid we're going to have to take witness statements from you all. DS Stickley will speak to you in turn. Oh yes, and DS Crip may want to ask you a few questions. I've requested some coffee and tea to be sent in while you're waiting.' He smiled at Chrissie.

Yes, Nick thought, we're getting special treatment, but it still feels awful. 'It could've been me,' he murmured. He caught Clive's eye.

'I know. Thank God you had the sense to stay in your car.'

'I nearly got out. If Matt hadn't warned me...,' he let his voice drift as once again metal smashed in front of his car and a torrent of chrome bumpers clattered from scaffolding racks. His only thought had been to escape. He'd imagined his car roof caving in. And then he'd caught a glimpse of Mustang: wild eyes, mouth pulled into a snarl, a sudden convulsive movement, and the contorted face as he'd dropped from view. At the time Nick hadn't understood why. He'd even thought Mustang must have been struck by some metal.

It was only when Matt yelled that he remembered the cable. In one flash his car turned from death trap to shield.

'What the hell were you doing there?' Clive asked, irritation sharpening his tone.

'I thought that was obvious. I was collecting my car. How was I supposed to know you had the place next door under surveillance?'

'You hadn't said.' Chrissie shot a defiant glance across the room. 'We wouldn't have gone anywhere near either place if we'd known. And anyway, why were you watching it?'

Before Clive had a chance to answer, the door opened and a young man wearing dark, suit trousers, shirt and tie strode in.

'Whose statement would you like me to take first, sir?' the voice grated.

'This is my sergeant, DS Stickley. Maisie, why don't you go first? Just tell him exactly what happened.'

No one spoke as Maisie followed the sergeant from the room. Her pink wellingtons looked incongruously cheerful.

Nick guessed Chrissie must have already told Clive everything she knew about their visit to Mustang's accident repair workshop. She was the one who'd rung for help, and

315

his would have been the first number she'd have pressed. Nick realised this was just a formality, but the mention of DS Crip struck a warm feeling. A spark of excitement lifted his spirit as he remembered a striking girl with intensely blue eyes. He hoped against hope DS Crip, rather than the rasping Stickley, wanted to interview him.

'DS Crip didn't tell me not to collect my car. If someone had explained, like Chrissie said, we'd never have gone near the place. It was alright until Mr Ravyt turned up.'

'Yes, and I nearly died of fright when I heard his voice. I mean, after the auction last Saturday, he's the last person on Earth I'd ever want to meet again. And when Mustang called him Mr Vatry…. What's going on Clive?'

'Yes, what was it all about? I was just about to leave and then suddenly Mustang goes mad, starts yelling and chases my car. And the next thing, Dodge comes at me with some kind of JCB.'

'Did I hear right? Is this Ravyt guy the same person as Vatry?' Matt asked as he slumped onto a chair and hugged his helmet.

Chrissie didn't say anything, but looked at Clive.

'Yes, Matt. He uses several names.'

'I knew it,' Chrissie muttered. 'His signet ring is all wrong. I know it doesn't prove anything, but I saw a large *M*, small *c* and large *A*.'

'Now that's enough. All of you stop. You guys walk onto a site we've got under surveillance. Something the organised crime team have been setting up for days. A main suspect turns up and before he's had a chance to lead us to his distribution outlets, you lot are driving around like fiends. Within ten minutes there's pandemonium and then a death. I mean what the hell were you thinking of?'

No one spoke for a moment, and then Chrissie said quietly to Nick, 'It was something to do with the phone call to Mustang. He said the police had picked up Jim and Darrel and you'd set them up. That's why they tried to attack you.' She turned to Clive. 'How'd they know Nick set them up unless someone on your side leaked it?'

'No one leaked anything, Chrissie. They'll have worked it out for themselves.'

'And Mr Ravyt's been there before,' Matt muttered, seemingly still following his own thread. 'Paid for takeaway pizza to be delivered. Remember I told you? An' Jim an' Darrel attacked the delivery guy.'

'But they knew him as Mr Vatry,' Chrissie added.

The door opened and a uniformed policeman came in carrying a tray of tea and coffee. A young woman with dark brown hair and wearing a butternut-coloured coat followed.

'Ah, good. Tea and coffee,' Clive said as the policeman put the tray on the table. 'Thank you. And this is DS Crip.'

'Good morning,' she said brightly.

Nick would have liked to think the cheery tones were directed at him, but he couldn't kid himself. The mascara-enhanced blue eyes didn't smile.

'Help yourself to some coffee, Nick. Then if you'd come with us next door, we can run through a few things with you and DS Crip can take your statement.'

Coffee slopped into the saucer as Nick filled his cup. He knew Clive was keeping the tone light but he wasn't fooled. They probably thought he'd messed up their sting on purpose. The injustice of it all smarted, and a glimmer of anger fired as he trailed after them into a small interview room across the corridor.

'Sit down, Nick,' Clive said mildly. 'Perhaps it would help if we explained that the statues and garden furniture, et cetera, stolen from Church Street, Lavenham, had been marked with trackers.'

'Yes, and Mr Sops was in on the sting,' DS Crip murmured.

'What? But I thought the police were going to catch them in the act of stealing the stuff. Red-handed. Why didn't you tell me that wasn't the plan when I rang you? I thought you'd messed up. You could have said.'

'You believing they'd been successful was all part of the illusion. We needed it to seem real. Not all informants can act,' she said.

'What? You let Mr Sops into your confidence but not me? That's not right. You expected me to take a risk and you didn't tell me?' He stared into her blue eyes before adding, 'You even said, "At least that way I'd get my car back." You as good as said it was OK to collect it.'

'All right, Nick,' Clive's voice cut in. 'Under the circumstances, I suppose we can't blame you for going to collect your car.'

'Yes, one could even say it might have looked suspicious to the gang if you hadn't arranged to collect it,' DS Crip reasoned.

'I'm really sorry it turned ugly.'

'If you'd kept me in the loop I wouldn't have gone near enough for them to try. So I nearly get electrocuted because Mr Ravyt was stashing the stuff in the Nissen hut, yeah? Is that it?'

'Actually, they'd already moved everything on from the Nissen hut, apart from the bronze statues,' DS Crip said quietly. A blotchy redness marked her peachy cheeks.

'Oh that makes me feel a whole lot better.'

'Enough. This is life, Nick. Criminals, like ill health, can be unpredictable. In retrospect, perhaps we should have warned you not to collect your car, but a lot has happened in the last twenty-four hours. I've been up to my eyes putting together a case to charge someone for the murder of Marlin Poynder. I didn't know I was supposed to be babysitting you as well.'

'Babysitting? A moment ago I was part of the illusion.' Nick thought his head would explode. He glared at Clive, but this time he noticed the shadows beneath his eyes and the ashen skin. 'So, is it Mr Ravyt? Is he your killer? Or was he just a prospective buyer for the bronzes and you can't even charge him for that?'

'Actually, we will be holding him. But not because of Marlin Poynder,' the DS said, clipping her words.

'So who? Who are you charging?'

'Gavin. Gavin Poynder, and we've already charged him.' Clive almost made the words sound like a sigh.

Nothing was making any sense. 'What? But Marlin was his father, or rather adoptive father. You can't be serious.'

Clive stood up. Exhaustion seemed to have etched lines in his face. 'Oh yes, I'm serious. Deadly serious. Now I want you to give an account of what happened this morning to DS Crip. I know you've been shaken by the experience, but please answer her questions to the best of your ability.'

CHAPTER 37

Chrissie smelled chocolate as soon as she opened her front door. Rich, sweet aromas led her by the nose past her narrow hall table. Nutty hints of caramel and coffee mingled with prunes and red wine as she followed the scent trail to her kitchen.

'Hi. You're back early,' she murmured and kissed Clive.

'I thought I'd take a half day to make up for all that overtime.'

Steam rose from a huge pan crowning the hob. A pudding basin with a tin foil top rattled and bumped in the boiling water.

'Let me guess. It's your infamous chocolate sponge pudding.'

'How did you know?' Cocoa powder smudged his cheek and dusted his nose. 'It's only just gone on. I thought I'd get a head start. What else are we cooking for this evening?'

'You mean, apart from chocolate sponge?'

'Yes, and with lashings of extra chocolate sauce, of course.' He turned back to the sink and wrestled with a milky measuring jug and an eggy mixing basin. He squirted washing up liquid as hot water jetted from the tap.

'Sarah is bringing the leftover fish pie she froze the other night, and I thought I'd do a spaghetti bolognaise. There'll be five or six of us.' She eyed up the top of the hob and wondered if there'd be space. 'On second thoughts, I might ring her and see how much fish pie she's got.'

Chrissie left him to his fight with a pile of utensils coated in pudding mix, and wandered into the sitting room. While she cleared the low coffee table to make space for plates and glasses, she juggled her list of options and decided on a large dish of peppers, courgettes and onions sprinkled with herbs and oil, and then roasted in the oven. It could go on a shelf above the fish pie, along with some baked potatoes.

She made her call to Sarah and then traced the chocolatey smells back to Clive. He worked at the sink while she perched against her small kitchen table and watched him.

'I still can't believe Gavin killed his adoptive father,' she said, not quite able to let go of the case.

'Well, believe it. He hated him and wanted him dead. If he could've chosen a father, I think it would have been Patrick Suffield, not Marlin. But he got that wrong, because when it came to it, Patrick wasn't going to cover for him. Not while his own skin was in danger.'

'They could've been working together.'

'But only Gavin had a motive and knew enough about automata. He had a finger in every pie. We know he tempted Marlin to the reclamation yard that night using the mechanism as bait. We have a log of Marlin's calls. Gavin even kept the phone as a trophy. It would have been simple enough to bash him on the head while he was looking at the mechanism and then string him up so he was strangled. That open, first floor staging was close enough.'

'Bait?' The word triggered something in Chrissie's brain. 'The housing for the Utterly automaton. The doll's house…. It was bait as well, wasn't it?'

'Yes, Gavin was the seller. Mr Ravyt was the catch. I expect he wanted a hold over him.'

'Hmm….' Chrissie remembered Nick saying Gavin had been watching Ravyt.

'Anyway, for the moment it's over.'

'Already?'

'He was remanded in custody. He appeared before the Magistrate's court first thing this morning. In fact, he could've been enjoying his second meal in Norwich prison's remand centre by now.'

Chrissie frowned. 'Well, I doubt they'd be serving chocolate sponge pudding,' she said.

'I wouldn't bet on it.'

'And Patrick Suffield?'

'He's been charged with dealing in stolen goods and withholding evidence. Now enough of that for today.' Clive smiled at her. 'This evening is downtime. Relax, unwind and enjoy.'

She gave him a hug and then wiped the cocoa powder off his nose.

Rat-at-at-at-at-at! The doorbell juddered its metallic notes. 'That'll be Matt. I bet he's come straight from the Academy.'

'Hmm, chocolate,' he said by way of a greeting, as she let him in.

'Isn't Maisie coming?'

'Yeah, but she don't finish work till around six. Nick said he'd give her a lift from Stowmarket. Figure he's showin' off his new wing.'

He headed towards the kitchen, homing in on the cooking smells.

'Hi, Matt,' Clive shouted above the bubbling of boiling water and clattering of pans. 'There's lager in the fridge. Now make yourself useful and stir this sauce, will you. And keep your fingers out of the chocolate.'

As Chrissie squeezed past Matt and dodged round Clive at the sink, she dispensed glasses of wine and lager. The temperature in the kitchen rose as the oven heated.

'So this is how you make a sauce? I reckoned you just opened a tin or squeezed a bottle,' Matt said, while Chrissie peeled onions and sliced courgettes and peppers. 'Flamin' hell. Those onions are a bit strong.' He rubbed his eyes.

'They'll be in the oven in a moment. Go into the other room and switch on the TV, if you like.'

She hardly noticed him slip away as she sprinkled herbs, and drizzled oil. A newscaster's voice rode in on the steam in the kitchen.

'Well Matt's found a channel all right,' she said over her shoulder to Clive.

Rat-at-at-at-at-at! The sound could have been mistaken for an automaton rattlesnake.

'Can you get that, Matt?' she shouted.

A second later she'd shut the oven door on her vegetable dish and hurried out of the kitchen to say hi. She heard voices at the front door, but the newscaster's words stopped her in her tracks as she passed the living room.

'*Gavin Poynder has been found dead. He was on remand in Norwich prison, charged with the murder of his adoptive father, Marlin Poynder. Details are still to be released, but it is thought he was found asphyxiated in his cell.*'

'Oh my God,' Chrissie murmured and nipped into the sitting room. She looked up to see Clive peer in after her. A million words were transmitted as she held his glance. She flicked off the TV.

'It's… he was always so… devious,' Clive said quietly, more to himself than Chrissie.

'Fish pie, fish pie! I hope the oven's on. Wow, the chocolate smells good.' Sarah's voice drifted down the narrow hallway.

There was nothing Chrissie could say. Gavin must have fooled the psychiatrist and avoided the suicide watch. He'd had a choice. Plead mad or bad. It sounded as if he'd chosen a sad option three, and she guessed Clive had known. She sighed and understood. This evening they needed to relax, unwind and find normality, and Sarah was part of that.

'Hi Chrissie,' Sarah screeched and enveloped her in an extravagant hug.

'Brilliant. You've brought the fish pie. You're a life-saver. Come on, let's get it in the oven straight away. Wine for Sarah, somebody.'

By the time Nick arrived with Maisie, the drinks were flowing and the savoury aromas coming from the kitchen were mouth-watering.

'This is great, Chrissie. You should do this more often,' he said and gulped from his glass. 'Has Matt really made chocolate sauce? I mean is that a subtle hint to go for the cream instead?'

'Not at all,' Clive said. 'The process is burn proof. The secret is in using two pans – you know, with boiling water in the bottom one. And,' he held up his hand for extra effect, 'the chocolate you use. If you like, I could make sticky toffee pudding next time.'

'The man's a genius,' Sarah squealed.

'Hi, Mais,' Matt said as Maisie sidled over. Chrissie caught the hints in the smile passing between them. Yes, she thought, Matt may have found a girlfriend at last.

He turned to Clive. 'There is just one thing that's botherin' me.'

'How much butter to put in the sauce?' Clive asked.

'The man needs another can of lager?' Nick shouted.

Matt seemed to ignore their questions as concentration flickered across his face. 'Clive, who or what is TARV? Did they know their place was bein' used?'

The atmosphere changed in an instant. Chrissie watched as Clive retrieved his glass of wine from the coffee table. How much was he prepared to say about the case, she wondered. Would he mention Gavin? Would the others say anything? Had they even heard the news yet?

'TARV was just a business name Mr Vatry used for trading.'

'So TARV, Vatry an' Ravyt are all names for the same bloke, yeah?'

'Yes, that's right, Matt.'

'While you're on names, what's DS Crip's first name?' Nick sipped his beer, but Chrissie saw the sudden high colour coursing his neck and cheeks.

'Zita. And before you ask, I've no idea if she's got a boyfriend. Now, one last question, and that's your lot for this evening. Who's going to ask it? Matt?'

'Yeah, thanks. So what's his real name?'

'If you mean Mr Ravyt, it's Mr McAvtry.'

Matt almost jumped to his feet. 'Do you realise,' he faltered, 'TARV, Vatry an' Ravyt are all anagrams from bits of his name? He's like McAvtry... the mystery cat.'

'No, Matt. I think you'll find it was Macavity. That's the name of TS Eliot's mystery cat,' Chrissie said, thankful for Matt's single mindedness.

'Not in my comic-strip book it aint, Chrissie.' He turned to Maisie. 'You brought the spare helmet, didn't you?'

'Yes, but what's an anagram, Matt?'

The End.

Lightning Source UK Ltd.
Milton Keynes UK
UKHW021114050921
389956UK00008B/331